# THE CAPTAIN

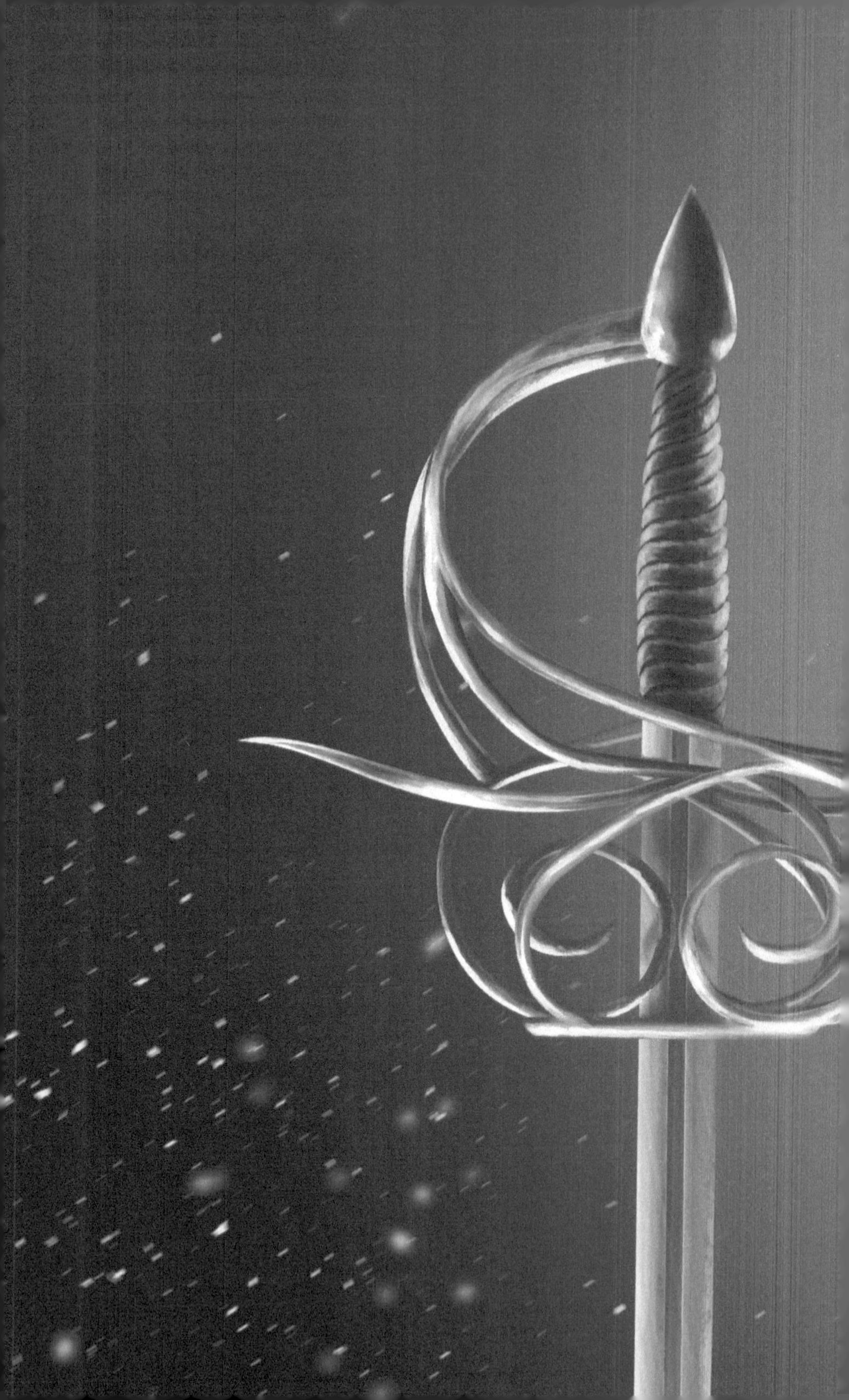

# THE CAPTAIN

ERIN MICHELLE SKY
& STEVEN BROWN

TRASH DOGS MEDIA, LLC

Library of Congress Control Number: 2025933329
(hardcover edition)

ISBN: 978-1946137111

Printed in the United States of America

Cover art by Benjamin P. Roque
Layout & design by Jordan D. Gum

Trash Dogs Media, LLC
1109 South Park St, Ste 504-327
Carrollton, GA 30117
trashdogs.com

10 9 8 7 6 5 4 3 2 1

For Dad,
who provided so much for so many,
asking nothing in return

The war council convened in the great hall of the Viking village, a structure of grand timbers and thatched earth built in the ancient Norse tradition. Like all buildings in Neverland, the lodge had the peculiar habit of growing or shrinking based on the size and number of its occupants.

At the moment, it was full up.

It was so full, in fact, that its walls now jostled against the neighboring homes, several of which had been forced to edge over a bit, sighing and grumbling at the inconvenience.

Inside, Captain Hook surveyed the motley gathering, careful to maintain his commanding presence even as he withered quietly on the inside.

How had his life come to this?

A war council ... with fairies.

He wondered where he had gone wrong—what decisions he might have made differently, somewhere along the line, that could have avoided this latest absurdity. But ever since he had met

Wendy Darling, it felt as though every step had led inexorably to this moment. As though fate itself were mocking him.

His gaze swept across the gathered assembly.

Tigerlilja, leader of the clan that had protected Neverland for centuries, sat at the head of the longhouse table, her lips set in a grim line. Her brother, Vegard, sat next to her, his massive arms crossed over his broad chest. They, at least, seemed to understand what their limited forces were up against.

"A war council," she had promised him.

"A war council," Vegard had agreed.

But what Hook had expected and what he now found himself a part of were two very different things. This, he thought, was not a war council. It was more like a drunken night at the pub, if that pub were chock-full of magical creatures shouting over each other and throwing bread rolls.

"We should invite the mermaids." The everlost twin scowled, pounding his fist on the table.

"No, we shouldn't." His brother pounded his own fist against the dark wooden planks, making both their plates jump and clatter.

(Hook hadn't spent much time with the winged crew and didn't know most of their names. But even he could see they were twins.)

The first surged to his feet. "Yes, we should."

"Don't be daft," the second shot back. "They're stuck in the lagoon. What are they going to do, man the cannons while they flop about like fish?"

Several of the innisfay protested in melodious, jingling chimes. Their flame-red hair cast an ominous glow over the wide map that lay spread out across the table, all but lost beneath a clutter of metal plates and mugs.

Hook's attention snagged on the figure in the center, a stick-figure giant marked with a hand-drawn "X"—Buri, who

wanted to destroy Neverland so he could finally kill Peter Pan. (A desire Hook understood perfectly.) But if Pan died, Buri's ancient powers would be unleashed, encasing the world in an endless winter of ice and snow.

And that, clearly, would not be in the best interest of the British Empire.

One of the imps stood up on his seat, planted his fists on his hips, and puffed out his chest. "The mermaids aren't stuck in the lagoon."

"Shut it, Barnaby." The golden-hued imp sitting next to Barnaby didn't even look up. He was too busy swiping a fistful of fried potato slices from his plate and shoving them into an overstuffed pocket. "You're just going to confuse things."

A third imp stood up on the other side of the table, mirroring Barnaby's posture. "Yeah, shut it, Barnaby! Shut it right now, or I'll rip your heart out and cut it up in my stew!"

Hook blinked slowly, then sighed. With the fate of the world hanging in the balance, this did not seem like a lot to work with.

Wendy, who was seated more or less across from Hook, must have had a similar thought. She winced at the imp's belligerence, and Pan (who was sitting next to her, of course) spoke up immediately.

"Don't be rude, Scrant. The Wendy doesn't like it."

"Say that again," Scrant yelled back. "Tell me what to do one more time and I'll have your liver for dessert!"

Hook's jaw twitched ever so slightly. He hadn't gotten to know the imps any better than he had the everlost, but he was starting to like that one.

Tinker Bell, however, took offense on Peter's behalf. In the blink of an eye, she transformed into a tiny red dragon and hurled herself toward Scrant, darting in and out of swatting range as she tried to bite him.

Wendy's innisfay companion, Charming, jingled merrily from his perch upon Wendy's right shoulder.

It was at this moment that Charlie Hawke, Hook's navigator and Wendy's childhood friend, cleared his throat in a meaningful sort of way—an effort that had no effect whatsoever.

Tinker Bell still flitted around Scrant, who waved his arms wildly in the air trying to defend himself. The twins were now wrestling each other, toppling off their seats onto the floor where the skirmish continued. The everlost contingent cheered them on.

"Ahem!" Charlie tried again, clearing his throat more loudly this time. The imps, innisfay, and everlost didn't seem to hear him. But the Vikings and the British in the room—including Wendy's brothers in arms, John Abbot and Michael Bennet of the Fourteenth Platoon—all gave him their attention, so he forged ahead, doing his best to steer the conversation toward a modicum of productivity.

"We've increased the size of our fleet here in Neverland considerably," he began. "Between the vessel we stole from Blackheart—the *Ravenhawk*, which still needs a captain—and Captain Darling's *Jolly Roger*, we don't have enough sailors to crew them all. Most of the everlost will stay with Pan, of course—"

"Except for Tootles," Pan interrupted. "Tootles sails with the Wendy. That's very important."

"Right," Charlie agreed quickly. "Except for Tootles. And the Fourteenth will be glad to follow her as well." Charlie paused, his eyes darting to Hook. "Assuming that's where they're assigned. But even then, one platoon isn't nearly enough. And we're already spread too thin. We need more recruits."

Tigerlilja's eyes narrowed. "If you think four flying ships are going to decide this battle, you don't understand Neverland at all. You have no idea what lives on this island—creatures like you've never even imagined, plenty of which could destroy any of our ships. And who knows how far Buri's influence has spread? Or

how large Blackheart's army has grown? You saw the wyverns for yourselves."

Hook grimaced. When they had breached Blackheart's defenses, the sight of the wyverns lifting off from the towers had chilled him to the bone.

"Worse than the wyverns?" John asked, echoing Hook's thoughts.

"Worse," Tigerlilja confirmed.

Charlie gulped. "Worse than the dragon on the mountain?"

"Much worse," Pan boasted. "Nothing scares me. I've brought all kinds of terrifying creatures to this island!"

"Of course, you have," Hook muttered.

"Will the dragon fight for us?" Charlie turned to Tigerlilja, hoping to cut Pan off before he could really get started.

"Only the dragon can answer that," she replied, "and only Pan can ask him. But the dragon isn't the biggest question. The real question is what the various denizens of Neverland will do. Blackheart's words will ring true to far too many of them. They don't trust humankind. Most of them are here because they were driven from your world."

Tigerlilja fell silent, glancing from Hook, to John, to Charlie, to Wendy, meeting each of their eyes in turn.

"But Blackheart's human too," Wendy protested. "Or he was, before he became an everlost. And he wants to help Buri destroy Neverland. Why would they ever help him?"

"He will lie to them," Tigerlilja said simply. "And they will believe him because he has aligned himself against England. They will not understand the truth until it is too late."

"They'll listen to Jokul," Vegard said quietly.

Tigerlilja's eyes flew wide, and she snapped her head around to glare at her brother. She didn't say a word, but this particular glare spoke volumes.

"I know." Vegard raised his hands between them in an unspoken apology. "But it's true. A lot of them will listen. That is, assuming we can convince him to help. He might be our only chance."

"Then we're already lost." Tigerlilja clenched the edge of the table, her knuckles bright as snow with the force of her grip.

"I'm sorry," Wendy interrupted gently, "but who's Jokul?"

"You don't know Jokul?" Pan crowed this at the top of his lungs, and the entire room fell silent, turning to stare at Wendy.

"Um ... should I?" She looked to Charlie for help, but he only shrugged.

Tigerlilja continued to glare at Vegard even as she answered the question.

"In England," she said, "you'd know him as Jack Frost."

# CHAPTER
# 2

"Jack Frost!" Wendy exclaimed. "But he's—"

She had been about to say that Jack Frost wasn't real when a bread roll came flying through the air, cutting off her words as it hurtled toward Charming. She caught it deftly in one hand, her fingers closing around the still-warm crust, then glanced at her shoulder to make sure the tiny fairy sitting on her shoulder was all right.

The tiny, magical fairy.

Sitting on her shoulder.

In a land where time stood still.

"Oh," she said quietly. Of course, Jack Frost was real. "And he lives here? In Neverland?"

"Aye." The single syllable rumbled from Vegard's chest.

Wendy leaned forward, curiosity overtaking her surprise. "Does he truly bring the winter?"

"He brings terror and destruction." Peter grinned. "And I found him."

"Of course, you did." Hook pinched the bridge of his nose with his good left hand.

Vegard glanced at his sister. "He brings an army of his own to this fight. If we can convince him to join us."

"Do you think we can?" Wendy asked.

Tigerlilja's expression hardened. "No. He won't listen to us."

"You don't know that." Vegard pronounced each word slowly, his voice firm but gentle.

"I do know that." The clanswoman's shoulders tensed. "Maybe once …" Her eyes dropped to the table, and Wendy caught a flash of something she had never seen there before—a profound, unhealed sorrow. But then, with a subtle shake of her head, the guarded mask of fierce determination snapped back into place. "It doesn't matter. Jokul is not our enemy, but he is not our ally either. He abandoned this clan a long time ago."

Wendy paused. She couldn't decide whether she should ask the woman what had happened or not. Tigerlilja had obviously been hurt by the history between them, and Wendy didn't want to pry. But it did sound like an *interesting* story, and Wendy loved stories almost as much as she loved flying ships.

Besides which, this particular story might hold the key to understanding where the man called Jokul stood when it came to the fate of humanity. If he was already working with Buri …

Wendy shuddered, but Peter interrupted her thoughts.

"He didn't abandon *me*," he told Wendy with a grin. "Jokul's my friend. Would you like to meet him? I'll take you if you like."

Given what little she had heard about the man, Wendy wasn't sure she wanted to meet Jack Frost at all, but Hook's growling baritone addressed the Vikings before she could reply. "Is there any chance this Jokul might join forces with us?"

Vegard met his gaze steadily. "There's a chance."

Hook turned to Tigerlilja, waiting for her assessment.

8

The woman sighed deeply. "I suppose there's a chance." She shrugged, running her thumb along a notch in the wooden table. "A small one. If it's Pan who asks him." Then she added wryly, "Assuming he can remember his mission long enough to ask."

Hook's eyes burned with frustration, reminding Wendy of the caged tiger she had seen in him back in England. She knew what he was going to say even before he said it.

"Then Captain Darling should go with him. We'll assemble a party."

"No," Tigerlilja countered. "If they're going at all, and let me be clear, I'm advising against it, they should go alone. The more humans Pan brings with him, the less chance Jokul will listen."

"Advising against it?" Hook's eyes narrowed. "Why?"

"Because," said Tigerlilja, "I can't guarantee her safety."

Hook's jaw worked back and forth as he watched Wendy in silence, his eyes locked on hers. "Can we gather enough forces to have a chance without him?"

"No." The Viking leader's reply was unequivocal. "We cannot."

A muscle in Hook's cheek twitched. "Then so be it." He rose from the table with fluid grace, his coat settling around him like a shield. "Captain Darling, you will accompany Pan to meet this Jokul. Report to my quarters for a full briefing before you depart."

When Hook, Wendy, John, and Charlie had arrived in Tigerlilja's village for the war council, they had discovered a small but serviceable barracks waiting for them on the outskirts of the settlement.

It was oddly cozy for a barracks, with warm furs draped across simple beds and small windows that framed the most beautiful

view of the mountains. Yet there was something distinctly temporary about it—something in the way the corners seemed to shimmer when Wendy wasn't looking at them directly—that gave her the unsettling feeling it might pop out of existence at any moment.

As a result, she had stored very few possessions in it, preferring to carry most of them with her in her travel pack. She collected what little she had left behind in a matter of moments, affording her almost no time at all to reflect upon her new circumstances.

"Captain Darling," he had called her.

Wendy's heart soared all over again. She was a captain. A real captain in the Royal Navy, and of a flying ship, no less! She hoisted her pack to her shoulder and smoothed the sides of her blue captain's jacket, her fingers running fondly over its polished gold buttons.

And then she sighed.

She hadn't wanted to leave her ship even long enough to attend the war council. Now, she would have to extend that absence when there was still so much to do. She had just been assigned the beginnings of a crew: part of the Fourteenth, a few of the imps, and Tootles, of course. It wasn't enough, but it was a start. She needed to be with them, training the Fourteenth to become true sailors and stitching her patchwork corps into the whole cloth of a ship's crew.

It was what she wanted, and it was what her crew needed.

But it wasn't what was best for England.

England needed an army. And it sounded like Jokul had one.

For the first time since she had put it on, the weight of her captain's jacket felt heavy on her shoulders. She wished she could talk to Nana about it, but even the dog was on the *Jolly Roger*.

"I'm grateful you're here with me," she said to Charming, who was riding opposite her pack on her other shoulder. "It turns

out there's a lot more to being a captain than commanding a ship. But sailing is the only part I was trained for. I don't know anything about recruiting an army."

Charming answered in a somber, chiming warble that Wendy couldn't understand at all. But then he stood up straight, looked her firmly in the eye, and nodded.

"Oh, I hope you're right," she said quietly.

Together, they left the small room and headed for Hook's quarters at the other end of the building. Wendy had assumed Hook's "briefing" would amount to a private, long-winded warning about keeping Peter in line, so she was pleasantly surprised to discover Hook, Charlie, Vegard, and Tigerlilja all waiting for her together.

"Captain Darling," Hook began, addressing her as she entered, "I asked Tigerlilja and Vegard to join us so they can brief you further about this Jokul before you depart."

"And I told you," Tigerlilja snapped, "that I have nothing more to say."

The two of them glared at each other so fiercely across the room's small table that Wendy thought either one of them might leap over it at any moment.

Hook drew himself up to his full height and practically snarled in reply. "I am about to send an officer of His Majesty's Royal Navy into unknown territory in an attempt to recruit an unknown entity into a war against unknown forces. I won't have her going out there unprepared. Tell her whatever you can."

When Tigerlilja refused to answer, Hook took a long, deep breath in through his nose and exhaled slowly. "Please," he added finally, "for her sake, if not mine."

Tigerlilja stared at him a moment longer, then turned to Wendy, her gaze softening at least slightly.

"There honestly isn't much I can tell you. I don't even know where he is. He came here a very long time ago, as did so many of the fay, seeking asylum."

Wendy's brow furrowed. "Asylum? From what?"

"From you."

"From me?" Her eyebrows shot to the height of their reach, arching together in extreme protest.

"No, not—" Tigerlilja shook her head. "Not you personally, of course. From humankind. If you do find him, be prepared. Jokul can be dangerous, especially when it comes to humans."

"But you're human too," Wendy pointed out. "And you obviously knew him."

"Like I said, that was a long time ago. And in any event, we're clan. That made it different … at least for a while." Her eyes took on the same sad look they had before when she spoke of him. "He blames humanity for driving the fay from your world. He won't trust you. Our only hope is that Blackheart has been bringing more and more humans to Neverland. Jokul won't like that. If you find him, be sure he knows that once Blackheart is defeated, you'll gather all the humans he brought here, and you'll leave this place forever. All of you."

*Leave Neverland?* Wendy thought. *Forever?*

But it was Hook who answered. "The sooner the better. Anything else?"

Vegard cleared his throat. "Pan will protect you, but don't let Jokul draw you away from him. And try not to provoke him either. He has a good heart, but Buri has poisoned it. If you can't get through to him, just leave—before he does anything rash."

"Buri's gotten to him?" Hook demanded, his voice sharp. "Then what's the point of going?"

"He doesn't follow Buri," Vegard insisted, "but Jokul has a natural affinity for snow and ice, and he hates humankind. Between the

two, it makes things ... complicated." He tried to smile at Wendy, but she didn't find this particular smile to be reassuring in the slightest.

"I've half a mind to call the whole mission off," Hook growled.

"No," Wendy said firmly, though her heart had begun to race at Vegard's warnings. "If we need an army, and if we can't defeat Buri without him, then we have no other choice." She held Hook's gaze. "England has no other choice."

The muscles of his jaw twitched twice during the silence that extended between them, but, at last, he relented.

"Then go. And Godspeed."

Nevertheless, as they were all leaving, Hook spoke to her again. "One moment please, Captain."

Charlie gave her one last hug for good luck, then slipped out with the rest, leaving her alone with Hook. Wendy braced herself for the long-winded warning she had expected from the beginning. She sighed and tilted her chin up bravely, prepared to suffer through it. But, as it turned out, that wasn't what he wanted to say at all.

"Captain Darling," he told her (and she had to admit, she very much liked the sound of him saying it), "do be careful."

"Of course, Captain," she said softly. And because she had tilted her chin up so bravely, she found herself staring suddenly into his forget-me-not blue eyes.

"The most important part of this mission," he said, just as softly, "is for you to return safely. I ... that is, we ... England needs you."

Before she could reply, he cleared his throat and spoke again. "You are dismissed." And then he stepped back, bidding her Godspeed once more on her mission.

13

"England needs me, Charming. Imagine that." Wendy turned to the innisfay, who was seated once again upon her shoulder. He had been waiting for her outside Hook's temporary quarters. Now, he cocked his head, looking puzzled.

"Well, yes, you're quite right," Wendy agreed. "I'm a captain now." She brushed her hands down the sides of her coat, a gesture that was quickly becoming a habit. "And I was a navigator before that, and a diviner before that. Of course, England needs me. But I didn't know that Hook knew it, if you catch my meaning."

Charming raised a pointed eyebrow and said nothing. Not a single note.

She narrowed her eyes in mild suspicion, but then Peter's voice pulled her from her musings.

"Ready?"

Wendy looked up to see him hovering a foot or two above the ground, his arms crossed over his chest and a huge grin on his face.

"I—" Wendy started, but Peter didn't wait to hear whatever it was she might have said, so now we shall never know what it was.

"Follow me!" he told her, and he darted off toward the distant tree line.

"Oh dear," Wendy said quietly. Peter was always a bit of a loose cannon, but he had a very particular look about him at the moment that spelled trouble. If there was one thing Wendy had developed during her time as a diviner, it was the ability to smell trouble from a mile away.

"I'm not sure you should come along," Wendy said, turning to Charming. "He seems even less predictable than usual. And I have no idea what we're about to get ourselves into with this Jokul fellow. It might be safer if you stayed here."

Charming frowned and shook his head.

"I could order you not to come," Wendy suggested, frowning a little herself.

The innisfay launched off her shoulder to hover in front of her nose. He brushed his hands down his sides as though smoothing an imaginary officer's jacket, then shook his head, crossed his arms, and glared at her.

"I suppose you're right," Wendy said slowly. "You're not technically part of my crew."

Charming nodded sharply, as though the subject had been decided.

And, apparently, it had.

"Well, come along then," Wendy said, relenting with just the barest hint of relief. "We'd best hurry or we'll lose him, and he'll forget he's supposed to wait for us."

In truth, Wendy was tremendously glad to know that Charming would be coming along. She adored Peter, but, given the curse and the resulting state of his memory, being alone with him some-

times made her feel even more alone than she might have felt without him.

And Wendy wasn't at all sure she felt ready to handle Jokul by herself.

Having come to a decision with Charming, Wendy looked up, only to discover that Peter was already nearing the forest. Instead of flying high in the air, looping and spinning through the sky as he often did, he was moving with a distinct sense of purpose.

"Oh!" Wendy exclaimed. "Charming, hurry! Don't lose him!"

Charming saluted sharply (despite having just established that he wasn't part of her crew), and he darted off to follow Peter into the forest.

Wendy broke into a hard sprint, doing her best to keep up despite the weight of her pack.

"Peter," she called. "Peter, wait!"

But Peter showed no sign of slowing down. He disappeared between the trees while Wendy was still a hundred yards away, and Charming had made up only half that distance, at best. Wendy's heart sank into the pit of her stomach. She had wasted too much time talking to Charming, and now they were going to lose Peter completely. This had been their best chance at stopping Buri, perhaps their only chance, and Wendy had failed before she had even begun—on her first official mission as a captain in the Royal Navy.

Spurred on by the thought, she sprinted even faster, saying, "No," under her breath with every quick stride. "No-no-no-no-no-no-no-no."

Then Charming disappeared after Peter, and Wendy was all alone in the field, her eyes focused on the spot where they had both faded into the shadows. Would Charming be able to keep up? Or was Peter already too far ahead, off to visit Jokul without them?

Precious moments later, Wendy reached the tree line and broke through into a world of perpetual twilight. She stumbled in the sudden darkness, her eyes too slow to adjust. "Peter!" she called again, her hands now splayed out in front of her as she ran blindly between the trees.

"Yes?" The answer came from just behind her left ear.

"Oh!" She spun, but her heel caught a root and she started to tumble backward. Instinctively, she reached for him, and his strong hands caught her own. As her eyes finally adjusted to the dim light, Peter came into view.

He smiled down at her, still holding her hands. "Hello, the Wendy."

"Peter," she said quietly. The relief that flooded through her was so overpowering and immediate that she almost hugged him. "I thought I'd lost you."

"Lost me?" Peter asked. "But we're on a mission together."

"I was afraid you might have forgotten," Wendy admitted, staring into his ice-blue eyes and feeling suddenly shy, and more than a little embarrassed.

"Forgotten? I could never forget you, the Wendy," said Peter.

Charming, who was hovering behind his right shoulder, chimed away at him angrily, his hair a fiery red.

"Don't be ridiculous," Peter said in reply, his gaze still locked on Wendy's. "I forget nothing."

Charming rolled his eyes, and Wendy smiled. She took a gentle step back and finally let go of Peter's hands. When she did, he reached into his shirt and pulled out the small leather pouch that hung around his neck.

"Innisfay dust!" Wendy exclaimed.

"Of course," said Peter. "That's why I came to the forest to wait for you. I know you don't like them to see you fly."

"You really did remember." Wendy stared up at him in wonder. Suddenly, she wanted to hug him again, though for a different reason than before.

And if Peter had been any other man, he might have recognized the sudden change in the way she looked at him. He might have stilled, watching her, hoping against hope that she might take one step closer.

But, of course, he was Peter.

"Are you ready?" he asked brightly.

Captain Darling sighed a little. If she was at all disappointed— just *if* she was, mind you, without saying anything for certain— she set the moment aside for the sake of the mission, as any good captain would have.

"Ready," she agreed.

And with a quick sprinkling of innisfay dust, they were on their way.

# CHAPTER 4

Hook awoke with a sudden pain in his chest—a pain unlike anything he had ever felt, as though an iron fist had taken hold of his heart, squeezing it until he thought the organ might burst. The pain eased for a moment, then gripped him again, harder than before.

He took a short, shuddering breath and clutched at his chest with his good left hand. But the moment his fingers touched his skin, the pain ebbed away, leaving him drenched in sweat. He waited through two shallow, cautious breaths. Then three. But the pain didn't return.

Afraid to sit up, he lay still, and a chill passed through him, racing from the top of his head to the base of his spine. Was he sick? Had he caught malaria from one of those dreadful innisfay?

Wouldn't that just be par for this godforsaken island.

And then, across the room, something moved.

Hook was still in Tigerlilja's village, resting in the temporary barracks under full light of day, but he had locked the shutters

tight and drawn the blinds against the eternal sun. The room was black as moonless night, but he could have sworn something moved, just there, in the far corner.

He strained his eyes against the dark, but he decided it must have been the last remnant of a dream. He couldn't have seen anything. It would have been impossible.

Perhaps the pain had been a dream too?

Keeping his good left hand pressed firmly against his chest nonetheless, he raised his hook before his eyes, testing the light. He could barely see the curve of its blade. Not even a single glint of steel. His own arm, mere inches from his face, was nothing more than darkness against darkness.

Slowly, carefully, he drew his palm away from his chest—no, from his heart. The pain had been in his heart, that much was certain. He let his fingertips rest there gently for a time, but then he lifted them away.

Nothing.

Hook scowled. What foolishness was this? He was letting the blasted island get to him—stories of old Norse gods and the end of the world. It was a weakness he could ill afford. Was he frightened of his own dreams now? Imagining terrors in the dark? Honestly.

He had witnessed the throes of battle many times over. He had lost dozens of good men—men he would not forget. He thought momentarily of Nicholas and his heart hurt again, but not like before. This was a quiet ache, one with which he was well familiar. It was the hollowed absence of grief. The simple weight of command.

He took in a sharp breath. And exhaled slowly.

And then the thing moved again.

In an instant he was fully alert, crouching in the center of his bed, his hook at the ready and his pistol in his good left hand.

But he didn't know where to look. It was as though he had *felt* the thing more than he had seen it.

And then he heard it. The quiet laugh of a young girl, beautiful and lilting—with the harsh, subtle undertones of nails clawing across slate.

"Don't call out," she warned him softly. "You'll want to hear what I have to say. If you call out, people will die. And you will hear nothing but their screams."

"You think I'm afraid of you?" Hook still couldn't see his adversary, but he leered into the darkness, nonetheless. "I'm not the one hiding in the shadows. Show yourself. Or say what you have to say and be done with it. I have no time for games."

Now the laugh sounded like a woman, not a girl, and it came from the other side of the room. A single exhalation followed by a guttural snarl. Lower, and far more dangerous.

Hook snapped his head toward it, but still he could see nothing. How many of them were there?

"No time for games?" the voice taunted, coming from the foot of his bed. "You're in Neverland, you fool. You have all the time in the world. And yet, only moments ago, you thought you had no time left at all. Such is the power of death. It can end even eternity."

Hook cocked his pistol, but the woman only laughed again.

"Your silver cannot harm me," she told him. "And if I wanted you dead, you would be dead. You are safe enough. For now."

As she spoke, her voice flitted about the room, first in one corner, then the other, then high overhead, as though floating near the ceiling.

"I thought the innisfay couldn't speak." Hook's eyes narrowed in the dark.

"I. Am. No. Innisfay." The words were clipped, almost whispered in their harsh declaration.

And then he saw it. A nebulous form in the dark. A woman, her shape uncertain. A silhouette of a hip. A hint of ... horns? Like his own arm before his face, she was darkness within darkness.

"What are you, then?" he demanded, careful to keep his voice from trembling. Careful to keep his good left hand steady.

"You may call me ... Shadow."

The final word came from everywhere and nowhere.

From every corner of the room.

From inside his own mind.

And the shape vanished.

Hook swallowed. For a moment he thought the creature had left, but then it coalesced again, perching at the foot of his bed like a predator. One leg remained folded beneath her, the other stretched out to her side. Her hands splayed across the bed as she leaned forward.

Hook pointed his gun squarely at her chest, but she didn't even flinch. "If Blackheart sent you with a message, you'd best deliver it."

"I speak for no man," she hissed. "I speak only for myself."

"Speak then," Hook snapped back. "Say what you have to say, or I *will* kill you. One way or another."

The voice chuckled. "I think you will find me a more worthy foe than an everlost child."

In that moment, all light was extinguished. Hook might as well have been crouching in a tomb.

He felt a breath on his neck, and the voice whispered in his ear. "Hello."

He swiped at the sound with his hook, but it met only air.

Then the dim light returned, what little there was of it, and the creature was sitting cross-legged at the foot of his bed. She held her face in her hands, her elbows propped against her knees, staring at him with coal-black eyes.

"At least hear me out," she told him. "Or you might lose your chance to save your precious—"

"Wendy!" Hook blurted out. "What have you done with her?"

Shadow laughed again, the mocking notes falling like sleet in the depths of Hook's heart. "I was going to say, 'your precious England,'" she told him. "But I find your mistake ... intriguing."

"Save it from what?"

Hook was starting to believe what she had said. That he couldn't kill her with his silver. But he trained his gun on her new position, nonetheless.

"First, a question." The creature tilted her head, considering him with a disturbingly innocent expression. "Do you think that if you defeat Blackheart, Peter will leave England alone?"

Hook said nothing.

After a long silence, the shadow continued. "You know that he won't. He will follow her back home. He would not be able to stop himself even if he tried. And he will be more invincible than he is even now."

"What's your point? I'll deal with Pan when I'm done dealing with Blackheart. He's the more immediate threat to England." But her words had echoed Hook's own thoughts, and now he wanted her to go on.

"You will not be able to 'deal with him,'" said Shadow. "You cannot kill Peter in a duel any more than you can kill me. But I can help you strike him down when he least expects it. While he still considers you an ally."

"How?" He spat out the word, unable to help himself.

Shadow chuckled. "I will get you the weapon you need, and I will tell you when to strike. I will even help you defeat Blackheart. This, I promise. But you must tell no one that we have spoken."

"Why do you want Pan dead?" He would not promise her anything. Would not admit the hope that had flared in his heart, not even to himself. "If you're as powerful as you seem, why not just kill him yourself?"

In the blink of an eye, her face was less than an inch from his own, her breath caressing his lips with the chill of the frozen tundra. "I am far more powerful than you know."

And then, just as suddenly, she was gone. Her form vanished, leaving only her voice, coming again from everywhere and nowhere, her words echoing through his mind with a touch of grief so ancient he thought he might drown in it.

"But I cannot kill Pan," she told him, "for reasons you cannot understand. Like you, I only want to be free of him."

CHAPTER

# 5

Wendy loved the way Neverland changed as they flew over it, transforming so completely between one zone and the next. Even in England, flying had given her a similar feeling as she raced across the countryside. Forests had given way to farmland, which had given way to the sea. But this was different. This was a world unlike anything she had ever imagined.

Which, of course, made it exactly what she had truly wanted.

Sunlit mountains turned to desert night in a heartbeat where a yeti had taken up residence next to a herd of nocturnal sand beasts.

When Peter rescued new creatures and brought them to Neverland, did he just drop them anywhere?

She had the sense, flying over the cacophony of habitats, that he did exactly that, setting them down and forgetting about them immediately as he flew off to some new adventure. She could see no rhyme or reason in it. No pattern in the transitions from noon to twilight, tropical paradise to frigid arctic.

Wendy shivered. Moments ago, she had been sweltering in the woolen sleeves of her thick captain's jacket, the open sides of the coat flapping in the wind like great blue wings. Now, she pulled them close, buttoning the garment up tight against the sudden chill.

They were here, she realized, without knowing quite how she knew. They had reached the outskirts of Jokul's domain.

Vast. And cold. And free.

Wendy took a deep breath. Even the air smelled different than it did throughout the rest of Neverland—so fresh she thought she had never truly smelled fresh air until this moment. She closed her eyes and took another breath, deeper than the last, letting it fill her senses.

The green of Neverland's magic was still present, but it was more subtle, laced throughout the more powerful scent of Jokul's own magic. Pine and snow. Woodsmoke and tundra. With a hint of … peppermint?

She opened her eyes, and the scene below had changed. Glancing behind, she discovered a lightly shimmering dome—a magical veil that had not been visible from the other side.

And on *this* side of that veil … Wendy inhaled sharply.

A winter wonderland.

Above, ribbons of light danced across the night sky, bathing the world in an ever-shifting aura of color. Green and gold. Blue and pink. Orange and violet.

Below, a ring of mountains stretched as far as the eye could see, covered in majestic pine forests and a pristine blanket of snow. Within that ring lay a wide, gleaming plain. A herd of reindeer grazed upon it, pawing at the snow, first blue, then green, then gold, then blue again.

"It's beautiful," Wendy breathed.

"Just wait," Peter told her. "You haven't seen the best part."

They sped across the plain, flying occasionally through small patches of gently falling snow even though there wasn't a cloud in the sky.

Eventually, they came upon a stand of ancient evergreens—a horseshoe-shaped grove right in the center of the mountain range. Peter landed just beyond its open edge.

It was a surprisingly gentle landing, Wendy noticed.

She touched down beside him feeling almost disappointed to mar the perfect plane of snow upon the ground. But as she took a step forward, her footprint filled itself in, the snow rising up from below in the span of three heartbeats until there was no sign she had ever stepped there at all.

"How curious," she said, speaking mostly to herself.

But, of course, Peter answered her, nonetheless.

"Isn't it wonderful?" He smiled at her gently. When Wendy met his gaze, the look in his eyes seemed clearer than usual. He reached out his hand, and she took it without any thought to the contrary.

As they entered the grove, Wendy felt as though she had stepped through the entrance of a palace. Grand sculptures lined a broad pathway, as white as the surrounding snow. There were huge, antlered deer—two or three times the size of normal deer, Wendy thought. And a minotaur, surrounded by smaller statues with pointed ears. And an enormous, winged lion with eyes as blue as the sky.

Suddenly, two tiny dragons that seemed to be made of living ice zipped toward them down the path, then veered off to land on the horns of the minotaur, watching Wendy and Pan with keen interest.

The minotaur shook its head, casting them back into the air.

"It's alive!" Wendy exclaimed.

"They all are," said Peter.

Sure enough, as Wendy looked around again, one of the deer blinked slowly and another bowed its head—whether to acknowledge their presence or simply stretch its neck, Wendy wasn't certain.

The tiny ice dragons circled the minotaur's head, chattering in annoyance. Peter laughed, so of course Tinker Bell turned herself into an ice dragon too and sped off into the fray. She spun and screeched, flying in spirals around the minotaur's horns, making Peter laugh even more.

Wendy turned to Charming, who sat quietly on her shoulder. "Would you like to join them?" she asked. "I don't want to keep you from the fun." But Charming frowned darkly, shook his head, and remained where he was.

When the ice dragons tired of the game and flew away, Tink stayed with them, speeding along the path ahead.

Wendy's gaze followed them to a towering throne of ice.

On either side of the throne sat a white wolf, each the size of a horse, and upon the throne itself sat a young man with pointed ears and sharp features. He appeared to be about the same age as John or Michael, but in Neverland, of course, that meant nothing. He wore a long, white coat, cut very much like Wendy's own captain's jacket, but his was adorned at the cuffs and down the front with silver embroidery that reflected the shifting colors of the sky.

The dragons flew straight to him. One took a moment to settle on the right arm of the throne. Another sprawled across the carvings at the very top. Was that Tinker Bell? Wendy wasn't sure anymore. The third landed on the man's left arm, perching there like a hawk. Its wings spread wide, flapping madly as it almost lost its balance, but then it found its feet and folded its wings gracefully to its sides.

The man stroked it absently with his right hand, contemplating his new guests. His features were fine and even, almost deli-

cate, but when he smiled, there was a distinct air of danger about him that sent a shiver of unease down Wendy's spine.

Peter, of course, wasn't concerned in the slightest.

"Hullo, Jack," he said brightly. "This is the Wendy. She's come to speak with you. I know you don't like humans, but she's not like the others. If any harm comes to her, our truce will end, and I'll have to kill you."

Peter said this last bit just as brightly as the first, as though exchanging pleasantries. *How have you been, Jack? Such nice weather we're having.*

But Jack only chuckled and offered up a smile, one that was much wider and easier than before. "So be it. We shall begin on friendly terms and see how things progress."

He shifted the ice dragon off his arm and onto the throne. The small creature puffed a disgruntled cone of frost from its nostrils, then settled down again, and Jack leaned forward, resting his elbows on his knees. "Tell me then, human," he said with a smirk, "what could be so urgent to have brought you all this way?"

Wendy, however, wasn't at all sure how to proceed. Despite his casual demeanor, the man was still sitting on a throne. Even if that throne happened to be made of ice, certain proprieties were in order. Should she address him as "Your Majesty"? Peter had called him Jack and the man hadn't seemed to mind.

But Peter got away with a lot of things that other people didn't.

Jack watched her intently, then frowned, just a little, a tiny crease forming between his snow-white eyebrows.

"Speak plainly," he said, sighing a little. "I have no patience for human *diplomacy.* The more time you spend choosing your words, the less inclined I shall be to believe them."

"I'm sorry," Wendy said at once. "It's just, I wasn't sure what to call you. Your Majesty? Jack? Jokul?"

"Ah," he said, brightening a bit, "of course. How rude of me."

Without removing his elbows from his knees, he pressed one hand briefly to his chest. "I am Jokul Frosti. Father Frost. Jack Frost. Old Man Winter. You may call me Jokul. Or Jack. Or any of them, as you prefer. I am known by many names."

"But which do you prefer?" Wendy asked. "Which of them is your true name?"

His frown deepened, his expression suddenly as cold as the air around her. "None of them. They are all human names. You could not pronounce my true name. It is beyond even you."

*Even me?* Wendy wondered, but Peter interrupted the thought before Wendy could speak it out loud.

"I can say it!" Peter boasted.

"I wish you wouldn't," Jack muttered.

Wendy decided she had best forge ahead before things got any worse.

"We have a common enemy," she said quickly. "You, Peter, and I. All of us. We came here hoping to combine our forces. To fight for Neverland together."

"Fight for Neverland?" Jack snapped. "Against whom? The British who first invaded our sanctuary thanks to this lovable dimwit? Or the British who have only just arrived? Ridding Neverland of one British threat would only help the other."

Jack thrust his chin toward Peter upon the word "dimwit," but if Peter took offense, he didn't show it in the slightest.

"If you help us defeat Blackheart," Wendy replied evenly, "you will be rid of the British all around. We will leave as soon as Neverland is safe and the threat to our homeland has been eliminated."

But Jack only scoffed. "When have the British ever left a land they claim to have 'discovered'? Tell me another tale, storyteller."

"It's not a tale." She drew herself up to her full height, and she brushed her hands meaningfully down the sides of her captain's jacket. "I give you my word. When Blackheart is defeated, we will

leave. Captain Hook wants nothing to do with this place. I assure you he has no desire to stay."

Jack smiled, but there was no joy in it. It was a smile of wrath and sorrow in equal measure. "I believe you," he told her. "But that, too, would be a problem. Even if you stayed and your precious captain left, he would return to his king. He would report everything he has found here. And then it would be out of his hands. They would send ships," he snarled, "and men. I have seen it before. Now that he knows how to reach Neverland, I can't allow that."

"If I ... stayed?" Wendy asked. "Why would you say that?" It wasn't as though it had never crossed her mind, but she was a captain now. She had her own responsibilities to crown and country. When the time came for the fleet to leave, she would leave. She had not given herself permission even to dream otherwise, let alone consider it.

"Why?" Jack echoed. His eyes trailed slowly down her arm to her hand, which was how Wendy suddenly realized that she was still firmly clasping Peter's hand within her own. With a start, she dropped it.

Peter merely shrugged, then flew off to start a game of tag with the winged lion. Jack's gaze traveled back to meet Wendy's own with an expression she found inscrutable.

"You don't even know," he said quietly.

"Know what? What don't I know?" She didn't like the way he was looking at her, so the question came out sounding more like a demand.

But Jack remained thoughtful, speaking more to himself than to her. "I wonder how Neverland will affect it."

"Affect what?" If anything, she sounded even more cross this time. "Is it about Peter's curse? Will being back in Neverland affect it somehow? What aren't you telling me?"

Jack removed his elbows from his knees, leaning back against his throne with an air of sudden indifference. "Does Tigerlilja know you're here?"

"Why?" Wendy shot back, utterly exasperated. "Do you want her people gone too?"

But he continued to ignore her questions. "What did she say about asking me for help? Speak truthfully. I will know if you do not. I am immune to your charms, *the Wendy*." When he used the title with which Peter had introduced her, his voice dripped with sarcasm.

"I won't tell you." She didn't think she had ever felt quite so infuriated by a simple conversation. What was he doing to her? "Why should I answer your questions when you'll answer none of mine?"

"Because you need my help," he reminded her. "Unless, of course, you've changed your mind. Would you prefer to defeat Blackheart's forces on your own?"

Wendy took an unconscious step forward. "I don't think you have any intention of helping us no matter what I say. Not me. Not England. Not Tigerlilja. Not even Neverland. Because that's who truly needs you. Neverland." She glared at him, then broke his gaze, turning her face to the glorious sky. "Peter. Let's go."

"Wait."

Reluctantly, Wendy turned back to face him.

"I have conditions." He watched her coldly, his face devoid of any emotion. "First, your captain must agree to destroy the portal. To cut your precious England off from Neverland forever. If he refuses, then I shall need your word that you will defy his orders and destroy it yourself."

"He won't refuse," she told him. But she remembered what Jack had said about Hook, and about England wanting to send more ships, and she didn't feel as certain as she might have wished.

"Beyond this," Jack told her, paying no heed to her assurance, "Tigerlilja and your Captain Hook must agree to meet with me to plan the attack. If you truly want Neverland to be safe, Blackheart must be killed. Not captured. Killed. Even if it comes to a surrender. There must be no quarter for him, or for any of the everlost who follow him."

"What else?" Wendy asked quietly. She wasn't at all sure how she felt about this new demand, but there would be time to consider it later. At least the lines of communication remained open, which was more than she had come to expect.

"When it is done, the British will leave. All of them. None may remain but you."

"Why me?" Wendy couldn't help asking, but Jack merely stared at her in silence until she finally spoke again. "I will convey your terms and return with your answer."

CHAPTER

6

Upon Wendy's return, the council reconvened. Tigerlilja and Vegard were present to speak for the Vikings. Hook, Charlie, and Wendy would represent England. But when Peter tried to follow Wendy into the longhouse, Hook stepped between them, raising his steel appendage to block the way.

"This is a proper war council," Hook told him, placing a distinct emphasis on the word "proper" as though the last one might not have been up to par. "You don't need to be here."

"I do need to be here because I'm on the council," Peter argued. "I'm the most important one."

Tinker Bell, who was sitting on his shoulder, chimed in his ear.

"Well, of course, you are," Peter agreed, and then he turned to address Hook again. "She's the most important one, too."

Hook sighed. "Just wait out there. Both of you. We'll let you know what we decide."

"But you can't decide anything without us." Peter puffed his chest out proudly. "We're dignitaries."

"Dignitaries," Hook echoed. "Really."

"That's right," Peter insisted.

"And who are you supposed to represent, then?"

"Myself," Peter declared at once.

Before Hook could reply, Tinker Bell chimed delicately in Peter's ear again.

"And the everlost," Peter added quickly.

Hook frowned.

"And the imps," Peter continued, folding his arms across his chest as Tinker Bell kept chiming new suggestions. "And Snaggleclaw. Yes, good form. And the yetis, the dinosaurs, the gazelles, the penguins, and all the other creatures I've rescued."

Tink's hair turned a warning shade of red.

"We've rescued," Peter said without missing a beat. "And Tink represents the innisfay. Make that all the fay. Plus, the rock people, the mermaids—"

Hook finally interrupted, slashing his hook through the air in a gesture that seemed both frustrated and resigned in equal measure. "Yes, yes, all right."

And that was that.

If Hook noticed that Charming came in with Wendy, riding as usual on her shoulder, he didn't say a word. And although the longhouse had shrunk a bit, returning to its more customary size, Peter's plate was still present, as were two tiny bowls for Tink and Charming, proving that Neverland felt they should all be invited even if Hook did not.

Once everyone was settled, Wendy took a deep breath, squared her shoulders, and began to list out Jokul's terms one by one, trying very hard not to look nervous. (An officer, she

35

thought, must never look nervous, no matter how understand-able that nervousness might be under the circumstances.)

"First," she said, "Captain Hook and Tigerlilja must agree to meet with Jokul to plan the attack."

Hook and Tigerlilja each nodded once, watching her intently.

"Second, Blackheart is to be killed, not merely captured. There is to be no quarter for him, nor for any of the everlost who follow him. Not even if they surrender."

"You'll hear no argument from me," Hook muttered.

Everyone else glanced at Peter, but he only had eyes for Wendy, smiling at her as though she were listing out a menu they might pack for a picnic later.

"All the British who have come to Neverland must return to England when the battle is won," Wendy said next. She left out the fact that she alone had been invited to stay, but that was only because she would be leaving with the rest of them. It was her duty as an officer.

"Finally," she said, her eyes locking onto Hook's, "we must agree to destroy the portal between England and Neverland. So that no one from our homeland shall ever return."

Wendy had expected Hook to object immediately, but instead, he only looked thoughtful, drumming the fingers of his good left hand against the table.

Tigerlilja nodded.

Vegard merely shrugged.

Wendy glanced at Peter, but he was still smiling. Did he realize that she would have no way to return once the portal was destroyed? Or had he realized it and then instantly forgotten?

She turned briefly to Charlie, but his expression held no reaction. Clearly, he was waiting to see what his captain had to say. He would never disagree with a superior officer, especially not in front of a foreign delegation.

"Destroying the portal would be best for England as well as Neverland," Hook said finally. "That is, if it's the only portal between the two. It would put an end to the everlost raids. And it would keep the infernal magic of this place away from England's shores."

It seemed to Wendy that Tigerlilja's face darkened at these words—but only for a moment. By the time Wendy could glance fully in her direction, the Viking's expression was as inscrutable as ever.

"But if there are others ..." Hook's voice trailed off as he, too, turned toward Tigerlilja. "If there are others," he repeated, his voice pitched so low it was more akin to a growl, "England will not allow the path between our two nations to run in only one direction."

Tigerlilja's face betrayed nothing, her words calm and even as she voiced her reply. "In all the time we have been here, we have found only one portal between our worlds. Not that it matters," she added. "Jokul won't budge on his demands."

"Any list of demands is merely the opening shot of a good negotiation," Hook countered.

"Not this list," Tigerlilja said softly. "Jokul doesn't want any humans in Neverland. He makes an exception for our people because we actively work to preserve this place, but even then, he barely tolerates our presence." For a moment, her eyes held an expression of profound sadness, but they hardened in an instant as she scoffed the moment away. "But the English? Believe me, if there's anything Jokul hates more than all of humanity, it's Englishmen in particular."

"And how much is that?" Hook surged to his feet. "Enough to hide some other portal he could use to reach England? To raid our lands once we have no way to return?"

Tigerlilja rose to meet him, matching his aggressive stance.

37

"I don't need a ship to visit England," Peter chimed in.

"You're not helping," Vegard muttered.

Wendy thought quickly, desperate to change the course of the conversation before the council could dissolve before her eyes. "What about the everlost?" she blurted out.

"What about them?" Tigerlilja turned to Wendy, looking puzzled, which seemed like a significant improvement over the brewing storm she had just interrupted.

"Jokul didn't say that Peter's everlost had to leave," Wendy clarified. "But all the everlost are from England, aren't they?"

Tigerlilja paused, choosing her words carefully. "The everlost are no longer fully human," she said finally. "Once they are turned, Neverland becomes a part of them."

"Then why does Jokul want to kill the ones who follow Blackheart?" Wendy persisted. "Why not give them a chance to renounce their allegiance?"

If Peter had any thoughts about this new turn in the conversation, he didn't show it. He watched first one woman and then the other with no sign of any particular feeling on the subject.

"Because their minds and hearts have been corrupted by Buri," Tigerlilja replied slowly. "You don't understand how deep that goes. Blackheart isn't the first to try to rule Neverland; he's just the first to channel so much of Buri's power here. The first to bleed so much corruption into the magic that maintains Neverland itself. That's what makes him so dangerous."

"Ha, I laugh at danger," Peter crowed. "Nothing can defeat me. I always prevail!"

Charming, who had finished his meal and was seated once again upon Wendy's shoulder, shook his tiny fist at Peter, turning red and chiming angrily.

"Don't be ridiculous," Peter responded. "I've defeated Blackheart every time we've ever fought."

The innisfay's protests grew louder, harsh and discordant in Wendy's ear.

"What are you talking about?" Peter shot back. "If he defeated us, then how did the Wendy steal his ship? That sounds like a victory to me."

At this, Charming dropped his chin to his chest, muttering melodiously and shaking his head. He didn't seem to be talking to Peter anymore, but Peter replied, nonetheless.

"Now, that's not fair," he said, finally sounding defensive. "Defeating your own shadow is very difficult. It's an exceedingly even match, after all. I'd like to see you try it."

Wendy couldn't be certain, but she thought Tigerlilja, Vegard, and even Captain Hook twitched a little, glancing uneasily around the room for no reason she could discern.

"So, Peter's everlost are safe?" she asked, trying to bring the conversation back around. "Jokul doesn't hate them for being from England?" Truth be told, she was growing quite fond of Peter's everlost. Especially Tootles, who was part of her crew now.

"Believe it or not, many of them are too old to be English. They became everlost long before England was England." Tigerlilja paused again, giving Wendy time to let that sink in. "Others are from far-off places. Still, Jokul will let all who are loyal to Peter remain here. Even the everlost who were once English belong to Neverland now. Of course, they could also choose to return with you and live out their natural lives on English soil. If they break their ties to Neverland, they will become again what they once were."

Wendy frowned. That seemed sad to her. The thought of losing their magic, returning to England and what they were before. It made her think about her conversation with Jokul. And the fact that he had said she could stay—if she wanted to.

The thing was, she wasn't sure *what* she wanted.

She had been working so hard to get where she was now that she hadn't even begun to think about the end of her adventure—about going back or staying, either one. Could she really accept going back to the way things were? Where the buildings always stayed the same size you built them and the world wouldn't change just to make you feel at home?

She didn't even have a place in England, let alone a way to fly.

After everything she had gone through to become a captain, she still wasn't sure she could depend on keeping her rank. Hook was a loyal officer of the Royal Navy. He would follow any orders he received, including an order to denounce her.

She wanted to think he would do what he could, but was she certain of it? Would he try to speak up for her at all? Maybe she was fooling herself. Maybe he wouldn't even try.

And maybe not knowing was why she hadn't told Hook about Jokul's final demand—that if Hook wouldn't destroy the portal, Wendy would have to do it herself.

Suddenly, she sensed Peter watching her. She turned to find him not quite smiling, and not quite frowning. His expression was more curious than anything. Interested. As though he cared very much what she might be thinking.

Which, of course, he did. He always did.

Peter would speak up for her, she realized, no matter what. Even if the gods of Asgard tried to take something away from her, he would stand against them.

He would change the whole world for her, just to see her smile.

# CHAPTER
# 7

After the council meeting, Tigerlilja retreated to the small, cozy sanctuary that served as her home. She needed some time alone—to think, and to consult the runes of her ancestors. The battle with Blackheart was coming.

The thought weighed heavily on her heart.

On the one hand, she was desperate to strike at the threat, to defend Neverland against this most recent attack. She wanted that more than anything. But she was also tired. Tired of the endless battles. Tired of having to defend this place over and over, winning every single fight yet somehow never winning the war.

And at what cost?

Why did she have the feeling that it would be her own people, yet again, who would bear the highest price for Buri's jealousy?

She still remembered that first battle like it was only yesterday. Buri had come to her village looking for the sword that Pan's mother had left in their care. The sword that led her to Neverland.

Buri had killed her parents that day. And her beloved Amma. And so many of the rest. Now, he might take all that she had left.

Her people might not age in Neverland, but that didn't make them immortal. If Blackheart's silver struck Vegard, or Argus, or any of the others, even the fay couldn't save them. They would be gone. Just like Mother and Father. Just like Amma. Blackheart could kill them all, and she would be powerless to stop it.

If she wasn't sworn to protect this place, she might be tempted to put her own people first. To sail away until the battle was over.

But then again, if Blackheart won …

No, their destinies were tied together now: the Vikings belonged to Neverland, and Neverland belonged to the Vikings. Her people would not abandon this place. They would not leave that battle to fate.

Not even if she begged them to.

Tigerlilja sat on the floor in front of her small fireplace and poured Amma's runes into her hands. She watched them roll back and forth between her fingers, their long-polished surfaces reflecting the low flames. One after another, the symbols spoke to her, twisting and turning to flash their messages before she had even cast them.

*Ancestors. Magic. Sanctuary.*

Neverland, Tigerlilja thought. The gift from Amma that had preserved their people so far beyond their years.

Wendy had asked her once how long she had been here. And whether she ever tired of it.

Too long, had been her first thought. Longer than any human beings could possibly deserve. Everyone else born in her time had crossed the veil centuries ago. Their bodies had burned to ash on funeral pyres, the sparks of their memories blown away on the wind.

But the runes continued to speak, interrupting her thoughts. She felt Amma's presence and almost smiled.

Yes, Tigerlilja agreed, there had been a time when she was happy. When the eternity of Neverland had felt like a blessing. How long ago was it now? It was impossible to know—and it didn't make any difference.

Despite appearances, time did move in Neverland. People found happiness. And lost it again. Things changed. But instead of moving forward, away from the past, time here had a way of wrapping back around itself, so that what came before remained fresh in her mind, every moment of it as clear as yesterday.

It seemed like only hours ago that she had opened her heart to another, letting that love influence the decisions she made for her people. For Neverland. At the same time, it felt like centuries since he had held her. Laughed with her. Made her time here feel less like a responsibility and more like a gift.

*Love.*

Her hands fell still, holding the rune that gleamed in the fire-light. But then she searched through the stones in her palm until she found another, answering her grandmother in kind.

This one meant *Endings.* Or *Death.*

Idly, she shifted her fingers, watching them argue back and forth as each caught the light in turn. *Love. Death. Love. Death.*

And then, suddenly, she sensed his presence. Jokul. She looked up to find him standing in her doorway, watching her.

Surprised, she dropped the runes from her hands, and they scattered across the floor.

*Love. Joy. Relationship. Gift. Magic. Light. Sanctuary.*

Tigerlilja frowned and snatched them back furiously.

"Enough, Amma," she muttered under her breath.

"What do they say?" He rubbed the back of his neck with one hand, his eyes uncertain.

"They say you're trouble. As usual."

But he only smiled. "That's not true. Your grandmother loves me."

Tigerlilja glared at him, refusing to give in to his charms. Not now. Not after he had made his position clear. "Why are you here? And why are you insisting on this mockery of a council? You'll dictate the terms of this alliance or you won't be part of it at all, and we both know it."

"Perhaps I'm here because you need me." His lips still hinted at a smile.

"Because Neverland needs you," she shot back, sounding more bitter than she had meant to. They locked eyes for a long moment, but she gave him nothing.

Eventually, his expression fell, and he sighed deeply. "You're the only one I trust," he admitted. "I needed to make sure you knew what they had asked of me. That you had sent them willingly, understanding what's at stake. What we're all risking."

His voice held concern now. Even affection. But that only fueled her anger. It reminded her of everything he could be when he wanted to. When he tried. But that was only part of him. A genuine part, to be sure, but not always the part that mattered. He carried the cruel tragedies of the past in his heart, always, holding them close, fresh as new-fallen snow.

He was as much a victim of Neverland as she was.

*Stop*, she told herself. *Stop rationalizing your feelings for him. Stop letting them seep back in. What's done is done. That's the one truth in all of it.*

He would always put his precious fay before everyone else. Before her. Before her people. Before Neverland. She needed to know what he thought was best for them when it came to the coming battle. Because no matter what he said, no matter what promises he made, deceit meant nothing to him if he thought it would serve the fay.

Not even love could change that. He had proven as much.

"I know the risks," she told him. "But Blackheart's forces grow stronger every day. And he has opened a portal for Buri. Already, the Old One has begun to step through." She paused to watch for his reaction, but he merely nodded.

"The fay told me as much," he admitted.

"And yet you did nothing?" Her voice betrayed the horror that flared within her, but Jokul raised his hands in a gesture of peace, answering quickly.

"I only found out when you did. *Because* you did. I swear I would have told you had I known sooner."

"Tinker Bell," Tigerlilja realized.

"Yes." He nodded. "I was considering what to do when your delegation arrived."

Tigerlilja finally cracked a sardonic smile. Peter would not have been her choice of delegates if she had had any better options.

Jokul took a deep breath and spoke again, his eyes not holding any hope, despite his words. "Do you think there could be any reasoning with Blackheart? Buri will destroy the very land Blackheart hopes to rule. Perhaps, if he could be made to see that—"

But Tigerlilja interrupted him sharply, already shaking her head. "You know the truth as well as I do. He has allowed Buri into his heart. He is beyond reason. You've said it too often not to believe it now: 'There is a void that lies within the hearts of humankind—one that is easily filled with evil.'"

A tear formed in her eye as she spoke his words back to him. She couldn't help it. It was cruel of her and she knew it. But instead of recoiling, he arced like lightning into the room and knelt before her in the space of a heartbeat, reaching out to wipe the tear away before it could fall from her cheek.

"Not all of them," he said.

His touch was tender. His words, gentle. But his movement had surprised her. It was too far beyond what she had expected of him. Before she could realize his intentions and reach for his hand, she acted on instinct, springing to her feet and drawing the dagger from her belt.

She regretted it immediately, but like so much that stood between them, she couldn't take it back once it was done. "Will you fight with us or not?" she asked quietly. "No more lies. If you ever held any love for me, if there was ever any truth to that, don't lie to me now. Not about this."

Jokul rose to his own feet, moving slowly now, and stepped away. When his eye formed a tear of its own, Tigerlilja wanted desperately to do the same thing he had just done—to drop her dagger and reach for him, brushing it from his cheek with her fingertips—but she couldn't give him that. She couldn't let him believe he could manipulate her through her emotions.

Not again. Never again.

"We will fight," he said. "That much, I promise. Although I fear we have waited too long. Their forces are stronger than ours, even together. Still, I will not hide my intentions. Not from you. If we are victorious, I will not allow the English to leave unless they cannot return. One must be destroyed: either the portal, or the English themselves. You know my preference."

"All too well," she snapped.

"I have kept my word," Jokul said gently.

"On that much, at least." The glare she offered back held no quarter, but Jokul returned it with a look of sorrow that almost broke her heart.

"We will need others," he said, clearly changing the subject. "As many allies as we can recruit. The Wendy should be able to help. We will need all the forces we can gather if we are to have any chance of turning the tide."

"Why was it so difficult?" she asked suddenly.

"I ... what?" He paused, and a tiny, perfect line formed between his eyebrows, reflecting his confusion.

"Why did it take you so long to get involved?" she demanded. "Why did we have to ask you? You might not have known that Blackheart had opened a pathway for Buri, but you knew he was building his forces. You must have known we were moving against him. Why didn't you join us then? If you had been there, we might have ended it—"

"You know why," he said, cutting her off and sounding angry for the first time since he had arrived.

Of all the emotions he had shown her, this was the first one she trusted. She noticed that fact quietly, inside herself, and it broke her heart a little more.

His chest rose and fell as his breath quickened, and the blue of his eyes turned cold as ice. "Do we agree about the portal?"

"I agree that they must not leave knowing how to return," she said carefully.

"Good," he replied. "It is enough. Then you have my sword— and whatever fay from the realm of frost might choose to fight beside me."

He left the same way he had arrived, swift and silent, moving like a force of nature.

Tigerlilja sheathed her dagger, her hand trembling, and she bent to retrieve the runes from the floor. When she did, her fingers brushed one by accident, and it turned on its side, a new rune gleaming in the firelight.

*Promises,* it told her.

It took every ounce of self-control she had not to hurl it into the fire.

Sometime later, high above the twilight glade where the *Jolly Roger* had first made its home, Wendy stood on the deck of her beautiful flying ship and breathed in the cool, sharp air of the mountains. The weight of her captain's jacket felt reassuring upon her shoulders, raising her spirits, its long tails flapping gently in the breeze.

*What a wonderful night*, she thought, even though days and nights didn't really mean anything in Neverland.

She was enjoying herself so much in fact that she almost felt guilty about it, knowing what still hung in the balance. But she needed this. They all did. Not just because her first round of recruits needed to come together as a crew, but because missions that could save or doom the world were simply too much to bear without a bit of fun in between. Which is why Wendy wasn't doing much to rein in the chaos that surged around her.

Her skeleton crew hadn't yet learned the whistles they would need for battle, so they had set up a chain of command to relay Wendy's orders from one end of the ship to the other.

As it turned out, this system left something to be desired.

"Hard to starboard," she announced.

"Aye, Captain." Charlie had come along to take the wheel, working on his flying skills while Wendy watched over the crew.

"Hard to starboard," John shouted, calling out the order.

"Hard to starboard," Goldie echoed, standing some yards away.

"Hard to port," yelled Barnaby, who was standing right next to Goldie.

Scrant exploded in a slew of cursing. "Shut it, Barnaby! You're not even part of the chain! The next time you say it backward, I swear I'll throw you overboard myself!"

In point of fact, Scrant had threatened this no fewer than seventeen times already. If Barnaby had looked a bit concerned in the beginning, it was clear he no longer felt even remotely threatened.

"Hard to—" Michael shouted, trying to yell in the midst of laughing and not succeeding very well at all. "Hard to—"

Wendy thought she saw tears rolling down his face and decided not to turn to starboard after all. She didn't want to surprise the crew stationed in the foresails and shake them from the rigging.

For everyone's safety, she had ordered Tootles to keep watch from the crow's nest and fly rescue missions in case anyone toppled overboard, but she was starting to wonder whether that had been a good idea. When she first came up with it, she thought Tootle's reputation for missing all the adventure might work a bit of magic to keep anyone from falling overboard in the first place.

But just because he missed all the excitement didn't mean it never happened.

It just meant he didn't see it.

Unfortunately, this new thought had occurred to Wendy only after they were underway, so she had decided not to rely on him too heavily in this capacity. Just to be on the safe side.

"Belay that order," Wendy said.

"Aye, Captain," Charlie agreed, chuckling quietly.

"Belay the order," John shouted, looking just as serious as before.

"Belay the order," Goldie echoed, sighing a little.

"Hard to port," Barnaby shouted again.

"Barnaby!" Scrant exploded.

Charming, who had been sitting on Wendy's shoulder this whole time, finally lost his temper. Turning bright red, he darted off to buzz around Barnaby's head, shaking his fist and jingling angrily. (He and Barnaby, after all, did have a bit of a history.)

"What do you think?" Wendy asked, turning to John. "Should we try firing the cannon again?" If there happened to be a mischievous twinkle in her eye, he missed it entirely—as she had known he would.

In the interest of safety, they had limited the crew to a single live cannon, at least for now. But their attempts to fire it had yet to be successful.

So far, Goldie had stolen five bags of powder, a dozen wads of rags, the flint (which had held things up for quite some time), and no fewer than seven cannonballs, imps being remarkably strong for their size. Still, it was only when he swiped a lit fuse and shoved it in his pocket, burning a hole in his pants and almost setting them on fire, that Wendy had finally put an end to their attempts.

"Oh, heavens, no," John protested, taking Wendy's suggestion quite seriously. Without warning, he chuckled in spite of himself, then coughed diplomatically and reinforced the reply, his face serious once again. "Best not."

Wendy only smiled.

"Well, I think they're shaping up, nonetheless," she declared. "It's a fine crew. We need more, to be sure, but it's an excellent beginning. Wouldn't you agree, Charlie?"

"Aye, Captain," he said, nodding solemnly. "A fine crew. Especially the imps. Best I've ever sailed with."

"They're the only imps you've ever sailed with," John protested.

"Doesn't make it any less true," Charlie said with a grin.

"A grand beginning," Wendy declared, putting the subject to rest. "In fact, I believe the occasion calls for a song."

"Aye, Captain," Charlie agreed.

"Must we?" John grumbled.

"Indeed, we must. Convey the order, Mr. Abbot," Wendy insisted.

"Give us a song, then," John shouted reluctantly.

"A song for the crew," Goldie echoed.

"No singing!" Barnaby shouted.

"For once, I'm with him," John muttered.

"Shut it, Barnaby," Scrant hollered. "Let him sing!"

The crew fell silent as a voice rose from the rigging, setting the pitch.

The voice belonged to Hurley, who was an imp, and although he looked perfectly imp-like from head to toe, his voice sounded nothing like the gravelly baritone or bass of the others. He sang in a crystal-clear tenor, smooth as silk and sweet as honey, and his tune was surprisingly gentle, almost like a lullaby.

*The moon is my love*
*It calls to me softly*
*"Come sail on the wind*
*And be free again"*

Hurley sang alone, but all across the deck, the imps among the crew stomped twice in perfect unison.

*Stomp. Stomp.*

His voice rose again into the evening air.

*A light in my heart*
*A dream I remember*
*I lived every breath*
*Full of confidence*

*Stomp. Stomp.*

Wendy had assumed by this point that Hurley would sing the entire song by himself, but as his voice rose into the first lines of the chorus, the imps answered him, singing every other line in a rough, deep reply.

*My soul has wings*
*I feel them growing*
*My soul has wings*
*They're still unfolding*
*My soul has wings*
*I'll touch the heavens*
*My soul has wings*
*Just wait and see*

They were already touching the heavens, Wendy realized. Right now, flying beneath the stars. A tear formed in her eye as Hurley sang the next verse.

*But try as I might*
*The night spins above me*
*Hurling me back*
*To the everyday*

*Stomp. Stomp.*

*I fall to my knees*
*Yet still I remember*
*The sun in my heart*
*Lighting up the way*

*Stomp. Stomp.*

This time, when the chorus came, the rest of the crew sang along with the imps. The voices of the Fourteenth Platoon rose into the night, and Charlie and Tootles added their own clear tenors to the mix. Wendy couldn't quite bring herself to join in, and neither did John. But he did at least hum a little in a lovely baritone.

*My soul has wings*
*I feel them growing*
*My soul has wings*
*They're still unfolding*
*My soul has wings*
*I'll touch the heavens*
*My soul has wings*
*Just wait and see*

The song finished just as it had begun, with Hurley's voice singing alone.

*The moon is my love*
*It calls to me softly*
*"Come sail on the wind*
*And be free again"*

The final note trailed away, but the crew didn't clap or cheer.

They simply went back to sailing, turning their faces silently toward the night sky.

As Wendy looked around, she noted an occasional exchanged glance. A nod here and there of quiet camaraderie. Between human and imp. Imp and everlost. Everlost and human.

*This crew will work,* she realized.

It was a thought she had had a hundred times before, but always the words had flowed through her mind consciously. Purposefully. As though she were willing them to be true.

Now, finally, they came to her unbidden. An innate response to what she saw. To what she felt. Which is how she knew that they were true.

That they always had been.

CHAPTER
**9**

Occasionally in life, amidst the humdrum of work and errands and quiet meals, we are blessed by moments of profound revelation. They may be tangible, like a newborn child, or they may be fleeting, like a dream. But no matter their form, they change us forever.

For Wendy, this was such a moment, and she felt a weight leave her shoulders—a weight she hadn't even known she was carrying. This crew was going to work. It was going to *work*.

Which meant that she, Wendy Darling, was truly a captain.

She had been a captain in name ever since Hook had assigned her a ship of her own. That much was true enough. But even as Wendy had celebrated that fact, she had also known that her transformation was incomplete.

For every great captain is keenly aware that it is not a ship that makes a captain, but her crew.

A captain alone on a ship is but a sailor. A sailor with a crew, on the other hand, is a captain no matter where she might find herself—commanding from the deck of her ship, at home in bed on shore leave, or even shipwrecked on an uncharted island. A ship may be a captain's pride and joy, but her crew is her greatest responsibility. Her crew is her family.

Wendy took a deep breath, letting this newfound truth fill her heart. She accepted that truth, holding her breath for one perfect moment as she embraced it completely, and then breathed out again with a small, joyful sigh.

Which, as is so often the case, was all the time she had to appreciate it before things began to go completely, horribly wrong.

The first sign of disaster was a cannonball rolling across the deck. It should be noted here that as serene as flying looks to those of us standing on the ground, it is often a wild and choppy affair in practice. Winds do as they please, jostling and wrestling each other whenever they're awake, much like children. So a flying ship gets tossed around a good bit, rolling this way and that, which is why everything on a ship has some way of being bolted down.

Cannonballs, of course, are no exception. They are stored quite carefully so as to prevent exactly this sort of danger. But that isn't much help if a certain member of the crew is in the habit of pilfering them and then leaving them lying about after the fun has been had. (We won't point any fingers because it doesn't really matter who was responsible, but still, if you wanted to take a guess, let's just say you would probably be right.)

Had there been only one loose cannonball, things wouldn't have been so bad. One certainly never wants to have a cannonball careening along the deck, picking up speed as the ship slides and rolls with the winds, but that isn't nearly as much trouble as ... well ... we're getting ahead of ourselves. Here's how things played out, revealing them one at a time, which is how Wendy discovered them.

First, she saw the one cannonball, rolling along the deck at an alarming clip and heading straight for Michael.

"Michael, look out!" she cried.

John followed her gaze and sounded the warning in an instant. "Michael! Loose cannonball! Watch your feet!"

"Loose cannonball," Goldie shouted. "Watch your feet! Loose cannonball!"

"No, there isn't!" Barnaby shouted. "All is well!"

Fortunately, everyone knew to ignore Barnaby by now, including Michael. He located the danger and leaped over it just in time. The cannonball, without Michael's ankle to break its momentum, crashed into the side rails.

"Report!" Wendy shouted, but even as she called out the word, she saw Michael's eyes widen. For the briefest of moments, time stood absolutely still. And then the rest of it seemed to happen all at once.

A wave of cannonballs hurtled along the deck toward the first one. At the same time, shouts of "Loose cannon!" rose from the other side of the ship, where a certain imp had tried to steal something that even he, as strong as he was, had no hope of carrying.

"Look alive!" Wendy shouted. "Secure the cannon!"

"Look alive!" John echoed faithfully. "Secure the cannon!"

In a small stroke of luck, the cannon had only just now broken loose. As heavy as it was, it hadn't had time to gain much momentum. The nearby crew members were able to wrestle it back into position and retie the ropes that had been securing it.

The same, sadly, could not be said for the cannonballs. Michael took two running steps and dove out of the way just in time to avoid them as they slammed into the rails en masse. With a resounding crack, they punched a hole straight through, sailed

gracefully into the open air, then plummeted toward the ground far below, picking up speed by the second.

You might think that this would be the end of it. After all, a ship could be repaired, and no one on board had been injured. But Wendy had always had a wonderful imagination. The moment those cannonballs careened over the edge, she imagined them hurtling toward any number of innocent creatures who might be wandering about below. A herd of deer, perhaps, or even a colony of innisfay in their quaint little homes of ...

Wendy paused. What were innisfay homes made of? She suddenly realized that she had no idea. She had never seen an innisfay village. Did they sleep in tree branches, curled up in leaves? Or did they build elaborate miniature castles out of driftwood and river stones? Why, that would be marvelous!

In Wendy's mind, the cannonballs were now hurtling toward a lovely settlement of innisfay castles that had been handcrafted of driftwood and river stones. Tiny children were nestled in their beds, begging in tiny jingling voices for bedtime stories. Their parents smiled tenderly. "Perhaps just one," they said, unaware that at this very moment, an iron rain of death was pelting toward them through the heavens.

"Tootles!" Wendy cried. "After those cannonballs! Protect anyone and anything that might be in their path. Hurry!"

"Aye, Captain," Tootles shouted at once. "At last, an adventure!" Quick as a wink, he leaped out of the crow's nest and dove after them.

Wendy sighed in relief. Nothing very exciting ever happened when Tootles was around. Now that he was on the job, there probably weren't any innisfay below them at all.

So why did she still have an uneasy feeling in the pit of her stomach?

Wendy's right eyebrow recognized it first, shooting up like a warning flag. (Like any good partner, the left joined in immediately, even though it still wasn't quite sure what was happening.)

There was something, Wendy thought, hovering on the horizon. Something that smelled a bit more like green than the imps, who were already swarming over the broken side rails, roping them off for safety. Something that wasn't Charming, who had returned to his usual perch on her shoulder. Something greener than the air of Neverland itself.

And this something, she now realized, smelled less like green and more like the underlying rot of late autumn, when dead leaves litter the forest floor with the pervasive scent of decay.

She scanned the skies, but the only thing she saw ahead was a small, dark shape. A raven, perhaps. She could just make out its wings. Still, there was something odd about it. It didn't move like a raven. And although it was too far away for Wendy to make out its true shape, she sensed its magic as it grew closer by the moment.

A powerful, twisted magic.

Magic that smelled like death.

Wendy reached for the spyglass at her hip, but her hand closed on nothing. She had loaned her glass to Tootles, who had taken it with him when he dove after the cannonballs.

"Charlie," she said softly. "May I see your spyglass, please?" She never took her eyes off that single dark spot on the horizon. She merely reached out her hand.

Charlie placed the instrument into her palm at once, without question.

Wendy raised the glass to her eye. For a long moment, she said nothing, and then she whispered a single word under her breath.

"Dragon."

CHAPTER

# 10

"Captain?"

Wendy's attention snapped back to Charlie, and their eyes locked. Charlie looked away first, his gaze turning toward the creature that sped toward them on the horizon.

"Snaggleclaw?" he asked, but he didn't sound very hopeful.

"That," Wendy said softly, "is not Snaggleclaw."

Charlie's eyes hardened and he gripped the wheel, his knuckles turning white under the pressure.

Wendy snapped into action.

"Dragon!" she shouted. "Battle stations! All hands!"

"You heard the captain. Dragon! Battle stations!" John yelled. "All hands!"

"Battle stations, all hands," Goldie repeated, adding quickly, "It's a dragon, Barnaby. Don't even think about it."

To his credit, Barnaby didn't say a word.

"Dragon," Michael shouted, last in the command chain. "Battle stations! All hands!"

Wendy raised the spyglass to her eye once more, but even without it, she could tell that the beast was coming fast. Too fast. And if she had to guess, its body was larger than her entire ship.

"Charlie," she murmured, "keep the wheel. But perhaps I should take the helm."

His eyes wide, he reached out his hand and pressed the knucklebone trinket into her palm with a grateful nod.

In an instant, the ship's magic surged through her.

"Hard to starboard, then full speed ahead," she told Charlie. "Man the sails. I need all the speed we can get."

"Hard to starboard! Man the sails! Hard to starboard!" Her orders echoed along the length of the ship without interruption. Without hesitation.

Wendy shifted her attention more intensely to the ship and its magic, urging the *Jolly Roger* to accelerate into the turn. She felt the sails turning to give her the full power of the wind. The rudder moving far below her feet.

"All hands, secure yourselves." Her voice sounded foreign to her ears—calm and commanding, as though it belonged to someone else. Someone she wasn't sure she knew.

"Brace yourselves." John, Goldie, and Michael repeated the call so quickly their words sounded like an echo rolling away against a mountain. Only there was no mountain—just the monstrous body of the dragon, still gaining on them despite their best efforts.

It wasn't going to be enough.

The thought terrified her, right down to her bones—not for herself, but for her crew. They didn't stand a chance, yet not one of them abandoned his post. Not one raised his voice in protest. They followed her orders in disciplined silence, and they watched as the mouth of hell grew closer ... closer ... until a roaring torrent of flame exploded from its depths.

It wasn't going to be enough.

It *had* to be enough. There was no other choice.

A scream ripped from Wendy's throat as she forced the ship harder to starboard, willing the turn with all her might. Her crew hauled on the sails with every ounce of their strength. Charlie raised himself up to his full height and threw all of his weight onto the wheel, forcing the rudder to hold its position.

And then she felt it. Something ... *new.*

At first, she thought it must be the heat of the dragon's breath, and she clenched her jaw against the pain that was sure to follow. But then she realized the warmth was coming not from without, but from within—as her heart opened like a blossom to the sun, embracing the full strength of every soul in her crew.

There was Charlie, with his calm endurance.

And John, full of stoic faith and grim determination.

Michael, whose unquenchable optimism held true, even now.

And Goldie, who stole as a habit, but who could also turn things up in the most surprising ways, just when they were needed.

Scrant was there too, facing down the dragon without an ounce of fear in his heart.

And Barnaby, who could deny even the most certain of deaths, refusing to believe in it right through the very last moment of his existence.

And, of course, Charming, with his rainbow shimmer of enthusiasm, loyalty, and unwavering confidence in her ability.

One by one she felt them—all of them—as clearly as she felt the ship, joining together to refuse the darkness. To oppose the inevitable.

And so the ship turned. It shouldn't have been enough, and yet somehow, miraculously, it was, avoiding the dragon's blaze by a hair's breadth.

"Full speed ahead!" Wendy shouted. "Give it everything you have!"

The warmth in her heart grew, and the ship picked up speed.

The dragon screamed, its wings beating faster, until it was catching up yet again. It opened its mouth wide, preparing to blast them from the sky.

"Hold fast," she shouted.

"Hold fast." Her order echoed down the line.

Just as the dragon roared a new stream of molten fire, Wendy released her hold on the ship, and it plummeted from the sky.

A scattered chorus of surprised shouts rose from the crew as the deck fell out from under them.

"Dive to port!"

She caught the *Jolly Roger* up again just enough to control its fall, sliding hard to port as molten dragon fire rained down from above. Only when they were clear of it did she set her will toward halting their descent. But their downward speed by that point was terrifying to behold.

The ship bucked in protest as the abrupt deceleration pushed the vessel to the limits of its endurance. At one with the ship, every sinew of Wendy's body screamed in agony as the very timbers of the hull threatened to rip apart.

Still, the *Jolly Roger* held. Shouts turned to cheers as they finally hurtled forward once more, but the ship had lost more than half its altitude. Wendy knew she couldn't pull that trick off again without crashing headlong into the ground.

Unless ... unless they didn't crash into the ground at all.

She scanned the terrain below. They were flying over twilight desert at the moment, but a bright, sunny lake loomed up ahead, slightly to starboard.

"Head for the lake!" she shouted.

"Pull to starboard! Head for the lake!" The order flew down the ship. Given their speed, with the force and noise of the wind, Michael's voice was lost to her now. But she could still see him as he raised his hands to his mouth, repeating her command.

The dragon was right behind them, and Wendy turned her full concentration back to the ship itself, urging it forward, hoping against hope that they would reach the water in time.

Gritting her teeth, she used their sloping dive to gain new momentum, building their speed, barely managing to keep them out of harm's reach. But the crew was still with her. She felt their firm presence filling her heart, adding their strength to hers, so she flew faster still. And when the dragon opened its mouth, she dove hard, plunging toward the water, sliding starboard yet again to get out from under the flames.

She watched the wall of fire raining down from above. They were edging out from under it, but there wasn't enough room left between water and sky. By the time they were clear of that molten death, the ship was going to crash at full throttle into the surface of the lake.

"Brace for impact!" Wendy shouted. "All hands! Brace for impact!"

Bravely, the crew echoed her command.

She spent their last, fleeting moment straining with all her might, but it was no use. The *Jolly Roger* was going down.

CHAPTER

# 11

*I must be the worst ship's captain in the history of the world.*

This was Wendy's last thought as the hull of the *Jolly Roger* was about to crash into the glassy surface of the lake.

And, to be fair, things did look rather grim. Even if the ship wasn't smashed to bits, even if anyone survived, they would surely be burned or boiled or steamed alive by the dragon's next roaring blast from above.

Not that Wendy was responsible for their current predicament. If anything, she had acted quite heroically from the beginning. Only moments ago, she had saved her entire crew from the breath of the dragon—the *dragon*, mind you—and not just once, but three times in a row.

Still, one of the most unfortunate truths about the human condition is that it can take a very long time to believe in yourself and almost no time at all to give it up. No matter who you are, no matter how much you've managed to accomplish, the second it looks like a dragon is about to crash your ship and burn the flesh off the

bones of your crew, you'll be back at square one, convinced that all your efforts have come to nothing.

This is how Wendy felt in that moment. Everything she had worked so hard for, everyone she loved and cared about, was about to be lost forever, and she could think of nothing that might stop it from happening.

Just about everyone goes through this sort of thing at some point—perhaps not a dragon, but some great loss that feels insurmountable—and there's no right or wrong way to deal with it.

For Wendy, for the first time in her life, believing this complete and utter failure to be both permanent and inevitable, she stopped thinking and simply reacted from the deepest, darkest core of her being. She didn't worry about how she might look in front of the men or how they might judge her later. The very idea of "later" was over—for all of them.

So she bounded toward the railing, slammed her body against it, arched her back to stare death in the eye, and screamed at the beast with all her might in one final show of defiance.

When the dragon opened its mouth, the flame that grew deep in its throat was already hot enough to warm Wendy's face.

And then the ship crashed into the lake.

The wave created by the *Jolly Roger* as it smashed at full speed into that huge body of water was enormous—taller and more massive than the worst storm Wendy had ever encountered at sea. Tall enough to block her view of the dragon as it spewed a fatal river of molten death toward the deck. Massive enough to turn that fire into an impenetrable bank of ... fog?

Wendy's mind reeled, trying to take in what had just happened. It didn't make any sense. The dragon was behind them, not in front of them. How had the ship created a wave behind itself?

As the fog lifted, Wendy had only a moment to wrap her mind around the impossible wall of water that surrounded the ship. The

lake had parted to catch the *Jolly Roger*, bringing its descent to a gentle halt far beneath the surface, but the waters weren't closing in. Instead, they held their shape, unmoving, mere feet from the railing where Wendy stood. She watched in wonder as colorful fish regarded her from the depths.

She reached out to the shimmering wall, brushing it with her fingertips, and then the ship started rising, slowly at first, then faster and faster, popping back to the surface like a cork.

The dragon still hovered above the vessel, but now an enormous funnel of water rose from the lake, adopting an almost humanoid form. As large as the dragon itself, the rippling water caught the beast mid-flight and pulled it under.

Recovering her wits, Wendy glanced about her, surveying her ship and its crew. She caught Charlie's eye for the briefest of moments, sharing a wide-eyed glance that could only mean one thing: *Did that really just happen?*

But there would be time to sort that out later. As far as Wendy could tell, the crew seemed to be alive and well. The imps had climbed into the rigging, the everlost had taken to the air, and the humans had lined up along the railing, doubling over it as far as they could—all of them trying to catch a glimpse of the dragon.

A battle raged far beneath the surface of the lake—too deep to make out most of it. A tail exploded out of the water some distance away, only to crash back into the lake and disappear. Then a taloned foot broke the surface and slashed at the hull. The crew shouted in alarm and leaped away, but a rippling tentacle of water snatched the offending foot back under before it could connect.

Wendy had just started to wonder whether the dragon might have drowned when the creature burst from the deep, taking to the sky with a giant coil of water wrapped around it several times—a serpent with no head or tail. The dragon fought to gain altitude, its wings struggling to breach the grip of the water that tightened

around it. With each powerful surge of its wings, sheets of rain poured down on the *Jolly Roger*, soaking the ship and its crew.

Without warning, a terrifying voice pierced Wendy's mind. She clapped her hands to her ears by instinct, but that did nothing to lessen its intensity. She fell to her knees under the onslaught of its cold, calculating scream.

"Undine, this is not your battle. If you continue to interfere, I will extract you from this pond, boil you into steam, and finish my task."

Water rose from the lake in long, thick ropes, reinforcing the coils that wrapped around the dragon's body, and a voice as deep as the ocean roared in reply. "Try it, and you shall become my guest at the bottom of this lake forever, feeding my aquatic friends for generations."

The dragon craned its neck, breathing a rippling, molten stream of fire back on itself. The air filled again with fog, and the water loosened its grip. The beast rose into the sky as the rest of the water finally fell away, dropping back into the lake below.

The dragon stopped and hovered, preparing to attack the ship, but a huge creature shaped like a wave rose from the lake. "Come down again, and these waters will be your grave."

Wendy held her breath as the dragon considered the threat, but then it snorted frustrated smoke into the air, spun on its tail, and flew away.

The crew of the *Jolly Roger* released a collective sigh of relief, then gasped as the wave curled toward the ship, towering over them.

In a voice as gentle as a burbling brook, the water spoke, addressing Wendy directly. "Daughter of Peisinoe, it is a pleasure to meet you. Your mother and I were close."

Peter sat cross-legged on a branch, resting his back against the trunk of an ancient oak. He peered down through the thick canopy of leaves, but nothing seemed to be moving on the forest floor. After a while, he tilted his head toward the twilight sky, but nothing seemed to be up there either. His latest adventure was turning out to be a lot less exciting than he had hoped.

He would have very much preferred to go with the Wendy. He loved being part of anything she was doing, or at least watching whatever she was doing. She always did such interesting things, and just being with her made him feel ... something. He couldn't quite put his finger on it, but she made him feel more alive somehow. More like himself.

He wasn't sure what that meant, which made him curious, so he closed his eyes and tried very hard to think about it. But the moment he thought he might be making progress, his mind drifted away again, remembering how the Wendy and Tigerlilja had insisted that he was needed here.

Well, not here in particular, but at least not on the *Jolly Roger*.

They had been so adamant, in fact, that he had started to feel a bit suspicious at the time. But then they had brought up a very good point: nobody was better than Peter at gathering an army of trusted allies to fight by your side. Even Hook had agreed, swearing it in a blood pact, which everyone knew was the greatest oath you could make.

Tigerlilja had tried to silence the English captain, shushing him dramatically, but Hook had insisted on honoring Peter's talent, biting his own tongue hard enough to make it bleed.

Peter had asked the Wendy where he should start, but she and Tigerlilja had left it in his capable hands. No, they had left it to his tactical genius. Yes, that's what they had said. Peter would never forget it. Hook had chimed in on that as well, biting his tongue harder and spitting the blood on the floor at Peter's feet.

Finally, the man seemed to be coming around. Maybe Neverland was rubbing off on him.

Perched in his tree, Peter smiled. There had to be someone or something around here that he could recruit. A bear maybe. Or a passel of raccoons. Maybe even thirty. Or one hundred.

Peter wondered if he should go check on Blackheart's army, just to make sure he was keeping things even. He didn't want to recruit such a big army that the game wasn't fair. That wouldn't be any fun at all.

Just then, Peter caught a hint of movement on the forest floor. He peered through the leaves, but he couldn't make out what it was. The broken edges of its shadow slid eerily over the ground as though the form that cast it was changing shape from one moment to the next.

Shadow.

He tensed with excitement. She was a great warrior, and it had been a long time since their last adventure together. If Blackheart hadn't already recruited her, she would be perfect.

As he watched, her form stilled, then slithered up a nearby trunk, circling around to the other side of the tree. When she didn't reappear, Peter stood as quietly as he could, spread his wings, and flew over to her, watching her from above. He wanted to make a good impression—he was trying to recruit her after all—so he crossed his arms over his chest and fell from the sky, catching himself dramatically at the last possible moment to hover by her side.

But Shadow didn't bat an eye. She just sighed wearily, as though the weight of the entire world lay upon her shoulders.

"Peter." If she sounded less than enthusiastic to see him, Peter didn't notice.

"Hi, Shadow. I'm looking for people to join my army. What are you doing?"

A shadow-dagger sprang from her hand and stretched into a sword, slick and sharp. "I sensed you were nearby, so I was trying to avoid you. If I had seen you before you saw me, I would have."

"Aha, a game of Hide and Seek!" His expression crumpled. "And it's already over, before I even knew we were playing."

"I'm not playing games." Shadow lunged at Peter, thrusting her sword through the air, but he was hovering too far away to reach.

"You should be in our army! It's not a game, but it's still going to be fun. So far, I've recruited a tribe of rogue innisfay, a gecko, and a whole school of fish." To emphasize this last triumph, Peter executed a perfect backward somersault in midair.

"A school of fish and a lizard?" Shadow scoffed. "Whenever I think you can't get any more daft, you find a way. I bet you don't even know what you're fighting for, do you? Tell me, Peter. Tell me why you're going to war, and I'll consider joining your ridiculous army. Go ahead. Convince me."

A strange expression flitted across his face. "My poor Shadow. Always so angry."

"I'm not your Shadow!" She threw back her arms, thrust her face toward him, and roared in defiance.

He answered her quietly, his voice unaffected by her wrath. "I fight for Neverland. And for Wendy. And for you, my sister. I wanted to be rid of you, once. But now ... now I'd save you if I could."

Shadow stared at him, too dumbfounded to speak. Before she could recover, his expression changed again.

"I hope you choose our side. It's going to be a grand adventure. I'm off to recruit the very wind itself!"

With that, he shot into the sky and flew away.

Shadow watched him in silence. As he disappeared into the distance, her sword shrank until it was just a dagger, then nothing but a point, merging at last into the unbroken edge of her hand.

# CHAPTER 13

"You knew ... my mother?"

Wendy stared at the wave of water that towered over the ship. As she watched, its surface flowed and shifted, the rippling wall reshaping itself into a massive being that looked very much like she had always imagined a genie might look. ("Aladdin and the Magical Lamp" was one of her favorite stories.)

His voice was deep yet surprisingly gentle, even soothing. "I did. Very well, in fact. I am Undine. Perhaps she spoke of me."

Across the deck of the *Jolly Roger*, the crew stared up at the enormous water creature, their mouths falling open in amazement, but no one was more shocked than Wendy herself.

Her eyebrows lifted to the most glorious heights they had ever achieved, and every hair on the back of her neck stood straight out from her skin, sizzling with energy. Was it really possible? Did this water being know something about her mother?

But then she thought about what he had said, and her stomach trembled in a horrible mix of anticipation and dread. "You said you were close. Meaning, in the past. Do you know if she ..."

Wendy couldn't say the words. Was she finally about to discover her mother's identity only to have her death confirmed in the same moment? Her eyes brimmed with tears.

Just then, Charming flew in and landed on her shoulder, returning from wherever he had darted off to during the crash. Wendy took a deep breath, taking comfort in his presence and doing her best to steady herself for whatever Undine might say next.

"I know not, little one. Peter brought me to Neverland ages ago. It's impossible to know how long. I've lived in this lake ever since, and I've never seen her here or felt her presence." He paused, regarding Wendy for a long moment. "But perhaps she lives. Like water elementals, sirens never age, of course—not even in your world. Still, they can be killed. And there is no shortage of hatred for our kind."

"Sirens?" Wendy echoed, her mind racing. "You're saying my mother was ... is ... a siren?"

"Yes. But, how is it that I know this when you do not? Did she really never tell you?" He opened his arms wide, and a wave of water spilled from them, splashing across the deck.

Charlie backed away from the wheel to stand by Wendy's side—whether for her protection or his, she couldn't be sure.

"I never knew her," Wendy admitted. "I was abandoned as an infant, raised as an orphan." She spoke softly, her voice laced with grief, but Undine was already shaking his head.

"Not abandoned. Hidden." He met her gaze with firm intensity.

"Hidden? I don't understand. Hidden from what?"

"From Buri."

Wendy gasped. "Buri?" Her eyebrows, which had only just now finally settled down, leaped back up to resume their posts on high alert.

Undine nodded sadly. "He has been hunting the fay for a very long time, trying to steal their magic from the world. Across the centuries, whenever he gets too close, many of the fay have left their children on human doorsteps, to be raised where they won't learn to use magic. Where they won't be discovered."

Wendy shared a glance with Charlie. Could he be a fay too? There were so many orphans in London. Too many. Even as a child, she had known it—what the grown-ups couldn't admit.

Magic. It was the only thing that made sense.

*But if my mother was a siren …*

She paused, her mind reaching conclusions she didn't like at all. "Well, in my case—" Wendy let the comment hang in the air, hoping the water creature would finish her thought without the need to speak it.

After a long moment, he frowned. "In your case, what?"

With the smallest of sighs, she forged ahead, steeling herself to face the truth. "Perhaps in my case it was for the best. I don't suppose a siren would make a very good mother."

"What? Why would you say that?" The swirling water of his body darkened like a storm, and Wendy took a quick step backward.

"I … I'm so sorry," she said, stammering an apology. "I didn't mean to offend you. It's just, well, the stories aren't very flattering—sirens always luring sailors to their deaths." Holding his gaze, she ducked her head and shoved her hands into the pockets of her captain's jacket.

Undine scoffed, shaking his head. "A few, perhaps. Like any creatures, some can be … unkind. But Peisinoe was not that way. She and I saved countless ships together over the centuries. I pro-

tected them from storms, waterspouts, kraken—and she soothed them with her voice, calming their minds so they would not be afraid. Most sirens use their magic to help sailors focus. To help them survive."

Before Wendy could reply, Charming crossed his arms over his chest and chimed in her ear, his face a mask of stoic skepticism.

"What is it, Charming? Are you saying that's not true?"

But the innisfay waved the idea away. He pointed at Undine, then at Wendy, tilting his head and raising his hands in confusion.

"Oh!" she exclaimed. "If he came to Neverland so long ago, and he hasn't seen Peisinoe since, how does he know she's my mother? Goodness, yes, that's a very good question."

The water creature grumbled, the sound echoing like thunder deep in his chest, but of course Wendy hadn't meant any disrespect. It wasn't that she suspected him of lying—she simply had an inquisitive nature. And anyone could make a mistake. No matter how much she wanted to believe him, she needed to be sure.

Wendy turned back to the giant water elemental looming over her head, addressing him politely. "Again, my apologies. But you must admit, he raises an interesting point. What makes you so certain this Peisinoe was ... *is* my mother?"

"She isn't," Barnaby yelled, suddenly deciding to chime in, which was a clear vote in the water creature's favor.

"Shut it, Barnaby, or I'll rip your face off."

Michael stepped in front of Scrant before things could get out of hand.

Undine shrugged, ignoring the interruption. "The resemblance is unmistakable." The waters of his body cleared as he spoke. "Your hair. Your eyes. Your voice. They are hers. I would know them anywhere. But, more than that, it is the feel of your magic. You are your mother's daughter."

With those words, the tears of hope that had pooled in Wendy's eyes spilled over, running down her cheeks in two tiny, perfect rivulets. All her life, she had felt as though she came from nowhere, completely on her own, with no connections to the world beyond those she managed to forge for herself. But that wasn't true at all.

She had a mother. A fay mother.

"Wait," she blurted out. "Is that why I can smell magic? Because I'm a fay?"

Without warning, Undine bowed toward Wendy until his face was terrifyingly close to hers, and he sniffed the air deeply, his water-formed nose making it sound as though he were gargling. "Half fay. Your father was a human."

He straightened again, and Wendy took a deep breath, letting it out in slow relief.

"But in any case, no," he continued. "The difference between the fay and humankind is not as great as it might appear. From the beginning, our blood has been shared. The rift that tore us apart was not one of magic."

The water genie swiped an agitated arm through the air, sending another wave of water crashing across the deck. Even as Wendy ducked, she heard his words as clear as day.

"There are few of us left who remember, but the fear and hatred that now stand between us are based on a lie."

CHAPTER

# 14

There are moments in life when one discovers something so extraordinary that all other thoughts must politely step aside and wait their turn. The revelation that one's mother is a siren is precisely such a moment.

"A lie?" Even as she posed the question, Wendy's mind was already pushing it aside, shoving it back into the crowd with all her other thoughts, which were milling about in a rather disorderly queue, jostling each other for her attention.

But Undine was already moving on, his watery form rippling with urgency. "There isn't time. This attack was not random. Blackheart has sent his forces to strike at your allies."

"Wait, what? Are you certain?" Wendy's mind reeled. Peter, Hook, Tigerlilja, Jokul—were they all in danger this very moment?

"I am as certain as your mother would have been. As *you* could be, if you focused hard enough. You are your mother's daughter, after all."

"But ... how? I don't understand."

Undine held out his hand, the water that made up his palm gliding smoothly across it. "Think of Neverland's magic like a river, flowing peacefully until disturbed." In several places across his palm, water rose up like rocks, causing the rest of the water to flow around them. "All water creatures sense these disruptions, including sirens. We sense danger to those who are under our protection."

Wendy's other thoughts, which had watched Undine's explanation with varying degrees of patience, all grumbled in protest as a new one crowded forward, shoving itself rudely to the front of the line. "Are you saying I could have sensed this attack before it happened?"

"In time, perhaps. You've always had good instincts about any threat to your crew, have you not?" Undine's massive form shifted, and Wendy braced herself for another wave. But he merely scratched at his side for a moment. When he pulled his hand away, he had plucked a small fish from inside his body. He held it out unceremoniously and dropped it into the lake. "Those instincts come from your siren nature. They could grow stronger, if you learn to trust them."

Before Wendy could sort through all the new thoughts this statement had produced, Undine disappeared. In a single moment, all the water that had made up his body fell back into the lake in one tremendous splash.

"Wait!" she called. "I have so many questions—"

But Undine was gone, leaving Wendy to contemplate this latest revelation for barely a moment before more immediate concerns demanded her attention.

"Captain!" Tootles landed before her, slightly out of breath. "I checked the path of the cannonballs, and I'm happy to report that no creatures were harmed." He paused, looking sheepish. "Though I did have to apologize to a rather indignant fish. Twice."

Poor Tootles. He had missed the dragon attack and the water elemental entirely.

"Thank you, Tootles. Well done." Wendy placed a grateful hand on his shoulder, and he blushed, beaming proudly. "Now, let's canvass the crew. I need a report on the ship's status."

The responses came back in a cascade that would have sent most Royal Navy captains straight to the brandy stores.

"Port rail's splintered, Captain," called Michael.

"Starboard's holding, but we've lost two cannonballs," Scrant announced. "I'll rip the throat out of whoever left them loose!"

"We didn't lose them," Barnaby corrected. "We know exactly where they went."

"Shut it, Barnaby!" This from at least three voices at once.

Charlie's assessment cut through the chaos. "She'll fly, Captain. Not as pretty as before, but she'll fly."

Wendy nodded, already calculating their next move. Peter was out there somewhere, recruiting allies, but she had no idea where. The Viking village, however, was much more findable—and just as much in need of a warning.

"Set course for the village," she ordered.

The crew jumped to obey—with perhaps more enthusiasm than coordination after everything they had been through, but they managed to sort themselves out, just the same.

As they flew, Wendy's thoughts turned to the village, Captain Hook, and the danger he might be in. She tried to focus on that protective instinct Undine had mentioned, hoping for some flash of insight about his safety, but nothing came.

Perhaps she was doing it wrong.

Or perhaps Hook was perfectly fine and there was nothing to sense.

Or perhaps she was too distracted by the question of how Hook would react upon learning that he had promoted a siren to

the rank of captain in the Royal Navy. (Well, half a siren, not that Hook was likely to care much about the distinction.)

Wendy had worked so hard to earn his respect, to prove herself worthy of command. And she had succeeded beyond her wildest dreams. He had given her a ship of her own. Called her "Captain Darling" in a way that made her stand straighter every time she heard it.

But Hook's opinion of magical creatures was about as warm as a British summer—which is to say, not at all.

"Charlie," she said quietly, ensuring her voice wouldn't carry beyond the two of them, "perhaps it's best if we don't mention the ... siren situation ... at least for now?"

He nodded, and Wendy was reminded yet again why she had always trusted him, right from the very beginning. He didn't need an explanation, didn't require justification. He simply understood, as he always had.

At last, the Viking village came into view, looking surprisingly peaceful beneath their approach. No dragons circled its borders. No horrifying creatures threatened its walls. They landed without incident, but Wendy descended the gangplank at a sprint, nonetheless.

She found Tigerlilja in the great hall, calmly sharpening an axe that looked capable of felling a medium-sized forest. The Viking had been eyeing the axe blade critically, tilting her head first one way, then the other, but she looked up sharply when Wendy burst into the room, clearly out of breath.

"Blackheart's forces ... are coming." She tried to force her heart to stop racing, to slow her breathing so she could speak. "We have to hurry. We need to warn ... everyone."

Tigerlilja paused, her hands falling still, but she looked more confused than concerned. "His forces cannot attack us here." She stared at the blade in her hands as though lost in thought.

"Neverland has a way of protecting its denizens, of keeping the peace. It always has."

Wendy remembered visiting Jokul's realm, feeling as though she had passed through some invisible force that held one region separate from the next. But then she remembered infiltrating Blackheart's fortress and stealing the *Ravenhawk*, too.

Clearly, there were exceptions.

"But we attacked their stronghold," she pointed out. "We stole their ship. Can't they attack us, too?"

A hint of a smile touched the Viking's lips. "Peter was with us then. Haven't you noticed? The rules don't apply to him. Neverland lets Peter do whatever he wants." She looked up, meeting Wendy's gaze. "What happened? Why do you think they're coming here?"

"A dragon attacked the *Jolly Roger*. We would have been killed if Undine hadn't saved us. He said the attack wasn't random—it was part of a coordinated effort. Blackheart has sent his forces to attack us all."

"Undine said that? He was certain?"

Wendy nodded. "He sensed the disturbance in Neverland's magic."

The Viking pressed her lips together tightly, then nodded. "We're safe enough here, but we can no longer travel freely without risking attack. Come. We need to tell the others."

In that moment, all of Wendy's thoughts about sirens and dragons and water elementals were shoved roughly aside by a single, terrifying concern: Peter was out there somewhere, on his own, almost certainly unaware of the danger.

# CHAPTER 15

Shadow remained beneath the ancient tree, letting her form drift between the leaves that rustled in Peter's wake. His words about saving her lingered in the air. He had seemed so earnest, so sincere.

Was it just another game? Perhaps. Then again, Peter's games were playful, not cunning. Whatever he was up to, surely there was no malice behind it.

There couldn't be. Shadow knew the truth of that all too well.

A sound caught her attention. Voices, carried on the wind. Deeper than Peter's. More cautious, more guarded.

More human.

She slid down the trunk of the tree, pooling into the grass below, where she could better hear what they were saying.

Three men emerged from the forest path, their forms backlit by the ever-present twilight. One of them held a chain that writhed and twisted in his grip, pulled taut against the darkness that followed behind.

No—not darkness. Shadow knew darkness better than any creature in Neverland. This was something else entirely.

This was true evil.

The hooded creature moved like liquid night, its scales reflecting what little light reached the forest floor. Even from her vantage point in the grass, Shadow could sense the waves of death that rolled off its serpentine form.

"Do we really have to keep it with us?" The man holding the chain spoke through clenched teeth, his knuckles white against the metal links.

A dry laugh answered him. "Having second thoughts already, Davies?" The second man's voice carried the sharp edge of intelligence mixed with arrogance. "And here I thought you were made of sterner stuff."

"You're not the one holding the bloody chain," Davies muttered.

"As I told you before, Peter can't be harmed by mere steel." The second man's tone suggested he was explaining something to a dim child. "We need the basilisk to poison him."

A basilisk? Shadow grimaced. No wonder they had a hood over its head. Meeting its gaze could turn a man into stone. Peter had brought all manner of creatures to Neverland, but even his dim-witted brain wouldn't try to rescue a basilisk. Wherever the beast had come from, this wasn't Peter's doing.

Davies shifted his grip nervously. "Pan's not going to let us get close enough. You know what he's like."

"What he's like," the second man retorted, "is an idiot."

"But he's clever," Davies protested. "Everyone knows that."

"Peter is a man without grief. Without anger. Without suspicion. That alone makes him the greatest fool in the world. We will tell him we want to join his army, and he will believe us. Trust me, it will work."

The third man, who had remained silent until now, muttered something under his breath.

"Speak up," the second man snapped.

"I said poison can't kill Pan. Everyone knows that, too."

"We don't know for certain what it will or won't do. That's the point. It's an experiment. Perhaps we'll petrify him instead. Honestly. Where's your sense of curiosity?" The second man turned, and Shadow's form constricted involuntarily. The sharp planes of his face, the glint of ancient knowledge in his eyes—this was no ordinary soldier. This was Loki's half-human son, Kaspar.

She watched them pass, her thoughts churning. She wanted Peter dead. Had wanted it for longer than she cared to remember. His death would mean her freedom, her chance to finally be more than just a shadow of his foolish games.

And yet.

Something about their plan struck her as wrong. Not because she cared for Peter—she refused to even consider that possibility—but still ...

A flash of movement caught her eye. High above the trees, a familiar figure circled toward them, his form silhouetted against the endless twilight. Of course, Peter would return. He never could leave well enough alone.

The men below had spotted him too. Kaspar raised his hand in greeting. "Hail, Peter. Well met, et cetera, et cetera. We heard you're recruiting an army. We've come to join your cause."

But the basilisk had plans of its own. With a terrible scream, it surged to its full height, ripping the chain from Davies's grasp and shaking the hood from its head.

Shadow burst into action. Her form stretched like smoke, racing toward the sky, toward Peter, toward the last person in all of Neverland she should want to save.

"Peter!" Her voice rang out sharp as steel. "Look out!"

The basilisk reared up, its eyes gleaming with deadly purpose, but Peter was already moving. He twisted in the air, wings flaring behind him like a shield. In the same instant, she poured herself between Peter and his would-be killers, her form expanding into an impenetrable blind.

"Shadow." Peter's voice held none of its usual playfulness. "Good form."

The monster struck, but its fangs passed harmlessly through Shadow's ethereal form. Folding in on herself, she wrapped her body around the creature's head, plunging it into absolute darkness. The basilisk thrashed wildly, but it couldn't shake the living hood that had stolen its vision.

Peter dove into the fray, drawing his sword, but he pulled up at the last moment to hover just beyond the creature's reach. "I don't suppose you've come to join my army after all?" he called out, sounding genuinely disappointed.

Kaspar drew his own sword with fluid grace. "You see?" he said to his companions. "The greatest fool in all of Neverland."

But Peter only laughed. "You're not the first to think so. Probably won't be the last. Shadow, let's show them how good we are when we fight together."

Shadow didn't answer—she had never appreciated Peter's banter—but she moved in perfect synchronization with him as he attacked. While Peter engaged Kaspar, Shadow stabbed the basilisk in the back of its neck, killing it instantly. Free of the beast, she flowed toward Davies and the third man, forcing them back.

Davies broke first, fleeing into the forest. The third man followed, leaving their leader to face Peter and Shadow alone.

At first, Kaspar held his ground, his sword work as elegant as it was lethal. But even he could see the fight was lost. He retreated one careful step, then another, his blade never wavering.

"It doesn't matter." His voice retained the same sharp edge of certainty. "If we can't kill you, we'll use you instead. You're their greatest weakness, Peter. Wherever you go, Neverland opens the gates between the regions. When you return to your base, we'll be waiting." His lips curved into a cruel smile. "They'll never be safe as long as you're on their side."

With a final mocking salute, Loki's son melted into the forest, and Shadow let him go. She would track him later, to see what she could learn. Buri and Blackheart were up to more than she had realized—that much was certain.

Peter landed lightly on a nearby branch, sheathing his sword. For once, he didn't launch into a victory celebration. Instead, he stood quietly, his expression thoughtful. "I have to warn Wendy," he said. "And Tigerlilja. And Hook, I suppose, though he's not nearly as much fun."

Shadow stared at him, entirely at a loss for words. This was not the Peter she knew—the eternal child who treated everything like a game, who forgot the most important moments of his life as soon as they happened.

"Thank you," he added, turning to face her. "For fighting with me. It felt like old times, didn't it? Before ..." He trailed off, a flash of confusion crossing his features.

"Before what?" She uttered the demand before she could stop herself.

But Peter merely shrugged, his usual grin returning. "Does it matter? We fought well together, and we could do it again. If Tigerlilja and Jokul can put death itself behind them, surely you can forgive me."

Her eyes narrowed. "Forgive you for what?"

"Why, for being cleverer than you, of course!"

With a laugh, he spread his wings and took to the sky, leaving her once again in his wake. But this time, he left behind something

else—a glimpse of someone she had never seen before. Someone who could think of others, who could plan ahead, who could even remember to say thank you.

Someone who might, Shadow realized with growing unease, be worth saving after all.

# CHAPTER
# 16

**H**ook leaned over his desk, choosing to squint in the lamp-light rather than open the blinds to the infernal sun of the Viking village. The flame cast dancing shadows against the crude collection of maps that lay before him. Despite what they lacked in detail and scale, his good left hand moved steadily, marking potential attack points.

A long flicker of the lamp caught his attention, but when he glanced up, the flame was steady. He returned to his work, making another notation. Perhaps here, at the border of the desert region ...

This time, when the lamplight wavered, he was ready, and the twinge of pain in his chest felt almost familiar. He offered no reaction beyond setting down his quill and placing his good left hand over his heart. The light flickered once more, then extinguished.

In the darkness, Hook smiled, though the expression held no warmth. "I was starting to wonder when you might return."

A quiet laugh, beautiful and terrible, echoed through the room. "Did you miss me, Captain?" Her voice carried the harsh whisper of a blade being drawn from its sheath.

He didn't bother trying to locate its source. He had learned that much, at least. "Miss you? I've been rather occupied commanding His Majesty's forces."

A shape formed briefly—a suggestion of wings, then horns, then nothing at all. "Your enemies have been equally occupied with their own plans."

"Have they?" He kept his voice light and steady, careful not to betray the depth of his interest. "And what might those plans be?"

The darkness shifted. Suddenly, she was perched on the edge of his desk, her form more solid than before. "They've found a way to breach Neverland's defenses. To strike at your allies wherever they hide."

Despite himself, Hook felt a grudging admiration for the strange creature. Her flair for the dramatic was impeccable. She had his complete attention, and she knew it. "Explain."

"Haven't you wondered why the different regions of Neverland remain separate? Why the predators of one territory cannot hunt in another?" Her form rippled like silk in a midnight breeze. "The magic that divides them is absolute. Or nearly so."

Hook's eyes narrowed. "Nearly?"

"Peter creates openings wherever he flies. The barriers part for him, and through those openings ..." She let the words hang in the air between them.

"Blackheart's forces can follow." His mind raced through the implications. "When Pan returns—"

"Yes. They will follow. Your safe haven will become your trap." Her voice held no sympathy, only cold certainty. "Even now, they gather at the borders, waiting."

Hook studied her warily, impressed despite his natural distrust of all things magical. There was a brutal efficiency to her methods that appealed to his tactical mind. "And you've chosen to share this information out of the goodness of your heart, I suppose?"

Her form began to fade. "I share it because your premature demise would be inconvenient to my plans."

Before Hook could press further, Tigerlilja called out from beyond his door. "Hook. War council. Now."

In an instant, Shadow vanished. The lamp sputtered back to life, but every flicker in the glow that danced across the maps, once warm and reassuring, now felt like a warning.

The great hall in the Viking village had shrunk considerably since their last council meeting, as though Neverland itself knew the gathering needed focus, not festivity. The thick timber walls pressed close in an atmosphere more suited to secrets than celebrations.

Even the everlost, who rarely sat still, perched like hawks in the rafters, awaiting the news.

Wendy caught Charlie's eye as they settled into their places around the broad wooden table. He gave her a slight nod, reminding her that she did not carry the weight of Undine's revelations alone. The thought made her touch her throat, wondering if anyone else could sense the siren's blood running through her veins.

Charming, perched on her shoulder, chimed softly in her ear.

She turned to him. "What is it, Charming? Is everything all right?"

Before he could respond, Tigerlilja strode into the room.

"We have a problem." She stood at the head of the table, not bothering to sit. "Blackheart's forces are on the move. We can no longer travel freely through the neutral territories of Neverland. The *Jolly Roger* was attacked while it was out on training maneuvers. By a dragon. They barely escaped alive."

A chorus of gasps erupted around the room. Even Hook, as accustomed as he was to the turning tides of war, seemed startled. He turned to Wendy, his forget-me-not eyes holding hers for a long moment before he looked away, his jaw twitching.

"Neutral territories?" The question came from Thomas, but every British eye in the room turned to Tigerlilja for the answer.

"Those toward which neither we nor Blackheart's forces hold any animosity. Neverland protects all who live here. They have not attacked our village because they cannot enter our home region with an intent to harm us. Neverland itself prevents it. But they will be lying in wait whenever we leave."

"We attacked Blackheart's fortress," John pointed out. "Does that mean Neverland isn't protecting them?"

"It's different with Peter." Tigerlilja shared a quick glance with Wendy, then lifted her shoulders and let them fall with a sigh, her shrug speaking volumes. "Neverland lets him go where he will, no matter his purpose. We crossed the boundary when he did."

Hook rose to his feet, commanding attention. "Couldn't Blackheart's forces do the same? When Peter returns, couldn't they follow him through?"

A crease formed between Tigerlilja's brows. "Perhaps."

From his seat across the room, Barnaby muttered sadly, "No, they couldn't. It's impossible. We're perfectly safe. Every one of us."

"Shut it, Barnaby." Even Scrant seemed subdued, his threats uttered in a tone that was considerably lower than his usual volume.

"For all we know," Hook continued, "they could be forming up outside our borders right now, watching for him. We need to send out patrols. Track their movements. We must be prepared."

The room burst into a cacophony of arguments. The everlost wanted to go on patrol immediately. Tigerlilja and Vegard counseled caution and further reflection. Goldie claimed he could steal all their weapons by himself.

Through it all, Wendy's heart sank. If she knew how to use her siren-linked abilities, she could sense that danger. She could warn them when Blackheart's forces were close. But even if she could learn how to do it, she couldn't reveal anything without explaining to Hook why she knew what she knew. As much as he had come to trust her, he wouldn't just follow her blindly.

And telling him could destroy that trust in an instant. After everything she'd done to earn it. She caught Charlie's eye again, and he nodded grimly, understanding her without a word.

No matter what it might cost her, she was going to have to tell Hook.

CHAPTER

# 17

Far too often, bad situations become worse in a very particular way—not slowly, with proper warning, but all at once, like a powder keg exploding. Wendy had barely stepped foot outside the longhouse, bracing herself to approach Hook, when Peter darted into view.

And behind him, one of Blackheart's ships emerged from the clouds like a nightmare.

"To arms!" Again, Wendy's voice carried the sharp edge of command, at once both strange and familiar. "Enemy vessel approaching!"

The rest of the allied forces poured out of the longhouse. Hook appeared first, his steel appendage glinting in the light, followed by Tigerlilja and Vegard, their weapons already drawn. One by one they spread out to either side with practiced efficiency—everlost and British, imps and Vikings—all staring upward at the horrors descending from the sky.

Dark shapes dropped from Blackheart's ship, wings unfurling as they fell. But it wasn't the everlost that made Wendy's heart stutter in her chest. It was their cargo: a massive serpentine form, hooded and bound, being lowered to the ground between them.

Peter landed beside Wendy and Charlie. "Don't look at its eyes," he warned. "It's a basilisk. Meet its gaze and you'll turn to stone."

Vegard, who had moved to stand with them, let out a sound somewhere between a growl and a laugh. "Outstanding."

If Wendy noticed Peter's unusual sense of gravity, she gave no indication of it, her eyes glued to the scene playing out before her.

The everlost removed the basilisk's hood with ceremonial care, as though unveiling a prize. The creature's scales gleamed like polished obsidian in the unchanging light, and though Wendy carefully avoided its gaze, she could feel the ancient malevolence radiating from its form.

All around them, the fight erupted as Blackheart's forces advanced. British soldiers loaded silver bullets with swift precision, and the sharp crack of musket fire split the air. From everywhere at once, Vikings charged forward, their battle cries and thundering boots shaking the ground. Even the imps darted through the chaos, their small size and quick movements making them difficult targets for the everlost's blades.

But it was the basilisk that commanded their immediate attention.

The creature moved with terrible grace, its fanged maw striking out with terrifying speed. Wendy, Charlie, Peter, and Vegard fell into formation instinctively, their blades flashing as they fought to it at bay.

Some of the English turned their weapons on the creature, but their bullets skipped off its scales like pebbles across a pond. The basilisk pressed forward, forcing them to give way, its attacks becoming increasingly difficult to dodge while keeping their eyes averted.

In a desperate attempt to track its strikes without meeting its gaze, Wendy found her attention drawn to a strange movement in the sky above. What she saw made her forget all about the basilisk, if only for a moment. Large, wingless men were walking off the edge of Blackheart's ship, plummeting to the ground below.

But instead of the sickening impact she expected, each one stood up and shuffled forward, their movements jerky and irregular, like puppets with half their strings cut.

Then the smell hit her.

Wendy had thought she understood the scent of dark magic after encountering the dragon, but this was corruption itself—ancient and ravenous. It spoke of graves torn open and souls twisted beyond recognition. The overwhelming stench pervaded her senses, turning her stomach.

As the creatures drew closer, she realized they weren't men at all. They looked more like corpses, their flesh gray and sunken, their eyes holding an unnatural gleam.

More disturbing still, they grew larger with each shambling step.

"Draugar!" Vegard's shout carried across the battlefield.

"What's a draugar?" Thomas was reloading his musket, his voice carrying the same calm precision he brought to all scientific inquiries.

"Draugr," Vegard corrected, ducking beneath one of the basilisk's strikes and redirecting it with his sword. "One draugr. Many draugar. Only two ways to kill them—take their heads or burn the bodies."

Wendy had never seen Vegard so animated. The stoic Viking tended to let his sister do the talking, but there was a savage joy in his voice that suggested he was finally in his element.

"And the basilisk?" Wendy ducked beneath another lightning-fast strike. Her sword felt useless against its scales. "How do we kill that?"

"Usually with a mirror." It was Peter who answered, his voice tight with concentration as he executed a perfect backflip to avoid the creature's fangs. "If it sees its own reflection, it'll freeze itself."

"Will this do?" Thomas produced a small mirror from his pocket and tossed it through the air.

Peter snatched it with his usual grace and flashed it toward the basilisk with a flourish.

The creature's reaction was immediate. Its entire body stiffened, its scales turning gray and lifeless as stone spread across its form. But in that final moment, as Peter held his position, one of its fangs grazed his hand.

The change in Peter was subtle at first—a slight tremor in his step, a dimming of the ever-present light in his eyes. Then his wings flickered like a guttering candle, and for the first time since Wendy had known him, his face showed something other than absolute certainty.

"Peter?" Wendy stepped toward him, her heart clenching as she watched his smile slip away, replaced by confusion, and something that looked unsettlingly like fear.

And then he crumpled to the ground.

Around them, the battle raged on. The draugar shambled forward, growing ever larger. The everlost clashed with Vikings and British soldiers alike. But Wendy barely noticed any of it. All she could see was Peter—the man who never faltered, the man who couldn't die—lying motionless beneath the eternal sun of Neverland.

"Peter!" The cry tore from Wendy's throat before she could think, raw and desperate. She didn't notice how her voice rippled through the air, or how the sunlight briefly shimmered around her.

All she could see was Peter's crumpled form lying on the ground, utterly still.

The draugar pressed forward, growing more monstrous with each step. What had started as human-sized corpses were now towering giants, their gray flesh stretching and expanding until they loomed twice the height of any man. The stench of death and dark magic grew stronger with their size, making even the hardened Vikings fall back.

"We have to help him!" Wendy took only one step forward before Vegard's iron grip caught her shoulder.

"You'll die before you reach him." He dragged her back as three draugar converged on their position. Their dead eyes gleamed

with horrible intelligence, and their movements, once shambling, had become terribly swift for their size.

"Hold the line!" Hook's voice carried across the battlefield as he parried a massive gray fist with his steel hook, turning it aside with precise control.

The British forces fought alongside Tigerlilja's warriors, their different fighting styles creating an unexpected advantage. Hook's men moved in disciplined formations, drawing the draugar into tight clusters where Viking berserkers could strike from the flanks with their silver-edged axes.

But for every draugr they managed to fell, two more seemed to take its place.

A young Viking warrior ducked under a draugr's swing and drove his spear through its knee. The creature howled, its flesh beginning to crumble, but as the warrior tried to withdraw his weapon, the shaft snapped. The draugr's retaliatory blow sent him flying.

Wendy knew Vegard was right—she could see it in the way their forces were being pushed back, could hear it in Hook's increasingly urgent commands. But leaving Peter felt impossible. He had saved her life more than once, had shown her wonders she'd never imagined. And now—

A familiar roar split the air.

Snaggleclaw burst from the clouds above the mountain, his massive form blocking out the light. For one glorious moment, hope surged in Wendy's chest. Dragon fire could burn the draugar. They still had a chance.

But then Snaggleclaw opened his mouth, and everything went wrong.

The great dragon's first blast of fire missed the draugar entirely, setting one of the Viking longhouses ablaze. His second at-

tempt nearly incinerated a group of British soldiers, who dove for cover with remarkable agility. Tigerlilja shouted something in Old Norse that was impolite, to say the least.

"What's wrong with him?" Charlie ducked as he watched the dragon careen through the air.

"He's half-blind," Wendy realized. "He can't see well enough to aim."

Hook's voice cut through the chaos. "Someone needs to guide that beast before he burns down the village!"

A draugr took advantage of the distraction, its massive fist swinging toward John's exposed back. Michael saw it coming and fired his pistol point-blank into the creature's face. The shot did little damage, but it bought John enough time to spin away.

Amidst the general chaos, Snaggleclaw made another pass, this time managing to catch two draugar in his flames. The creatures screamed as they burned—a jaw-aching sound of stone grinding against stone—their massive forms collapsing into ash. But the victory came at the cost of three more buildings catching fire.

"At least he's trying," Thomas offered, though he winced as another blast went wide of its mark.

Beyond the battle, a dark shape emerged from Blackheart's ship. A tall figure in an elaborate black coat walked calmly through the fray, his face hidden beneath a deep hood.

"Kaspar!" Tigerlilja's shout carried equal measures of recognition and hatred.

The hooded figure turned at her cry. Wendy still couldn't see his face, but she felt the weight of his gaze. A chill ran through her that had nothing to do with the chaos of battle.

The draugar seemed to respond to Kaspar's presence, their attacks growing more coordinated, more precise. One of them seized a burning timber from a longhouse and hurled it at Snaggleclaw, forcing the dragon to veer away sharply. Another pair worked in

tandem, one drawing the attention of Hook's men while the second circled behind to cut off their retreat.

"They're herding us!" Michael fired another useless shot at the advancing wall of gray flesh. "Trying to split us up!"

He was right. The draugar had stopped their random assault and were now moving with horrible purpose, forcing wedges between the different groups of defenders. Vikings found themselves separated from their shield-mates, British soldiers cut off from their ranks.

A fresh wave of the giant corpses surged forward, forcing Wendy and the others to retreat even farther from Peter's still form—a wall of death and decay cutting off any chance of rescue.

Tigerlilja rallied her warriors, shouting commands. "Fall back to the great hall! Draw them in!" Her axe caught the sunlight as she pointed toward the longhouse.

Wendy and Hook understood immediately. If they could get the draugar to cluster together, Snaggleclaw might have a better chance of hitting them. As one, they added their own commands to her efforts. "Fall back! To the longhouse! Fall back!"

The retreat was anything but orderly. Vikings and British soldiers moved backward in stages, small groups doing their best to provide cover while others fell back, leapfrogging past each other in a desperate attempt to maintain the defensive line. Above them, Peter's everlost clashed with Blackheart's forces in a deadly aerial dance, their wings catching the light as blade rang against blade.

"Watch the flanks!" Hook bellowed. A massive draugr tried to circle wide around their position, but John's platoon pivoted smoothly to meet the threat, their disciplined volley forcing the creature to stumble back into the main group.

A familiar voice rang out overhead. "Left side clear!" Curly swooped low enough to be heard before banking sharply to avoid a sword thrust from one of Blackheart's warriors. The twins fol-

lowed in his wake, harrying their opponent until he was forced to retreat toward the clouds.

Tigerlilja's berserkers worked in pairs, one warrior occupying a draugr's attention while the other struck with silver-edged weapons at joints and weak points. But even their success came at a cost—each fallen monster seemed to release something into the air, a visible miasma that made the nearby draugar grow stronger, more aggressive.

"Keep moving!" Wendy's voice joined the chorus of commands. "Draw them in tighter!" Their only chance was to bunch the draugar together enough to give Snaggleclaw a clear target. But the dragon's wild passes made coordination dangerous for both sides.

Charlie ducked as one of Blackheart's everlost shot past him, locked in combat with two of Peter's crew. "They're starting to bunch up. But we'll be caught in the fire ourselves if we're not careful."

"Better than being caught by those things," Michael muttered, reloading his pistol. Another draugr fell to Viking axes, its death-essence making its companions surge forward with renewed fury.

The plan was working—slowly, brutally, but working. The draugar pressed forward, their massive forms crowding together as they closed in on the defenders now clustered near the longhouse's entrance. Above them, Snaggleclaw wheeled into position, his huge shadow sweeping across the battlefield.

"Now!" Hook's command cut through the din of battle. "Everyone back!"

The defenders broke as one, diving for whatever cover they could find as Snaggleclaw opened his maw. This time, with the draugar packed together in the clearing, there was no chance of

missing. Dragon fire erupted in a searing torrent, engulfing the creatures in flames hot enough to melt stone.

The sudden chaos disrupted whatever control Kaspar held over them. The few draugar that remained fought as individuals again rather than as a unit, making them vulnerable to the Viking berserkers' axes. When Snaggleclaw wheeled around for another pass, his wild attack scattered the everlost warriors who were trying to coordinate from above.

But Wendy barely noticed the victory. Her eyes were fixed on the hooded figure as he moved through the chaos with deadly purpose, heading straight for Peter's unconscious form. Before anyone could stop him, he slung Peter's body over his shoulder and waved down two of Blackheart's everlost, who plucked them up together and carried them toward their ship.

"No!" Wendy's cry held rage and despair in equal measure, but this time there was no magical response, no summoning of ancient allies. There was only the horrible sight of the hooded figure disappearing into Blackheart's ship with his prize.

The ship rose and turned, its dark sails filling as it moved away from the village. Within moments it had vanished into the clouds, taking Peter with it.

There is a peculiar hush that follows in the wake of disaster, when the screaming has ended but the true weight of what happened has not yet settled in. Wendy Darling stood absolutely still, her hand reaching toward the sky where Peter had been only moments before.

Around her, the village burned. Behind her, the wounded called out for aid. But Wendy's entire world had narrowed to a single point of focus—they had taken Peter, and he was dying. "Charlie, get the crew together. We're going after them."

Vegard's grim voice cut through the chaos, his leather armor scorched from battle. "I'm coming with you."

"We all are," Charlie added. Behind him, John and Michael were already reloading their weapons.

"No." Tigerlilja's firm command brought them all to a halt. The Norse leader stood before them, her hair streaked with ash and blood. "Their lead is too great. By the time we reach Black-

heart's domain, they will have marshaled every force at their disposal. We need a plan."

Wendy's fingers tightened around the hilt of her sword. "Every moment we wait—"

"We need to attend to our wounded and put out these fires." Tigerlilja gestured at the blazing structures. "Literally. Someone please tell the dragon the fight is over."

Wendy forced herself to look—truly look—at the chaos surrounding them.

Flames licked the edges of the longhouse roof as Snaggleclaw's massive form loomed behind it. Warriors lay scattered across the ground, some moving, some terrifyingly still. The air was thick with smoke, and the sharp crackle of fire competed with cries of pain. Snaggleclaw lumbered into a burning home, sniffing the air for any remaining draugar as the walls crashed at his feet.

"How long?" Thomas's quiet voice drew everyone's attention. He clutched his mirror in his hand—the one that had reflected the basilisk's gaze—holding it against his chest like a shield. "How long do we have? With the poison?"

Tigerlilja's expression wavered. "I don't know. But if anyone in Neverland knows how to cure basilisk venom, it's Jokul."

"Then we send for him." Wendy's mind raced ahead, trying desperately to formulate a plan. "But how do we reach him with Blackheart's forces waiting to ambush us, ready intercept any messenger?"

A grim smile crossed Tigerlilja's face. "There is one among us they cannot intercept." She turned to Tinker Bell, who was hovering over the spot where Peter fell. Her hair had dimmed to a deeply worried gray, streaked throughout with blue hints of grief. "Go. Find Jokul. He is our best hope."

Before Tink could dart away, Wendy stepped forward, her heart thundering in her chest. "Charming, go with her. Please."

The two innisfay streaked into the smoke-filled sky, leaving Wendy to face the impossible task of waiting while every muscle and sinew in her body screamed at her to *do* something. Anything. She watched them disappear, remembering how still Peter had gone when the basilisk's fang pierced his skin, how his bright eyes had dulled as the poison took hold.

"Right then," Charlie said softly beside her. "Where do you need us first, Captain?"

Wendy's nostrils flared, and she drew in a sharp breath. Peter needed her, now more than ever. And her crew needed her. To be steady. To be the leader she had become. She looked to Hook, her ranking officer, but he merely nodded, giving her permission to convey the orders.

"Thomas, care for the wounded. Charlie, get the crew of the *Jolly Roger* working on those fires." She turned to Tigerlilja. "We'll need a plan ready the moment Jokul arrives."

They had to save Peter. Somehow, they would find a way. No matter what it might cost.

But Wendy had no idea at the time just how high that cost would be.

Captain James Hook was not one to doubt his own observations. He had seen too much in his years of service—had lost too much—to waste time questioning what his own eyes and ears told him to be true.

And what they told him now, as Wendy Darling stood before him in his quarters, was that she had somehow managed to summon a dragon from an impossible distance.

"There was no way that dragon could have heard you." He watched her as he spoke, searching her face for any sign of deception. "Not from that far away. Not through the chaos of battle." His tapped his hook once, lightly but firmly, against his desk. "And yet, he came."

Wendy's fingers curled at her sides, then straightened. She brushed her hands down the sides of her blue officer's coat, mustering her courage—a tell, Hook realized. One she didn't even know she had.

"I ... I believe I did call him, sir. Though I'm not entirely certain how."

His eyes narrowed. The set of her shoulders, the way she met his gaze directly—she wasn't lying. But she wasn't telling him everything either. "Explain."

She drew in a careful breath. "I recently learned that I may have some fay blood in me, sir. From the water spirit that saved the *Jolly Roger*."

Hook's jaw tightened, the implications of her confession cascading through his mind. "And you had no inkling of your heritage before this moment?" The words came out sharper than he'd intended. "Do your loyalties lie with us, Miss Darling, or with the fay?"

Her eyes flashed with pain, veiled quickly by indignation. "My loyalties?" Her voice trembled. "I have given everything to this cause—to England—to *you*."

Regret twisted in Hook's chest. He had seen her risk her life countless times for their mission. Had watched her agonize over every decision that put her crew in danger. The accusation was unfair, and he knew it.

"He said many humans have some fay blood in them," Wendy added, her chin lifting slightly. "You might even have some yourself, sir,"

"There is no fay blood in me." His reply was automatic, but even as he said it, a new thought struck him. How had he known it was Wendy who called the dragon? Had he sensed it? Was it even possible?

Her expression shifted, and Hook suddenly noticed how exhausted she looked. How worried. The weight of command lay heavy on her shoulders—he recognized it because he carried the same burden.

And now, with Pan captured ...

"Are you going to take my ship away?" The vulnerability in her voice made his chest ache.

"No," he said immediately, the words rushing out before he could consider them. "I would never take your command. In some ways, I believe in your abilities as a leader even more than my own."

The moment the confession left his lips, he wanted to call it back. Not because it wasn't true—God help him, it was absolutely true. He had watched her care profoundly for her crew, had seen her refuse to give up under impossible circumstances, no matter how bleak the odds.

But he hadn't meant to reveal quite so much of his regard.

Their eyes met, and for a moment, something dangerous flickered in the space between them. Something he could not afford to entertain.

Not here. Not now.

Hook straightened, forcing himself back behind the walls of proper military decorum. "That will be all, Captain Darling. You're dismissed."

He turned away before he could do something truly regret-

table, waiting until he heard the door close behind her before he allowed his shoulders to sink, just slightly, under the weight of everything left unsaid.

CHAPTER

20

If anyone had asked Wendy how long she had been waiting for Jokul to arrive, she would have sworn it had been several days at least. In reality, it had been about two hours—though in Neverland, time being what it was, the matter was somewhat debatable.

She had managed to organize the aftermath of the battle, tend to the wounded, and still find time to wear a path in the ground with her anxious pacing. Nana, who had long since given up trying to calm her mistress, had settled for following two steps behind, adding her own set of paw prints to Wendy's trail.

The first sign of the frost king's arrival was a sudden chill in the air, followed by a small snowstorm contained entirely within the space of ten feet. From within this meteorological phenomenon emerged Tinker Bell, Charming, and the snow-white lion she had first seen in Jokul's domain, its magnificent wings looking for all the world as though they had been carved from ice crystals.

Upon its back sat Jokul himself, looking undeniably regal and more than a bit heroic. "I hear Pan's gotten himself into a bit of trouble." The lion settled to the ground, and Jokul dismounted with an air of casual grace.

The allies gathered quickly—Hook, Tigerlilja, Thomas, and the rest forming a rough circle around Jokul while maintaining a respectful distance from the winged lion, which had settled onto its haunches and was now grooming its crystalline feathers with fastidious attention.

"How long?" Wendy's voice was barely more than a whisper. "How long does Peter have?"

"That depends on several factors. The poison wasn't mixed with any other toxins, which works in our favor. And time..." Jokul gestured vaguely at the sky. "Time works differently here. That should slow the process, at least somewhat. But precisely how long?" He shrugged. "In Neverland, even the simplest questions rarely have simple answers."

"But there is a cure?" Tigerlilja pressed.

Delicate frost patterns formed on the ground at his feet. "We'll need two things: an alchemist capable of brewing the antidote, and a griffin feather. The griffins are here in Neverland, but as for an alchemist ..." He trailed off with another shrug.

Thomas cleared his throat. "I'm not an alchemist," he said, adjusting his spectacles, "but if you can provide me with the formula, I should be able to follow it. It's all rather scientific when you break it down, isn't it?"

Jokul nodded. "More or less. As long as you believe it is."

"The formula," Tigerlilja added, "would be in the Library."

Wendy's eyebrows rose together, each of them desperate for anything that might be interpreted as good news. "The Library? What's that?"

"It's where everything ends up," Tigerlilja explained. "All the odds and ends Peter has brought back to Neverland over the years. Trinkets and books and scrolls. Magical objects too. He's quite the collector, though I doubt he realizes it."

"I know where to find the griffins," Jokul offered. "Though I should warn you, the journey will be … challenging."

A series of chimes interrupted him as Tinker Bell darted forward, her tiny form glowing with determination. She addressed Jokul in the language of the innisfay, sounding like a fleet of wind chimes in a storm.

Jokul tilted his head, his expression grave. "The griffins live far from innisfay territory for good reason, little one."

Her hair flashed brilliant red, and her chimes took on a distinctly angry tone.

"You're only proving my point," Jokul replied dryly.

"None of this matters if we can't protect ourselves." Charlie's voice was tight with worry. "Whether Blackheart's forces realize it or not, they can go anywhere in Neverland now that they have Pan. They could return at any moment."

"And once we have the cure," Michael added, "how do we rescue Pan? We haven't got … well, Pan."

Thomas, who had been scribbling notes in a small book, looked up. "Traits often run in families. Does Pan have any relatives who might share his abilities?"

A heavy silence fell over the group. Finally, Tigerlilja spoke. "Shadow. She's Pan's sister. I've never thought about it before, but she does seem to move freely throughout Neverland."

"Then we need two teams." Hook's forget-me-not eyes gleamed with strategic purpose. "One to create a diversion, and one to obtain what we need for the cure. While they're gone, we'll work out the rest of the plan."

"The *Jolly Roger* could draw their attention," Charlie suggested. "She's the fastest of our ships, and Blackheart knows it. He won't be able to resist pursuing her."

Wendy shook her head. "He'll suspect a trap if we send our best ship."

"Precisely why we should send her," Hook countered. "Blackheart will know it's a trap, but he'll also know we'll know he'll know." He paused, frowning slightly. "The point is, he'll have to pursue regardless, because he can't risk being wrong."

"And while they're chasing the *Jolly Roger*," Michael added, catching on, "a smaller team can slip past their defenses."

"I can fly with innisfay dust," Wendy said. "Jokul can travel on his lion." She glanced at the magnificent creature, which had stopped grooming itself and was now watching the proceedings with interest.

"Two of you won't be enough." Tigerlilja glanced from Wendy to Jokul, then back to Wendy. "The path to the griffins is treacherous, and the Library ..." She hesitated. "Let's just say Peter's collection has developed a mind of its own over the years."

"Three are better than two," Thomas offered. "I should come along. I'll need to see the formula firsthand to understand it properly."

"And four are better than three," Charlie said firmly.

"No," Hook interrupted. "You'll be needed on the *Jolly Roger*, Mr. Hawke. The crew trusts you, and they'll need steady leadership if this diversion is to be convincing."

Charlie opened his mouth to protest, but Wendy caught his eye and gave him a slight shake of her head. He subsided, but his expression suggested the discussion might not be over.

A thunderous footfall interrupted their planning, making the ground tremble. Vegard smiled grimly. "Too bad you

can't bring the dragon. Blackheart would think twice about attacking Snaggleclaw."

"Poor thing," Wendy said softly. "If only there were some way to help him see properly again."

Thomas had fallen silent, staring thoughtfully at his notebook ever since he suggested coming along. Now he looked up, a familiar gleam in his eye—the same look he always had before attempting something brilliant. Or impossible.

Or brilliantly impossible.

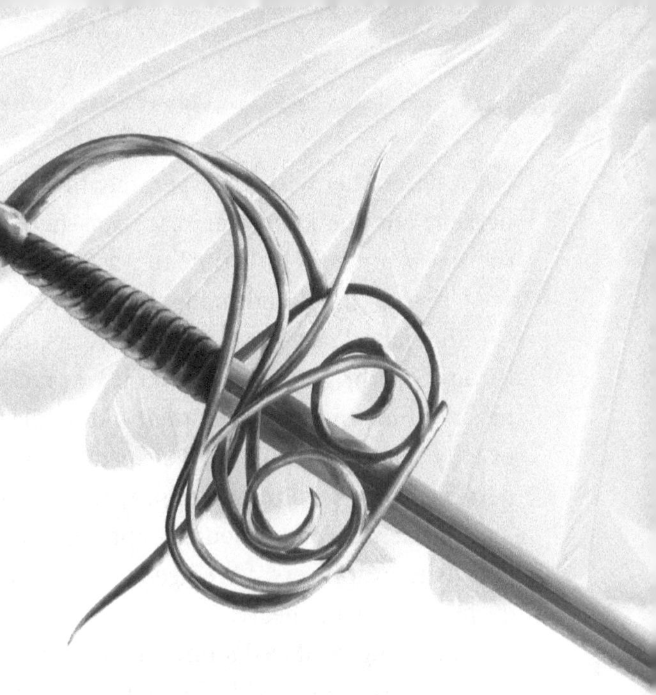

# CHAPTER 21

In the short time Wendy Darling had held command of her own ship, she had discovered that a captain's courage comes in many forms. There is the courage to lead a charge, the courage to give difficult orders, and then there is this—the courage to stand aside while others fly into battle without you.

Wendy waited at the edge of the Viking settlement, her blue officer's coat doing little to ward off the morning chill as Jokul Frosti's presence beside her turned each breath to vapor. The sky above the village remained stubbornly empty, though she knew that would change any moment now.

"Soon," he said, as though reading her thoughts.

She nodded, clenching her fists around the lapels of the coat and drawing it more tightly around her. Charlie was a fine sailor—one of the finest she'd ever known—and she had every confidence in him. But this was her ship, her crew. Her responsibility. And she was sending them straight into danger while she remained safely on the ground.

A part of her wished desperately that she could be at the wheel herself, but she knew her place was here. Pan needed her, and there was precious little time to waste if they hoped to save him.

"There," Jokul said suddenly. "Look."

The *Jolly Roger* rose into view, its dark silhouette cutting through the bright blue sky. But it was not alone. Three of Blackheart's ships emerged from their hiding places around the village, exactly where Tigerlilja had suspected they would be—like spiders, sensing the vibration of prey in their web.

*Godspeed*, Wendy thought, but she could spare no more time for wishes or prayers. "We need to go." She kept her voice steady despite her racing heart.

Charming produced a tiny bag of innisfay dust and sprinkled it over her. Jokul, meanwhile, mounted his winged lion with practiced grace. "The odd human can ride with me, if he's still even coming."

Tinker Bell, who had taken her tiny dragon form, settled onto Jokul's shoulder with a soft chiming that sounded suspiciously like a snort.

Wendy glanced around, suddenly realizing that Thomas was nowhere to be found. "Thomas?" she called out.

"We're here!" His voice carried from somewhere behind them. "Sorry, we're coming."

"We?" Wendy wondered aloud. Her question was met by the thundering approach of footsteps that could only belong to one creature.

Snaggleclaw emerged from between two longhouses, and there, perched upon the dragon's neck, sat Thomas, his face bearing an expression of barely contained excitement.

"I made him some reins," he announced proudly. "Look! So I can show him where to go." He held long leather straps in his hands, and a strange contraption adorned the young scientist's

head—a pair of goggles unlike any Wendy had ever seen, festooned with various lenses and what appeared to be actual clockwork.

"What in all of Neverland is that?" Jokul's tone held more skepticism than curiosity, but Thomas's enthusiasm wasn't doused in the slightest.

"They're like spyglasses," he explained, demonstrating how different lenses could be flipped up and down. "I've been working on them ever since we arrived. I can adjust the magnification to see at different distances. I thought they might come in handy."

Wendy smiled, ever so slightly, until the grim sound of cannon fire wiped it away. Without further discussion, they took to the air, leaving the village—and the battle beyond it—behind them.

But Wendy's gaze remained glued to the *Jolly Roger*, following it long after it had disappeared into the distance.

"There." Jokul gestured ahead with a graceful sweep of his arm. "The Library."

Wendy's breath caught in her throat. Rising before them was a sprawling castle that looked as though it had sprung fully formed from the pages of an ancient fairy tale.

Its pale stone towers spiraled toward the clouds, its windows catching the light like scattered diamonds. A moat encircled the entire structure with waters so still and deep it looked almost as though someone had inked it on the ground. Only the battlements belied the storybook image. Between the traditional crenellations, the parapets were adorned with enormous brass telescopes, all pointing at different parts of the sky.

"We'll land outside," Jokul called over his shoulder. "The Library's guardian doesn't take kindly to unexpected visitors dropping in from above."

They touched down before an impressive gate of wrought iron and copper, its metalwork forming intricate patterns that seemed to shift and change when viewed from different angles. As they approached, Wendy noticed that what she had taken for decorative statues along the walls were in fact suits of armor, complete with swords and shields.

From within the castle, another suit of armor stepped forward, this one unarmed. It strode toward them with military precision, addressing them through the gate in a voice that sounded melodiously mechanical. Or perhaps mechanically melodious. Wendy couldn't quite decide between the two.

"State your names and purpose."

Wendy took a deep breath. "I am Captain Wendy Darling of the *Jolly Roger*. I'm here with Jokul Frosti of the Winter Realm, Thomas Pettigrew of the Royal Society, and our companions Charming and Tinker Bell." She gestured to each in turn. "We seek knowledge to save Peter Pan, who lies dying of basilisk poison in Blackheart's fortress."

The knight raised its visor, revealing an intricate assembly of gears and clockwork that conveyed as much expression as flesh and blood could manage, if not more. "Peter Pan is in danger?" The mechanical features shifted in what could only be concern. "Oh, that's terrible news. Terrible. He has always been most kind to me, bringing such fascinating objects to study. Indeed, half of my improvements have come from his discoveries."

Thomas gave a strangled sort of gasp. "Good heavens. You're Leonardo's knight. The mechanical man from his notebooks. But … but you're meant to be theoretical. A sketch. A dream."

"I was. Now, I'm Sir Galahault." The knight's gear-work face arranged itself into what might have been a smile. "Dreams have a way of becoming real in Neverland. Though I must say, I've made quite a few modifications to the original design. Leonardo was brilliant, but even genius can be improved upon over time."

The great gate swung open, and the knight led them into a magnificent gallery that spanned the soaring entrance hall. Wonders upon wonders clamored for Wendy's attention—mechanical birds perched on high windowsills, craning their necks at the guests below; captured light danced like flames in a variety of bottles and flasks; huge floating globes rotated slowly, revealing unfamiliar terrain; and several animated books appeared to be reading themselves.

"The information you need is certainly here." Sir Galahault approached an enormous apothecary's cabinet with drawers that opened and closed on their own, one after another sliding forward hopefully only to snap shut again, as though eagerly awaiting his request. "I remember cataloging a treatise on basilisk venom some time ago ... now where did I ... ah!" A drawer shot open (with perhaps more enthusiasm than was strictly necessary), and a card floated up to the knight's mechanical hand. "The Bestiary Room, of course. Third floor, east wing."

They followed their guide up a grand staircase whose steps started to move as soon as Wendy and the others were on board.

"Oh," Wendy exclaimed. "How marvelous!"

Thomas craned his neck over the edge, trying to inspect the mechanical gears that carried them along before coming to a gentle stop at the third floor.

"Here we are," the guardian announced. "Watch your step."

The Bestiary Room proved to be a vast chamber with shelving on all sides that reached up into shadows too deep to fathom.

Books of every size lined the walls, some growling softly, others emitting exotic perfumes or gentle glows.

Wendy caught glimpses of titles as they passed: *A Complete Accounting of Dragon Subspecies*, *Practical Applications of Phoenix Ash*, *The Proper Care and Feeding of Wyverns*.

Sir Galahault retrieved a thick volume bound in scales that changed color from one moment to the next and presented it to Thomas, who immediately began scanning its pages. "Most of these ingredients are quite simple," he announced. "We should be able to find them easily enough. But the last one …" He looked up, his expression grim. "For the griffin feather, there's a catch."

Wendy's heart sank. Of course, there was. In her recent, though limited, experience, nothing involving mythical creatures ever turned out to be simple.

# CHAPTER 22

Flying toward the griffins gave Wendy a lot of time to think, which, as you've probably realized by now, was not always a good thing. When she had a clear problem to solve, thinking time was exactly what she needed. But when there wasn't anything useful to ponder and fix, Wendy Darling tended to get lost in her own worries, spinning her responsibilities around and around like juggling plates, terrified that she might drop one.

For example, Wendy had known for some time now that Thomas harbored a particular fondness for mechanical things—the more intricate, the better. But watching him in the Library, surrounded by the greatest collection of magic and mechanics she ever could have imagined, she had come to realize that calling it a fondness was a bit like saying the ocean harbored a particular fondness for salt.

In truth, it was a part of his very nature.

Thomas Pettigrew of the Royal Society had discovered a place that was perfectly matched to every fiber of his being. And yet, in

almost no time at all, he had been ripped away from it, never to return again.

For a brief moment, Wendy allowed herself to imagine a different future—one in which, after they rescued Peter and defeated Buri and Blackheart (if they succeeded, of course, which was rather a significant "if"), Thomas might return to this magnificent place. He could study Sir Galahault's ingenious workings, catalog the Library's countless treasures, and perhaps even add his own discoveries to its vast collection.

But one glance at Jokul's stern profile banished that fantasy. The terms had been quite clear: no British subjects would remain in Neverland.

None at all.

Which brought Wendy's thoughts rather uncomfortably to her own future—a matter she had been studiously avoiding whenever possible. Would she stay in Neverland? Or would she return to England?

Or would she die in battle before she ever had the chance to choose?

That last one didn't seem like the best option, but at least she wouldn't have to pick between her friends—go back to England with Hook, Charlie, John, Michael, Thomas, and the others; or stay here with Peter, Charming, Jokul, Tigerlilja, and all the wonders of Neverland.

Fortunately, her mind was soon diverted by other, more pressing concerns. Had the *Jolly Roger* and her crew managed to outrun Blackheart's ships? Was Peter still alive, or had the basilisk venom already consumed him? Every moment they delayed could mean the difference between life and death.

"We land here," Frost announced, breaking through her clamoring thoughts so effectively that they all breathed a collective sigh of relief.

The group descended into a valley that felt as though it had been crafted from pure magic itself. Crystalline streams wound their way through meadows of impossibly tall grass, shimmering with colors that had no proper names in English. And rising from the otherworldly landscape were scattered rock formations that appeared to have been carved by giants—towering, twisting waves of stone that stretched toward the sky in graceful, sweeping arches.

"This is as far as the rest of you go," Frost declared, his tone brooking no argument. Even his great snow lion would remain behind.

Wendy could see the poorly concealed disappointment on Thomas's face—after all, how often does one get the chance to study a living griffin? Even Charming's hair took on a distinctly sulky shade of purple.

Tinker Bell's reaction, however, was far less subtle: she turned a violent shade of red and exploded into an extremely unladylike string of discordant hexes and curses, punctuated by various tiny gestures that made Wendy more than a bit nervous.

But Frost was already walking away, clearly expecting Wendy to follow. As she hurried to catch up, he spoke without turning. "Move carefully now. Griffins see the world differently than humans do. They're rather particular about their protocols—and they have excellent reason to be suspicious of your kind."

"Actually," Wendy said, choosing her words with care, "I'm only half human."

At this, Frost did turn, one pale eyebrow raised. "Ah," he said, his voice carrying more than a hint of amusement. "So you've worked that out, have you?"

"Undine told me. Perhaps … perhaps the griffins will sense it?"

"Perhaps." The corner of Frost's mouth twitched. "If you're fortunate, maybe they'll only eat half of you."

Before Wendy could decide whether he was joking (one could never be entirely sure with him), she caught a flash of movement

from the corner of her eye. Atop one of the stone towers, something massive shifted against the sky.

"Now, listen carefully." Frost's voice dropped to a whisper. "When you ask for the feather, you must accept their answer completely. Not just in your words, but in your heart. There can be no doubt, no reservation, no hidden plan should they refuse."

"But we need it," Wendy protested. "Peter will die without—"

"No." His voice rose for a moment, sharp as midwinter ice. "That sort of thinking will doom us from the start. The griffins must be free to choose, and you must fully acknowledge that freedom, no matter what lies in the balance. A griffin's feather cannot be taken, only given. Even if we managed to steal one, it would be worthless—the antidote wouldn't work. The asking must be as pure as the giving."

Suddenly, Wendy understood why Tinker Bell had to be left behind. It wasn't just that the griffins might eat her. The innisfay and her tiny loyal heart would never have accepted the possibility of returning empty-handed.

Not with Peter's life at stake.

"That's why you brought me?" Wendy asked.

"That's why I brought you," Frost confirmed. "I believe you can do this. I wouldn't have bothered bringing you here if I didn't."

Wendy wished she shared his confidence. The weight of Peter's life pressed against her chest like a physical thing, making it hard to breathe. "Couldn't you do it? You certainly seem composed enough."

Frost pressed his lips together in a grim line. "I may not care about Peter's life as deeply as you do, but there's more than one man's life at stake here. If Peter dies ... well, best not to put any more pressure on it than there already is."

But Wendy knew what he had been about to say. *If Peter dies, Neverland falls.*

"Try not to fret too much," he added, his voice softening. "Griffins despise basilisks—they're ancient enemies. And it was Pan who brought the griffins to Neverland when they were hunted almost to extinction in your world. They owe him their lives, and griffins have long memories. They'll likely grant your request." He took a deep breath, letting it out slowly. "But they must know without question that you would accept their refusal."

The words had barely left his mouth when an enormous shadow passed over them. Wendy glanced up to see a magnificent creature descending from the stone towers. It was larger than a warhorse, its great eagle head crowned with feathers that shimmered gold and bronze in the light. The powerful front legs ended in talons that could have easily clasped a grown man, while the hindquarters of a lion rippled with barely contained strength.

Two more griffins flanked it, only slightly smaller, their feathers gleaming silver and copper.

As the three creatures landed before them, Wendy became aware of movement all around the valley. Dozens of griffins peered down from the towering rocks, their fierce eyes fixed upon the visitors who had dared to enter their domain.

Frost's hand pressed gently against Wendy's back, urging her forward. She turned to him, her heart thundering in her chest "What do I do?"

"Speak to them," he said simply.

Wendy drew in a steadying breath. "Honored griffins," she began, "we come seeking—"

"No, no. In their language. They don't speak English."

"I don't speak Griffin," Wendy protested in a whisper, though she dared not take her eyes from the magnificent creatures before

her. The largest griffin's gaze pierced straight through to her soul, as though reading every doubt, every fear, every hidden thought.

"Of course, you do," Frost replied with absolute certainty. "You're part siren. You speak more languages than you know."

"How?" The word came out barely louder than a breath.

"First, you must want to," he said. "Then, you must believe you can. Then …" He gave an elegant shrug. "Then you simply do it."

"It can't possibly be that simple."

A touch of amusement crept into Frost's voice. "Oh, but so many things are simpler than we make them. We simply never try, because we've already decided we cannot. Perhaps try before accepting defeat?"

Wendy closed her eyes, focusing on her desperate need to save Peter. She thought of him lying helpless in Blackheart's fortress, time slipping away like grains of sand. She thought of all the children he had saved, all the magical creatures he had brought to Neverland—including these very griffins. The desire to speak, to make them understand, grew until it filled every corner of her being.

When she opened her eyes again, something had changed. The world shifted ever so slightly, like looking at a reflection in water that had finally grown still. The words rose up from someplace deep inside her that she hadn't known existed, flowing past her lips in sounds that were definitely not English but felt as natural as breathing.

"Great Ones," she heard herself say, "Peter Pan lies dying, struck down by basilisk venom. Only a griffin feather, freely given, can save him. I come to ask—knowing it is fully your choice to make—if you would grant us this boon."

The griffins remained motionless, their golden eyes unblinking, and in that moment, something extraordinary happened. All of Wendy's fear and desperation melted away, replaced by a profound sense of trust.

She believed in Neverland, in its magic, in its wisdom. She believed in these magnificent creatures. Whatever they decided would be the right choice, even if it meant losing Peter forever.

The largest griffin held her gaze for what felt like an eternity. Then, with an almost imperceptible dip of its neck, it bowed its proud head. Maintaining eye contact with Wendy, it reached back with its wickedly sharp beak and, with infinite care, plucked a single feather from its wing. The feather gleamed like captured sunlight as the griffin extended its head, offering the precious gift.

With trembling fingers, Wendy accepted the feather. It felt warm against her skin, thrumming with its own kind of magic, freely given and freely received.

CHAPTER

# 23

Returning home from a successful mission is normally a joyful event, filled with a sense of triumph and camaraderie. But Wendy felt only fear as their strange convoy sped toward the Viking village.

The mission *had* been successful—they had both the alchemy formula and the griffin feather—but Peter remained poisoned, and every moment they spent in flight was another moment lost.

Had they already taken too long?

Was it too late to save him?

No, she couldn't afford to think like that. She needed to stay focused. As long as there was any hope at all, she had to believe.

And in her darkest moments, when she couldn't believe, when she felt to the very depths of her soul that all hope was surely lost, well ... even then, she still had to try.

It was no more than Peter would have done for her.

Her hand drifted down to hover over the pack she had cinched to her waist. The griffin feather tucked safely within seemed to pulse with life, as though eager to fulfill its purpose.

Wendy glanced at her companions, taking comfort in their presence. Thomas leaned forward over Snaggleclaw's neck, urging the great best faster, clutching his precious notebook with unwavering focus as the dragon's massive wings cast dancing shadows across the fields below. Jokul, astride his magnificent snow-lion, wore Tinker Bell like a living bracer—her tiny dragon's form wrapped securely around his forearm. He sat so perfectly upon the lion's back that he hardly moved, the set of his shoulders determined and fierce, his ice-blue eyes fixed on the horizon ahead.

Sensing her distress, Charming burbled a soothing trill in her ear. The sound of it helped somehow, even though she still didn't understand it. Whatever magic she had tapped into with the griffins had already faded.

At long last, the Viking village finally appeared in the distance, and Wendy's heart leaped at the sight of the *Jolly Roger* nestled proudly in the field beyond the great wooden halls. Her ship had returned safely. But before she could fully process her relief, something utterly unexpected caught her eye.

Shoved amidst the traditional Viking structures, a building that had clearly escaped from one of Leonardo da Vinci's notebooks rattled in protest, jockeying its neighbors for space. Copper pipes twisted up its sides like metallic vines, letting off occasional puffs of steam. Glass cylinders and oddly shaped vessels protruded from various points in the walls, and a series of intricate weather vanes spun at different speeds atop a domed roof that somehow managed to look both precisely engineered and completely haphazard.

"What in the world is *that*?" Wendy murmured. Even Charming, who had gone back to dozing in her coat pocket, poked his head out to investigate, his hair shimmering with curiosity.

They descended toward the village center, where Tigerlilja stood waiting with Nana, who was wriggling all over with barely contained excitement at Wendy's return. The massive Newfoundland's tail wagged with such enthusiasm that it nearly knocked over the young Viking warrior standing beside her—though the boy seemed far more interested in gaping at Thomas atop his dragon than in maintaining his balance.

Wendy landed gracefully beside Tigerlilja to greet Nana, while Thomas's descent with Snaggleclaw was considerably more adventurous, involving a series of last-minute adjustments, several alarmed shouts, and a resounding crash that left Thomas dangling awkwardly from the dragon's neck.

Meanwhile, Jokul's snow-lion touched down with effortless precision, a landing that would have been quite impressive had anyone been watching—but all eyes remained fixed on Thomas's efforts to disentangle himself from Snaggleclaw's reins without dropping headfirst to the ground.

"That's new." Wendy nodded at the peculiar structure as she scratched Nana behind the ears.

"It appeared while you were away. I took it as a sign your mission had been successful." Tigerlilja turned to Thomas, who had finally managed to land on his feet. "It seems Neverland wanted you to have a proper place to work."

Thomas's eyes widened as he took in the unusual structure. "A laboratory," he whispered. "Wonders upon wonders."

"We have the feather." Wendy reached into her pack, carefully withdrawing the precious gift. "And the formula. Thomas will need a few other items to prepare the antidote though."

Tigerlilja nodded and turned to the young Viking who was still staring at Snaggleclaw. "Erikson, please assist our guest. Bring him anything he requires, without exception."

Thomas took the feather reverently. He nodded to Wendy and then held it up to watch it shimmer in the sunlight before striding off toward his new laboratory, Erikson hurrying to keep pace.

Finally, Wendy asked the question she had been dreading. "My crew?"

"Alive and well."

Wendy closed her eyes and took a long, deep breath, exhaling slowly. "And the plan to rescue Peter?"

"We're working on that now." The Viking leader gestured toward the great hall. "Come. There is much to discuss."

Stepping into the longhouse, Wendy felt the weight of Peter's absence like a physical thing.

She spotted Charlie, John, and Michael among the assembled group, loosening a small knot in her chest, but her relief was short-lived as she took in their grim expressions. Even Hook looked more dour than usual.

The imps and everlost scattered around the table sat with bowed heads, as though they were already in mourning. Without Peter's infectious laughter and boundless confidence, the very air felt heavier, more serious.

More dangerous.

Wendy sank onto the bench between Charlie and John, while Tigerlilja took her place at the head of the table. Jokul remained

standing near the door as though he might need to escape at any moment.

But the conversation was already well underway.

"What good is any of it?" As Curly spoke, the rest of the everlost nodded. "We can't reach Blackheart without Shadow, and Shadow isn't going to help us. She hates Peter. She'd probably be happy if he died."

Tigerlilja turned to the everlost, her face inscrutable. "Tensions between family are more easily set aside in times of need." She glanced at Vegard, then Jokul. If the frost king had any thoughts on the subject, his gaze betrayed nothing. "If I know anything, I know this: We won't know what Shadow will or won't do for Peter until we ask her."

Vegard nodded slowly. "But first, we need to find her. We could ask the innisfay to help. Blackheart won't be targeting them. They'll be free to search for her across every region of Neverland."

Tinker Bell, who had been hovering near Charlie's shoulder, let out a series of discordant chimes that needed no translation. Her color shifted from gold to a deep crimson as she added several rude gestures to her commentary.

From his post in the back of the room, Jokul translated for her. "She says Shadow's always hated Peter. Why should we trust her now?"

Tink chimed angrily again.

"That was the gist of it," Jokul said, addressing her directly. "I'm not translating the rest."

"We have to trust her. We have no choice." Hook's voice cut through the quiet murmurs of agreement that had followed Tinker Bell's comments. "Without Shadow, we can't breach Blackheart's domain. Without access to his domain, we can't save Pan. Without Pan, England falls. God help us all."

"Without Pan, Neverland falls," Jokul countered. "And all the beings it protects."

Hook glowered at the frost king, but Charming interrupted, chiming from Wendy's shoulder.

"Charming will go." The words tumbled from Wendy's lips before she realized what she was saying. She didn't know exactly what Charming had said, but she had understood his intention clearly enough. She turned to the innisfay to find him grinning back at her, nodding in earnest.

"Yes," Jokul confirmed, watching her closely. "He'll spread the word among the innisfay to look for Shadow. Wherever she is, they'll find her."

Charming darted from Wendy's shoulder, pausing briefly to offer a midair salute before zipping out the door.

John cleared his throat. "And if we can't find Shadow? Or if she doesn't want to help? What then?"

Vegard shifted in his seat, exchanging a meaningful look with Tigerlilja. "There might be another way into Blackheart's domain—someone Blackheart might not see as an enemy, at least when it comes to Pan. Someone who, in his heart of hearts, might not want to save him."

All eyes in the room turned to Hook.

His forget-me-not eyes blazed. "You want me to act like a turncoat? You can't be serious."

"You've tried to kill Pan before," Curly pointed out.

"You do threaten him a lot," Tootles added.

"Almost as much as I do," Scrant muttered.

"Enough." Hook pounded his good left hand against the table. "Pan's fate is tied to England. If it proves to be the only way to save them both, I will do what must be done. But if any of you want to question my loyalty, do it now. And prepare to suffer the consequences."

In the silence that followed, Wendy stared at Hook, but he refused to meet her gaze. If Hook entered Blackheart's domain alone, even if he managed to rescue Peter, there would be no escape for him—not for a mere human who had betrayed Blackheart in front of his own men. They would shoot him with their precious silver and tear him limb from limb.

Wendy felt her breath catch in her throat. The thought of losing Hook struck her with unexpected force. When had that happened? When had the intimidating captain with the distant air and those haunting forget-me-not eyes become someone she couldn't bear to lose?

"Perhaps," Jokul suggested, "we should send Tinker Bell to gather information. Find out Pan's condition, where they're keeping him." His ice-blue eyes flickered briefly to Tink. "But Neverland won't let you in if you're looking for revenge. Your only thought must be for Peter's safety."

Tinker Bell's angry crimson faded to a worried amber. She looked to Tigerlilja, her tiny features twisted with indecision.

"Time grows short," the Viking leader said. "But we will wait for you to return as long as we can. We need to know where Pan is being held—and whether Shadow can be found and persuaded to help us."

*And whether Peter's still alive to save.*

Wendy's hand clenched into a helpless fist as the Viking rose from her seat, signaling the end of the council.

"Until then, we prepare for both possibilities."

Before Tigerlilja had even finished speaking, Jokul slipped out the door, disappearing without a backward glance.

"Now, what's that about?" Wendy spoke the words softly, the comment meant only for herself, but Vegard overheard her and paused, then gestured, inviting her to follow him out.

They moved between the longhouses together, blinking as their eyes adjusted to the sunlight. When they were far enough away from the rest, Vegard stopped and turned to her, his words barely more than a murmur.

"Look, it's not my story to tell, but you and your men, you're risking your lives fighting side by side with us. You have a right to know."

Wendy waited, watching him choose his words.

"There was a time," he finally said, "when Jokul's forces worked together with ours. He and Tigerlilja … they came to care deeply for each other."

She nodded—she had suspected as much. "What happened?"

"One of our people broke one of their laws. Not our law, mind you, but an important one. An obvious one. Any fool should have known better." He shook his head, his eyes full of sorrow. "Jokul wanted the man's head, but Tigerlilja insisted that the man had the right to have his case heard by council. She even offered to let some of Jokul's people sit on it."

Vegard's expression grew distant, as though seeing it all again. "But Jokul's hatred of humans ran too deep. The things they'd done to the fay …" He shrugged. "That was it. He took his people and left. They both chose duty to their own kind over what they felt for each other. Since then, there's been no trust between them."

He paused again, watching Wendy closely. "When the time comes, I don't know what side Jokul will be on, but I promise you—it will be his own."

Hook stormed through the village. He needed to get away. Away from Vikings and voices and people who had lived impossibly long lives—people who had all the time in the world. Time to live. Time to fall in love and get married and raise families.

*Time to fall in love.*

His strides lengthened, quickened, until he passed the last of the longhouses and reached the open fields beyond.

Only there did he feel like he could think.

Like he could breathe.

He glanced up at the nearby mountain, noting that Snaggle-claw was sprawled across the ridgeline, back in his usual spot, as though nothing had changed.

That's how Neverland tricked you, he thought. The very idea of endless, unchanging time was a lie. The sky might remain in eternal sunlight. The snow might never melt off a mountain. But unchanging?

No. In Neverland, everything could change in a single moment.

A longhouse could grow larger or smaller depending on who was in it. An alchemical lab could appear overnight. Undead creatures could attack a village, killing Vikings and Englishmen alike, and people could die.

The funeral pyres had lain at least a dozen souls to rest. But now, it was as though nothing had ever happened. The smoke had cleared. The damage to the village had been repaired. The sun still hadn't moved.

But those people were gone, just the same.

Soon, he might be gone too.

Hook expelled a long breath. The irony was insufferable. After all these years of wanting Pan dead, he was actually contemplating a suicide mission to save the insufferable idiot.

But of course, it wasn't really about Pan at all. It was about England. About stopping Buri and Blackheart before they could destroy everything Hook had sworn to protect.

Still, if he could get Pan an antidote, the overgrown child would simply fly away without a second thought, leaving Hook to face Blackheart's forces alone. Pan would forget his sacrifice immediately—literally forget it, thanks to the curse.

And Neverland would erase him too. From history. From memory.

From Wendy's memory.

When he was gone, would she ever think of him again?

He doubted it. Certainly not any time soon. If he died in Blackheart's fortress, Wendy would become the ranking officer of their expedition. The fate of England—of all the world—would rest in her hands.

Yet, somehow, that thought didn't trouble him in the slightest.

When had he started believing in her so completely?

Like everything else in Neverland, it had simply ... changed.

But there was no doubt about it in his mind. The fleet, such as it was, would be in fine hands under her command. It might even be better off. Wendy belonged in this place—with the Fourteenth Platoon and the fay alike.

Hook couldn't even get his own ship to leave the ground.

He sighed again, watching as his shadow lengthened in the late afternoon sun, stretching across the field before him.

*Wait. What?*

Glancing at the sky, he confirmed that the sun hadn't moved. And yet he watched as his shadow grew longer, darker—and then, impossibly, split in two.

The second shadow rose up from the ground, coalescing into a dark form that was hard to look at directly, even in the bright sunlight. Its edges blurred and shifted, as though it couldn't quite decide where it ended and the light began.

"Not now," Hook growled.

"Something on your mind?" Shadow's voice was soft, almost melodic, but its taunting undertones set his teeth on edge.

"They're looking for you," he said curtly.

"Do tell." She drifted closer, her form rippling in the air.

He refused to look away, but watching her in the sunlight was unsettling—even more so than usual. Seeing her like this felt less like looking at something and more like trying to see the absence of something. "They want your help stirring up trouble," he told her. "Seems right up your alley."

"Oh, I know why they're looking for me." Shadow melted back into the field, rippling over the grass to circle around him before forming back up again, whispering in his ear. "And I know exactly why you want them to find me. I was there in the long-house, watching from the rafters."

Hook suppressed a shudder. "Then what do you need me for? Go talk to Tigerlilja."

"But I don't want to talk to Tigerlilja." Her form condensed, becoming more solid, and she ran a tender hand through his hair. "You're so much more … interesting."

She moved like a cat stalking its prey, each motion designed to unsettle, to threaten. It took every ounce of self-discipline he had not to flinch away from her. Instead, he stood perfectly still, turning his head only enough to glance at her in cold, calculated disdain.

Her voice hardened. "You promised your friends you would try to save Peter." Her form morphed until it mirrored his own, parroting his words back to him. "Pan's fate is tied to England. I will do what must be done." In an instant, she looked like herself again, an impossible hole in the fabric of the world. "You promised *me* you'd help me kill him. So, tell me, which promise should I believe?"

"My intentions haven't changed. But Buri and Blackheart must be dealt with first. The threat to England—"

"Oh, your precious England." Her snarl echoed with the sound of ice cracking under pressure. "And yet your fellow Englishmen are so perfectly willing to let you die. Why do you think they chose you for this particular mission? Was it because you're the most annoying, perhaps? Or are you the most expendable?"

"Because I would make that sacrifice," he snapped. "What would you know of true loyalty? A creature trying to kill her own brother."

"He's not my brother!" Shadow's form exploded outward like ink suspended in oil, her edges jagged with rage. When she pulled herself back together, her voice dropped to a dangerous whisper. "Let's test that loyalty you're so proud of, shall we? You won't have to save Peter alone because I'm coming with you. I'll appear to one of those conniving little innisfay who are out looking for me, and I'll gladly add my steel to your efforts."

"Why? What are you up to?" The trust he held for this creature wouldn't fill a flea's teacup, but he had to admit, if only to himself, he held a certain admiration for her cunning.

From somewhere inside her form, she produced a small vial of thick glass, pulling it out of thin air as though she had conjured it from nothing. And yet, despite its provenance, it looked for all the world like an innocent inkwell. "Peter was poisoned by a basilisk, but that shouldn't be enough to kill him. This, on the other hand, is far more potent—a fully brewed potion no alchemist can cure. It will end him in moments."

She reached out her hand, the bottle resting on her palm, but Hook made no move to take it. He just watched her in silence, hoping that the less he spoke, the more she would reveal.

"Do you want to know something funny?" She cocked her head, taunting him. "Your precious Wendy doesn't even need me for this mission. Neverland wouldn't stop her from trying to rescue Peter. The very thought of it is absurd. As long as she and her band of misfits intend to save him, they can waltz right into Blackheart's lair."

Shadow brushed a finger along his jaw, leaning close to whisper in his ear again. "But since you'll be trying to kill him, you'll need me after all."

"I told you, I'm not killing Pan until Buri's been dealt with."

"Why do you think I'm going with you? While everyone's focus is on Peter, I'll slip away through the shadows and put an end to Buri, once and for all." She dropped to the ground, sliding along the grass to circle him before rising in front of him again. "I'm giving you this so that when I hold up my end of the bargain, you can hold up yours. Buri's life—and the safety of your precious England—for Peter."

"Buri's life?" He eyed the vial in her hand. "How?"

"Don't worry about that. I have a plan. You just focus on your end of the deal."

"And how am I supposed to know if you've kept up your end? I'm not doing anything to jeopardize England's alliances here in Neverland until I'm sure the threat has been … eliminated."

"I'll send you a signal you won't be able to miss. When Buri dies, you'll know. But you mustn't tell anyone about our little arrangement. If you do, I might be angry enough to kill someone else— someone you care about protecting even more than England."

Hook remained perfectly still, but the threat hung in the air between them, as tangible as the jet-black inkwell that rested in her hand.

"Take it," she hissed. "If you test me on this, I promise you'll regret it. And that's a promise you can count on."

He regarded her for another long moment, weighing her words. Finally, he reached out with his good left hand and closed his fingers around the bottle, lifting it from her hand.

He had been right, as it turned out. The sun still hadn't moved in the eternal Neverland sky, but in the space of a single moment, everything had changed.

CHAPTER<br>25

Tinker Bell had always prided herself on her ability to be inconspicuous when the occasion called for it, which was why she'd chosen the form of a dragon no larger than a hummingbird for this particular mission.

Shadow, she decided, with no small measure of satisfaction, wouldn't have thought of that.

The very idea of her superior sneaking abilities caused her scales to shimmer with a conspicuous golden gleam—rather defeating the purpose of being so tiny in the first place. Hovering above the dark water of Blackheart's harbor, she forced herself to think of Peter instead. Her scales promptly shifted to match the troubled blue of the waves below.

The fortress loomed before her, its stone walls rising from the water like the spine of some ancient sea beast. New ships had been added to Blackheart's fleet since her last visit—sleek vessels with strange runes carved into their hulls, their rigging eerily still in the absence of wind.

Tink counted three additions, though the newest appeared to be the smallest, barely larger than a fishing boat.

Movement caught her eye—two innisfay, their wings giving off an unusual gray aura she'd never seen before, were making their way toward the small vessel. There was something odd about them, something that made her tiny dragon whiskers twitch.

Curiosity overcame caution (a common affliction among innisfay, truth be told) and Tink followed them, slipping over the side of the ship not far behind. The strange innisfay navigated the deck with unwavering purpose and dove through a hatch near the stern. Tink darted between coils of rope and ducked behind a barrel, watching for a moment before diving in after them.

She followed them to a cabin door that opened with a loud creak. Waiting until the innisfay had entered, Tink landed on top of the exterior door frame, hooking her claws into it and stretching her neck down to peer cautiously into the chamber beyond.

*Blackheart!*

Tinker Bell pulled her head back, allowing herself to flash bright fiery red before getting her emotions under control. Slowly, carefully, she lowered her head again to peek into the room.

The captain's quarters were surprisingly austere. A single oil lamp cast looming shadows across a chart-strewn table, where Blackheart himself stood in conversation with a man Tink recognized as Kaspar, Loki's son.

Digging her claws deep into the doorframe, Tink settled in to observe. The strange innisfay positioned themselves on either side of the room like sentinels, their gray light dimming to barely a glimmer.

From her vantage point, Tink could see every detail of the cabin: the worn spots on the floorboards where someone had paced endlessly, the half-empty bottle of wine on a shelf, and most importantly, the door to what appeared to be a smaller compartment behind the main cabin.

Something about that door made her scales prickle—a faint trace of magic that seemed familiar.

Before she could give it more thought, Kaspar spoke, his voice carrying the faint echo of an ancient language, long forgotten. Tink held perfectly still. Whatever was about to be said, she had a feeling it would be worth hearing—assuming, of course, she could keep her scales from betraying her.

Kaspar leaned against the chart-strewn table, his fingers idly tracing the coastline of what appeared to be England. "So, tell me. What has Buri promised you in exchange for helping him kill Peter Pan?"

Blackheart straightened, a proud smile playing across his features. "He's letting me have Neverland as my own, to rule as I please."

"Really." Kaspar's brow rose in quiet skepticism. "What makes you think he doesn't want it for himself?"

A harsh laugh escaped Blackheart's throat, and he waved a casual hand through the air, dismissing the idea. "Buri doesn't want Neverland. He wants England." His grin turned savage in the lamplight. "He plans to use it as a base and reclaim the world of men, destroying anyone and anything that refuses to serve him, poor buggers."

Kaspar pushed away from the table, moving to stand before one of the cabin's small windows. "I see. You do realize that if Peter is slain, Neverland may very well cease to exist. The land is tied to him through a powerful enchantment."

From her perch, Tink's scales nearly flickered into red with the sudden force of her rage, but she managed to calm herself just in time.

"Buri must know that isn't true," Blackheart protested, but he didn't sound as certain as before. "I've been loyal to him. Neverland is my reward. You're not making any sense."

Kaspar turned to face him, the light casting strange shadows across his angular features. "Oh, my dear Mortimer, I fear you may not understand how far Buri is willing to go for revenge. Or how little value he places on any deal he's made with you. With anyone, for that matter." He shrugged elegantly. "I wouldn't take it personally."

Blackheart snatched a dagger from his belt and slammed it into the table, neatly severing England's shoreline. "How do we find out? I won't risk destroying this place. Neverland is mine."

"I may know a way." Loki's son turned from the table to pace slowly back and forth, his boots oddly silent against the wooden floor. "In the meantime, I propose we keep Peter here on this ship. If all goes well, he can be a wonderful surprise gift. His presence will only gain you more favor once Buri can come through the portal. Then Buri can kill Peter himself." He paused, regarding one of the strange innisfay with apparent interest. "Peter won't awaken from the poison without an antidote, but I don't think it will kill him."

Blackheart poured himself another measure of wine and downed it in a single gulp. "And what is it you'll get out of all this? Nobody does anything unless there's something in it for them."

"Curiosity." Kaspar resumed his pacing, his voice taking on an almost musical quality. "There are few things I hate more than my own curiosity left unappeased. I've tried to reach Neverland many times, but I've been unable to locate a way here until now."

He picked up a small figurine from a shelf—a carved mermaid—turning it over in his hands. "That said, I have no great love for humankind or what they've done to our world. Buri's talk of reclaiming it is an idea I find quite interesting." A smile played across his face. "Plus, if I'm being honest, I do love the sheer chaos of it all. It amuses me."

Setting the figurine down with exaggerated care, Kaspar continued. "But now that I've seen this place for myself, I believe it may be worth preserving if there's a way to do it. And I couldn't care less who claims to be its king. Or emperor. Or whatever title you prefer—your choice, of course."

He gestured expansively at the maps covering the table. "I would prefer to be rid of its infernal sense of order, but that's just me. What you do with Neverland is up to you. My primary interest, if I have one at all, is to bring some of its magical creatures back to the world of humanity." His voice dropped to a silken whisper. "A world that will not belong to humankind much longer."

Tink's scales rippled through a mixture of horror and fascination, but thankfully the combination blended well enough into the shadows above the doorframe to keep her safe from detection.

Blackheart moved to stand before the cabin's windows, his reflection ghostly in the glass. "So be it. I see no harm in holding Pan here until you find the answers we need. Or until Buri makes it fully through the gate." A cold smile played across his lips. "They can't attack us now that we have Pan, and soon enough our forces will grow beyond anything they can withstand."

"Excellent." Kaspar gestured to one of the strange innisfay, whose gray light pulsed in response. "I'll have Chronwick here guard Peter while we send Pendulum to seek out our answer: Can Neverland survive the death of Peter Pan?" He paused, studying Blackheart's reflection. "By the way, why do you hate Peter so much? I thought he was your friend."

Blackheart turned from the window with a bark of laughter. "I don't hate him. He was a means to an end." His voice took on an edge that reminded Tink of broken glass. "I learned a long time ago not to get attached to anyone or anything. I simply play their games long enough to get what I want. Pan's just a fool who didn't understand the game we were playing."

He whirled to yank the dagger back out of the table. "It's my destiny to rule, and here in Neverland, I can rule forever. It doesn't matter who has to die for that to happen." He looked up suddenly, fixing Kaspar with a skeptical glare. "But I'm not convinced by your choice of guards. What good is one innisfay if someone shows up?"

Kaspar's lips twitched in a sly grin. He turned to the innisfay he'd called Chronwick. "Show him."

The creature made a sound unlike anything Tink had ever heard—a single, pure note that stretched into infinity. As it filled the cabin, the two men slowed to a crawl, then stopped altogether.

They didn't move. They didn't even blink.

Apparently, they couldn't.

This, Tinker Bell thought to herself, might be the greatest thing that had ever happened to her in all her days. Just imagine the things she could do while they were trapped in place! A torrent of mischievous ideas flooded her mind, and she launched herself off the doorframe in a fit of glee.

Only she didn't launch at all.

In fact, she couldn't seem to leave her hiding place. No matter how hard she tried, she couldn't move a single taloned foot even one iota. She was just as stuck as the flame in the oil lamp, now frozen in place, its light caught in a single, endless moment.

As suddenly as it had begun, the effect ceased. The flame resumed its dance, and time flowed normally once more. Tink's scales flashed white with shock, then red with frustration, then back to a safe, shadowed sort of gloom.

Thankfully, no one had been looking in her direction.

"You see? He can slow everything around him, at least for a short distance, but he doesn't slow himself." Kaspar's smile turned predatory. "He could easily kill a dozen men, casually flitting from one to the next and slitting their throats."

"Impressive," Blackheart admitted. "He can stay in the room with Pan, but I'm still posting a couple of my own guards at the door. We don't want anyone else finding out about our little surprise."

*Peter!*

Tink had heard enough. With movements so careful they would have made even Shadow proud, she slipped away from her perch, back down the corridor, and out the hatch. Her wings carried her swift and silent across the harbor, her scales trembling between sorrowful, midnight-blue worries and frost-white horror.

She had to warn the others. Not just about where they were keeping Peter, but about everything—Buri's plans, Kaspar's involvement, and the strange innisfay who could control time. Her tiny dragon heart pounded as she darted straight through the sky, leaving Blackheart's fortress far behind.

Not once did she spare a single thought for whether she was better at sneaking than Shadow.

CHAPTER

# 26

As small as they are—or perhaps *because* they're as small as they are—innisfay tend to be uncommonly good at gathering intelligence. The trouble, of course, is that they all know it. As a result, their reports tend to arrive in a rather dramatic fashion, amidst a trail of golden sparkles and a chiming so frenetic it would set your teeth on edge if you ever heard it.

The first to arrive in the Viking village was a young male innisfay, quite out of breath yet miraculously shouting at the top of his lungs nonetheless that he had located Shadow (or so Jokul was kind enough to translate) and that she had agreed to come along on their rescue mission.

She wasn't here yet, mind you, but she had promised to appear shortly.

The second to arrive (yes, you've guessed it) was Tinker Bell. She, however, refused to divulge her news until everyone was present. The longhouse quickly filled with Vikings, British sailors, everlost, imps, Jokul Frosti, a smattering of innisfay, and one

very expressive Newfoundland dog, all summoned to hear what she had discovered.

The fairy's golden glow only brightened as her audience filed in, until she finally felt the gathering was sufficiently impressive to warrant her report.

"Well?" Hook demanded. "What did you find?"

Tink's reply came in a multitude of chimes that started out quietly enough, then built to such a crescendo that Wendy wanted to cover her ears.

Jokul translated, his voice cool and measured. "Blackheart has expanded his fleet. Pan is being held aboard the smallest vessel, guarded by two of Blackheart's crew—likely everlost—and an unknown innisfay that can slow time itself, at least within a limited area."

A murmur of concern rippled through the assembled crowd.

"There's more," Jokul continued. "Buri hasn't fully passed through the gate yet. They're keeping Pan's capture secret until they can determine whether killing him would destroy Neverland. Apparently, Blackheart intends to rule it for himself."

"Killing Pan?" Wendy whispered.

"Destroy Neverland?" Thomas whispered in the same moment.

Wendy turned to meet his gaze. "If we can get Peter the antidote, how long will it take him to recover?"

Thomas ran a hand through his disheveled hair. "There's no way to know. The formula didn't say, and even if it did, the effects might play out differently for an everlost—especially him."

"Actually, I'm not sure it matters." John leaned forward, foregoing his usual military bearing to rest his forearms on the table. "We've stolen one of Blackheart's ships before. We should do it again. Especially if his fleet is larger now. Let's take the ship— with Pan in it."

Hook nodded in grim approval. "Abbot's right. We can't let Blackheart turn the tides so far against us that this war is unwinnable."

"We can do it." Wendy tapped her fingers against the edge of the table as she spoke. "We already know we can fly an enemy ship as long as we can locate its trinket."

Thomas shifted nervously. "We know *you* can. We've never tested the theory with anyone else."

Charlie turned to Tinker Bell. "Did you see the ship's trinket?"

Her golden light dimmed as she considered the question. After a moment, she responded with a series of delicate chimes.

"She isn't sure," Jokul translated, "but it might be a mermaid figurine in the captain's quarters."

"We should bring Goldie, just in case." Wendy glanced at the imp, who froze at the sudden attention—right in the middle of shoving a butter knife up his sleeve.

The knife slid back out, but Goldie caught it before it could fall. "Can't say I've ever stolen anything as big as a ship, but it'd be my honor to try."

"She means steal the trinket, you numbskull!" Scrant hollered from across the table. "Shut your trap or I'll gouge your eyes out!"

Goldie shrugged. "Steal the trinket, steal the ship. I still say it counts."

"We need a small, elite team to take out the guards." Jokul surveyed the gathering. "Fast and lethal. Me, Vegard, Tigerlilja."

The Viking leader straightened in her chair, her braids catching the light. "You and Vegard, yes. And Michael, for the English. I must stay here to command the village in case of attack." Her fingers tightened around her cup. "As long as they have Pan, no one is safe."

Hook's gaze locked onto Wendy, his expression unreadable.

"Hawke stays here too. I can't risk both of my navigators on the same mission. It's too dangerous."

"So be it." Frost crackled across Jokul's shoulders. "I'd prefer to bring my own forces. They're faster than anyone we have here. But there isn't time. We need to strike while our information is still good."

Tigerlilja's scowl deepened, but she remained silent.

"We're coming too." Curly jumped to his feet, his wings snapping to the ready.

The other everlost erupted in a chorus of agreement. Each face showed the same determination—they would not be left behind when their leader needed them.

"Curly and the twins should go." Tigerlilja's voice cut through the commotion. "As for the rest, we'll need your aid here if the village is attacked."

"And Tootles." Wendy's left eyebrow lifted slightly as she spoke. "He should come with us. To make sure nothing goes wrong."

Hook turned to Charlie. "Hawke, you'll command our forces here until I return."

Charlie straightened. "Aye, Captain."

"No." Jokul stared at Hook, his eyes glittering dangerously. "We have too many as it is. You'd just be a liability."

Before Hook could respond, Vegard interrupted. "I don't know. Hook's pretty good at dueling, I suspect. He and Pan go way back."

Hook slammed his steel appendage into the table with enough force to make the Vikings' mugs jump. "I'm coming. The matter is not up for debate."

After several moments of abrupt silence, Thomas cleared his throat. "So, I've been thinking." When all eyes turned to him, he shifted nervously in his seat, his fingers fidgeting with the edge of his sleeve. "Would Peter really have brought the draugar here?" He glanced around the table. "I know he's brought all manner of creatures to Neverland. But none of the others seem … unnatural."

Tigerlilja's hand tightened around her cup. "No, he would not. There have been no draugar in Neverland until now."

"I doubt he brought Kaspar either." Jokul's breath frosted in the air as he spoke. "Although that one's been trying to find his way here for ages."

Vegard pounded his fist on the table, matching Hook's outburst and earning a sharp look from Tigerlilja. "Nothing could be worse than the draugar."

"Nothing?" Thomas's voice dropped to a whisper. "Perhaps …"

"Thomas?" Wendy leaned toward him. "What is it?"

He stared down at his hands. "Well, it might not be anything. But it just seems an unlikely coincidence. The draugar, your greatest enemy, suddenly showing up in Neverland." He looked up, his eyes troubled. "I wonder if perhaps Buri has found a way to do it on purpose. To bring our worst enemies to bear."

A heavy silence fell over the longhouse, broken only by the crackling of the fire.

"Let us pray you're wrong." Tigerlilja's fingers traced the runes carved into her cup. "There are far worse things we could face."

At that moment, a shadow dropped from the rafters, materializing behind Tigerlilja. The Vikings tensed, their hands darting to their weapons as Shadow took form. The horned creature glided around the table to position herself behind Hook, who didn't even turn to look at her.

*How peculiar*, Wendy thought. For someone who claimed to hate all things magic, he seemed remarkably comfortable to have her at his back.

Shadow's voice whispered through the room, rustling like dead leaves over stone. "I have no time for your small talk. I am ready." She melted back into the darkness, her final words trailing behind her. "I will join you when you depart."

CHAPTER

## 27

"I don't like it," Michael muttered.

Wendy could not have agreed more. First, Charming hadn't returned from the hunt for Shadow—not even after Shadow had been found—and now, the *Jolly Roger* sailed through empty skies toward Blackheart's domain, transporting its cargo of rescuers without a single hostile vessel in sight.

Everything about it made her uneasy.

Had Blackheart's forces gotten bored and left? Had they retreated to investigate Pan's ties to Neverland? Or, without Pan, had England and its allies been deemed unworthy foes who could simply be ignored?

Then again ...

Wendy stole a glance at Tootles.

He must have noticed the movement because he turned to meet her gaze, grinning from ear to ear. "It's a fine day for an adventure, don't you think?"

His expression in that moment reminded her so much of Peter that she couldn't help but smile back, despite her worries.

Whatever the reason, Charlie was able to fly them to Blackheart's region without incident, dropping the raiding party in the fog, as close to the fortress as possible without being seen.

Even sneaking closer on foot proved suspiciously easy, although the sight that greeted them was anything but reassuring. Countless enemy forces scurried in and out of Blackheart's castle—far more than Wendy remembered.

And yet, oddly enough, there seemed to be fewer guards posted on lookout duty than before. Every creature of every shape and size seemed intent on going somewhere or doing something. But what those intentions were, Wendy couldn't tell.

She was watching one of Blackheart's imps argue with an everlost when Goldie let out a piercing shriek. She spun and drew her sword, only to discover the small creature hopping about on one foot, holding the other in his hands.

Wendy aimed a look at Michael, asking silently, "What in the world happened?"

"Stubbed his toe on a rock," he murmured.

The glare that Hook aimed at Goldie said something else entirely, but it's probably best not to repeat it.

Fortunately, there were so many imps in Blackheart's own crew hollering this way and that—at each other, at the everlost, at the odd assortment of creatures shambling in and out of the castle's gates—that none of them took notice.

The group stayed well away from the fortress, moving along under the cover of the fog and the tree line until they could finally see the docks. That's when their luck ran out.

Wendy stopped so abruptly that Michael walked straight into her back.

"That's not possible," she whispered.

But there they were: Blackheart's entire fleet of flying ships, every one of them hovering in the air without a soul at the helm that she could see.

For Wendy, this was quite a shock. As far as she knew, ships could only fly when they were actively being flown. In fact, she had forgotten to fly a ship on more than one occasion only to have it drop through the air like a stone until she remembered what she was doing and caught it again.

These vessels hung suspended as casually as washing on a line, each one secured to the docks below by nothing more than a pair of ropes, each pair of lines stretching longer than the last. The ship that held Peter, naturally, was tethered a full three hundred feet in the air.

"Well," Hook said dryly, "I don't suppose anyone thought to bring a ladder?"

Jokul turned to Hook, his crystalline eyes glittering. "Like I said. Liability."

Hook glared back at the winter king. "It isn't as though you can fly either."

"I don't need to fly." His rebuttal emerged in visible puffs of frosted breath. "I can climb that rope without being detected. Can you do the same?"

"Even if we could all fly," Wendy interjected, stepping between them, "we'd be in plain sight of the entire fortress. We'd be captured or killed before we ever got to Peter."

Shadow sighed, the eerie sound grating across Wendy's nerves. "As much as I hate to suggest it, there may be a way." She turned to Jokul. "Can you form a snow cloud over that ship?"

He nodded, eyeing her with suspicion. "I can, but I don't see what good a snowstorm is going to do us."

"Not a storm. A shadow." Her form rippled lightly as she spoke. "If you can cast a big enough shadow on the deck of that ship, I can get a few of us in. As long as someone's holding my hand, walking just behind me, I can take them with me."

"Well, well." Jokul raised a snow-touched eyebrow. "Aren't you full of surprises."

Hook's jaw twitched at the revelation, but he said nothing.

Before Wendy could ponder his reaction, Curly stepped forward. "The rest of us could fly up at the same time," he suggested. "We'll just have to take the ship quickly—"

"No." Wendy cut him off, afraid he and the twins might launch straight into the air in their eagerness to save Peter. "There's an innisfay on that ship that can stop time. We can't afford to rush up there and be seen. The battle might take much longer than we think, which would give Blackheart's forces time to come stop us."

Hook nodded. "Right. No one's flying anywhere."

Wendy paused, considering their options. Finally, she turned to Hook. "We should take a small team, to preserve the element of surprise. Me, to fly the ship. Goldie, to find the trinket. Jokul and Vegard to fight if there's trouble."

"And me." Hook's tone left no room for debate.

Jokul shrugged. "You can take my spot with Shadow. I can hide in a cloud of ice shards and climb the rope—far faster than any human. I'll meet you on deck."

Shadow merely shrugged.

Wendy turned to the everlost. "Wait here until we signal you, or until Blackheart's forces spot us—whichever comes first. When that happens, cut the anchor lines and fly up to the ship, bringing Michael with you. We'll need those sails set quickly if we're to have any hope of escape."

"I can handle the anchor lines," Michael promised. "If the twins can't wait for me, I'll climb the rope myself."

Jokul took a step forward, frost crackling beneath his feet. "Once we're up there, I'll go in first. Even if the innisfay slows time, I'm fast enough to—"

Shadow took a single step and reappeared beneath a tree several feet away. "You were saying?"

"Fine." The crystals of Jokul's breath hung in the air between them. "We can charge in together if you'd like to join me in risking your life."

Shadow only shrugged again. "I was merely making a point. I'd hate to take away your chance to shine."

But Wendy wasn't about to let their best chance of saving Peter duck out of the fight so easily. "You should go in with him," she told her. "If anyone can stop the innisfay, it's you. The rest of us can follow behind—hopefully the innisfay's spell won't extend past the captain's quarters."

Shadow blinked but said nothing.

"Please?" Wendy asked.

With a sigh, Shadow took a step and reappeared in the group, right where she had been standing before. "I'll do what I can."

The plan settled, Wendy and Goldie took hold of one of Shadow's hands.

As their fingers made contact, Shadow flinched, and a wave of sorrow crashed through Wendy's soul, so deep and vast she thought for a moment she might drown in it.

Hook and Vegard grasped Shadow's other hand. If they experienced anything similar, their faces didn't show it.

Just as Shadow prepared to step forward, Tootles rushed up and squeezed his hand into the small space next to Wendy and Goldie.

"Wait—" Wendy began, but it was too late. Shadow had already taken that impossible step through the dark, and suddenly they were standing on the deck of Blackheart's ship.

"I'll take care of the time-stopping innisfay," Tootles announced cheerfully. "Don't worry, nothing exciting ever happens when I'm around. If I go in first, he probably won't even be there anymore."

Before anyone could grab him, Tootles disappeared through the hatch.

Wendy raced through the ship after Tootles. Wooden planks creaked angrily beneath the heels of her boots, the flickering lamplight painting wild shadows on the salt-stained walls.

"Tootles, wait!" She kept her voice to a loud whisper. They couldn't risk alerting anyone to their presence, not when they'd come this far without detection. But it was no use. She was too far behind—she could only pray that Jokul or Shadow would reach him in time.

Remembering the sight of him disappearing through the hatch, her chest tightened in fear. He had moved with such clear intention, such uncharacteristic purpose. After a lifetime of missing every adventure, it seemed Tootles was determined not to miss this one.

The thought sent a chill down Wendy's spine.

*You've always had good instincts about any threat to your crew, have you not?* Undine's words came back to her as clearly as if he had just spoken them.

If she could have run any faster, she would have, but she was already sprinting as fast as she could go.

The smell of tar and damp wood grew stronger as she moved deeper into the vessel. Her ears strained for any sound of pursuit or alarm, but she heard only the creaking of the ship's timbers and the muffled footsteps of her companions up ahead.

Even Neverland itself seemed to be holding its breath, waiting to see what would happen next.

A final turn brought her to a wider section of the ship where several corridors met. The space opened up enough for two people to walk abreast, though the ceiling remained oppressively low. Here, the lamplight fought a losing battle against the shadows that gathered in the corners, and Wendy had to blink several times before she could make out the scene that lay before her.

An innisfay hovered near the ceiling. Its wings caught and scattered the glow of the lamps like fragments of starlight. But it wasn't the creature's beauty that made Wendy's breath catch in her throat—it was what it held in its hand.

A silver stiletto, no larger than a sewing needle. The weapon radiated malevolence, despite its size.

Before Wendy could shout a warning, the air around her changed.

She felt it first as a strange resistance, like trying to run through honey. The sensation rippled from the innisfay in visible waves, distorting the lamplight as it spread. She could see Jokul up ahead, just far enough back that the spell didn't take full hold of him, but Tootles had rushed in too quickly.

He moved now as if he was deep underwater, each motion stretched and slowed by the innisfay's magic. His eyes widened with dawning comprehension, but even that expression took an eternity to form. His hand reached for his sword with agonizing

slowness, the muscles in his arm flexing at a pace that would have been imperceptible if Wendy hadn't been watching so intently.

The innisfay, unaffected by its own magic, darted forward with terrifying speed. Its wings hummed at a pitch that made Wendy's teeth ache, the silver stiletto catching the light as the creature moved.

Wendy saw exactly what was about to happen, but she could do nothing to stop it. She was too far away, her movements sluggish even though she was only at the edge the spell, her body refusing every command her mind screamed at it.

She could only watch as the stiletto found the gap between Tootles's ribs with surgical precision, angling upward toward his heart. Time slowed even more as the blade slid home, and Wendy knew in that moment, with devastating certainty, that it was a mortal wound.

A dark shape materialized behind the innisfay—Shadow, appearing from nowhere. But she had broken through the magic too late.

In one fluid motion, she eliminated the threat, her blade as quick and precise as the innisfay's had been. The tiny creature crumpled without a sound, its wings falling lifeless around its form.

The two guards at the door to Pan's chamber remained frozen in the time-spell's effect, their faces caught in expressions of mild confusion. Neither had even begun to draw his weapon, trapped in that moment of dawning realization that something was wrong.

Jokul dispatched them with efficient grace, his movements leaving trails of frost in the air that lingered like frozen cobwebs before dissipating.

But Wendy saw none of this. She was already moving to catch Tootles as he fell, the time spell dissipating around him. She reached him just as his knees buckled, her arms wrapping around

him with desperate strength. His sudden weight nearly took her down, but she managed to guide them both to the wooden deck with some semblance of gentleness.

"Tootles," she whispered, cradling his head as she eased his body to rest against the planks.

The wound was deceptively small, but she could feel the heat of it beneath her fingers. Blood welled from the puncture, staining the fabric of his shirt in an ever-widening circle that looked black in the lamplight.

"Captain." Incredibly, he was smiling. His face was pale as chalk, but his eyes were bright with feverish excitement. "Did you see? I was right in the thick of it this time. Right where everything was happening."

"You were," Wendy agreed, her voice threatening to break. She blinked hard against the tears that wanted to fall. She wouldn't cry, not now. Tootles deserved better than that. "You were so brave, Tootles. So very brave."

He reached for her hand, and she took it, trying not to notice how cold his fingers felt against her palm. His grip was still firm though, as if he was channeling every bit of strength he had left into that one point of contact.

"Don't be sad," he said, still wearing that strange, peaceful smile. "I've spent my whole life missing adventures. Always too slow, always too late, always in the wrong place at the wrong time." He drew in a shaking breath that rattled in his chest. "But not this time. This time, I was part of something real. Something that mattered."

"You've always been part of something real," Wendy insisted, but Tootles shook his head.

"This was different," he whispered. His eyes found hers with intense clarity. "This was ..."

His voice trailed off as his gaze grew distant, focused on something Wendy couldn't see, but the smile never left his face, even as his hand went limp in hers and his breath left his body in one small, final sigh.

"Tootles?" Her voice was barely audible now, but it didn't matter. Tootles had already embarked on his last great adventure, one from which there would be no return.

# CHAPTER 29

Shadow slipped back to the ship's deck, her form stuttering as the eternal daylight pressed against her. Her outline shifted, dispersing like smoke, then sharp as a knife's edge as she stared toward Blackheart's fortress.

An ancient rage coiled within her.

The time had come.

She stepped into the dark, letting it fold around her like wings. When she emerged, she hugged the shadows between the stones of the fortress, where even torchlight failed to reach. The castle walls loomed above her, their crevices holding secrets as old as the stone itself. Here, darkness pooled all around her—in corners where two walls met, in the space beneath worn stairs, in the hollow arch of a doorway.

Each shadow called to her, offering passage deeper into Buri's lair.

There were so many guards, but they all passed unaware, unseeing—their shadows betraying their movements long before

they reached her. She watched them from the spaces between the torchlight—their unchanging forms, their predictable patterns, their weaknesses. They were men playing at war, unaware of the true power stirring beneath their feet.

She descended through the levels of the fortress, each step taking her closer to Buri's presence. The wrongness of him pulled at her, trying to unravel what she was, what she had become. The deeper she went, the colder the air grew, until even the torches seemed to burn with less heat.

The everlost who patrolled the lower halls moved with confidence, believing themselves masters of this domain, but Shadow slipped between them, formless as grief itself. Their immortality meant nothing to her. She had existed before they had ever drawn breath. Their borrowed time was nothing compared to the weight of the years she carried.

The narrow passages twisted ever downward, stone steps worn smooth by countless feet. She felt the age of this place in every surface she touched. The darkness had seeped into the very rock itself.

Shadow was almost there now, she could feel it—the source of power that thrummed through the fortress like a heartbeat.

At the lowest level, frost formed along the stone, spreading in patterns that mirrored the ancient runes carved above. The cold intensified until even the shadows of her skin felt brittle.

Just ahead, the entrance to Buri's temple rose from the rock, torchlight catching on gold-leafed symbols that writhed in her presence. His pillars loomed above her like silent sentinels, their shadows stretching toward her in recognition, offering their strength for what was to come.

She ignored their call. She had strength enough of her own.

Power thrummed through the space ahead—old power, twisted into something that should not exist. Shadow emerged into

the temple proper, where darkness pooled deep between the massive columns.

The arena spread before her, but in her presence, the torches burned lower, their light retreating from the edges of the space. The empty stone seats loomed above, row upon row curving into darkness, an audience of shadows waiting to witness what was to come.

With each flowing step, frost crackled beneath her feet. Here, in this sacred space corrupted by Buri's presence, even the shadows felt wrong—stretched too thin, pulled toward the center like water spiraling down a drain.

Shadow felt their distress, their ancient stillness twisted by Buri's power.

The massive statue dominated the center of the temple, its white marble surface gleaming in the wavering torchlight. Buri's form hung suspended through the gate, caught between two worlds, neither fully here nor there. His upper body thrust into this realm while the rest of him remained anchored in another.

She watched him long enough to know his pattern too—the ripple of transformation that passed through him every few moments, stone become flesh become stone again.

As she drew near, the strength of his intentions pressed against her like a physical force. Each new ripple sent waves of distortion through the chamber, making the shadows recoil. The ancient runes carved into the pillars shivered in response, reflecting the light in brief, desperate flashes.

Shadow gathered herself, pooling her strength. Darkness swirled around her like a cloak as she moved forward, ready to end this.

The statue's eyes flicked to her, cruel and ancient. She felt his gaze trying to pierce her very being, trying to freeze her in place. But his power could not hold her—she had been born of a cruelty that matched his own.

As another ripple passed through the statue, the weight of his attention settled over the chamber like a shroud.

*Shadow.*

*Join me.*

His voice invaded her mind like sharp tendrils of ice racing through water. The words echoed in the spaces between thought and memory, between what was and what could never be. She held her form steady, refusing to disperse under his gaze, though the shadows around her trembled at his presence.

"I've come to kill you." The words carried the weight of all she had endured, all she had become.

In reply, Buri's laughter filled the chamber, the sound of glaciers cracking, of mountains falling into the sea. Each ripple through his form sent new waves pulsing outward, forcing the shadows to recoil even further. They pressed against the walls, trying to escape him, but Shadow stood her ground.

*Why?*

His massive head tilted almost imperceptibly, the movement too fluid for stone, too jerking for flesh.

*To serve Peter?*

*Pity.*

*So many years*

*to stand*

*in his shadow.*

Her form deepened, edges hardening into angles sharp enough to cut. The darkness around her condensed, becoming solid with her fury. "I am not Peter's shadow," she snarled. "And I am no one's servant. I have never served him."

The statue's next ripple lasted longer, flesh replacing stone for several heartbeats. His coal-black eyes fixed on her with terrible knowing, with an understanding that cut deeper than any blade.

The shadows between the pillars writhed as his power pressed down on her, trying to force her to submit, to acknowledge what she was.

*Sorrow.*

*Fear.*

*Pain.*

Buri's voice sliced through her mind.

*No one serves Peter*

*better than you.*

Fury erupted within her, cold as the space between the stars, sharp as splintered ice. She watched, motionless, every fragment of her being focused on the ripple building within Buri's form. The transformation moved through him like a wave. There—flesh become stone become flesh.

The moment it began, Shadow struck.

Her blade formed from darkness itself. She aimed for his throat, putting all her rage into the strike. But the weapon passed through him like smoke through air, finding no purchase in either flesh or stone.

Buri's laughter crashed against the temple walls, shaking loose fragments of marble that fell like snow.

*Nothing can touch me*

*while I pass*

*between worlds.*

Her form became solid as iron, the dark aura around her roiling with her fury, with her determination.

"Let's fix that." She drew on the strength of every shadow in the chamber, pulling their power into herself until the very air grew thick with them. The runes on the pillars dimmed, their golden gleam fading as she drained the light until there was nothing left.

169

Surging forward, she seized Buri's marble arm. "You're in my world, now."

Using every scrap of power she had gathered, every fragment of darkness she could command, she pulled.

For a long, agonizing moment, nothing happened. Then, slowly, terribly, Buri began to move.

The great form shifted forward, first inches, then feet. She felt the weight of worlds in her grasp as she dragged him through the portal. His laughter had stopped, his eyes fixing on her as more and more of him emerged into this realm.

When only one leg remained behind, anchored in that other world at the knee, he stopped. She pulled harder, reaching further than she ever had before, gathering more darkness, more strength, but still he wouldn't move.

Couldn't move.

Buri's laughter returned, soft at first, then building like an avalanche.

*Thank you, little shadow.*

*You've helped me more than you know.*

*I am almost here now.*

She tried to release him, to retreat, but his power held her fast.

*I will not step through until you are gone.*

*Don't bother trying to stay and hide.*

*I can feel your presence.*

His voice filled her mind, filled the chamber, filled every shadow and dark corner with its terrible certainty.

Then, suddenly, she was free. She slipped back into the shadows, racing away, as his final words echoed through her mind.

*There is no hiding from Buri.*

# CHAPTER
# 30

There are moments in battle when even the most hardened warriors find themselves frozen in place, unable to look away from what unfolds before them. For Hook, this was such a moment.

He watched, transfixed, as Tootles's form broke apart into glowing embers that drifted up from Wendy's trembling arms, each spark extinguishing itself in the still air of the captain's quarters.

Hook had seen it before, of course—an everlost dissipating into nothing, leaving not even ash behind. But this was different. This was Wendy's crewman. Her responsibility. He knew how that felt, had lived with that weight since his first command. Since his first loss.

The silence in the room was absolute. No one moved. No one spoke. They simply watched as the last ember floated upward and winked out, leaving Wendy's arms empty, her hands still curved as though she could somehow hold onto him.

He had expected her to cry out, to rage against the loss. But she did not. Instead, she sat perfectly still, her face a careful mask that made her look far older than her years.

This, more than anything, told Hook how much she had grown as a leader. She was already learning the hardest lesson of command—that sometimes there was no time for grief.

Jokul was the one to break the silence, his voice little more than a whisper, but urgent, nonetheless. "We cannot linger here. Blackheart's men will have heard the commotion. And there's no telling where Shadow has disappeared to."

At the mention of Shadow, the weight of the vial in Hook's pocket grew heavier. The basilisk poison that could end Pan's life in an instant. The bargain he had struck seemed darker now, in the wake of Tootles's death.

He found himself wondering what sort of captain he would be—what sort of man—if he chose this moment to fulfill his end of that devil's bargain.

When Wendy straightened her shoulders, he recognized the gesture. It was the same way he had learned to push through his own grief, to put duty first when lives depended on quick action. He had done it countless times before.

They both had, when they lost Nicholas.

She rose gracefully to her feet and crossed to the chamber door. Her hand hesitated for just a moment on the latch before pushing it open.

Peter Pan, the greatest enemy of the Royal Navy and terror of the sea, lay still as death on a narrow cot. His ethereal beauty was marred by the gray pallor of basilisk venom, making him look almost human. Almost mortal.

Hook had never seen him so vulnerable, not even in his most vengeful dreams.

Wendy knelt beside the cot, already reaching for her pack, in which Thomas's antidote was carefully stored.

"Wait." The word escaped before he could stop it.

She looked up, her eyebrows knitting together in concern. "Why? What's wrong?"

His mind raced. He could hardly tell her about his arrangement with Shadow, about the poison burning a hole in his pocket.

Not that he was going to use it, was he? In truth, he wasn't sure. He needed a reason—a good one—to delay giving Pan the antidote.

He needed time to think.

"We have no way of knowing how he'll react when he awakens," he said finally, and was relieved when Vegard nodded in agreement.

"He's right," Vegard said. "Pan would try to take on Black-heart's entire army without thinking twice. He'd get us all killed. Better to wake him when we're safely away."

Wendy's hand retreated, the antidote safely tucked away. She didn't look entirely convinced, but she nodded. The measured necessity of the argument had won out over her instinct to help Pan.

But that same strength might well be her undoing, Hook thought grimly, should he choose to use Shadow's poison.

He clenched his jaw tight to keep it from twitching.

Thankfully, Goldie's voice cut through his thoughts. "Captain!" Addressing Wendy, the imp held out a small mermaid figurine carved from driftwood. "Found the ship's trinket, I did!"

Wendy accepted it carefully, her expression shifting to surprise as she made contact with the carved figure. "I can feel its connection to the ship. But I still don't understand how the vessel stays aloft without someone actively controlling it."

"Questions for another time." Hook glanced around the small room. "Where's that godforsaken innisfay?"

Tinker Bell, currently sitting on top of the door in the form of a tiny dragon, turned bright red and chimed at him in a rage.

"Belay that tirade. Do you want to help Pan or not? Go signal the ground crew. Let's get everyone aboard before—"

She didn't wait for him to finish. Still chiming discordantly, Tink shot through the doorway and back toward the main deck. Hook followed at a fast clip, reaching the rail just in time to see her signal the crew below as Michael started slashing at the mooring ropes with his sword.

The everlost moved with their usual speed, positioning themselves around Michael. As soon as the last rope separated from the dock, they lifted him into the air, speeding toward the ship.

Just then, a bell tolled in the distance, loud and insistent. Hook's hand touched the vial in his pocket. Was that Shadow's signal? Had she killed Buri?

He frowned.

No—the alarm only meant they had been spotted. All along the castle's battlements, Blackheart's forces burst into view.

The everlost crew were already unfurling the first of the sails, their movements quick and efficient. Hook hoped they would be fast enough. A lot could go wrong in the time it took to prepare a flying ship for departure.

"Captain Darling," he shouted. "The alert's been sounded. We need to set sail."

He wondered for a moment if Tootles's death had been too much for her, but he dismissed the thought immediately. He knew her better than that. He had seen Wendy sail England's first flying ship in a harrowing chase to Neverland not long after they lost their youngest crewman.

He remembered the set of her shoulders. Her determination.

The sheer force of will that had made him realize she had all the qualities of an officer in the making.

A bright arc of flame shot through the sky, interrupting his musings—the first projectile from the castle's catapults.

Could that be Shadow's signal?

But no, Hook watched its trajectory, realizing the truth.

"They're ranging their weapons," he muttered to himself. "That can't be it."

The everlost unfurled the second sail as a round of cannon fire exploded from the castle walls, the familiar boom bringing Hook's hand once again to the vial in his pocket.

Was that the signal?

His jaw started to twitch uncontrollably.

When people made plans to give each other signals, he thought irritably, they really ought to be more precise about what those signals might be.

"Captain Darling!"

"I'm here, Captain."

He turned to the ship's wheel, where Wendy had taken her place at the helm. She stood straight-backed and resolute, just as he had known she would, ready to fly them all to safety.

Despite the blow she had just taken, the loss she had endured.

That simple recognition changed something in him, making his decision crystal-clear and absolute.

Dark shapes streamed from the castle like a tide of living shadow, but Hook no longer cared whether it was Shadow's signal or not.

He had no intention of killing Peter Pan. Not tonight.

He couldn't do that to Wendy.

It would break her heart, and he wouldn't do that to her. Not for anything.

Not even for England.

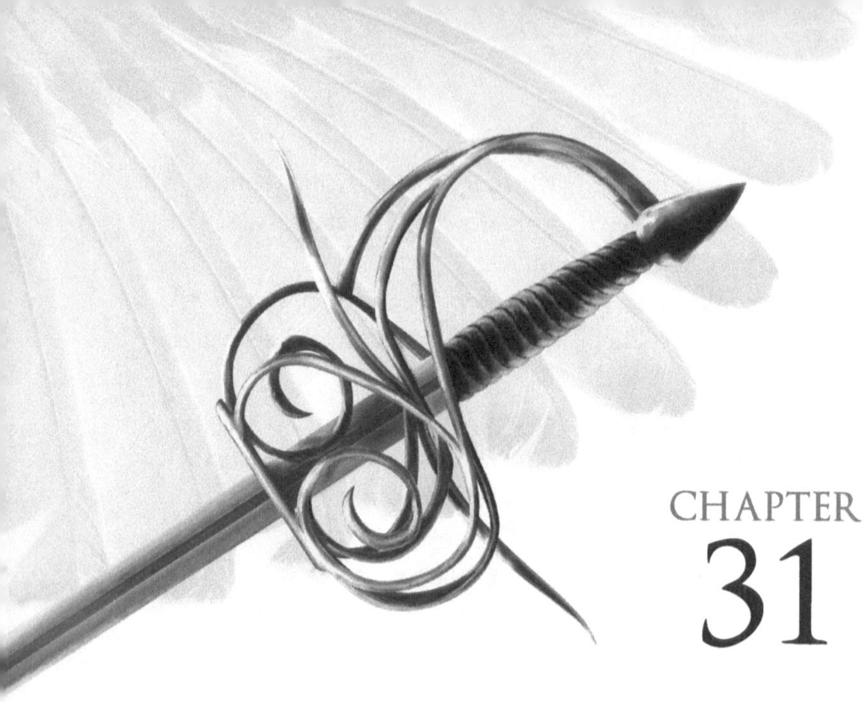

Wendy's hands gripped the wheel of the stolen ship, her knuckles white as she guided the vessel through the air. It was small—hardly more than a sloop, really—but what it lacked in size, it made up for in speed. Blackheart's forces had been caught entirely off guard, giving them a late start to the chase, and now their pursuing ships were falling steadily behind.

Still, the victory felt hollow, matching the ache in Wendy's heart. Her mind kept straying to the cot where Peter lay unconscious. And she could hardly bear to think about the spot where Tootles had dissolved into embers.

The fog that perpetually encircled Blackheart's fortress loomed ahead, thick with the promise of safety, which also meant they were that much closer to the moment Wendy was dreading more than any battle.

Her eyebrow, usually so quick to express its opinions, remained stubbornly still, as though it too were in mourning.

She turned to Curly, who had stationed himself nearby. He wasn't quite hovering, but he wasn't keeping his weight fully on the deck either. Like her, like all of them, he was clearly on edge.

"Can you fly her?" she asked, although she already knew the answer. Every one of Peter's crew could fly anything the innisfay had touched with their magic.

He nodded, saying nothing.

"Would you take the wheel?" Her voice caught slightly. "I need to ... that is, I should ..."

"Aye, Captain." He spoke softly, with such gentle understanding in those two words that Wendy nearly broke down then and there. He knew, as they all knew, what she would have to tell Peter when he awoke.

Even if he would forget it moments later.

Which meant her heart was doomed to break twice—once with the telling, and again when Peter's entire history with Tootles was erased from his mind forever.

The rest of the crew found various tasks to occupy themselves, all of them careful not to meet her gaze. Even Hook remained silent, his eyes focused on the fog ahead.

It was a peculiar sort of kindness, this studied avoidance. They all knew she had insisted on bringing Tootles along.

They knew his death was her fault.

What a fool she had been.

These were her thoughts as she made her way across the deck, each step feeling heavier than the last. She wished someone else could deliver the news—someone who hadn't led Tootles to his death. Still, it needed to be her. She needed to face Peter, to tell him what had happened, even if his curse meant he would forget it instantly.

*Especially* because he would forget.

With trembling fingers, Wendy opened her pack to check on the vial Thomas had prepared. The liquid inside caught the light, shimmering with an otherworldly gleam that made her heart ache all the more.

Closing the pack carefully, she made her way into the belly of the ship.

When she reached the captain's quarters, she opened the door to the small chamber beyond, where Peter lay unconscious on the small cot. The door creaked on its hinges, the sound unnaturally loud in the stillness. The chamber was small, but someone had thought to hang a lantern.

Its gentle light cast undulating shadows on the walls, making the tiny room feel almost like an underwater cave.

She crossed to where Peter lay, his form unnaturally still. His breathing was so shallow his chest barely moved. But the light softened his features, and for a moment, she simply looked at him.

In this strange state that hovered somewhere between life and death, his face held traces of the ancient being that lurked beneath his usual boyish grin.

The sight made her heart ache in an entirely new way.

*Well,* she told herself sternly, *you wanted to be a captain. And this is what captains do—they face the consequences of their actions, no matter how painful those consequences might be.*

With a deep sigh to steel her nerves, she uncorked the vial and carefully poured its contents into his mouth.

For a long, terrifying moment, nothing happened. But then Peter's eyelids fluttered, and Wendy held her breath.

She had seen him awaken before, usually with a laugh already forming on his lips, as though sleep were just another grand adventure. But this time was different.

His movements were slower, more deliberate, as though he were swimming up from the depths of the ocean.

"The Wendy," he murmured, making her name sound like a title from a fairy tale. But his brow furrowed with concern. "I had such a dream. A frightening dream."

Her heart stuttered in her chest. In all their time together, through battles and storms and countless near-death experiences, she had never heard Peter admit to being frightened of anything.

"I was in darkness," he continued. "Complete darkness. And you were there too, trapped in it somewhere. I called for you over and over, trying to find you so we could escape together." His hand found hers, gripping it with surprising strength. "But you never answered."

The secret kiss in the corner of Wendy's mouth trembled, threatening to dissolve into tears. She tried to speak, but no words came.

"I should have known, though," Peter said, his voice growing stronger. He looked up at her with those ice-blue eyes that had first captured her attention at Dover Castle. "I should have known I didn't need to find you. That you would find me. You're still the best navigator of them all." His lips quirked into a hint of his usual smile. "Becoming a captain doesn't change that."

The awareness in his voice caught her off guard. This wasn't the Peter who forgot everything that brought him pain. This wasn't the eternal innocent who lived in a perpetual present, un-marred by grief or regret.

This was ... something else. Someone else.

"Peter." She paused, her voice already catching. "I've done a terrible thing. I brought Tootles with us to rescue you. I thought ... his luck, you see. Nothing bad ever happened when Tootles was around. But he—" Her voice broke as the words stuck in her

throat, but she forced them out, nonetheless. "He was killed. Because of me. Because I brought him here."

Before she could dissolve into the tears that threatened, Peter pulled her into an embrace, gentle and tender—almost protective.

"It's all right," he murmured into her hair. "Listen to me. This isn't your fault. Some people ... they just want to take everything, even in a world that has plenty for everyone. The fault lies with them—the ones who won't let anyone else live in peace."

He drew back slightly, keeping his hands on her shoulders. "Neverland was meant to be a safe place for everyone. That's what it was always supposed to be." His eyes hardened with determination. "We have to fight to protect that. We have to. We'll mourn Tootles. He was our friend and we both loved him. But his death was never your fault. It was—"

Something shifted in his expression, that familiar glazed look creeping back into his eyes. She had known it was coming, of course—the moment when grief became too much for Peter's cursed mind to bear.

But Wendy's heart couldn't bear it either. And now he was going to leave her alone, carrying the weight of that grief for them both.

"No," she pleaded. "You can't leave me now. Please, Peter. I need you."

In a flash, his gaze locked onto hers with surprising clarity. "I would never leave you. I'm right here." Still, even as he spoke, a bright, cheerful expression forced its way across his features.

No, that wasn't quite true, Wendy decided. There was something different this time. The glazed wonder in his eyes seemed less ... lost, somehow.

When he spoke again, his voice had an odd quality to it, as though it were coming from very far away. "I'll miss Tootles," he said softly. "But I'll never forget him."

Then, as quick as a change in the wind, his bravado returned. He sat up, that familiar spark of mischief lighting his face. "Wendy! There you are. Where are we going? Are we on the way to avenge Tootles?"

Wendy stared at him, hardly daring to breathe.

Peter's grief had vanished, yes, as it always did. But the memory ... the memory of Tootles remained.

"No," she told him, her mind racing. "Not yet."

She looked back at Peter, who was chattering excitedly, his eyes bright with schemes and adventures and plans for revenge. But beneath the familiar enthusiasm, she could see something new.

Something that suggested even curses—much like the rules about who could or could not be a captain—were made to be broken.

CHAPTER

# 32

It's a peculiar experience, returning from battle. The body wants to race home and leave the horror behind, while the mind often drags its feet, weighed down by memories too fresh to process. Hook had experienced this phenomenon countless times before, but never quite like this.

Their small party trudged up the path to the Viking village in silence. The only bright moment was Wendy's reunion with her innisfay companion, Charming, who must have returned while they were gone.

Even Pan, who normally couldn't keep his mouth shut for more than five seconds at a time, seemed lost in thought. He was walking rather than flying, which was unusual enough on its own, but stranger still was the way he kept glancing at Wendy as though to make certain she was still there.

And yet, Hook found himself doing much the same thing.

The entire village had gathered to meet them, eager for the news. But despite Peter's obvious recovery, the looks on the faces

of the returning crew prevented any celebration. Instead, the silence stretched out before them like a blanket of fresh snow, pristine and untouchable.

Tigerlilja stood at the front of the crowd, her expression impossible to read. Charlie and Thomas flanked her on either side, and Hook could see the moment they realized Tootles wasn't with the returning party. Charlie's face fell first, then Thomas's, and finally Tigerlilja's careful mask cracked just enough to show she understood as well.

It was Wendy who spoke, her voice steady despite everything.

"We recovered Peter," she said, gesturing to where Pan stood beside her. "But we lost Tootles."

The crowd shifted as the news rippled through them. Peter's crew bowed their heads, honoring the fallen, and the Vikings followed.

"How?" Charlie asked quietly.

"He died saving us all." Wendy squared her shoulders, clearly determined not to cry. "He knew the danger he was putting himself in. He died a hero. We owe him our lives."

In the silence that followed, Jokul stepped forward. "I must return to my kingdom. There are matters I must attend to."

Tigerlilja's jaw tightened, but she said nothing.

"If something happens before I return," he continued, his eyes fixed on Wendy, "send word with one of the innisfay. I will come."

As the winter king departed on his great snow-lion, its wings stirring up flurries in the evening air, Hook found himself wondering how much time they had left before everything changed again. Before they would need to call on Jokul and his people.

Before the final battle that would decide the fate of worlds.

The crowd began to disperse, breaking into small groups that huddled together, sharing grim smiles over Peter's safe return and quiet condolences over Tootles's loss.

Hook watched as Tigerlilja led Wendy, Peter, and the rest of the rescue party toward the great hall, where they would no doubt spend hours discussing everything that had happened.

He should join them, he knew. There were plans to be made, strategies to consider. But for a moment longer, he stood in silence, remembering the way Tootles had smiled at the end. The way he had seemed almost happy that he had finally been part of a real adventure.

Some victories, Hook had learned long ago, felt remarkably like defeat.

Inside the great hall, the fire threw dancing shadows across the small gathering. Hook found himself studying Pan's face, searching for … what? Some indication that he understood the weight of what had happened?

What he saw there instead was something far more subtle, but perhaps more significant.

Pan hadn't left Wendy's side since they'd returned. He fidgeted about, as he always did—never quite still, never quite settled. But his movements formed a careful orbit around her, as though she had become his own true north. And the strangest part was that he seemed to be remembering—truly remembering—his fallen crewman.

"Do you remember," Pan was saying, "the time Tootles missed the entire fairy rebellion because he was reading a book?"

"I remember." Curly's voice was rough with grief. "He was so upset when he found out. Said he'd finally found a good part and couldn't possibly put it down."

"The fairies were quite offended." There was something different in Pan's voice. Something other than his usual careless joy. "But then Tootles begged them to tell him what he'd missed, and suddenly they all wanted to tell him at once, his absence immediately forgiven."

Wendy smiled softly, and Pan's demeanor shifted. He became ... not subdued, exactly, but more focused, more present. As though she was anchoring him somehow to this moment, preventing him from floating away.

It was Tigerlilja who finally brought them back to the matter at hand. "We need more information. About Buri, about Blackheart's forces, all of it. We can't plan our next move until we know what we're facing."

The others all nodded. Even Pan seemed to understand the gravity of the situation, though he kept glancing at Wendy as though to gauge her reaction.

"Tinker Bell could go," Pan suggested. "She's our best spy, and she knows Blackheart's fortress better than any of us."

The innisfay in question, who had been perched on Pan's shoulder, blazed a brilliant pink. She took to the air, her tiny form casting rapid shadows as she darted back and forth in a riot of indecision.

"Come now, Tink." Pan's voice held that strange new quality again. "You know how important this is."

Her light dimmed, shifting to a subdued shade of blue. She had barely left Pan's side since his rescue, but they needed information. And she was, indeed, their best option.

"Please, Tink," Pan added softly. "We need to know what we're facing."

With a resolute sigh, the fairy's color shifted again, this time to a determined golden hue. She flew once around Pan's head and shot toward the door.

"Well," Hook said, speaking for the first time since they'd entered the hall, "I suppose that's settled then."

He tried not to notice how everyone started at his voice, as though they'd forgotten he was there. He was developing a knack for being forgotten lately, at staying in the shadows and watching. He told himself it was simply a tactical choice that kept him silent, not the terrible weight in his chest that only grew with each passing hour.

"We should all get some rest while we can." Tigerlilja rose from her seat at the head of the table. "Tomorrow will bring new challenges, I have no doubt."

As the others began to disperse, Hook caught one last glimpse of Pan and Wendy. The everlost was telling another story about Tootles, something about a missing boot and an angry mermaid, his eyes clear and present.

Whatever curse had affected Pan's memory seemed to be weakening, at least when Wendy was near. Hook wasn't sure if that was a good thing or not.

Then again, he wasn't entirely sure of anything anymore.

Back in his own quarters, Hook had removed his jacket and gratefully closed his blinds. He was contemplating whether exhaustion or duty should win out when Shadow appeared out of nowhere, as though she had been there the whole time, lurking in the dark corners of the room.

"I don't recall inviting you in," Hook growled, but his heart wasn't in the reprimand. He was too tired for verbal sparring.

"If I waited for invitations, nothing would ever get done." She moved closer, her form shifting and rippling in the candlelight.

"I'm guessing your plan for Buri didn't go as expected." Hook sank into his chair, removing the dark ribbon that bound his hair so he could run a tired hand through it. "If you sent me a signal, it wasn't a very good one."

"That's not why I'm here. The fact that you haven't killed Peter isn't my concern at the moment."

Her voice held an unusual edge, piquing his interest, though he was careful not to show it. "No? Then what *is* your concern?"

"Let's just say you've guessed correctly. Things with Buri did not go as planned." When she spoke his name, the lamplight guttered, sending shadows leaping wildly around the room before the wick caught again. "As it happens, I may need your help with that."

"What if I don't want to help?" Hook snarled, though he already knew the answer. "What if I'm tired of being caught up in your schemes?"

"Don't be ridiculous." Shadow's form solidified, becoming more distinctly feminine. "We both know you don't have any choice in the matter. You can hardly admit to your men, or to Wendy, or to any of your allies, that you've been scheming with me all this time. Like it or not, we're in this together."

Hook glared at her in silence, the muscles of his jaw twitching painfully.

"I tried to kill Buri and failed," Shadow confirmed. "But as you were running away in your precious little ship, I was *investigating.* I've discovered many interesting things, only two of which you need to know."

His only reply was to shrug and raise his eyebrows, waiting for her to continue.

"First, the closer Buri gets to clearing the portal, the more of his power he can bring to bear here. He can call more things through now. Worse things."

"Worse than those undead draugar?" Hook shuddered. The sight of those monsters tearing through the village still haunted him.

"Worse than anything you can imagine." Her voice had softened, which somehow made it more terrifying.

"Fantastic," he growled. "And the second thing?"

"The protections of Neverland will start breaking down. If you and your allies intend to strike, it must be soon. Very soon."

A chill ran up his spine that had nothing to do with the mountain air. "How long? How much time do we have?"

Shadow moved closer, her form drawing every ounce of light into herself. "He's moving through much faster than anyone thought. In less than the time it would take you to reach England's shores, Buri will be in Neverland."

Hook closed his eyes, a new weight settling on his shoulders like a physical thing. Less than a voyage home. Weeks, perhaps. Days, even.

When he opened his eyes again, Shadow was gone. But her words remained, echoing in his mind like a death knell.

They were running out of time.

Meanwhile, somewhere in the village, Pan was still telling stories about Tootles to anyone who would listen, while Wendy kept him anchored to his grief. And a tiny fairy winged her way toward their enemies, seeking information they might not live long enough to use.

Hook remained in his chair for a long time, staring at the shadows in the corners of his room, wondering which ones might be watching him back.

Wendy stood near the edge of the ship they had just stolen, running her hand along a rail so polished it could have been made of glass. Even the planking beneath her feet had been laid with meticulous precision, each board fitting snugly against its neighbors without the whisper of a gap between them.

This wasn't the work of common shipwrights—whoever had built this vessel had studied the art of shipbuilding over a lifetime.

Or perhaps many lifetimes, she realized. If the ship had been built here in Neverland, who knew how many centuries had gone into perfecting their craft.

Hook paced the length of the deck, his hair loosely bound as though they were at sea. It caught the light as he turned. "It's very small," he declared, noting the ship's dimensions with practiced eyes. "I don't know if it's worth splitting our resources to crew it."

Wendy understood his hesitation. The ship was indeed compact compared to the *Pegasus* or the *Jolly Roger*, but there was

something about it that called to her. Maybe it was the way it sat so lightly in the air, as though it might dart away at any moment.

John cleared his throat. "Maybe we can use it as a decoy. Or a command post." He stood with his hands clasped behind his back, unconsciously mirroring Hook's own military bearing.

Charlie leaned against the mainmast, watching the exchange with keen interest. After their recent battles, any advantage, no matter how small, could prove decisive.

Thomas was off to one side, examining the ship's unusual construction just like Wendy had, which gave her an idea.

"Thomas," she said, turning to face him, "do you think you could figure out what keeps it flying when no one is controlling the trinket?" She moved closer, warming to the idea. "If we knew how to replicate the effect, we wouldn't have to worry about any of our ships crashing to earth accidentally. Maybe we could even train others who aren't as well tuned to magic to pilot a ship."

His face lit up at first—he was clearly intrigued by the challenge—but then his natural caution reasserted itself.

"It's well beyond my range of knowledge," he admitted, adjusting his spectacles. "But with Erikson to help me, and perhaps an everlost or two, or someone else who understands magic and its inner workings, it might be possible." He glanced around the deck. "Actually, I should probably be working with whoever will be flying the ship. Do we know who that will be?"

Wendy glanced at Hook, but the captain remained silent. "Not yet," she said finally.

Thomas nodded thoughtfully. "I wonder if there might be any helpful information in the Library. It seems to have a way of providing the knowledge we need, just as Neverland provides us with food and lodging."

Wendy's eyes flew wide. What a curious suggestion. Was that part of Neverland's magic?

Even Hook was nodding along, a fact Wendy found almost equally remarkable. For a man who had flatly refused to believe her reports of flying ships, interrogating her for hours when they first met, he was awfully quick these days to accept new magical hypotheses.

She was about to ask Thomas more about this new idea when a familiar figure dropped from the sky, landing in their midst with characteristic flair. (Thankfully, he didn't slam his knee through the beautiful timbers of the deck, sparing the ship that indecency.)

"Greetings to you and your crew, the Wendy." Pan turned to the others with a slight bow. "Please excuse us. The Wendy has something very important to do. Charming? If you would be so kind." Peter pantomimed sprinkling dust through his fingers.

The innisfay turned to Wendy from his customary perch on her shoulder, clearly asking what she wanted to do even as Peter reached for her hand.

"Wait." Although Wendy was exceedingly glad Peter was awake now and able to extend random invitations whenever he'd like, that didn't mean accepting those invitations was any wiser than it was before. At least, not without asking questions. "Where are we going?"

His eyes sparkled with barely contained excitement. "Now that we know your mother was a siren, we need to see what you can do!" He gestured expansively. "Maybe your powers could help us when we fight Blackheart. I can't teach you how to use them, but I know someone who can."

Wendy turned to Hook, uncertain. They were in the middle of a strategic discussion, after all, and she had other responsibilities to consider. The captain studied her for a long moment, his forget-me-not blue eyes unreadable.

Finally, Hook gave her a slight nod. "Go. Learn quickly and return soon. We'll need every advantage we can get." He paused,

then added under his breath, "Maybe bring back a few dragons while you're at it."

With a grin, Wendy nodded to Charming, who sprinkled her with innisfay dust. A chance to learn about her siren nature! Ever since Undine had told her she might be able to hone her magic, using it with more intention, she had been excited by the possibilities, but she had assumed her duties to England would prevent it, at least for the time being.

"Are you ready?" Peter asked.

"Is it all right if Charming comes too?" As excited as Wendy was by the idea of learning more about magic—and maybe even about her mother—the prospect also made her feel nervous. She wanted all the support she could get.

"He can come," Peter agreed. "But he probably shouldn't fly too close to the lagoon. The sirens aren't the only ones who live there. And there are lots of things that would eat an innisfay for breakfast."

Hook flashed Peter a look that very clearly said, "Oh, there you are. I thought you had gone, and yet here you are, back again, just like you never left. How wonderful for all of us." That is, if you can imagine a look saying all that with a healthy dose of sarcasm.

Wendy only smiled. "I'm sure Charming will be careful."

Thomas ran a nervous hand through his unruly hair. He leaned forward as though he might protest, but Charlie placed a gentle hand on his arm, shaking his head. Wendy had waited all her life for this, and Charlie knew better than anyone how much it meant to her to learn more about where she came from.

Besides, some things were simply too important to pass up, especially in Neverland. And learning to master siren powers clearly took precedence over examining a stolen ship, no matter how intriguing its magical mechanics might be.

<h1>CHAPTER 34</h1>

The golden Neverland sun stretched across the fields to brush the Viking village, transforming the thatched roofs into shimmering illusions of peace, hope, and prosperity. Tigerlilja might have found it beautiful under other circumstances.

But beauty had a way of making terrible things feel worse somehow, as though the world was only mocking her pain.

Standing beside Jokul in the open field, she couldn't shake the feeling that everything she loved stood balanced on the edge of a blade. The battle that was coming would change everything—one way or another—and she had seen enough battles to know that victory could be as devastating as defeat.

She turned to the man beside her, as handsome and confusing as ever. "What's so important that we couldn't meet in the village? First you leave, then you're back, without any explanation. The closer we get to our borders, the greater the danger. You know that as well as I do."

His presence felt both foreign and familiar, an ancient memory that refused to fade. Jokul's otherworldly grace had always made him seem more like the winter wind than actual flesh and blood, but there was something softer in his bearing now—something that made her heart ache with remembrance.

"We're in no danger here," he assured her. "I would never let anything happen to you."

"That's not—" She took a steadying breath, trying desperately to let go of the past. This was no lovers' quarrel. She had to focus on what mattered here and now. "I don't need your protection. My people do. Neverland does. The battle that's coming isn't about you or me. It's bigger than both of us."

"Is it?" There was a note of intimacy in his voice that she hadn't heard in far too long—a hint of the connection they had once shared. "We've let so many things become bigger than both of us. Too many."

The words hung in the air like frost itself, delicate and dangerous. She felt the pull of old feelings yearning to bridge the distance that separated them. But the past was there too, a towering wall of loss and responsibility. She couldn't forget what he had done—what he was still capable of doing, if he decided his precious fay required it.

Her hesitation must have shown because something in his posture shifted, becoming more guarded. More like the Jokul she knew now than the one she had known before.

"What is it you want?" She left the question open, uncertain whether she meant from this meeting or from her. Maybe both. The line between love and politics had always been blurry where Jokul was concerned.

The light caught in his pale hair as he turned to face her fully, and for just a moment, she could see both versions of him at once—the one who had held her heart, and the one who had proven that some things were more important to him.

"The same thing you do. To fight side by side. We're stronger together. We're going to need each other when the time comes." He paused, and frost crackled beneath his feet, spreading in delicate patterns across the grass. "But I need your word—that my people will not be in danger from yours."

Tigerlilja's fingers curled into fists, her knuckles white with the effort of maintaining her composure. "You can't hold all of my people responsible for the horrific acts of one man."

"If I had held you all responsible," he said quietly, "you would not be standing here."

The calm certainty in his voice made her blood boil. "Because you get to decide? No. We have a system of justice. You should have let us serve that justice. You should have respected our laws—"

"He should have respected ours," Jokul cut in, and the temperature around them plummeted. Even the golden sunlight seemed to dim. "He wore the skin of my friend upon his shoulders. If you truly understood that, you would not have asked me to wait. Humans understand no life but their own."

The accusation stung all the more because she had heard it before—had even agreed with it in her darker moments. But now she lifted her chin, meeting his hard gaze with defiance. "And what about me? I'm human too. Why do you want to fight by my side if you hate us all so much?"

Something shifted in Jokul's expression—the light of the sun daring to break through a winter storm. "I never hated you," he said quietly. "You are the best of humankind. As long as they follow you, I have hope for all your people."

He reached toward her face, perhaps to brush away a strand of hair that had escaped her braids, or perhaps simply to close the space between them.

But caution caught up with him mid-gesture, and he lowered his hand. "Still, not all people are like your people. Too many

follow fear or greed or hate. They follow Blackheart. They follow Buri. Neverland is a sanctuary, and they would destroy it for their own ends." His gaze locked with hers. "I can't let that happen, not to those I have sworn to protect."

He paused, a hint of anguish flickering in his eyes before he continued. "That *we* have sworn to protect. And so, I simply ask, in the name of peace, can I trust you to make sure my people will not be murdered and skinned by yours?"

Tigerlilja dropped her gaze to stare at the grass beneath her feet, where frost still lingered in intricate patterns between them. The weight of leadership settled heavily on her shoulders. "Yes," she said finally, the word barely more than a whisper.

"Then you shall have our aid."

With that, Jokul lifted his fingers to his lips, letting out a clear whistle that pierced the air. For a long moment, nothing happened.

Then, over a distant rise, they came.

They emerged in waves, stepping out from the shadows of the forest and pouring over the folds of the land itself. Great bears lumbered forward, their fur gleaming with frost despite the sunlight. Enormous deer stepped delicately through the grass, their antlers spreading wider than a man's height, adorned with crystals of ice that never melted. Wolves padded silently beside them, larger than horses, their eyes holding ancient wisdom.

Minotaurs strode among them, their battle-axes gleaming. Massive owls swooped overhead, their wingspans casting shadows across the golden field. And there as well—slipping between the larger creatures like moonlight through trees—came the elves, their frosted armor catching the sun in flashes of silver and blue.

These were Jokul's people—the creatures of frost and shadow, of wisdom and wild places. The sight was breathtaking, and despite everything that lay between them, Tigerlilja felt her heart lift with hope.

Whatever came next, whatever battles lay ahead, her people would not face them alone. The force before her represented power beyond anything Blackheart could have imagined. And yet …

She glanced at Jokul, catching the proud set of his jaw as he watched his forces gather. The past still lay between them, but perhaps they could find a way across it—if only for the sake of Neverland itself.

After all, some things truly were bigger than both of them.

CHAPTER

# 35

Hook lay on his narrow bed in the Viking village, staring at a ceiling he could barely see in the darkness. Despite the eternal sun that blazed beyond his shuttered windows, he had managed to create a pocket of night within these four walls.

Not that it helped him sleep.

His mind refused to quiet, spinning endlessly through the preparations for battle. Jokul's promised reinforcements had arrived—a veritable menagerie of creatures that Hook would have dismissed as fairy tales if he hadn't seen them with his own eyes. Wolves prowled the perimeter of the village while bears lumbered between the longhouses, and he found himself counting them in his head like sheep that might lull him into dreams.

*Bears and wolves, owls and deer.* His lip curled at the thought. What sort of naval captain went into battle with wild animals as allies? But they needed every sword—or claw—they could muster. He had seen enough of Blackheart's forces to know that much.

His thoughts drifted inevitably to Wendy, as they so often did these days. She was out there somewhere, learning to master her newfound powers. *Siren powers.* What would she discover about herself? What new abilities would she master?

He lifted his good hand to his face, though he could barely see its outline. Who was he to judge? Look what he had become—allied with magical creatures, protecting Peter Pan, of all people. Pan, who had taken his right hand and earned his eternal hatred. Yet, here Hook was, guarding the man's life as though it were precious.

And Wendy … Hook let his hand fall back to the bed. Was he protecting her because he chose to? Or was she somehow compelling him? He didn't truly believe she would use her powers against him—the woman's sense of honor was painfully evident in everything she did.

Then again, would he know it if she had?

The thought should have troubled him. Instead, he found himself picturing her face, that determined set of her jaw when she was about to do something particularly noble and foolish. The way her eyes sparked when she was angry. The slight smile that appeared as she ran her hands over her captain's jacket when she thought no one was watching …

Sleep was finally creeping over him when a voice shattered the silence.

"Would you sleep better if I watched over you?"

The words drifted from the darkest corner of the room, and Hook's entire body tensed. There was something different in Shadow's voice tonight—a lilting quality that made it more unsettling than usual. It reminded him of a cat toying with its prey.

"The very thought of you watching me as I sleep has cost me countless hours of rest already," Hook said, not bothering to sit up.

Her answering laugh was barely more than a whisper. "Oh, I wouldn't harm you—not as long as you're useful to me. Besides,

your mere presence in Neverland is making you suffer. Do you know how rare that is? I find your angst more entertaining than I could have imagined."

"So glad to be of service."

The playfulness vanished from her voice, replaced by an edge of urgency. "Did you warn the fools that we must move quickly?"

"Why don't you warn them yourself?"

"Do you honestly think they would listen?" Shadow's form wavered, a flickering void at the foot of his bed. "I've been trying to kill Peter ever since we got here."

Hook pushed himself up on his elbows, anger finally overcoming his exhaustion. "And I'm the better choice? What exactly would you like me to tell them? That I've made an unholy alliance with you, the one person they *don't* trust in a sea of imps and owls and polar bears. That, on your advice, we're supposed to take whatever rag-tag army we can pull together and go attack a far superior force, in their fortified position, full of things so evil they're beyond our imagination?"

Shadow's silence filled the room, but Hook wasn't about to stop now.

"I'm certain, of course, that even though I've conspired with you and promised to kill the one person whose death could make this whole place collapse on itself, for reasons I can't possibly understand, they'll trust me completely. We'll all just miracle ourselves into a victory without any kind of strategy or tactical advantage."

His voice had risen despite his best efforts to keep it controlled. He forced it back to a harsh whisper. "For some strange reason that I can't quite put my finger on, I don't think my advice or admonitions will compel them to move forward on your behalf."

The words drained the last of his strength, and he fell back against his pillow, staring into the darkness that concealed his unlikely confederate. How had it come to this? How had James

Hook, decorated captain of His Majesty's Navy, found himself conspiring with shadows in a land of nightmares?

"Well, poor you." Her voice dripped with mockery. "Is that what you're looking for? The great Captain Hook, seeking my pity?"

His fingers tightened on his bedsheet. "Not your pity, for God's sake. Your reason. If you want me to warn them, give me something to work with."

"You need more to work with? Since when?" The voice circled around his bed. "I didn't choose you because I thought you needed someone to hold your hand, helping you figure out how to accomplish your objectives. I chose you because you have a dark cunning and a ruthless edge. Or you did, anyway. Maybe Neverland has changed you."

Shadow paused, and though Hook couldn't see her clearly, he felt the weight of her regard. It unsettled him deeply, how close her words hit to his own earlier thoughts and the doubt that had been gnawing at him since he'd first set foot in this impossible place.

"You'd best hold on to your ruthless cunning and use it," Shadow snarled. "Because if you don't, there will be no Neverland, no England, and no Wendy."

Hearing her speak Wendy's name made his jaw clench. "Or maybe I should just confess everything and be rid of you once and for all."

"You can't." The words came quick and sharp. "If you confess, there will be no one left to warn them."

"I still think you should warn them yourself."

"Do you think I haven't tried?" For the first time, genuine emotion colored Shadow's voice—something raw and desperate that made Hook's skin crawl. "It's not just that they won't listen; I can't speak the words. Do you think I like wanting to help them? To help *him*? Even when I try, I can't. Maybe it's the curse, but I

can't. The moment I try to speak, I'm pulled back to the shadows. Your hatred for Peter is the only hope I have."

Hook sat up fully now, his exhaustion forgotten. "The only hope for what?"

But Shadow was already gone, leaving him alone with his thoughts in the manufactured darkness of his quarters. The eternal sun kissed the edges of his shuttered windows, a constant reminder that he was far from the world he knew.

A world where sirens didn't train sailors, bears didn't fight alongside men, and shadows stayed where they belonged.

He lay back down, knowing sleep would elude him now more than ever. Shadow's words echoed in his mind: *Your hatred for Peter is the only hope I have.* What did that even mean? And, more importantly, was his hatred for Pan still strong enough to serve whatever purpose Shadow intended?

Hook stared into the dark, remembering the everlost who had taken his hand. The demon who had haunted his dreams. The leader who now fought alongside him against a greater evil. His enemy. His ally. Both at once, somehow, in this impossible place where nothing made sense anymore.

At least he wasn't the only one changing. Even Shadow, it seemed, was fighting against her nature. Perhaps Neverland did that to everyone who stayed too long—broke down their certainties, blurred the lines between what they were and what they might become.

The thought offered little comfort as Hook lay awake, awaiting a night and a new dawn that would never arrive.

# CHAPTER 36

Wendy had always imagined that if she ever discovered the truth about her parents, she would feel different somehow. More complete. As though the final piece of a puzzle had clicked into place revealing the full picture at last.

But as she flew over Neverland's ever-changing landscape toward the lagoon, she felt exactly like herself—only with several more questions than before.

The air was cool against her face, and the soft rustle of Peter's wings next to her was a constant source of comfort—a tangible reminder that he was alive, despite Blackheart's efforts.

Far below, forests gave way to meadows, then forests again, in the peculiar way of Neverland's geography. Yet everything seemed sharper somehow, more vibrant, as though the very air was charged with possibility.

Or perhaps Wendy was merely paying more attention than usual, searching for any sign that might tell her more about her

mother. Had Peisinoe flown these same skies? Had she walked those winding paths through the trees below?

Was she still alive somewhere, searching for the daughter she had left behind?

*To protect you from Buri*, Undine had said. The thought settled like a stone in Wendy's belly. She had always assumed she had been abandoned because no one had wanted her. But the truth, it seemed, was both far better and at the same time much worse— her mother had left her behind to save her life.

Because of Buri.

The realization struck her suddenly: she and Peter had more in common than she'd ever suspected. Both of them had lost their parents to forces beyond their control, and in each case, that loss had been marked by Buri's influence, though in very different ways.

She glanced at Peter, flying steadily beside her. There was something different about him since the basilisk poisoning—a focus she wasn't used to seeing, as though some of his perpetual scattered energy had been replaced by a sense of purpose.

Even now, he was watching their surroundings with careful attention rather than darting about in his usual fashion.

Charming, perched on Wendy's shoulder, gave a quiet trill that might have been concern, or perhaps curiosity. Despite her success with the griffins, she still hadn't had much luck understanding the innisfay language—certainly not as well as she would like to.

"The lagoon," Peter said suddenly, pointing ahead. "We're almost there."

The familiar rock formations came into view—living statues that weren't statues at all, though Wendy had mistaken them for such on her first visit. She raised a hand in greeting as they passed

overhead, but Peter didn't pause for a visit this time. Instead, he led them straight across the water to the far shore.

The lagoon was as beautiful as she remembered, its waters shifting between deep blue and bright turquoise. But there was something different about it now—a sort of resonance she hadn't noticed during her previous visit, as though the water itself was humming a song just below the range of hearing.

Peter descended toward a clear stretch of shore, and Wendy followed, her mind racing ahead to whatever might await them. As her feet touched the ground, Peter turned away from the lagoon to face the surrounding hills.

Wendy took a deep breath, steadying herself for whatever might come next. After all, she told herself firmly, she was still the same person she had always been. Learning about her heritage hadn't changed that.

But as Peter drew in a deep breath, she couldn't quite silence the small voice in her head that whispered: *Hadn't it?*

"Thelxinoe!" His voice rang out across the hills, startling a flock of birds into flight.

Wendy waited, her heart thundering in her chest.

But nothing happened.

"Thelxinoe!" Peter called again. "Are you here? There's someone I'd like you to meet."

The hills remained stubbornly empty for several long moments. Then, just as Wendy was beginning to wonder if they had come all this way for nothing, a figure appeared over the crest of the nearest rise.

Wendy's breath caught in her throat. The woman walking toward them sparkled green in the sunlight as though she were made of living crystal. At first glance, Wendy thought she must be one of the mermaids somehow walking on land. But as the wom-

an drew closer, Wendy realized the emerald flashes came from an elaborate gown that captured and reflected every ray of light it touched.

The woman's skin and hair were not green, as Wendy had first believed, but rather a deep, rich brown with striking bronze undertones. When the woman's eyes fell upon Wendy, they widened in shock.

"Peisinoe!" she exclaimed. "Is it really you?"

"No, I'm sorry." The words tumbled out of Wendy's mouth, half apologetic and half hopeful. "I'm Wendy. I'm her daughter, or so I'm told." She hesitated, then asked the question that felt like it might shatter her if she held it in any longer: "You know her?"

"By the stars, you must be. You look just like her." The woman's voice held a note of wonder, and she drew herself up with unconscious grace. "I am Thelxinoe, and yes, I know her well. Although I haven't seen nor heard any sign of her since I came here." Her expression softened. "I thought for a moment that Peter had finally found her after all this time."

"Oh, I see." Wendy tried not to let her disappointment show. "I was hoping ..."

"You were hoping I might know where she is. I'm so sorry. I wish I did."

"Don't worry, the Wendy," Peter chimed in. "I'll keep looking."

"I know you will," Wendy said quietly. "Thank you."

"We were hoping," Peter continued, addressing Thelxinoe, "that you might be able to help the Wendy learn more about her siren nature. About her powers, and how she might be able to use them in the fight against Blackheart."

Thelxinoe's gaze sharpened. "Against Blackheart?" she asked carefully. "Or against Buri?"

At the sound of that name, Peter's face transformed with sudden fury. His hands clenched into fists, and his wings snapped out as though he might leap into the air and fly away. But then, as quickly as it had come, the rage drained away, leaving his expression clear once more.

"Of course, against Blackheart," he said, as though the moment had never happened. "No one else has a fleet of ships that could stand up to ours. It would hardly be fair."

"Interesting," Thelxinoe murmured. Then, more clearly: "No, of course not. I do see your point."

Peter nodded, his usual brightness returning. "I knew you would. You're very clever."

A hint of a smile darted across Thelxinoe's mouth. "If I do you this favor, I'd like one in return. From now on, I'd like to have a say about what you do or don't bring to Neverland. I'd like to know what I might run into as I fly about."

"You can fly?" Wendy couldn't keep the excitement from her voice, though it dimmed slightly as she added, "Oh, with innisfay dust, I suppose."

In answer, Thelxinoe spread her wings—magnificent, iridescent black wings that caught the light like a raven's feathers. She turned back to Peter, wings still extended. "Do we have a deal?"

"It's a fair exchange," Peter said solemnly. "I'll consider it, but you'll have to uphold your end of the bargain first."

Thelxinoe sighed. "If you do consider it, if you even remember it at all, I suppose that's more than I could hope for." She folded her wings gracefully behind her. "All right, then. Let us begin."

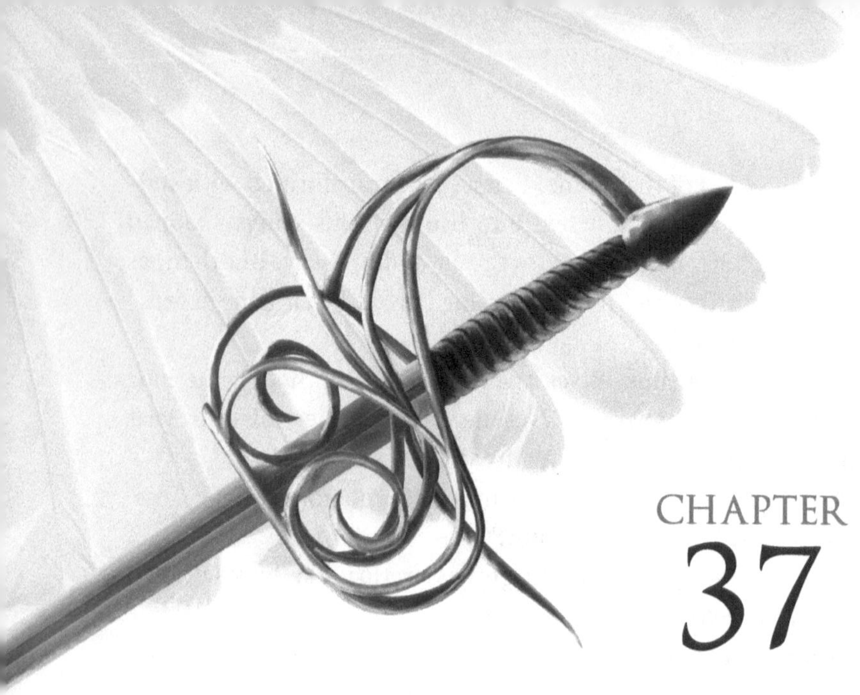

Thomas Pettigrew stood beside Peter Pan's docked ship, fidgeting with the brass buttons of his coat as he contemplated his next move. Wendy had tasked him with solving an excellent mystery: how their newly acquired vessel was able to maintain flight even when no one held its trinket.

Now, the scientific method usually requires a well-reasoned hypothesis followed by careful observation. But here in Neverland, where magic defied every natural law he'd ever studied, observation alone seemed woefully inadequate. What he needed was an expert—someone who understood both flight and magic—which led him, inevitably, to the everlost.

They were, after all, magical beings who had inhabited Neverland longer than anyone could remember. Thomas, by contrast, was decidedly not magical, and his experience with this realm could be measured in mere days—probably.

Besides, as everyone knows, when conducting research in foreign territories, it's generally best to consult with local authorities.

The problem, of course, lay in how to properly request such assistance.

"Hello?" he called up to the ship.

"How do you do?" came the response from above. (At Peter's insistence, Curly had been studying proper British etiquette ever since his first unfortunate encounter with Wendy back at Dover Castle. His training hadn't come in handy until now, so he was pleased to find the opportunity to use it at long last.)

"Why, I'm quite well, thank you. How do you do, sir?" Thomas replied.

"Quite well, yes. Thank you."

"Very good. I'm on a mission, you see. To visit the Library." Thomas straightened his shoulders. "I need to investigate the magical flying mechanics of our newest ship. I thought an expert in magic, and in flying, such as yourself, might be invaluable to the expedition."

Frankly, Curly was disappointed. Despite Thomas's well-considered compliments, the everlost had expected their last exchange to be followed up by a comment on the weather. Now that the conversation had gone off-script, he had no idea how to continue.

The word "mission" had sparked a moment of interest, but at the mention of "Library," his enthusiasm had visibly deflated.

"Right. You'll want Loamly for that. I'll send him down." Curly disappeared from view, only to return a moment later, leaning over the railing to add, "He looks young, but don't worry. He's as old as any of us. Just didn't feel like growing up, I expect."

The everlost who appeared at the ship's rail shortly thereafter proved to be the shyest of his kind Thomas had ever encountered—though, upon reflection, he was also the *only* shy one Thomas had ever encountered.

True to Curly's warning, Loamly appeared no older than thirteen or fourteen, with an air of solemnity about him that belied his youthful countenance.

Thomas, feeling it only proper to attempt some conversation, soon discovered that neither of them possessed any particular talent for small talk. Moreover, Loamly considered each new question with painstaking thoroughness before offering any response, a trait that Thomas appreciated but that also slowed their exchange considerably.

In the end, their departure proceeded quickly enough, with minimal conversation. Thomas and Erikson mounted Snaggleclaw—Thomas still marveling at how quickly one could become accustomed to riding a dragon—while Loamly took to the air as their guide.

They had extended an invitation to Captain Hook as well, but the captain had seemed unusually distracted. When Thomas had requested formal permission to depart, Hook had merely waved a dismissive hand. "Yes, yes. By all means," he'd muttered, though he'd called after Thomas as an afterthought: "Report back to me as soon as you learn anything of value."

Most of the flight was uneventful, but as they approached the Library, Thomas noticed something that made him straighten in his saddle. A dark patch marred the verdant landscape below, cutting through the lush grass like a wound. No ordinary path, it stretched nearly thirty yards across and seemed to lead directly toward the castle before veering abruptly at the moat's edge.

Thomas couldn't resist the pull of scientific inquiry. He guided Snaggleclaw to land beside the peculiar trail, dismounting with much more precision than he'd managed in their earlier flights. Erikson and Loamly followed, the latter hovering uncertainly near Thomas's shoulder.

Drawing closer, Thomas realized his initial suspicion of fire damage was incorrect. The vegetation hadn't burned—it had rotted, as though time itself had accelerated along this particular path, reducing every plant to immediate decay.

The scientist in Thomas reached forward, his hand extending toward the darkened earth, but before his fingers could make contact, an unholy sound split the air. Loamly's scream of warning carried notes Thomas had never heard in a human voice, much less an everlost's.

In a blur of motion, Loamly seized Thomas's arm, yanking him backward with surprising strength. Then he plucked a handful of grass from beside the trail and tossed it into the affected area. Thomas watched, transfixed, as the healthy blades withered and blackened the instant they crossed into the dark path.

"Thank you," Thomas managed, his voice shaky as he realized how close he'd come to touching the corrupted ground. "What manner of thing could cause this?"

Loamly's response, when it finally came, was characteristically brief. "Dunno. Feels bad."

Thomas straightened his coat, gathering his composure. "Well then, I think we'd best investigate that while we're here too."

At the main gate, Sir Galahault greeted them with a notable mix of warmth and enthusiasm. "Master Pettigrew! A pleasure to see you again." The knight bowed with precise dignity. "I must say, your presence is most welcome—unlike my last visitor, whom I was forced to repel at the castle moat."

The knight's jointed fingers clinked together as he gestured toward the trail of decay. "Just imagine what that would have done to the books!"

"If you don't mind the inquiry," Thomas said, his scientific curiosity piqued, "who—or what—exactly was your last visitor?"

"Odd thing, that." The knight's head tilted with a soft whir. "I believe it was a dullahan, although how one arrived in Neverland I couldn't even guess. It's not the sort of creature Peter would have brought. Of that much, I'm quite certain."

"Really? What's a dullahan?"

"Nasty thing. Makes everything around it wither away in an instant." Sir Galahault's mechanical voice grew somber. "They say if it calls your name, you're doomed to die."

Thomas glanced back at the path of destruction. "Does that decay follow it everywhere it goes?"

"It does, although it doesn't last forever. The area outside the moat should start to regrow soon enough." The knight's armor creaked as he turned toward the entrance. "There's a book inside that contains some information about them. You're welcome to take a look."

"Thank you." Thomas started to follow, then hesitated, remembering his original purpose. "You don't happen to have any books on flying ships, do you? I'm looking for information on their trinkets and how they function."

"There may be one that covers the subject." The guardian's voice carried a note of consideration. "I try to keep the catalog current, but the specifics about each book's contents aren't always as detailed as I'd like." He gestured toward the grand doors. "Come. Let us see what we can find."

# CHAPTER 38

Thelxinoe led Wendy to the water's edge, where wavelets lapped gently at the shore. Peter settled cross-legged on a nearby rock. For once, he seemed content simply to watch and listen.

Charming remained on Wendy's shoulder. Whether he was there to protect her or merely because he was curious, she wasn't sure. But his presence was comforting either way.

"Your mother," Thelxinoe began, "had the most remarkable voice I've ever heard. When she sang, it wasn't just beautiful—though it certainly was that. It was as though she could reach right into your heart and strengthen whatever emotion was already there, making you feel it more deeply than you ever had before."

"Like the mermaids?" Wendy asked, remembering their hypnotic voices.

"No." Her answer was firm and immediate. "The merfolk can force emotions upon you, even emotions you don't wish to feel. But that is not our way. We are ..." She paused, considering. "We

213

are more like a looking glass, reflecting what is already within you. We cannot—and will not—create what isn't there."

Wendy thought about this. "But I've never had any particular skill with singing," she pointed out.

Thelxinoe smiled. "Not every siren sings. When you speak to those around you, when you make requests or offer encouragement, surely you've noticed how well they respond, have you not?"

"Well, yes, but that's just ..." Wendy stopped. Just what, exactly? She remembered how the Fourteenth Platoon had always listened to her, even before she held any official rank. The way John and Michael had considered her input from the very beginning, when she was nothing more than a young diviner fresh on their doorstep in Dover.

"Your gift has always been with you," Thelxinoe said gently. "You simply didn't know what it was. When you speak with conviction, with passion—you magnify the courage that already exists in those who hear you. The loyalty. The desire to be part of something bigger than themselves."

"But I've never tried to make anyone—" Wendy began, distressed at the thought.

"Of course you haven't." The siren raised a calming hand. "You cannot make anyone feel what they do not already feel. You can only help them find what lies within themselves. It is a gift of inspiration, not control."

From his perch on the rock, Peter spoke up. "Like when you told us all stories and my crew started treating you like their mother," he said. "They already wanted a mother. You just gave them what they needed."

Startled, Wendy turned to stare at him, but Peter merely smiled back.

"Exactly so," Thelxinoe agreed. "Now then, shall we see what happens when you try it consciously?"

Wendy swallowed hard. "What do I do?"

"Begin with something simple. Something you already know how to do." Thelxinoe gestured toward Peter. "Give him an order, just as you would give an order to your crew."

"But he's not part of my crew," Wendy protested. "He's never taken orders from anyone."

Peter's smile widened. "Try it anyway," he suggested. "I promise not to be offended if it doesn't work."

Taking a deep breath, Wendy squared her shoulders and tried to summon the same calm certainty she felt on the deck of her ship. "Peter," she said firmly, "stand up."

But nothing happened. Wendy's eyebrows huddled together, trying to figure out what had gone wrong.

"It's all right." Those simple words were filled with great kindness, reminding Wendy very much of Mr. Equiano. He had always been such a patient teacher. "You're trying to force him. Remember—you cannot create what isn't there. Think about what he already feels. What he already wants."

Wendy considered this. What did Peter want? To play games, usually. To have adventures. To show off …

"Peter," she said again, but this time she let a hint of challenge enter her voice, "show me how quickly you can reach that cloud." She pointed to a particularly fluffy specimen drifting overhead.

Peter was in the air before she finished speaking, his delighted laugh trailing behind him as he shot upward.

"Oh!" Wendy exclaimed. "I didn't expect … I mean, I didn't think it would be quite so—"

"Easy?" Thelxinoe chuckled. "That's how true inspiration feels. You helped him act on a desire that was already there—his

love of showing off, his eagerness to impress you. Now, shall we try something a bit more challenging?"

For what felt like an hour or so, Wendy practiced finding the thread of emotion in various simple requests. Most of them worked well—especially with Peter, who contained enough enthusiasm for a dozen ordinary people. But some produced no effect at all, and Wendy couldn't quite determine why.

"It's not working," she said at last, frustration creeping into her voice. "I can't tell when it will work and when it won't. I don't understand it at all."

"That's because you're thinking about it logically." Thelxinoe offered up another gentle smile. "You're trying to create a list of rules in your head, aren't you? If I say this, then that will happen."

"Well, yes," Wendy admitted. After all, that was how navigation worked—if you took this bearing and sailed for that number of days, you would arrive at your destination. If you adjusted the sails just so, the wind would carry you in the direction you intended. "Isn't that how it should work?"

"It's how we'd often like it to work," the siren admitted. "But those kinds of rules don't apply here. To see why, try this. Close your eyes."

Wendy did as she was told, though not without a small sigh that made Peter chuckle.

"Don't think about what you want to happen. Think about what already is. Listen to the lagoon. Feel the wind. Sense the currents of connection flowing around you, just as you sense the currents of magic."

Wendy concentrated as hard as she could. She heard the gentle lapping of waves against the shore, the rustle of leaves in the breeze, the soft beating of Charming's tiny heart next to her ear. She smelled the particular scent of magic that always surrounded Peter—pickles and cool water and the color green.

And then, beneath it all, she heard a melody.

It was so subtle at first that she could barely make it out. But as she focused on it, listening more closely, it grew in volume until it filled her mind—the most complex, beautiful music she had ever heard.

Deep drums filled her chest with their rumbling. Horns heralded the joy of the water, earth, and sky. Strings carried each leaf, each bird, each ripple of the waves. Everything had a place in the whole. And everything had its own melody, she suddenly realized. Songs within songs within songs.

"What is it?" she whispered.

"It is the song of the universe," Thelxinoe said softly. "The magic of connection. Every movement, every thought, every emotion affects the whole."

"And those changes affect us too," Wendy realized. "They change the song, moment by moment."

"Yes. Moment by moment, ever changing. Always perfect, but never the same.

Wendy thought about that for a long moment, letting it sink in. "So the effect you can have in one moment won't always be the same later," she said finally.

When she opened her eyes, Thelxinoe was nodding.

"That's right. There are no rules to siren magic. There are only instincts. You must feel the truth of what needs to be said moment by moment." She paused, watching Wendy closely. "When you can do that, you can change the very fabric of the world."

Tigerlilja stood at the edge of the gathering, her arms crossed, watching the circle of warriors. Vikings and frost-folk alike had formed a ring in the clearing, their breath visible in the cool air as they cheered and shouted.

At the center, Vegard faced off against one of Jokul's polar bears—an enormous white beast that walked upright and spoke with the voice of a warrior.

The bear towered over her brother, his massive shoulders blocking out the sun as he lunged. But Vegard was quicker than his size suggested. He ducked under the bear's reaching paws, shoved his shoulder low into the bear's thick waist, and, in a move that drew gasps from the crowd, lifted the creature clear off his feet.

For a moment, the bear's surprised expression was almost human.

Then Vegard twisted, using the bear's own weight against him, and slammed his opponent onto his back with enough force to shake the ground.

The bear lay there for a moment, blinking up at the sky. Then a deep, rumbling laugh emerged from his chest. "You're unnatural, Viking." He accepted Vegard's offered hand and climbing to his feet. "No man should be able to do that to a bear." He brushed the dirt from his white fur, still chuckling. "I've fought frost giants who couldn't throw me like that."

"Perhaps you need to fight better giants." Vegard's quip earned another laugh from the bear and appreciative shouts from the crowd.

As two more fighters took their places in the circle—this time an elf facing a young Viking warrior—Tigerlilja made her way to where Vegard stood catching his breath.

"Show-off," she said quietly.

Vegard's grin widened. "The frost-folk respect strength—that hasn't changed. Best to give them confidence in our alliance."

She couldn't argue with his logic. These practice bouts had done more to unite their forces than any number of formal meetings. Still, other matters required their attention. "Hook has called a council aboard the new ship." She nodded toward the vessel that floated above the trees. "Can you keep watch here? Make sure no one gets too … enthusiastic?"

He followed her gaze to where the delicate ship hovered, its silver-white hull catching the light like fresh snow. "Of course."

Tigerlilja made her way toward a rope ladder that hung from the ship's rail, swaying slightly in the breeze. Some twenty-five feet up, Hook's men gathered on deck, their voices carrying faintly on the wind.

She grasped the ladder, testing its strength. The rope was surprisingly warm to the touch—elven craft, without doubt. Their magic infused everything they created, down to the smallest detail. As she climbed, the sounds of the wrestling matches faded below, replaced by the gentle creak of the ship's timbers and the murmur of voices above.

Tigerlilja pulled herself onto the deck just as Thomas gestured to an open journal. His diligent work at the Library showed in the tightly scrawled notes that filled the page as well as the ink stains on his fingers.

"The texts are frustratingly vague," he was saying. "Flying a ship appears to require a unique combination of self-belief, innate magical affinity, and"—he paused, frowning at his notes—"what I can only describe as positive emotional resonance. It's not a precise formula like calculating a trajectory or measuring the angle of the wind. It's more … abstract."

Hook held up the ship's trinket, sunlight catching its well-worn surface. "Then perhaps the simplest way to determine who might pilot this mouse of a ship is for each man to hold the trinket and—"

The ship suddenly lurched to port, causing several of the men to grab the rail. Hook's fingers opened immediately, dropping the mermaid figurine onto the deck with a soft clatter. "Just the wind," he announced, though the air was nearly still. His eyes found Tigerlilja by the ladder, and something flickered across his face—relief at having a reason to excuse himself, perhaps.

"I was about to suggest," he continued smoothly, "that we might see if anyone from your village wanted to attempt piloting the vessel." He strode toward her, calling over his shoulder, "Thomas, continue with the testing."

Tigerlilja couldn't quite suppress her smile as she followed Hook to the opposite rail, well away from his crew. Captain James Hook, the great non-believer, accidentally making a ship respond to his touch.

"So, Captain," she said, keeping her voice low, "are you part fay yourself, or are you simply learning to embrace the magic that surrounds us all?"

His eyes hardened. "Thomas has garnered information that requires our immediate attention." He glanced back at his men, who were taking turns holding the trinket with varying degrees of skepticism. "We should discuss how best to share it with the others."

Tigerlilja studied his face. There was something in his tone, in the careful way he chose his words, that gave her pause. "What is it?"

"Thomas has discovered that a dullahan has come through the portal. Are you familiar with such creatures?"

The word struck Tigerlilja like a physical blow. *Dullahan.*

The nightmare that had brought her people here had been bad enough. She still missed her Amma, her parents, and all those they had lost that night. Her people had found relative safety here, but now the horrors of the old world were seeping through like poison. This had to end.

"I know them," she said carefully. "Though even in my time, dullahans lived only in tales passed down through generations. Headless riders who bring death in their wake. When they speak a name …" She paused, remembering her grandmother's warnings. "That person is marked. And once a name has been spoken, the dullahan cannot be stopped."

"Thomas said as much," Hook confirmed. "But there's more. They leave a path of decay wherever they travel. Any living thing that comes within their reach begins to rot. Thomas observed the effect firsthand. And the affected area spans at least thirty paces, possibly more."

A chill ran through her, settling low in her gut. If that was true …

But wait, the news, she realized, had other implications. "Blackheart can't be keeping a dullahan in his fortress. It's far too

dangerous to contain, especially where he's building up his forces. He wouldn't risk losing his entire army. So where—"

"You're right. Apparently, it's roaming around Neverland. Thomas encountered its aftermath near the Library. But that's not the worst of it." He lowered his voice even further, though they were well away from the others. "If Buri can bring creatures of such power through the portal, it means he's close. Very close. Once he crosses over, he could bring anything through—armies, monsters, demons. We must act soon."

Something flickered across his face as he finished speaking— was it relief? Perhaps he was simply glad to have conveyed the news, as grave as it was. Or maybe it was the look of a warrior who had grown tired of waiting and was ready for battle.

Still, Tigerlilja couldn't shake the feeling that there was something he wasn't telling her. She had never fully trusted Hook, and she wasn't about to start now.

"I will inform Jokul and the village council," she said finally. "When Peter and Wendy return, we can meet to determine our course of action."

Below them, the distant sounds of wrestling and laughter continued. Soon enough, they would all be tested in ways far more dangerous than friendly bouts with polar bears. Tigerlilja cast one last glance at Hook, who had turned to watch his men's attempts with the trinket, his steel appendage gleaming in the light.

Whatever Hook might be hiding, whatever battles lay ahead, one thing was certain—the time for preparation was over. War was coming to Neverland, and it would spare no one.

CHAPTER

# 40

Wendy soared through the air next to Peter, with Charming glowing a happy gold just below. The familiar scent of Neverland surrounded her—pickles and green and cool, clear water—but it felt different somehow.

It was more than the simple smell of magic. It was the scent of possibility.

A surge of hope filled her chest, so strong it nearly lifted her higher into the air of its own accord, but she had no idea why.

It certainly had nothing to do with her training. That, in Wendy's opinion, had been almost no help at all.

She'd felt relief, certainly, to discover that she couldn't actually control anyone's actions—that she never had. But relief had quickly given way to confusion. There were no rules to follow, no patterns to master, no way to know whether her abilities would work from one moment to the next.

All she could do was amplify what people already felt, strengthen the desires they held in their hearts. What use was that in the coming battle?

Everyone already wanted to defeat Buri. Everyone understood what was at stake. The very fabric of Neverland hung in the balance. What extra motivation could anyone possibly need beyond that?

At least they hadn't come away empty-handed. Peter had secured the allegiance of the mermaids, along with Thelxinoe and any other sirens she might be able to gather to their cause. In exchange, Peter had promised to consult with them before bringing new creatures to Neverland.

That is, unless lives were at stake and he had to act immediately. He was quite clear about that.

Wendy glanced at Peter, who flew with uncharacteristic focus, his eyes fixed on the horizon. The way he'd handled the negotiation still astonished her. He'd thought through his responses, considered the consequences, and found a middle ground that served everyone's interests.

This wasn't the same Peter she had met in Dover—the one who acted on whims and forgot any conversation he didn't like when he was still only halfway through it.

Of course, she realized. That was it—the source of this newfound hope. Peter had changed, fundamentally changed, and with him, Neverland itself had been transformed.

Ever since Peter's mother had tied him to the land, he had been its champion, and that champion had finally chosen to fight. For the first time, Wendy truly believed Peter would do whatever was necessary to defeat Buri. She could count on him—really count on him—and somehow, that was changing the way she felt about him too.

She glanced at him out of the corner of her eye to find him smiling at her.

Perhaps her siren nature could help her share this feeling with the others back at the village. Well, not *this* feeling, exactly. This feeling was something she would have to explore later.

But the hope—that was something they all needed.

Wendy glanced at the landscape below, trying to gauge how far they were from the village. The familiar patchwork of Neverland spread out beneath them—eternal summer beside eternal winter, jungle next to desert, mountain peaks overlooking valleys filled with mist.

That was when she felt it.

Something was wrong. Terribly wrong.

She glanced at Peter, but he must have felt it too. He was scanning the ground below, his troubled eyes darting back and forth. Turning her attention back to the hunt, Wendy tried to feel out the source of the danger.

There.

Peter pointed in the same instant that she spotted it: a trail of blackened earth that split into two paths, forking like a serpent's tongue.

"What is it?" Wendy asked.

"I don't know. But it feels like an adventure!" Peter grinned, then halted in midair and let himself drop like a stone, making her want to take back everything she had just been thinking.

Maybe he hadn't changed quite so much after all.

Wendy dove after him, landing next to him just a few paces beyond the edge of the dark trail. What she had thought was scorched earth was actually decay—raw, creeping decay that spread outward from the trail's center.

The stench of it hit her like a physical blow, worse than anything she'd encountered before. There wasn't a single hint of green in this magic. Instead, it smelled only of death and rot, like meat left too long in the sun.

And she could sense something else too.

The very magic of Neverland was fighting against it.

As she focused more closely, Wendy could feel the battle between them. She closed her eyes, trying to hear the music of the land the way Thelxinoe had taught her. Two symphonies clashed in her mind—one full of life and joy and endless possibilities, the other a screech of metal on metal, of endings and entropy and despair.

"Be careful," she warned Peter. "Don't touch it. Don't even get close. There's something terribly wrong here."

"I feel it too." His voice was an uneasy murmur. "It's so very sad and frightening. Like knowing Tootles is gone forever."

Wendy glanced at him sharply. It was very much like that, she realized. Exactly like that. "What could have done this? Have you ever seen it before?"

"Not that I can remember." Peter's eyes rose from the decaying ground. "But I think we're about to find out."

That's when they heard it—the sound of thunderous hooves approaching. But it wasn't just a sound. It was a feeling that penetrated straight to Wendy's bones, a sensation of inevitable doom that made her want to sink to her knees and give up. If she had been alone, she thought the feeling would have overwhelmed her completely.

Even as it was, standing there next to Peter, she could feel it haunting her—the horrible, depressing weight of futility.

Two riders were approaching fast, each astride a massive warhorse. But these were not living animals—they were rotting even as they galloped, pieces of flesh falling away with each thundering stride.

But the creatures that rode on their backs were more terrifying still.

Where their heads should have been, there was only emptiness beneath their hoods. Not like Shadow's familiar darkness,

which at least had substance to it. This was a complete void, a nothingness that pulled at the very light around it, consuming everything it touched.

Their cloaks writhed behind them, and Wendy realized to her horror that they weren't cloaks at all—they were swarming masses of insects, thousands upon thousands of them.

She didn't realize she had frozen in place until she heard Peter screaming her name.

"Wendy! Please, I can't move you. We have to go. Wendy Darling! Move! Now!"

Snapping back to awareness, she felt Pan tugging desperately at her arm, trying to lift her into the air while Charming jingled in alarm. Her mind been so focused on that terrible weight that it had pinned her to the ground. Even Peter's strength hadn't been enough to lift her.

She could still feel the riders pulling at her, trying to leach every ounce of hope from her heart. It took everything she had to tear her eyes away.

As the riders bore down on them, Wendy finally broke free, her mind reaching desperately for the sky. Peter's hand dragged her upward, pulling her out of harm's way just in time.

The creatures pulled their rotting mounts to a halt where she and Peter had been standing only moments before. As one, they turned their empty faces toward the sky, and one of them raised its arm to point at her.

"What are they?" Wendy whispered.

"Death," Peter said with a shudder. "I think they might be death itself.

At last, the Viking village lay ahead, its familiar longhouses a welcome sight after what they had witnessed. But even the comfort of returning couldn't dispel the chill that had settled in Wendy's bones.

She had known from her first day in Neverland that this was a dangerous realm. One didn't survive long here without a healthy respect for its perils, from merfolk who could drown you with a smile to dragons who might burn you to ash.

But those creatures they had just encountered—those *things*—were different. The very air around them had reeked of despair, as though reality itself were decaying in their presence.

Something must have gone terribly wrong in Neverland for such abominations to exist here.

Still, as they approached the village, Wendy felt a wave of relief wash over her—even if the respite would be temporary at best, she was grateful for it. When had this place become home? She couldn't pinpoint the moment, but there was no denying the

truth of it now. Even the smell of fish smoking over wood fires felt welcoming.

A familiar chiming drew her attention skyward. Tinker Bell was flying toward them, her glow shifting rapidly between colors that suggested both urgency and agitation.

Peter translated as the fairy jingled excitedly. "She says she's only just returned. She has news, but she's insisting on talking to me alone." He turned to Wendy, his ice-blue eyes showing uncharacteristic concern. "Will you be all right?"

"Why yes, thank you, Peter." Wendy was touched by his consideration. "I need to report to Captain Hook anyway."

Peter nodded and flew off, following the still-chiming Tinker Bell. Wendy watched them go, noting how the fairy's light cast a warm glow across Peter's face that made him look older, more serious somehow.

Looking down, she spotted Hook and Charlie standing alone on the deck of the *Pegasus*. Not long ago, she would have landed discreetly some distance away, hiding the fact that she could fly using innisfay dust. But after everything that had happened, such deceptions seemed pointless.

She angled her descent and landed gracefully beside them.

Hook didn't look surprised in the slightest. "Captain Darling, welcome back. Is this a new siren thing, being able to fly? What other wonders do you have in store for us?"

"Oh! No, Captain," Wendy replied hastily. "It's just innisfay dust. I can't fly on my own."

"Pity." Hook regarded her with a look of ... what was it? Wendy wasn't sure whether he was disappointed or relieved to discover she was as land-bound as he was—most of the time, anyway. "I trust you have something helpful to report. Tigerlilja has called a war council. Thomas is back. The news isn't good."

Wendy frowned, steeling herself. "What happened?"

"Buri's almost here." Hook's jaw clenched. "New horrors trotting about. As if this place wasn't bad enough already. Tiger-lilja and Thomas will provide a full report."

"I'm afraid my own news isn't any better." Wendy brushed a strand of hair from her face, buying time to choose her words. "Being part siren doesn't seem to be very useful. It's more about inspiring people and sensing danger than anything else. And I could already do those things." She took a deep breath. "But that's not the worst of it."

"And what, pray tell, would be the worst of it?" The look he gave her in that moment suggested he would rather start blowing things up than hear any more bad news.

Still, it was her duty to report what she had seen, so she took a deep breath and forged ahead. "There appear to be two life-leeching, headless horsemen blazing trails of rot wherever they go."

"Wait," Hook's eyes narrowed sharply. "There are *two* of them now?"

The glance that passed between Hook and Charlie spoke volumes.

"Now?" Wendy's left eyebrow shot up of its own accord. "You've seen one?"

"Not yet," he growled, "but with our luck, it's just a matter of time before we all do."

Wendy considered telling him more about her near-death experience, but the look on his face said he was carrying enough burdens already. Instead, she smoothed her jacket and suggested quietly, "Perhaps we should head to the war council. If there's more bad news, we'd best hear it all at once."

As they made their way toward the longhouse, Charlie fell into step beside her. "We tried again with the ships," he murmured. "A few of the lads managed to move them a bit, but only Mr. Starkey could properly fly one."

Charlie glanced at Hook. For a moment, she thought he might say something else, but then he shook his head, clearly deciding to keep whatever it was to himself.

Soon enough, the longhouse doors stood before them, but Wendy's steps faltered at the sight within. Even after everything she had seen in Neverland, she could hardly believe her eyes.

Tigerlilja's clan leaders were there, of course, their leather armor adorned with runes that seemed to shift in the firelight. The British were there too, along with the imps and the everlost. But now the frost-folk had joined them as well—elves and polar bears, minotaurs and owls, wolves and deer, all of them armored, all engaged in conversation.

A minotaur nodded at Wendy's arrival just as an owl dropped something from the rafters for Nana, who waited eagerly below.

Slowly, almost reverently, Wendy moved into the room, greeting Nana with a scratch behind her ears. They all found their seats among the assembled warriors, Wendy settling between Hook and Charlie while Charming perched on her shoulder. The room fell silent as Tigerlilja rose to her feet, her bearing every inch that of a Viking warrior queen.

"I've called this meeting because we have far less time than we thought." Her voice carried to every corner of the now enormous hall. "As Tinker Bell has confirmed, Buri is almost through the gate to Neverland."

A wave of murmurs passed through the gathering.

"There are rumors that Buri intends to preserve Neverland for Blackheart to rule," she continued, her hand resting on the hilt of her sword, "but that simply isn't true. Buri wants to kill Peter and destroy Neverland so he can spread his realm of ice across the world." Her eyes swept the room. "We've sent the innisfay to spread the word—the time has come. We must take a stand, together, while there's still a Neverland to save."

The fire crackled in the hearth, casting an ominous glow across the faces of the gathered crowd. "Even now, Buri's creatures are already putting a strain on Neverland's magic. Thomas has returned from the Library to explain."

Tigerlilja gestured to Thomas and took her seat. Wendy watched as her friend rose, clutching a leather-bound book to his chest like a shield. His spectacles caught the firelight as he pushed them higher on his nose.

"They're called dullahans." Around the room, several Vikings exclaimed in horror. "Yes, I'm afraid so." Thomas opened his notebook. "Where Neverland preserves life, the dullahans destroy it. Anything that gets within about thirty paces of them decomposes at a highly accelerated rate."

A new round of murmurs filled the room, and it wasn't just the Vikings who looked disturbed. Even the everlost shifted in their seats.

"Alchemists of the past say it works much like fire," Thomas continued. "Something small thrown into their path will decay immediately. A larger creature, like a human being, can stand in it for a few moments—exactly how long, we don't know—but their boots will decay out from under them. When it reaches the flesh, the rot eats the skin away and continues from there."

Wendy felt Hook tense beside her as Thomas added, "The closer you are to them, the stronger and faster the decay becomes."

Thomas looked up from his notebook. "Wherever they have tread, Neverland is striving to heal itself, but it's a process. Stay out of those areas until you're certain it's safe."

Heads nodded as several of the Vikings made subtle warding gestures.

"All right then." Thomas swallowed hard. "As for the creatures themselves, the sound of their approach has the potential to paralyze anyone in their path—especially if you're the subject of

their attention. If you hear hoofbeats in the distance, avoid them at any cost. Once in their thrall, there are very few who escape it."

Wendy's hand crept to her throat as she remembered that horror. She felt Charlie's concerned glance but kept her eyes fixed on Thomas, determined not to show how deeply his words affected her.

"They also wear cloaks made of insects," Thomas continued, his voice growing less certain. "But how they use them isn't exactly clear. Something about targets outside their reach? Just ... try to avoid those, obviously."

"Obviously," Vegard interjected, his dry tone drawing nervous chuckles from the assembled warriors.

Thomas cleared his throat, pushing his spectacles up his nose again. "Right. Don't look directly into their faces—or, rather, into the void where their faces should be. If you do, you can be lost to this world." He muttered the last part almost to himself. "Whatever that means."

The fire popped loudly in the hearth, making several people jump.

"There does seem to be at least some defense against them, but we aren't sure what it is or how it works," Thomas pressed on. "One of them approached the Library, but it was unable to cross the moat. It's possible that Neverland is shoring up its defenses around strategic targets, but again—"

"Let me guess," Hook interrupted. "You don't know what that means."

"I'm afraid not." Thomas turned a page in his journal to scan the page beyond, then turned it back again. "They've never been in Neverland before that I can tell, so there isn't any historical knowledge of how their magic interacts with this place. But there's one thing we do know—" He looked up and paused, his expression grave. "We should never, under any circumstances,

call anyone by name in their presence. Once they know someone's name and speak it aloud, they'll always know where that person is, coming for them no matter where they are until they're dead."

"Wait," Curly piped up, "until who's dead? The dullahan or the person they're tracking?"

"Well, either one, I suppose."

"Oh, right. Yeah, that makes sense." Curly nodded as a chorus of murmurs spread through the room, then quieted.

Thomas adjusted his grip on the book. "That's all we really know, except that there's one in Neverland already."

"Two, actually."

The murmurs rose again as Wendy turned to Peter in surprise. She hadn't expected him to remember their encounter.

As if reading her thoughts, Peter met her gaze across the table. "I'm sure I wouldn't remember them, you know, if things had gone the other way."

Before Wendy could reply, Jokul rose to his feet. "The dullahans should be proof enough, to all who doubted, that Buri has no intention of preserving Neverland or anyone in it." The winter king's words fell like ice in the silent room. "He has unleashed abominations that destroy everything they touch."

Tigerlilja rose to meet him, her hair catching the firelight. "You have all heard everything we know at this time. I suggest we end this larger meeting. A smaller council will convene to plan our tactics for the battle ahead."

As the crowd dispersed, Wendy glanced at Peter, only to discover that his characteristic smile had disappeared entirely, replaced by a haunting mixture of confusion and concern.

She couldn't help but wonder if his smile would return, or if—like so many things in Neverland—it too would be forever changed by what was coming.

# CHAPTER 42

There is a particular silence that falls over warriors before a great battle—not the empty quiet of peace, but a loaded stillness that feels like drawing back a bowstring. It settles into corners and weighs upon shoulders and makes every word spoken feel monumentally important.

Such a silence had descended upon the Viking longhouse, broken only by the crackling of the fire in the hearth and the occasional clink of weapons as their bearers shifted uneasily in their seats. Even Jokul, tucked between an elf and a polar bear, seemed to feel the gravity of the moment—his cold distance tempered by something that looked a lot like concern.

"Before we begin," he said quietly, "I'd like to make it known that we're reclaiming our ship."

The elf beside him nodded, and the polar bear crossed his massive arms over his chest in what was clearly intended to be a show of support.

Hook, sitting next to Wendy, tapped his steel appendage on the table. "What ship is that?" His voice was dangerously calm.

"The *Sparrow*," Jokul replied. "Gerdrek built it. It belongs to him."

Hook's eyes narrowed. "And who's Gerdrek?"

The elf next to Jokul sat up straighter, eyeing the British captain with thinly veiled suspicion. "I'm Gerdrek. I built the ship that hovers in the air above the village."

Wendy's eyes widened. "How did you do that?" She glanced down the table to share a meaningful look with Thomas, then back to the elf. "I didn't know ships could fly on their own."

She realized, of course, that she was interrupting a delicate conversation about the vessel's ownership, but the possibility of learning how it flew seemed more important, at least to Wendy, than discovering who would be flying it.

"They can't," Gerdrek confirmed, much to Wendy's disappointment. "I had nothing to do with that. But I carved and laid every plank of that ship by hand. Blackheart stole it from me. Thank you for retrieving it."

As for Hook, he wasn't nearly as concerned about how the ship stayed aloft as he was how it might be used in battle. Unfortunately, he hadn't worked that part out yet—at least not when it came to the *Sparrow*—so he wasn't sure who he wanted to see on her crew.

Then again, he had sent so many crewmen back to England along the way to Neverland that he had precious few British sailors left to work with. The *Sparrow* would need a captain, and at the moment, England was fresh out.

"Consider her return a gesture of goodwill," he said finally, "as long as you're willing to add her sails to the cause."

Gerdrek nodded.

"I'll captain the *Pegasus* of course," Hook continued, as though anyone might have doubted it, "flown by Mr. Hawke. Once we infiltrate the fortress, I'll be with the landing party, and Mr. Hawke will take the helm." He glanced at Charlie, who acknowledged this with a slight inclination of his head. "Captain Darling has the *Jolly Roger*. That leaves one more."

*Blackheart's ship*, Wendy thought. *The Ravenhawk*—the one she had stolen when they'd first attacked his castle. The one that used his mother's note as a trinket.

Hook was looking at Tigerlilja.

"As I've told you before," she said firmly, "our people don't fly. We'll gladly risk our lives by the sword, but sails are your concern."

His forget-me-not eyes darkened to a midnight blue, which didn't seem like a promising start to the proceedings.

"I'm sure we can sort out the *Ravenhawk* later," Wendy suggested.

Jokul seized the opening. "For the moment, I'd like to use it to transport the rest of my people here—those who won't be fighting. For their protection. The *Sparrow* doesn't have enough room for us all."

Hook considered this for a long moment, then finally relented. A request to protect civilians was more than reasonable—it was honorable. But he wasn't about to turn the ship over to the frost-folk completely.

"So be it. Mr. Hawke can fly her." Turning to Charlie, he added, "Take whatever crew you need—enough to man the cannons—and be ready for anything. There's no telling what's out there waiting for you."

"Aye, Captain."

Jokul nodded. "It's best if they leave at once."

Hook waved in agreement, prompting Charlie and Gerdrek to rise from the table and depart.

"We need to be ready for anything here too." Tigerlilja turned to Vegard. "Let's double the watch duty. We can't be too careful."

"Agreed." Vegard rubbed the back of his neck, then dropped his arm heavily to the table. "Do we have any idea what else Buri might have brought through the portal? Anything that might call for special preparations?"

At the mention of Buri's name, Wendy glanced at Peter, but he replied without any sign of reacting to it. "Tink said it's harder to get in there now, but she did see a dragon. Plus, some draugar. And trolls."

Tinker Bell chimed in his ear.

"Right," Peter added, "and more than one giant."

"Trolls and giants. Perfect," Hook growled. "Anything else out of fairy tales? Witches? Ogres, perhaps?"

Peter turned to consult with Tinker Bell, who jingled briefly.

"No witches yet, but she wouldn't rule out the ogres."

Hook blinked, sighed heavily, then stared at him in silence.

"Assuming we manage to fight our way through dragons, draugar, trolls, and giants"—Tigerlilja spoke each creature's name as though it were a weight to be measured— "do we have a way to kill Buri himself? Or at least push him back through the portal?"

For a long time, no one said anything.

"I could go back to the Library and do some research, if that would help?" Thomas offered.

"We should ask Shadow."

Every head at the table turned to Hook, who had spoken the words as though they weren't completely mad.

"What? Is that really so unreasonable?" He raised his good left hand in supplication. "She killed a time-stopping fairy. She might know something useful."

"She's only been trouble for us in the past." Tigerlilja paused, clearly weighing their options. "But I suppose if Neverland was destroyed, she'd be just as lost as the rest of us. We should pursue every possible path, just in case. Including sending you back to the Library, Thomas. That's definitely worth a look."

"The mermaids and sirens have agreed to help us too," Wendy added. "Do you think they would know anything? Or Undine?"

Tigerlilja shared a glance with Jokul. "Either way, we should consider our water-bound forces in our planning. Perhaps we should gather everyone at the lagoon."

"Not yet." Hook's response was immediate and firm. "It's too close to the enemy. But it would serve well as the last rally point before our attack."

Wendy watched Hook's expression carefully. She had expected him to struggle more with the idea of fighting side by side with mermaids and sirens. Then again, these were desperate times— Hook knew that as well as any of them. They would need every ally they could muster.

"Actually," she said, "Undine's trapped in his lake, I think. Is there any way to move him?"

Thomas turned to Peter. "How did you carry him here?"

"In a bucket," Peter replied, as though this were the most natural thing in the world.

"The giant water creature that fought a dragon." Hook's voice was flat. "You carried him here in a bucket."

"Well, it was a pretty big bucket." Peter brightened considerably. "I'm sure it's around here somewhere. I'll ask Curly to find

it. Meanwhile, the Wendy and I could escort Thomas to the Library and then visit the griffins. They might be willing to join us."

Jokul turned to stare at him. "I can't believe I'm saying this, but that's an excellent idea."

Tigerlilja nodded, her expression grave. "Let's gather our water forces at the lagoon, but only them for now. Bring the griffins back here."

"Good," Hook agreed. "We'll marshal most of our troops here, then move to the lagoon just before the attack. We can use the ships for transport. Although I'm not sure how much use our water forces will be. It's not like we'll be fighting anyone at the lagoon. Blackheart won't leave a fortified position."

"Still though …" Vegard's unfinished thought hung in the air.

Everyone turned to look at him, waiting. The Viking wasn't known for speaking unless he had something important to say.

"Well, I mean, it's not a bad plan." He gestured vaguely with one massive hand. "If we could lure them into fighting us at the lagoon, we'd have a massive army there. They'd have to hit us with everything they have."

"Leaving the fortress relatively unguarded," Tigerlilja finished, a dangerous light entering her eyes.

"I don't see how we'll lure them away," Hook countered. "I doubt they'll chase our ships again. They already fell for that once."

"They will for the right bait." Jokul's voice had gone cold as midwinter. When he and Tigerlilja shared another glance, something passed between them that made Wendy's skin prickle.

"Let us work on that." The Viking leader's gaze darted up to the rafters, then scanned each corner of the room. "And let's see if we can find Shadow again, too. Maybe she has some answers."

At the mention of Shadow, Hook's eyes narrowed, just for a moment—making Wendy wonder, not for the first time, what secrets the captain was keeping.

<h1>CHAPTER 43</h1>

Flying over Neverland was still a marvel, even now. You might think the novelty would wear off eventually, but it hadn't—at least, not for Wendy. Especially not with the Library's gleaming spires visible in the distance, stretching between earth and sky like a castle of dreams.

First the Library, then the griffins.

She smiled at the thought of seeing the griffins again. With the battle against Blackheart and Buri looming ever closer, their strength and loyalty would be invaluable allies.

*The battle.*

Wendy's smile faded. Tootles's death was still a raw wound in her heart, the memory bringing a lump to her throat.

How many more would they lose before all was said and done?

She glanced at Thomas and Erikson, perched together on Snaggleclaw's back. Just ahead of them flew Loamly, the everlost who had taken such a shine to Thomas's research. He looked terribly young in flight, his face set in concentration, and for a moment

all Wendy could think about was Nicholas—another young man who had died too soon, protecting those he loved.

It seemed she wasn't the only one dwelling on dark thoughts. Erikson and Loamly both wore expressions better suited to a funeral than a flight to the Library.

A new worry crept into Wendy's eyes as she glanced at Peter. Usually, he would have done something outrageous by now—perhaps convincing Snaggleclaw to do a barrel roll, or challenging everyone to fly backward while singing sea shanties. The curse had made any sense of gravity impossible for him, keeping him forever light and carefree.

But lately … well … lately things had been different.

The curse appeared to be weakening, letting him hold onto memories that once would have slipped away like water through his fingers.

It ought to be a good thing, Wendy thought. After all, one couldn't stay a child forever, not even in Neverland. Still, watching everyone's solemn faces, she couldn't help but miss Peter's irreverence.

Like when he had raced to touch a cloud during her training with Thelxinoe, just because she had challenged him to do it.

And *that* gave Wendy an idea.

Reaching for her siren nature, she called out to the lot of them, "Last one to the Library is a rotten goose egg!"

Peter's shout rang out immediately, bright and infectious. "Ha! That's hardly fair when everyone knows I'm the fastest flyer in all of Neverland!" With that, he shot ahead, trailed by the echo of his laughter.

Snaggleclaw let out an indignant snort—which was quite something coming from a dragon—and surged after him.

Only Loamly hung back, maintaining a steady pace just ahead of Wendy. She wasn't sure whether he was sticking close to her

out of courtesy or strategy. There was no doubt he could have flown faster, but perhaps he was simply keeping the real competition in view.

He didn't need to be first to avoid being the rotten goose egg, after all—he just needed to avoid being last.

And last, Wendy realized, was almost certainly going to be her position in this impromptu race. Still, if she was going to be a rotten goose egg, she might as well enjoy the view. Below, a spectacular field of wildflowers stretched out like a painter's palette gone mad with color.

Grinning from ear to ear, she dipped lower, hoping to catch their fragrance on the breeze.

That was when she saw it.

The dullahan moved across the meadow like a blight, leaving a trail of death in its wake. Where moments before there had been vibrant blooms, now there was only decay—the flowers withered and blackened as if weeks of rot had been compressed into seconds.

Wendy jerked her gaze away, remembering all too well their last encounter. She pulled up sharply, climbing as fast as she could. But then—

*Wendy Darling.*

The whisper slithered into her mind, startling her so profoundly that she looked down, responding to her name by instinct.

From this height, the dullahan should have appeared tiny, barely visible against the ruined flowers below. Yet somehow, Wendy could see it with terrible clarity. Its empty hood turned up toward her, and though it had no face, she could feel its attention fixed upon her with dreadful certainty, one arm raised high in the air, pointing directly at her with inexorable purpose.

*Wendy Darling,* it whispered again, the sound like desiccated bones scraping across a tomb.

And then the whole world went black.

Racing toward the Library, Thomas couldn't help but smile at Peter's antics. No matter how many times the everlost darted ahead, he never quite disappeared from view, always staying close enough for Thomas, Erikson, and Snaggleclaw to hear his voice carried back on the wind. "Come on, you can do it. I think you're catching up!"

This was the third time he'd said it, glancing over his shoulder with a huge grin, and Thomas was starting to think Peter might be enjoying their company more than the race itself.

But then Peter glanced back once more time, and everything changed. The playful expression vanished from his face, replaced by something Thomas had never seen there before: pure terror.

In the space of a heartbeat, Peter executed an impossibly fast twisting somersault and shot back the way they had come, moving faster than Thomas would have believed possible.

Something was terribly wrong.

The scientist yanked hard on Snaggleclaw's reins, urging the dragon into a sharp turn that made his stomach lurch.

As they wheeled around, he saw it. Wendy was falling from the sky, her unconscious form plummeting toward a dark path that cut through the field of wildflowers below like a gaping wound in the earth.

And in the middle of that corruption stood a dullahan, its empty hood tilted upward to watch her fall. The rot spread outward from its feet in a steadily expanding circle of death.

Loamly dove through the air after Wendy, his slight form arrowing downward as he raced to intercept her fall. But Thomas's mind was already plotting their trajectories.

The terrible truth was inescapable: Loamly wouldn't reach her in time.

Even Peter, despite his incredible speed, was too far away. And if Peter couldn't make it, there was no way old Snaggleclaw would be fast enough.

Still, they had to try.

"Faster!" Thomas's fingers tightened on the reins as he watched the nightmare unfold before him, each second stretching out with excruciating clarity as they raced toward their falling friend.

Wendy was only moments from crashing into the ground when Loamly finally reached her. He grabbed her arm, but she was falling too fast. No matter how frantically his wings beat against the air, they couldn't overcome the force of her fall.

As Thomas watched, his heart caught in his throat. He wanted with every fiber of his being to change the force of gravity, if only for one moment, to slow Wendy's fall and return her to the sky.

But, of course, he couldn't. And neither could Loamly.

So the young everlost made the only choice he had left. He wrapped his arms around Wendy's waist and spun in midair, placing himself beneath her. His wings spread wide, shielding her from the corruption below as they took the full force of impact with the ground.

The sound of Loamly's scream tore through the air.

Peter reached them just as they hit, one arm wrapping around Wendy's waist as Loamly held her up toward him.

He stretched desperately toward Loamly with his free hand. But before their fingers could meet, the dullahan's cape exploded into motion, the writhing mass of insects swarming between them like a living wall.

"Loamly!" Peter's voice cracked with anguish as he shot upward with Wendy, the dark cloud of insects forcing him back. "LOAMLY!"

Thomas was almost there. He urged Snaggleclaw into a dive, and the dragon's throat glowed red beneath his hands, releasing a massive burst of flame at the dullahan. But the creature's cape swirled inward, forming an impenetrable shield against the fire.

Thousands of tiny insect bodies crackled and burned, and the dullahan backed away a few paces, his mount screaming and pawing in agitation.

But then a second dullahan crested a ridge in the distance, thundering toward them.

Snaggleclaw hovered over Loamly's crumpled form, his wings beating dangerously close to the ground, but they were still too high. Thomas couldn't reach him, and the second dullahan was closing fast.

Without thinking, Thomas thrust the reins into Erikson's hands and launched himself from the dragon's neck.

The moment he hit the ground, Thomas could feel the rot corrupting his boots, transforming the hard leather soles into brittle flakes that deteriorated beneath his feet. He grabbed Loamly, lifting the everlost's body upward. The boy's wings were disintegrating before his eyes, crumbling away like ancient parchment.

As Erikson leaned down from Snaggleclaw's back, hauling Loamly to safety, Thomas screamed in agony. His boots had decomposed completely. Now, the blight surged through his flesh, rotting his feet out from under him.

He tried to jump for Erikson's outstretched hand, but the decay was already halfway up his calves, pulling him down into the abyss. As he started to fall, Erikson threw him the reins. Thomas's fingers closed around the leather just as his knees buckled.

"Hold on!"

The Viking's shout sounded so very far away.

Snaggleclaw rose higher, and Thomas thought he felt someone grab him—first his wrist, then his arm, then the waist of his pants, dragging him across the dragon's neck.

The last thing Thomas remembered was a wave of pain so intense it consumed all thought. Then darkness took him, and he knew nothing more.

CHAPTER

# 44

Wendy drifted slowly into consciousness, first becoming aware that she was lying on something soft and then taking in the gentle whisper of fabric above. Her eyes fluttered open to find herself in an enormous canopy bed, its gossamer drape rising and falling in a light breeze.

She stared up at the elegant fabric, trying to make sense of her surroundings. There had been a race, hadn't there? Yes, she remembered that much. They had been flying toward the Library. She had suggested the race to lift everyone's spirits, to push back against the weight of everything that had happened.

And then …

The memory hit her like a physical blow—the dullahan, its empty hood staring up at her, speaking her name.

A jolt of fear sent her heart racing, and she sat up so quickly that the room spun. A wall of windows stretched up to the ceiling, tilting wildly, their diamond-shaped panes catching the light like prisms.

She thought she might lose consciousness again, but then she saw Peter, perched on the sill of an open window with one knee drawn up to his chest, watching over her. And there was Charming too, sitting at the foot of the bed, his hair flickering through various shades of concern.

Their presence was as comforting as a warm hand on her shoulder, and her racing pulse begin to slow, at least a little.

"What happened?" Her voice came out as a whisper. "The dullahan ... it knew my name."

"There were two of them, actually," Peter said, which was not at all comforting.

He pushed off from the windowsill and drifted to the foot of the bed, hovering just above the coverlet. "When it spoke your name, it did something to you. Some kind of power. You just ... fell." His brow furrowed and his eyes started to glaze over, but just as Wendy thought she had lost him, they cleared again. "But Loamly caught you. Well, he slowed you down anyway. That's probably what saved you." He brightened. "The first time, at least."

"The first time?" Wendy pressed a hand to her head. A dull throb was making it hard to think.

"You fell into the rot after that." He spoke as casually as if he were discussing the weather, but there was a tightness around his eyes that betrayed something else. "But then Loamly saved you again. He used his wings to shield you from it."

"Loamly!" Wendy's hand flew to her mouth. "Is he all right?"

"I think ..." Peter's face scrunched up with the effort of remembering. "I think something bad happened to him, but I can't ..." He shook his head as if to clear it. "Sir Galahault is helping him. And Thomas too."

"Thomas?" Wendy glanced at Charming, whose normally bright glow had dimmed to a worried flicker. Her heart clenched,

and the throbbing in her head hurt worse than before. "Was he hurt trying to save me as well?"

"Oh, no. I saved you the third time. I carried you up into the sky." Peter grinned, showing just a hint of his canines. "But Thomas jumped down to save Loamly, and then Erikson and Snaggleclaw saved Thomas. So really, everyone got to save someone!"

"Everyone except me," Wendy said quietly. She looking down at her hands, twisting them in her lap. "And it's my fault they needed saving in the first place."

Charming shook his head so vigorously that sparkles of innisfay dust scattered across the bedspread.

"I didn't need saving," Peter pointed out. "Neither did Charming or Tink."

"I couldn't bear it if something happened to Loamly or Thomas because of me." The weight of that guilt pressed on her chest until she could hardly breathe.

Peter tilted his head, regarding her with an unusually thoughtful expression. "Everything that's happening now started a very long time ago. So long ago that even if my memory was always perfect, I still might not remember it." His mouth twisted into a wry smile, and he drifted closer, sitting cross-legged in midair about a foot above the coverlet. "My crew and I have saved each other countless times. We don't keep track of those things—except, of course, when it makes a good story."

The smallest corner of Wendy's mouth turned up in a hint of a smile, but then she thought of Loamly and Thomas and started worrying all over again. Which, of course, reminded her of the horrible creatures that had almost killed them. "Wait, how did you manage to get rid of the dullahans?" she asked.

"Oh, we didn't," Peter said cheerfully. "They're just outside the castle."

"What?" The word came out as a horrified gasp.

"Don't worry," Peter assured her with a shrug. "They haven't tried to cross the moat. They're just standing there, staring up at your window." His eyes lit up with curiosity. "Would you like to see?"

Wendy shuddered, pulling her knees up to her chest. "No, I would not." She wrapped her arms around her legs, trying to make herself as small as possible. "One of them said my name. It will never stop hunting me now." Her voice dropped to a whisper again. "I'm putting you all in danger just by being here."

"You're not in any danger when you're with me," Peter declared, but then his voice softened. "And I'm not in any danger when I'm with you." A mischievous grin spread across his face. "At least, not unless we both pass out at the same time." He rose higher, still hovering cross-legged above the bed. "We could fly to see the griffins together and figure out what to do along the way if you like. The dullahans can't fly, after all."

But Wendy wasn't convinced. "Peter, I can't go to see the griffins with those … those things chasing after me."

Peter scoffed. "They can chase us all they want. The plateau where the griffins live is very hard to reach on foot." He spun slowly in the air as he spoke. "We can fly there quickly, talk to the griffins, and be gone long before the dullahans could ever reach it." He paused in his rotation to face her. "If they can even get there at all."

Wendy opened her mouth to protest again, but the words died in her throat as an entirely new sensation washed over her.

She could feel them—the dullahans—waiting just beyond the moat.

That was why her head hurt so badly. Their presence was a terrible disturbance in the flow of Neverland's magic. Their very essence raged against the land, not with violence or fury, but with something far worse.

They were consuming it, Wendy realized, drawing every drop of magic from everything they touched. She could feel their reaching hunger, grasping not just for her but for everything around her.

Because she was here, because they were so close, the dullahans could sense the ancient power of the Library itself. They could feel Peter and the magic that bound him to Neverland in ways even he didn't understand. And somewhere within these walls, they could sense Loamly and Thomas, fighting for their lives.

Even Snaggleclaw wasn't safe. Wendy could sense the dragon sleeping on the roof, exhausted from the rescue, completely vulnerable. And if she could feel him, so could they.

She was putting them all in danger just by being here.

"Peter." Her voice came out steadier than she'd expected. "Are you absolutely certain we can reach the griffins long before the dullahans?"

His eyes met hers, and for once there wasn't a single hint of playfulness within them. "I promise."

"All right." Wendy squared her shoulders. "Then we have to leave. Now."

Peter didn't hesitate. "Tink!"

The fairy darted in through the window, her glow leaving a golden trail of light in her wake. At the same moment, Charming floated up from his perch and showered Wendy with innisfay dust.

They left through the window, Wendy being exceedingly careful not to look down, given what waited below. She didn't need to see them; she could feel their presence all too clearly.

"We need to go straight up," Peter said. "As high as we can. We'll get far away from them, then hide in the clouds."

Wendy hesitated, her heart stuttering as she remembered the terrible sensation of falling, of losing consciousness as the dullahan's power dragged her from the sky.

As if reading her thoughts, Peter grabbed her hand. "Don't look at them," he said firmly. "Just hold onto me. If anything happens, I'll be right here to carry you away. I won't let you fall again."

Wendy nodded, not trusting her voice to speak. She gripped his hand tightly, and together they rose into the sky.

As they climbed higher, she could feel the dullahans' influence weakening, like a weight slowly lifting from her heart. But she hadn't broken free of them—not really.

Even as she and Peter soared above the clouds and turned toward the griffins' plateau, she could feel their attention fixed upon her, their insatiable hunger reaching across the distance between them.

And she knew, with a certainty that chilled her to the bone, that they could sense her too.

CHAPTER<br>45

Inside the longhouse, something peculiar was happening. The walls, which usually stretched up into shadows, were slowly drawing inward and downward, as though the building itself was attempting to create a more intimate setting.

Tigerlilja noticed it first in the way the firelight reached the ceiling, casting a warm glow over the wooden beams that had previously been lost in darkness.

The massive table where she held her war councils had also transformed, shrinking until it was little more than a cozy spot for two, with barely enough room for the maps spread between them. If Tigerlilja had been the sort of person to believe in such things, she might have thought the longhouse was conspiring against her better judgment.

*Not that there is anything to conspire about*, she told herself firmly. After all, this was a war council. The fact that Jokul's eyes caught the firelight in a way that made them look like midwinter stars was entirely irrelevant.

She forced her attention back to the maps and the tactical discussion at hand. "My people could line these cliffs." Her finger traced the rocky outcroppings that overlooked the lagoon. "With enough archers, we could rain arrows down on Blackheart's forces before they even reach the shore."

Jokul's face was serious in the firelight, every line of it etched with concentration. He was watching her the way he used to, back when ...

But no, he was simply focused on the battle plans. That was all.

"Your archers would even be more effective if they could move," he said, his voice carrying that slight accent that had always made her think of frost forming on a windowpane—and a small, warm room with a cozy fire.

She closed her eyes, just for a moment, and took a deep breath to clear her head. When she opened them again, he was gesturing upward. "From the ships, they would have a clear line of sight to any target."

"My people don't like flying." Tigerlilja wrapped her fingers around the smooth edge of the table. "We are children of the earth. We fight with our feet planted firmly on solid ground, the way our ancestors did."

"The way your ancestors did," Jokul repeated softly, "until they didn't."

There was something in his tone that made Tigerlilja look up sharply. But his face revealed nothing beyond polite attention, and she wondered if she had imagined the hint of ... was it regret?

The fire crackled in the hearth, its light undulating across the walls of their now-intimate space. The longhouse had never felt quite so small, and Tigerlilja had never been quite so aware of how little distance separated them across the table.

If she reached out, she could almost—

But she didn't reach out. Instead, she turned her attention back to the map, focusing on it with determination. "The cliffs

provide natural cover," she insisted. "And my people know every handhold, every hidden path. We could move our forces quickly if needed, without relying on ..." She waved her hand vaguely, refusing to say the word "flying" again.

Jokul leaned forward slightly, and Tigerlilja caught the scent of winter pine and wood smoke. It was distinctly unfair that he should smell like everything she had ever loved about the first snow of the season.

"My people prefer the ground as well," Jokul said quietly. "It's one of the reasons we worked so well together, once upon a time." He traced a pattern in the frost that had formed at the edges of the map. "Our forces complemented each other perfectly. Winter and autumn meeting at the edge of the world."

Tigerlilja found herself drawn into memories she had tried hard to forget—when frost-folk and her own people had shared these very halls, when laughter had echoed from every corner and the mead had flowed freely. When the children of autumn and winter had found ways to bridge their differences, creating something entirely new and beautiful in the process.

She glanced at Jokul, watching the firelight play across the planes of his face as his expression changed, turning grim.

"But with the dullahans on the move ..." He shrugged, but the tight set of his lips spoke volumes.

"No one on the ground will be safe." The words tasted bitter on her tongue.

"I don't want your people to get hurt."

For a moment, anger sparked in her chest. Why did he always have to remind her that his forces were so much stronger, so much faster?

But when she looked into his eyes, there was no hint of arrogance or condescension there. Instead, she saw something she hadn't known in what felt like centuries: genuine concern.

Not just for her people, but for her.

The anger drained away as quickly as it had come, leaving behind a strange ache that she couldn't quite name.

(Or perhaps wouldn't name, which is not at all the same thing.)

"Blackheart's ship will need a crew." This wasn't what Tigerlilja wanted to say. It certainly wasn't what she was thinking. But the feeling that stretched in the air between them was too tenuous to address.

She was afraid that speaking it out loud would snap it like a thread. And, much to her surprise, she didn't want it to break. In that moment, she wanted to protect it with every fiber of her being.

"Our people could crew it together." Jokul's voice was soft but certain, like the first snowfall of winter blanketing the autumn leaves.

The silence that followed expanded until it filled every corner of the longhouse. The fire crackled and popped in the hearth, and Tigerlilja found herself counting heartbeats—though whether she was waiting for him to speak again or gathering courage to speak herself, she couldn't have said.

"I should have respected your laws."

She looked up sharply, certain she must have misheard. But Jokul's face was open and sincere, filled with a vulnerability that made her heart ache.

"I reacted out of anger," he continued, his eyes fixed on some distant point beyond the wooden walls. "My people were hunted in our world—a world that belongs to humans now. Hunted like animals." His voice caught slightly on the word, and Tigerlilja felt an echo of that ancient pain. "I had thought we were beyond it. And then, when it happened here …"

Before she could think better of it, Tigerlilja reached across the table and laid her hand on his sleeve. The fabric was cool beneath her fingers, as though it held the very essence of winter within its weave.

"I'm so sorry," she said softly. "It shouldn't have happened—not here. Not anywhere."

He turned his hand over, reaching for hers, and for a moment she felt the weight of centuries lifting between them.

"Maybe," he said, "when this is over—"

The door of the longhouse creaked open, admitting a blast of cool air and the looming form of Captain Hook, who paused in the doorway, watching them with an expression of keen evaluation. "Am I interrupting something?"

Reluctantly, Tigerlilja withdrew her hand. She was suddenly aware that the longhouse had begun to expand again, its walls stretching back up and out into their proper places as though nothing unusual had happened at all.

"The ships have returned," Hook said after a moment, his eyes moving between them with careful neutrality. "I thought you might be interested in joining us for some training exercises."

"Yes, of course." Tigerlilja rose with a quick nod.

"As would I." If Jokul's voice was slightly rougher than usual, well, that could have been attributed to many things.

Emerging into the crisp sunlight, Tigerlilja couldn't help but wonder what Jokul had been about to say. And if her hand still tingled where her skin had touched him, well, that was nobody's business but her own.

The wind whipped past Wendy's face as she soared through the sky next to Peter on their way to the griffins. Tinker Bell and Charming had accompanied them at first, two bright spots of light darting and weaving through the air between them.

But once Wendy's panic about the dullahans had subsided enough to clear her head, she and Peter had made the difficult decision to send their innisfay companions back to the Library.

"Keep watch for Shadow." Peter's voice had taken on an edge of seriousness that still surprised Wendy whenever she heard it. "If she crosses your path, see what she knows about the battle ahead."

The real reason, however, for sending their friends away had less to do with Shadow and far more to do with the griffins' notorious appetite for anything small and glittering. The chance of Charming or Tinker Bell ending up as a griffin's afternoon snack was too terrible to contemplate.

At least the dullahans' single-minded pursuit offered one small comfort: Wendy knew they weren't threatening the Library. She and Peter were leading them away at a pace that left the horrifying creatures far behind, their rotting horses no match for the speed of flight.

And Peter's presence beside her was helping too.

He flew so close that their shoulders nearly touched, his hand wrapped firmly around hers. "Just to be safe," he had said. Wendy had agreed without hesitation, trying not to think too much about how natural it felt to have her fingers intertwined with his.

She hadn't planned to hold his hand for the entire journey, but then again, very few things in her life had gone according to plan lately. The dullahans were proof enough of that.

A rueful smile tugged at the corner of her mouth as she considered just how far she'd strayed from any future path she might have imagined.

Had it really only been a year since she had joined the Fourteenth Platoon in Dover? When she was laying careful plans to rise slowly in the ranks, barely believing she might one day be lucky enough make her way onto a small, coastal vessel?

And now here she was, the captain of her own flying ship, soaring hand-in-hand with Peter Pan toward a gathering of griffins, all in service of preventing an ancient evil from destroying the world.

If there was one thing Neverland had taught her, it was that the best path forward wasn't always the one you'd mapped out in advance. Sometimes, it was the unexpected route that opened up before you, full of dangers and wonders you'd never imagined. The trick was recognizing those moments when they appeared and having the courage to seize them, even if it meant

abandoning your carefully constructed plans in favor of something wild and unknown.

Besides, some deviations from the expected path were worth every moment of uncertainty they brought with them.

She glanced at Peter, who seemed perfectly content to fly in silence, as though just sharing the sky with her was enough. When he caught her looking, his smile held none of its usual swagger. Instead, it was gentle and genuine—the kind of smile that made it easy to forget she had ever believed he was her enemy.

The rocky plateau that served as the griffins' domain soon came into view, its stone spires reaching toward the clouds like the towers of some ancient cathedral. The dullahans, which had seemed so terrifying before, were now so far away they had faded to a small, quiet awareness in the back of her mind, barely worth a thought.

When Peter finally released her hand, Wendy wasn't scared at all anymore, but she still felt a small pang of disappointment, nonetheless.

"Follow me," he called out, adding with a wink, "if you can."

He plunged into a steep dive between the towering spires, each of which held a full complement of griffins, all watching him with their eagle eyes. As he passed each formation, the magnificent creatures launched themselves into the air behind him.

Soon the sky was filled with hundreds of griffins, their wings catching the light like burnished bronze. Wendy had once attended a lecture at the Royal Society about murmurations—those mysterious clouds of starlings that moved as one across the twilight sky, shifting and flowing like ink in water.

But this … this was something else entirely.

Peter had orchestrated an aerial ballet of mythical proportions. The griffins followed him in perfect synchronization, their

ever-shifting patterns defying logic. They moved as one, contracting into a tight spiral, only to explode outward in a starburst of wings and talons. Then they flowed together again, the entire mass of them weaving between the spires in an intricate dance that left Wendy mesmerized.

When Peter finally descended into a clearing, Wendy held her breath, certain that the innumerable flock would end up in a catastrophic tangle of feathers and fur. But the griffins possessed a grace that belied their size.

They separated with fluid precision, some following Peter to land in the clearing while others returned to their perches on the surrounding spires. Their movements were so perfectly coordinated that it seemed less like individual creatures making decisions and more like watching the separate droplets of a waterfall, each knowing exactly where it needed to go.

As the griffins settled into place, Wendy recognized the magnificent creature that had gifted her the feather during her previous visit. It stood regally in the center of the clearing, flanked by the same two others, its golden eyes fixed on Peter with what could only be described as fond exasperation—an expression Wendy knew well.

But what happened next caught her completely by surprise.

Gone was the formal, ceremonial atmosphere of their last encounter. Instead, Peter bounded toward them like a schoolboy and threw his arms around the griffin's neck, and the creature responded in kind. It curved its head around Peter in a gesture remarkably similar to a horse nuzzling its favorite rider, though Wendy had never seen a horse with quite so many sharp edges.

As he spoke to them, Peter's voice took on a vibrant, musical quality, explaining their dire situation in a blend of melodious trills and plaintive cries. He described Buri's imminent threat, the

gathering of allies, and their desperate need for the griffins' help in the coming battle.

Even though Wendy didn't understand Peter's words, she discovered that if she concentrated, she could catch a vague impression of what he was saying.

The griffin's response needed no translation—the fierce pride in its bearing said everything—but Peter provided one just the same: "They said they'll fight. Neverland is their home too, and they won't see it fall to Buri's corruption."

Then his serious expression cracked into a grin. "They even promised not to eat Tinker Bell when she comes to get them." He cast a pointed look at several of the younger griffins, who managed to look both innocent and disappointed at the same time.

The griffin leader dipped its massive head, and Wendy could have sworn she saw amusement glinting in those intelligent eyes.

Their farewell was brief but touching. Peter and the griffin shared another embrace, and then, to Wendy's utter astonishment, one of the younger griffins glided down from its perch to envelop her in a careful hug. Its warm feathers tickled her face as the creature wrapped its neck around her shoulders.

The gesture was so unexpected and gentle that tears prickled at the corners of her eyes, and she hugged it right back, just as carefully.

As she and Peter took to the air once more, the griffins escorted them to the edge of their territory in an echo of their earlier dance. The magnificent creatures swirled around them, their powerful wings stirring the air into small eddies that carried the scent of sun-warmed feathers and wild places.

Wendy's heart swelled with gratitude for their willingness to join the fight, but the feeling was soon tempered by a sharp pang of guilt. These noble creatures were pledging their lives to

a cause that she and Peter had brought to their doorstep—she couldn't help but feel responsible for every risk they would face in the coming battle.

Her worry only deepened as she sensed the dullahans growing closer again, their corrupting presence hovering at the edge of her consciousness. They were still pursuing her, still hunting, their rotting horses eating up the miles between them with tireless determination.

Wendy glanced back one last time at the griffins' domain, silently praying that she wasn't leading the proud creatures to their doom.

# CHAPTER 47

High above the open fields of the Viking village, Captain James Hook stood on the deck of the *Pegasus*, surveying the training exercises of the allied fleet.

The mock battle spread out across the heavens like an ambitious circus performance gone awry. Some of the crews were doing well enough, but "well enough" had never been sufficient for James Hook, and it certainly would not be sufficient against Buri's monstrous horde.

Still, there were bright spots among the chaos. The *Sparrow*, for instance, was proving to be a revelation. Despite Gerdrek's tales of the small vessel's remarkable speed, Hook had been skeptical. But now, watching her outpace the *Ravenhawk* with casual grace, he had to admit the truth of it.

As if to emphasize the point, the *Sparrow* glided elegantly past the larger vessel with a row of frost-elves and Vikings stationed along its rail. As soon as her archers were out of range, the elven ship pivoted sharply, slipping through the sky in a full

180-degree turn that brought it back within boarding distance in moments.

Hook's eyes narrowed thoughtfully. Such maneuverability could prove useful in the coming battle, especially if they could maintain that level of precision under fire.

"Three more." Charlie stood beside him at the helm, piloting the *Pegasus*. "At least three more ships of that size in Jokul's domain. Although none of them can fly. Not yet, anyway."

Hook nodded, calculating the possibilities. A quick application of innisfay magic could get them in the air soon enough. The real limitation was their complete lack of cannons, which was significantly more problematic.

His strategic musings were interrupted by a massive shape forming in the air before them: a ship made entirely of clouds, courtesy of Jokul Frosti.

The frost king stood aboard the *Sparrow*, his arms raised as he conjured more phantom vessels to serve as target practice. Several of the cloud-ships even managed to return fire after a fashion, hurling snowballs that approximated the size of proper cannonballs.

Hook had to admire the ingenuity, even if he couldn't quite suppress a curl of his lip at the theatrical nature of it all. Still, proper target practice was essential, and he couldn't very well risk any of their actual vessels playing the role of the enemy.

Not when they needed every craft they had for the coming battle.

Despite his general distrust of all things magical, Hook found himself oddly transfixed by the spectacle before him. Pan's ship, under Curly's command, executed a perfect broadside against one of Jokul's phantom vessels. It fired a cannonball right through the cloudy construct, leaving a perfect circular hole that trailed wisps of vapor in its wake.

The crew's triumphant cheers echoed across the sky, their voices ringing with an odd combination of boyish enthusiasm and deadly intent. Hook might detest the everlost, but he couldn't deny their effectiveness in battle.

Unfortunately, his moment of grudging appreciation was shattered as the *Ravenhawk* lumbered into view. Mr. Starkey's handling of the vessel was surprisingly competent—the man had taken to aerial navigation with unexpected aptitude. But John ...

Hook watched in mounting frustration as the lieutenant's commands led the ship directly into the line of fire between the everlost vessel and its cloudy target.

The ensuing collision was almost graceful in its complete inevitability. The *Ravenhawk* plowed straight into one of Jokul's phantom ships, dissipating the illusion in a spectacular display of meteorological destruction.

Hook released a long-suffering sigh, shifting his attention to a squadron of winged frost-elk that pawed its way through the sky. The magnificent creatures moved with unexpected grace, their massive antlers gleaming beneath the eternal sun.

Each beast carried a frost-elf archer on its back, working in perfect coordination with Pan's vessel. The flanking guard maintained a precise formation while their riders loosed arrows into any cloud-ship that ventured too close.

Yet again, Hook found himself reluctantly impressed by the everlost's ability to adapt to these new circumstances. Their maneuvers accommodated the frost-elks' movements seamlessly, as if they'd been drilling together for years.

That professional assessment faltered, however, as he spotted what could only be described as an aerial catastrophe waiting to happen.

A massive polar bear—whose idea had it been to put a *polar bear* on a flying mount?—clung desperately to the back of

an enormous, winged frost-moose. The impromptu cavalry unit carved an erratic path through the sky, resembling nothing so much as a drunken albatross attempting to navigate a hurricane.

The sight would have been comical if it weren't so potentially lethal to anyone unfortunate enough to drift into its path. Hook watched in mounting horror as John's panicked response to the careening bear-and-moose combination sent the *Ravenhawk* into a desperate dive. The ship plummeted well below the minimum altitude Hook had explicitly set for the exercises, an oversight that would have had fatal consequences in actual combat.

The gravity of the error tightened his jaw.

Both Jokul and Tigerlilja had emphasized—repeatedly and with grave concern—the necessity of maintaining sufficient elevation above the dullahans' reach. The headless horsemen's aura of decay could reduce a proud sailing vessel to driftwood.

Hook bristled at the thought of watching one of his ships literally rot apart in mid-flight, spilling its crew into the waiting darkness below. And those damnable cloaks of insects the dullahans commanded were just as dangerous, if not more so— massive clouds of pests that could envelop a ship's helm in moments, rendering navigation impossible.

If this had been a real battle, John's entire crew would have been massacred by their captain's poor judgment.

Hook's eyes narrowed as he reached an unpleasant but necessary conclusion. John simply wasn't ready for command, not of a flying vessel, and certainly not with so many lives hanging in the balance.

Even years of intensive training might not be enough to overcome his fundamental unsuitability for aerial warfare. The man was a fine soldier, but this required something else entirely—the kind of instinctive grasp of three-dimensional combat that both Wendy and Charlie displayed so naturally.

Lost in thought, he ran his hook along the ship's rail, its polished gleam almost matching that of his own steel appendage.

They had the beginnings of a fleet, but whether it would be enough to stand against Blackheart's ships remained to be seen. The coming battle would test them all, and Hook had no intention of allowing poor leadership—or drunken polar bears—to doom their efforts before they'd even engaged the enemy.

As Wendy and Peter flew back toward the Library, the scent of Neverland surrounded them—green as spring leaves and cool as cave water. Only now, it held a faint undertone of decay wherever she went.

The thought of it made Wendy's stomach turn.

While they had been visiting the griffins, the dullahans' presence had retreated—a mere whisper of dread hiding in the dark recesses of her mind.

Even on their way back, she was able to shove it aside for a while by focusing on other things: the wind in her hair, the bright sensation of innisfay dust lifting her into the sky, the warmth of Peter's smile.

But as they drew closer, that small, nagging sensation grew into a scream that drowned out everything else.

No matter where she went, no matter what she did, she could not outrun them forever. They never got tired. They never got

hungry. They never slept. They pursued her with a single-minded purpose that would not end until one day, eventually, they would catch up with her.

And that would be that.

Her body would rot away until there was nothing left. And then there would be no more flying ships. No more nights spent gazing at the stars. No more quiet moments with Peter or Charlie or Nana or Charming or even Captain Hook.

Because there would be no more Wendy.

The closer she flew to the dullahans, the more that cold certainty invaded her mind until a significant part of her wanted to give up altogether—to fall like a stone to the hard earth below and be done with it. What point was there in trying to hold onto anything, to protect anything, to love anything if one day it would all be gone?

The dullahans would catch her eventually.

Everything ended eventually.

The hopelessness crushed her chest until she could hardly breathe. She could only stare into the distance ahead.

Watching for them. Waiting for them.

Knowing that when she finally saw them, they would rip her from the sky.

And then Peter called her name.

His voice seemed to come from very far away, as though she were walking hand in hand with Davy Jones along a peaceful stretch of sand at the bottom of the sea, and Peter was calling to her from the surface.

There was something in his tone that tugged at her mind, but it was already too late. She was about to lose consciousness. She could feel the cold tremors taking hold of her body.

"Wendy." His voice was sharper now. More urgent. "Wendy, look at me."

It took every ounce of strength she had just to turn her head.

To wrest her gaze from the ground and look into his eyes.

"It's all right," he told her. "I won't let you fall."

His hand clasped hers—warm and solid and present. Peter was real. He was right here.

And so was she.

It wasn't too late to share one last moment together.

He smiled at her. "There you are."

Well, all right, perhaps two moments.

And suddenly, the world snapped back into focus.

With a gentle, insistent tug, Peter guided them upward and to the left, his wings arcing through the air. They soared higher and higher, away from the dullahans and their terrible magic.

As the distance between them grew, Wendy's racing heart began to slow. The tremors ceased, and her thoughts became clearer.

The crushing sense of dread gradually receded, becoming smaller and smaller as it retreated once more into the dark corners of her mind and other, more immediate concerns were able to take its place.

Like how Thomas and Loamly were doing—and what news of their fate might await her upon her return.

Finally, the magnificent structure of the Library came into view, its spires reaching toward the clouds. Snaggleclaw's massive form was still curled in the same spot where they'd left him, his sides rising and falling in peaceful slumber. But the window they'd departed from earlier was now firmly shut, its stained glass gleaming in the perpetual daylight.

So Wendy and Peter descended toward the grand entrance instead, their feet touching down softly on the stone.

They had barely crossed the threshold, calling out for Sir Galahault, when two familiar figures appeared in the entry hall. Wendy's heart leapt at the sight of Erikson and Thomas walking toward them.

Without a moment of hesitation or a single thought for propriety, Wendy launched herself at Thomas, embracing him with so much enthusiasm that he staggered back to keep his balance. But instead of showing any sign of pain or discomfort, he just smiled his familiar, scholarly smile and returned her hug with equal warmth.

As Wendy turned to give Erikson a hug too, just for good measure, her eyes darted around the vast hall, searching for any sign of Loamly. When she didn't spot him, she turned back to Thomas, a tear already forming in her eye.

"His injuries were more extensive than mine, I'm afraid," he said gravely, "but I think he'll be all right. Sir Galahault is still working on the repairs."

"Repairs?" Wendy echoed.

Thomas bent down to lift the hem of his trousers, and Wendy gasped. Where flesh and bone should have been, his feet and calves gleamed with the warm luster of freshly polished bronze.

"Remarkable, isn't it?" His eyes sparkled with enthusiasm. "The elves created this alloy specifically for alchemical transmutation." He lifted one foot and then the other. "They aren't any heavier than my previous feet—perhaps even a bit lighter."

"They're incredible," Wendy breathed, still staring at the metallic limbs.

"The bonding process is equally impressive," Thomas continued, clearly delighted to share the technical details. "There's no need for straps or other securing mechanisms. Galahault merged

them directly with what remained of my legs somehow—something to do with elven metallurgy, though I'm afraid the specifics are beyond my current understanding."

Guilt crashed over Wendy like a wave. "Oh, Thomas, I'm so sorry," she whispered, her voice catching. "Your feet ... and that sounds so terribly painful."

But Thomas was already shaking his head.

"No, no. Quite the opposite. They're extraordinary." His eyes held the same enthusiasm as before as he flexed his right foot, making Wendy gasp. "The transmutational junction is seamless. Besides which, I could step on every horseshoe nail in London and never feel a thing. Just think of the possibilities when we return to England—the scientific applications alone are staggering. If we could understand how to craft this material, it would change everything. Everything!"

Peter, who had been hovering nearby throughout their exchange, suddenly dropped to the ground beside them. "Can you walk through fire?" he asked, then added without waiting for an answer, "What about swimming? Have you tried swimming?"

Thomas blinked, clearly delighted by these suggestions. "I hadn't even considered ... well, the fire is an interesting question. I'd need to study their thermal conductivity first; wouldn't want the heat traveling up to my natural legs. But swimming ..." His eyes grew distant with calculation. "Yes, I believe I could swim quite well. The alloy is remarkably lightweight, and the articulation is perfect."

The knot of guilt in Wendy's chest loosened a bit as she watched Thomas's genuine excitement over his new limbs. Before she could respond, however, a familiar chiming filled the air.

Tinker Bell burst into the great hall to circle Peter's head, followed immediately by Charming, who settled on Wendy's shoulder, his warmth a comforting presence against her neck.

"The innisfay told us about your mission to the griffins," Thomas said, straightening his spectacles. "Were you successful?"

Wendy was about to ask how the innisfay had managed to communicate such a complex message, but Peter spoke first, his chest puffing out with pride. "The griffins will fight for Neverland. They said they'd do anything for me."

Tinker Bell's hair turned bright red, and she chimed at him angrily.

"Well, of course I know you'd do *more* than anything for me," Peter told her. "That goes without saying."

With the barest hint of a smile, Wendy turned back to Thomas. "What about your research? Is there anything we can do to help?"

"Actually, the Library's catalog system is excellent. I was able to find every reference I requested, though it didn't amount to very much. Still, I did find some interesting entries that suggest certain magical items might be effective against Buri."

"My sword is magic," Peter declared, drawing the weapon with a flourish.

"Yes, enchanted weapons were mentioned." Thomas nodded thoughtfully. "But there's a catch. Buri can't be killed until he's fully manifested through the portal. And even then ..." He hesitated for a moment. "Even if we do manage to kill him, the texts suggest he'll return after about a thousand years."

"That's true. I've killed Buri lots of times." Peter brandished the weapon through the air, demonstrating. "The first time, I killed him like this." Peter flew up and thrust his sword through the open air as though stabbing the giant in the heart. "The second time, I killed him like this."

Before Peter could continue, a resonant voice filled the hall. "Sadly, sir, I do not believe that to be the case." Sir Galahault's metallic form whirred and clanked as he strode toward the small

group, and behind him stood Loamly, swaying slightly as if he'd just woken from a deep sleep.

When the young everlost's eyes found Wendy and Peter, a broad smile spread across his face. "Look what I have!"

With obvious pride, he unfurled a pair of magnificent new wings.

The shimmering metal caught the light like burnished autumn foliage, their surface a warmer, redder shade than Thomas's bronze feet. With a single downward beat, the air whispered around their edges and he launched into the air, rising to meet Peter. He saluted sharply, then executed a graceful turn before landing with precision.

"Oh! Why, they're wonderful!" Wendy turned to Sir Galahault with tears in her eyes, and her voice caught in her throat. "Thank you."

Peter sheathed his sword and landed in front of Loamly as Charming and Tinker Bell darted around them in excited circles, their light reflecting off each metallic feather to cast a riot of color across the Library's walls. Their bell-like voices chimed in what could only be admiration as they examined every angle of the magnificent plumage.

"Can you make me a pair of metal wings too?" Peter asked.

Sir Galahault grimaced. "Let's hope it doesn't come to that." He turned to Wendy, his tone growing more serious. "Forgive me for asking, miss. But does your return mean that the dullahans are back?"

"No, they're still distant, but moving quickly. They follow me everywhere now." She shivered, wrapping her arms around herself. "If I stay here too long, they'll be back soon enough, right where they were before."

"That reminds me," Thomas said, adjusting his spectacles on his nose. "I noticed something interesting. Where the dullahans

stood, all the plant life around them withered and died, but the moat remained untouched. There don't seem to be any dead fish, and the water plants show no signs of decay."

"Really?" Wendy asked, hope creeping into her voice. "Do you think water might harm them?"

Thomas shook his head slowly. "Nothing in my research suggests they're vulnerable to water. In fact ..." He sighed a little, then forged ahead. "Nothing seems to harm them at all."

"We tried fire," Sir Galahault added. "While you were still unconscious, Peter convinced Snaggleclaw to try burning them, maintaining a safe distance from their decay field, of course." The mechanical knight's voice carried a note of concern. "Given Snaggleclaw's age, I worry about his ability to withstand their aura for long. But it proved futile regardless. The dullahans' insect swarms simply grew larger, absorbing the flames. Even when reduced to ash, new swarms materialized instantly to replace them."

Wendy shivered again. She sensed them even now—racing across Neverland, drawn to her presence like iron to a lodestone.

And nothing was going to stop them.

Captain James Hook lay in his bed in the Viking village, trying to think as little as possible. The past few hours had been taxing, to say the least. He needed his rest if he was going to be any good to anyone—let alone lead his forces into battle for the very fate of the world.

The wooden shutters of his quarters creaked softly with the light breeze, so different from the familiar groaning of ship's timbers. He sighed, forcing his neck and shoulders to relax. He couldn't wait to be done with this strange, magical place and get back to the sea.

The coming battle loomed over them all, and there were still a thousand details to be worked out. A thousand ways it could all go wrong.

But those were problems for another day—if "day" meant anything anymore on this godforsaken island.

Finally, Hook's eyes drifted closed. He was bone-weary—the kind of exhaustion that promised sweet oblivion for a few blessed

hours, free from thoughts of strategy and responsibility and the weight of command.

The very best kind of exhaustion, really.

So, of course, Shadow chose that moment to appear.

She coalesced from the darkness at the foot of his bed, taking shape gradually until she sat there watching him with her glittering eyes—two black diamonds that managed to shine even when there wasn't any light to reflect.

"The training exercise was impressive." She sounded sultry tonight, her voice like silk brushing over steel.

Honestly, he didn't need this. Not tonight. Not from her. "Tell me, what impressed you most? Was it the drunken polar bear on the frost-moose? Or perhaps when the *Ravenhawk* crashed through the exercise floor? Personally, that part was my favorite."

"Tsk, tsk." She tilted her head and pursed her lips in a petulant moue. "Believe it or not, I'm quite serious. I thought it was going to go far worse than it did." She grinned then, resting her chin in her hand. "Admittedly, I'm something of a pessimist."

"What do you want?" The words came out a low growl, rough with fatigue.

"Honestly, Captain. I'm wounded." She pressed a dramatic hand to where her heart might be, assuming she had one. "I'm only here to help."

Hook fixed her with a cold stare. "If you want to help, tell us how to kill Buri."

"If only I knew." Her form rippled, reminding him of heat waves rising from summer-baked cobblestones. "All I can say with certainty is that he must come fully through the portal first. That's when he'll be vulnerable." She paused, her mouth grim. "Of course, that's also when his power will be at its greatest."

"Fantastic." Without intending it, Hook's expression mirrored her own.

Shadow's shoulders rose and fell in the smallest of shrugs. "It is what it is. We'll know when the time comes."

He propped himself up on one elbow, wondering if he was ever going to get any rest again in his entire lifetime. "What about the dullahans? Could you at least dispatch them the way you did that time-stopping innisfay?"

Shadow's form contracted slightly, drawing in upon itself. "I … I'm not certain. Frankly, I've been avoiding them." Her voice held an edge of unease. "Their magic is … different. I fear it might be able to absorb me entirely, or corrupt my mind. It's darker than anything I have ever known."

Hook fell back against his pillow, turning his gaze to the ceiling. "The sooner this bloody magical war is over, the better." His head was starting to ache, whether from lack of sleep or from the conversation, he wasn't sure. Probably both.

"That's even more true than you realize." She leaned toward him, her head darting to one side like a hawk eyeing its pray. "I know about your plan to draw Buri's forces to the lagoon while sending a small force to kill him. It won't work."

Hook's eyes narrowed. "And why is that?"

"Your allied forces grow by the day, it's true. But Buri's army grows faster still. Even half his current forces could overwhelm your entire army with ease." Her dark outline condensed with the gravity of her words. "And Buri isn't fool enough to commit everything to the lagoon. He'll hold back enough forces to make any attack on his fortress suicidal."

"So we'll fight on two fronts and die on them both." Hook's mind raced through the implications, but what Shadow said next drew every ounce of his attention back to the present. Back to her.

"Perhaps not." Her skin undulated with … what? Was it excitement? Or something else? "Buri hasn't yet stepped through the portal, so most of their strategy comes from Blackheart. When he

listens to Kaspar—Loki's son—their plans are brilliant. But Blackheart's arrogance often gets the better of him." She leaned forward even more, her black eyes shimmering in the dark. "If I could convince Buri and Blackheart that I've joined their cause, I could exploit that arrogance. Push him toward mistakes."

Hook sat up, his loose hair falling around his shoulders. "Enough. I'm done with your backroom schemes." His voice was harsh with frustration. "If we're making battle plans, we need to consult with the others. This affects us all."

"The fewer who know, the better." Her voice dropped until it was barely more than a whisper. "Convincing Buri of my loyalty will be difficult enough. He'll need to believe in me completely before he'll allow Blackheart to accept me into their inner circle." She moved closer, inching forward at the foot of his bed. "The more people who know the truth, the more likely the plan is to fail. For this to work, everyone—even our allies—must believe I've turned against them."

"Turned against them?" Hook's lip curled in a sneer. "From where I stand, you were never on our side to begin with."

Shadow flickered, then sharpened. "I tried to kill Buri," she admitted, her voice sharp as broken glass. "In the end, that's all that matters. I want him dead more than anything." Her outline faded again, until it was hard to make out where her form stopped and the room began. "Whatever happens, whatever you see me do, remember this: I will never truly join Buri's cause. No matter how convincing it may appear."

Despite her theatrics, Hook was hardly convinced. "And how can I be certain this isn't just another layer of deception? Another trap? Lies within lies."

A dagger materialized in her hand, its glittering blade matching her eyes. "We could seal it with a blood pact, if you like." Before Hook could respond, the dagger dissolved back into her hand.

"Or perhaps"—she glided across the bed until her face was mere inches from his own—"you'd prefer a kiss?"

Hook didn't flinch, didn't even blink. "Neither would make me trust you any more than I do now."

"But you already trust me." Her whisper brushed his skin with surprising heat. "I know you, James Hook. Know you better, perhaps, than anyone ever has." She drew back slightly, her cruel smile mocking him. "When the time comes to act, I'll find a way to signal you. Something only we would recognize."

"What signal?" Hook demanded, his voice harsh. "Act how?"

But Shadow had already melted away, leaving Hook alone with his thoughts and the creaking of the shutters in the wind.

And despite his exhaustion, sleep was now the furthest thing from his mind.

Wendy stood at one of the Library's tall windows watching the curling, rotting edge of decay spread across the ground like ink seeping through parchment. The dullahans weren't visible from this angle, but their presence was undeniable—even if the Library was protecting her from the worst of it.

"We need to get back to the village," she said quietly. "They'll be preparing for the attack. They need us there. But I can't—" She pressed her hand against the glass. "I can't lead those things back with me."

Peter, who had been watching her in silence, suddenly brightened. "What we need," he declared, "is a plan. And I know the perfect place to make one. Come with me."

Wrenching her eyes away from the horror below, Wendy turned to face him, but Peter was already halfway across the room, striding with purpose. She had to take several quick steps to catch up. "Where are we going?"

"The Treasure Room," he announced, as though that explained everything. He beckoned for everyone to follow—waving vaguely at Thomas, Erikson, Loamly, Sir Galahault, and of course Charming and Tinker Bell—and exited the great hall through a side door without waiting for a response.

Now, Wendy had read enough stories to have built up certain expectations about what a treasure room might look like—mountains of gold coins and glittering jewels, perhaps even a crown or two resting precariously atop a hodgepodge of ornate wooden chests.

What she discovered, however, was decidedly different.

The room itself was large enough, but there wasn't a hint of gold to be seen anywhere. Instead, the chamber was dominated by a sturdy wooden table and an odd assortment of chairs that appeared to have been collected across a wide variety of centuries and cultures with no particular rhyme or reason. But that was nothing compared to the walls.

Every inch of that towering space was jam-packed with rows upon rows of tiny drawers, punctuated here and there by the occasional small cabinet. They reminded her a bit of the hutch in Mr. Equiano's study where he had kept his navigational charts, except these drawers were far smaller—most no larger than the size of her palm. Each one bore a number, penned in a meticulous hand, the figures marching in order around the room.

"Go on. You can look." Peter smiled and tilted his head toward the nearest wall, which happened to be on his left. "Open any drawer you like. They hold the greatest treasures I've ever found in all my adventures."

Unsure what to expect, Wendy stepped forward hesitantly, her fingers hovering over the graceful pull of a tiny drawer about waist-high. What would she find there, she wondered. Rubies? Emeralds? An ancient scroll? A missive from a pharaoh, perhaps, or even a spell written by the great Merlin himself.

What she found instead was a baby's rattle made of clay, ancient and unadorned, worn smooth by countless tiny hands.

"That's from Egypt," Peter said proudly. "Someone lost it near a river back when they used to build pyramids. Go on, open another."

Intrigued, Wendy opened the next drawer to discover a wooden hairpin, its surface darkened with age. The craftsmanship was exquisite, though the design was utterly simple—just a smooth curve with a blunt point at each end.

"A little girl gave me that one," Peter told her. "She had lost a baby goat up on a mountainside, and I found him for her."

The next one contained a small wooden flute nestled in a careful bed of green velvet. Despite its apparent age, the wood retained a warm honey color, and the finger holes were worn to perfect smoothness.

"Peter brings them to me from time to time," Sir Galahault explained, his mechanical voice carrying a mixture of fondness and pride. "I catalog each one and store it here in the Treasure Room. They're very precious."

Her fingers itched to open another, but the weight of their current situation was too pressing. With a small sigh of regret, Wendy closed the drawer, promising herself that she would return one day if she ever got the chance.

When she turned to the table, she found Peter waiting for her. He had gallantly pulled out what looked like a small Egyptian throne at the head of the table, clearly expecting her to sit in it.

She hesitated for a moment, but he gestured to the seat with such a flourish that she would have felt it impolite to refuse.

"Right," he said, addressing her once she was settled. "Now then. Start us off by explaining the problem. Every last detail, leaving nothing out." His serious expression dissolved into a grin. "That's the most important part of solving any problem, and I should know—I'm excellent at solving problems."

But Wendy had no idea where to begin, mostly because she couldn't help but feel that the problem, ultimately, was her.

There was an argument to be made, of course, and a good one at that, that the dullahans were the real culprits here. But since they were both intent on following Wendy to the ends of the earth for all the rest of her days, it felt very much as though that was tantamount to the same thing.

"I think ..." she said finally, acutely aware of everyone's attention, "I think everyone understands the problem well enough. The dullahans are following me. Which means I'm a danger to everyone around me." She glanced apologetically at each of her companions. "We need to return to the village to help with the preparations, but I don't see how I can go with you. There's no moat at the village, nor even a surrounding wall to protect it."

Charming, sitting on her shoulder, reached down to pat it gently.

"Even if there were a wall," Thomas added, "it might simply crumble in the dullahans' presence. Though the moat here seems to be protecting us." He turned to Erikson. "The village does have a river. How long do you think it would take to divert it into a moat that ran all the way around?"

"The whole village?" Erikson's eyes widened.

"Even if we *could*," Wendy interjected, her tone suggesting gently that they most likely could not, "we can't be certain it's the moat. Whatever's protecting the Library, there might be more to it than that."

Sir Galahault nodded slowly. "Indeed. The magic of Neverland itself may be contributing to our defenses. The Library is very special to Peter."

"That's what worries me," Wendy admitted. "I'm afraid Neverland's magic is exactly what's holding them back, and I'm afraid the dullahans' presence here is placing a terrible strain on the land

itself." She shook her head firmly. "We mustn't rely on it any more than absolutely necessary. We need another solution."

"How many rivers and streams lie between here and the village?" Sir Galahault asked. "The dullahans do seem to have trouble with water, at the very least. Each crossing might buy you time. Perhaps enough to reach the village and plan your next move before having to depart again."

"I'm honestly not sure how many," she admitted. "But we crossed over more than one river on the way to the griffins, and they followed us in a straight line. I'm sure of it."

"That's true," Thomas mused. "They must have some way of crossing water to have followed us as well as they have. Yet they can't seem to cross the moat here at the Library." He leaned forward, tapping a finger on the table with scholarly intensity. "If we could observe how they manage it, that might reveal something about their nature—perhaps even a clue as to how we can defeat them."

"That seems simple enough," Peter said, and all eyes turned his way. "We'll fly back to the village, leaving someone behind to follow them and watch how they do it. After all, we happen to have the greatest spy in all of Neverland right here with us."

He turned to Tinker Bell, whose hair brightened instantly to a brilliant gold. "What do you say, Tink? Would you follow them and see what they do when they reach the water?"

Tinker Bell rang like a tiny bell and nodded, her light pulsing with determination.

"Even the smallest detail could help," Thomas added. "It could be anything. The way they approach the water. Whether they use any particular magic. Each and every observation could be very important."

Tinker Bell shone more brightly with every word he spoke, until her enthusiasm for the mission bathed the room in an aura of sunlight.

"But you must stay very far back," Peter insisted. "Promise me, Tink. I couldn't bear it if anything happened to you." She nodded again, glowing so brightly that Wendy was forced to look away.

With the plan agreed upon, Sir Galahault led them through the Library's winding corridors to an inner courtyard. Peter let out a piercing whistle, calling Snaggleclaw down from his perch on the roof. The dragon's massive wings stirred the air as he landed to let Thomas and Erikson climb onto his back.

They all bid farewell to Sir Galahault, and then, one by one, they took to the air. Peter and Wendy climbed highest of all, putting as much distance between them and the dullahans as they could—as quickly as possible.

Only Tinker Bell remained behind, hovering above the castle, her golden glow dimming to a subtle shimmer as Peter and the others dwindled into the distance. Then she turned her attention to the ground below, where two dark figures on rotting horses galloped across the fields in relentless pursuit, leaving trails of decay in their wake.

# CHAPTER 51

Through the crystalline air of Neverland, a tiny point of light darted between the clouds, following two dark riders as they raced across the land. The light dimmed and brightened with each new thought that passed through Tinker Bell's mind.

*Spying,* she mused with golden pride, *isn't difficult at all.*

But then she rolled her eyes, her glow flickering with mild irritation. The creatures moved with singular purpose, leaving trails of decay in their wake as they pursued their quarry toward the Viking village. Honestly, how hard would it be for anyone to follow creatures that were so intent on following someone else?

Then again, Peter had called her a good spy. No—she positively glowed at the memory—he had declared her the best spy in all of Neverland. Perhaps she was only making it *seem* effortless. That must be it. After all, true mastery often makes the most difficult tasks look deceptively simple.

A warm glow of satisfaction spread through her diminutive form. She was quite exceptional at everything she set her mind to—far superior to the others in practically every way.

Well, except for Peter. And even then, only sometimes.

But she was definitely better than the Wendy. The sorry, landbound human couldn't even fly without help. Pathetic.

Tink's glow took on a distinctly reddish tinge. What Peter saw in that woman, she would never know.

Shaking her head—and then her entire body (which is another thing innisfay can do much better than people)—she returned her attention to the dullahans below. Yes, this assignment was almost tediously simple for someone of her capabilities. Even maintaining a safe distance from their decay field was easy—she could sense its boundaries as clearly as she could feel the pulse of Neverland itself.

Being an innisfay meant having an intimate connection to the land, after all. She could feel how it recoiled from these blighted creatures, trying to resist their corrupting influence with every blade of grass they touched.

Her beloved Neverland was dying, and there wasn't anything Tinker Bell could do about it—which gave her all the more reason to want to blame someone else.

Naturally, her thoughts circled back to the Wendy.

If the Wendy hadn't been foolish enough to draw their attention in the first place... Yes, the more she considered it, the more certain she became that everything about this entire situation could be traced back to that horrible woman.

Come to think of it, the mere fact that Blackheart had had to deal with the Wendy the whole time he was growing up was probably what made him go mad in the first place.

It seemed a reasonable conclusion.

After all, whenever Tink herself acted in ways that other people deemed inappropriate, it could invariably be traced back to the Wendy's influence.

Tink's hair flashed through several colors in quick succession, none of them good. She needed something to take her mind off her troubles, but she was far too accomplished at spying for this assignment to be any help at all. If only it could offer her more of a challenge—or at least more entertainment.

She tried indulging herself in some of her favorite daydreams—the Wendy being swallowed by a whale, the Wendy tumbling into a volcano—but even these weren't enough to hold her interest.

No, she needed a better distraction. Something thrilling. Something epic. Something truly delightful.

At long last, an approaching river promised something worth reporting. Tink swooped down for a closer look, watching carefully as the riders changed direction. They galloped along the riverbank until they found a shallow place where they could cross more easily, but that wasn't interesting at all.

Any rider would do that. In fact, just about any creature that couldn't fly would do that, poor flightless things.

But when the dullahans entered the water, something much more unusual happened. Tink felt their decay field contract, drawing inward until it barely extended beyond their forms. Their progress through the water became almost incomprehensibly slow. Infinitesimally slow—slower than anything she'd witnessed before.

Well, she corrected herself, that wasn't quite true. Tinker Bell had been alive long enough to watch entire mountains flatten into hills, and oceans rise up into mountains. Not in Neverland, of course, but still.

The dullahans weren't moving as slowly as rocks.

Tink giggled, chiming brightly. It was a good joke, but the comparison lacked precision. As Neverland's premier spy, she had her standards to maintain. Her report to Peter had to be nothing short of exceptional.

She hovered idly above the scene, her light waxing and waning by turns as she searched her memory for the perfect analogy to capture the speed of the spectacle unfolding below—or rather, the lack thereof.

Did they move as sluggishly as the everlost whenever anyone besides Peter told them to do something? No, she decided. Even the everlost weren't this slow.

Perhaps they moved as slowly as the moon in the Wendy's world, that great silver disk that crept across the London sky.

*The Wendy again.* The thought irritated her to no end.

Maybe the dullahans' pace might match that of a scorpion placed beneath the Wendy's pillow. Tink's glow took on a mischievous glint. Maybe she should try leaving a scorpion under the Wendy's pillow to find out.

Just for the sake of accuracy.

A veritable eternity passed before the dullahans finally approached the opposite bank. But just as Tink was about to despair of anything interesting happening at all, a dark figure emerged from the forest.

*Shadow.*

Now *that* got Tinker Bell's attention. She watched intently as Peter's ancient nemesis approached the riverbank where the dullahans would emerge. Was Tink about to witness Shadow's demise? The thought didn't trouble her in the slightest. If anything, she would be pleased to report it.

Shadow had always been cruel to Peter—in Tink's world, that was a capital offense.

As the dullahans neared the shore, Shadow raised one hand

in what appeared to be a gesture of command. *Silly Shadow*, Tink thought, as the riders continued their relentless advance, ignoring her. But then Shadow lifted both hands, and something extraordinary happened—something that made Tink's hair dim to the ashen gray of instinctive dread.

The poisonous darkness that surrounded the dullahans seemed to reach out, long tendrils of decay stretching toward Shadow. But instead of destroying her, the darkness merged with her form, creating an aura of corruption around her that mimicked the dullahans' own, though far weaker.

Tink's mind raced. Was Shadow working with Buri? She had to be if she could command these abhorrent monsters.

The encounter lasted only moments before Shadow vanished back into the darkness, and the dullahans finally hauled themselves onto solid ground to resume their galloping pursuit of the Wendy. But Tink filed this new information away for her report: Shadow's obvious alliance with Buri, her ability to communicate with the dullahans, and her strange immunity to their decay.

*Of course, Shadow can't decay*, Tink reasoned. *She's only a shadow, after all.* Maybe this was how Buri communicated with his gruesome servants. The logic pleased her, and she added this conclusion to her mental report.

But simply observing didn't seem enough anymore—not for the greatest spy in all of Neverland. Her report would be sensational, stirring the hearts of all who heard it. And surely stirring Peter's heart most of all.

Far more than the Wendy ever had—or ever could.

Unfortunately, this new thought only drove Tinker Bell to imagine greater heights for her impending glory. What if she did more than just watch the dullahans? What if she managed to destroy one of these creatures?

Tink could see it so clearly in her mind—the look of adoring

rapture on Peter's face when he learned that she and she alone had managed to destroy a fearsome dullahan.

Now, Peter had pleaded with her to be safe, that much was true, and in Tink's defense, the memory did give her pause for a moment—but only a moment. After all, he hadn't explicitly ordered her not to kill one. And the dullahans seemed much more vulnerable in the water.

No, this was an exceptional plan. The most exquisite plan anyone had ever come up with. A plan worth executing immediately.

Tinker Bell glanced down at the dullahans, which were now galloping across the land again. She hoped they'd reach another river crossing soon. Maybe they'd move faster if she could get them to follow her instead of the Wendy, just for a little while. She could probably make them mad enough to chase her—Tink was almost as good at that as she was at spying.

Then, she could lead them on a chase to the next river, keeping well above their decay field, of course. It would all be perfectly safe.

Quick as a wink, Tink swooped toward the dullahans. She darted just above their corruption aura, then zipped in front of them, careful to keep her eyes averted from their absent faces. She thought she was probably immune to their gaze, but still, she wasn't taking any chances. (Or at least, she wasn't taking any more chances than she was already taking.)

But to Tink's utter indignation, the dullahans paid her no attention whatsoever. They just continued galloping straight ahead, making a beeline for the Wendy.

And *that* was simply intolerable.

Without another thought, Tinker Bell found the largest rock she could fly with, carried it very high over their heads (well, a good bit ahead of them to be honest—innisfay are excellent at timing when it comes to dropping things on people's heads), and dropped it at the perfect moment.

As the rock plummeted toward its target, a writhing mass of insects erupted from the dullahan's cloak, batting the speeding projectile aside as if it were nothing more than a leaf.

And then the swarm turned its attention to her.

With a string of chimed innisfay curses, Tinker Bell turned and fled. She easily outpaced the insects, of course, but their noxious existence offended her. The horrible creatures pursued her higher and higher as she tried to put as much distance between herself and their repulsive forms as she could.

In her haste to escape—and, perhaps, in her pride at bring able to escape so easily—Tink failed to notice two very important things. First, she was glowing spectacularly. Second, she had just crossed over into a region of eternal dusk.

Soaring high in the air, her brilliant light trailing behind her like a comet, she created quite the beacon in the darkening sky.

The shadow that fell over her was her first and only warning.

The wyvern had nearly closed the distance before she even registered its presence. In that terrible moment, Tink realized with perfect clarity that the creature was faster than she was—*much* faster.

Her only hope was the dense forest canopy she could barely make out below. She dove for it, hoping to lose the enormous creature in the trees.

She breached the uppermost branches of the tree line just ahead of the wyvern's snapping jaws, weaving desperately between ancient trunks as the beast crashed through the canopy behind her.

And then her tiny, racing heart nearly stopped as she sensed the dullahans' decay field approaching on her right, the trees dissolving into rot as they passed.

The forest seemed to collapse around her—trees withering into nothing on one side while ancient trunks splintered and fell beneath the wyvern's relentless pursuit behind her. With mounting panic, Tink pushed herself faster, trying to break free of the closing trap.

But in her desperation to see how close the wyvern was, she forgot to watch where she was going. The impact with the tree sent her spinning, her ears ringing and her vision blurring as though she was flying through a fog.

As she struggled to clear her head, her connection to Neverland screamed a warning—the dullahans' corruption was spreading toward her, the trees around her blackening and twisting into nothing. Behind her, she heard the wyvern land with a thud that shook the few healthy branches that remained.

She was trapped.

The wyvern's shadow loomed over her.

This was exactly the sort of situation Peter had warned her to avoid, and Tinker Bell's final thought dimmed her light to a profoundly sorrowful gray, as she thought how very disappointed he would be in her.

But before the creature could strike, it let out a horrific shriek. Tink watched in astonishment as the wyvern fell to the ground, thrashing on its side, its flesh rotting away where it had strayed too close to the dullahans' path.

In the blink of an eye, Tink shot skyward. Looking back, she saw the wyvern dissolve into nothing, its massive body too large to avoid the field of decay as the dullahans passed. They didn't even acknowledge its death, although it had clearly been one of Buri's servants.

The dullahans, she realized, cared nothing for allegiance or loyalty. They existed solely to reach the Wendy and destroy her.

A sentiment Tink could appreciate, if she was being honest.

But watching Neverland's trees wither and die in their wake stirred something deep in her innisfay soul. As much as she despised the Wendy, she hated these creatures more.

She had seen enough. It was time to deliver her report to Peter.

CHAPTER

# 52

When Wendy had first returned to the Viking village, she had pulled Hook aside, as her superior officer, to give him her report. Solemnly, she had informed him of four new developments, none of which struck him as especially good news.

First, only magical weapons could kill Buri. Hook didn't love the fact that none of his forces had any magical weapons, but the discovery was not unexpected. If he had thought he could simply stab the ancient giant in the stomach and be done with it, he would have found a way to do so a long time ago.

Second, the griffins would fight for them. This seemed at least somewhat helpful, but after what Shadow had told him about the size of Buri's forces, Hook doubted it would make as much of a difference as Wendy clearly hoped it would. Still, any advantage was worth having, even if it wasn't quite the advantage he might have wished for.

Third, Thomas had lost his lower legs to a dullahan, proving them to be just as dangerous as everyone had believed. At least the Royal

Society fellow had survived it, but he had only stood in the dullahan's presence for a few moments, which didn't bode well, to say the least. Hook found himself wondering how long a man might last in actual combat with such creatures, and then immediately wished he hadn't wondered at all.

Fourth, the dullahans were now following Wendy wherever she went, so if she was going to be part of their next war council, they needed to hold it right away.

But the worst of it, as far as Hook was concerned, was that upon hearing this last bit of news, he had not wanted to send her away. On the contrary, his fingers had itched to touch her, as though her presence before him was not enough to assure him of her current state of health.

He had not, of course, yielded to the impulse. Instead, given the pressing nature of their circumstances, he had informed Tigerlilja that Wendy had important news to impart, everyone had gathered in the longhouse, and then he had listened to her share that same news all over again.

He didn't like any of it any better than he had the first time.

They were about to begin planning for the lagoon battle when a streak of light burst through the doorway, followed by the distinctive sound of innisfay bells gone mad with excitement. Tinker Bell shot to Pan's shoulder, her glow so bright that Hook had to squint to look in her direction, and she launched into what had to be the most agitated series of chimes and rings he had ever witnessed. (Which, much to his annoyance, was saying quite a lot at this point.)

Throughout the innisfay's report, Pan hovered cross-legged in midair—a habit that Hook found particularly irritating as it served no purpose whatsoever, especially when there was a perfectly good chair not two feet below him.

Hook glared across the table at the everlost, whose expression grew more serious with each new trill and arpeggio.

When Tinker Bell finally fell silent, Pan fixed each person in the room with an unusually solemn gaze, one after the other. As his eyes lingered on Wendy, Hook decided he'd had about as much of these theatrics as he could tolerate.

"For the sake of time itself," he growled, "whatever else has gone wrong, whatever fresh disaster has befallen us, spit it out." He glanced at Wendy, acutely aware that the dullahans were no doubt galloping toward her at a breakneck pace. "We need to get Captain Darling in the air."

"Tink," Pan announced, maintaining his air of profound gravity, "has brought us the most important spy report that has ever been given. And I'm afraid it's terrible news."

"Of course it is," Hook muttered.

"Shadow has switched sides," Pan continued. "She appears to be commanding the dullahans now. Or at least relaying information to them from Buri. And she's absorbing their destructive energy to use for her own nefarious purposes."

"Of course she is." The fingers of Hook's good left hand closed into a fist. It occurred to him, not for the first time, that he really ought to have stabbed Shadow in his quarters when he'd had the chance.

Or at least he ought to have tried.

"On the bright side, the dullahans' powers are significantly diminished in water. They move as slowly as the moon across the sky, and their auras of decay draw into them completely. However," Pan added, holding up a dramatic finger, "they can still command their insect swarms to attack. Tink discovered this when she tried to crush one with a rock."

Hook snorted and Tinker Bell glared at him, her hair flashing red before returning to its bright golden hue.

"That explains the Library's defenses, at least partially," Thomas noted. "The moat goes right up to the walls, so the dullahans' decay field can't reach them."

"Wait." Vegard's eyes flew wide even as his brow furrowed. "Are you saying these monsters can bring even stone walls to ruin?"

"Well, the book didn't specifically say that." Thomas shifted uncomfortably. "The material used in construction would likely affect how long the process takes, but it did say that structures and fortifications don't offer any real protection because everything decays eventually."

"There's more," Pan added, drawing everyone's attention back to Tinker Bell's report. "Apart from Shadow, the dullahans care nothing for their own allies. Tink says that when they're pursuing someone truly worthy of their attention, they won't stop for anything—not even their own forces. Their path of decay washes over everything, friend or foe alike. They simply cannot be controlled. They will stop at nothing."

Hook's jaw twitched. Every moment they spent discussing this was another moment Wendy remained in danger. "The lagoon plan won't work," he blurted out.

"What? Why not?" Frost formed on the table where Jokul's hand rested. "This information only makes the plan stronger. We'll fight Blackheart's army over the bay. The dullahans will be trapped on the shore, and if they try to enter the water, they'll be useless. They might be able to stop one rock with their insects, but a hundred arrows and dragon fire together?" A cruel smile spread across his face. "I think not."

"Blackheart's forces have grown too strong," Hook insisted. "He won't need to send them all. His army is far larger than he's revealing. He could easily destroy our forces at the lagoon while maintaining a substantial defense at his fortress."

Tigerlilja's eyes narrowed. "How do you know this?"

"Because Shadow came to me a few hours ago." He paused to glance up at the rafters. When the horned woman failed to materialize, he forged ahead. "She's been watching our meetings here in

the longhouse. She knows our plan. And she told me that Black-heart could destroy us with less than half his army."

"Why would she tell you this?" Tigerlilja demanded, her voice sharp as steel. "How do you know she isn't feeding you false information for her own ends?"

"I asked her the same thing." Hook forced himself to meet her gaze steadily. "She said she wanted me to go with her. She believed we shared the same feelings about Pan." He gestured toward the everlost, who merely smiled and started spinning in midair, as though the conversation had nothing to do with him.

"I refused, of course," Hook continued. "If Buri succeeds, England falls. And with all this magical nonsense, we need every ally we can get. So whatever crazy, hopeless battle plan we devise, England will play its part. But trying to draw all of Buri's forces to the lagoon is a lost cause."

The silence that followed was broken only by Tinker Bell's soft chiming as she shifted restlessly on Peter's shoulder, but whatever she was saying, he kept it to himself.

"We'll need to change our tactics." Jokul's frost spread far enough along the table to make Vegard back away, the Viking's chair grating along the stone floor. "We should attack them with everything we have."

Hook ran the fingers of his good left hand through his hair. "How quickly can we get the rest of the elven ships to fly? Even without cannons, they could at least serve as platforms for archers."

"With the help we've gathered, preparing the ships wouldn't take long." Jokul glanced at Gerdrek.

"Not long at all," the elf agreed.

"We can't trust Shadow," Tigerlilja interjected. "We change nothing."

"I have a thought." Thomas cleared his throat, and all eyes turned to the Royal Society fellow. "I haven't studied much battle

strategy," he admitted, glancing first at Jokul, then Hook. "And this may be a terrible idea, but what if we used the dullahans against them?"

"Explain." Hook leaned forward, eager for any solution that sounded like it might have a chance.

"Well, I was thinking, maybe we could hide a small ship in one of Jokul's clouds above the fortress, with Wendy on board, you see. And let the dullahans do some of our work for us."

"I like it!" Vegard raised his fist to pound the table, then eyed the frost that covered the space before him and thought better of it. "But we'll need to do more than that. They'll have their own ships watching the skies. If they discover ours, it'll all be over, and it will take time for the walls to come down." The Viking glanced at Thomas, who nodded. "We'll have to infiltrate the fortress, so we're ready to strike."

"We can still use the lagoon," Tigerlilja added. "We'll gather enough of our forces there to make Buri believe he can decimate our ranks. That will draw some of his forces away, and we can use the distraction to sneak in."

The Viking glanced at Peter. He stopped spinning to face the table with a confused frown, but he displayed no further reaction to their conversation.

Hook nodded slowly. "We should hold some of our own fleet back too, keeping them in reserve to attack the fortress once the dullahans breach the walls. That should keep them busy while we make our way down to Buri's temple."

"And if Buri's still in the portal, where we can't kill him, maybe Wendy can lure the dullahans down to Buri's arena and destroy the portal altogether."

"That's a death trap," Hook protested, glancing at Wendy.

"I don't know," Thomas said at the same time. "Decaying the outer wall might work, but with so many walls inside the fortress,

Buri's inner sanctum would take far longer to breach. Unless you plan to run around opening doors for them."

Vegard surged to his feet and pounded the table after all, careful to avoid the frost. "Then that's exactly what we'll do. We'll let the dullahans wreak havoc on Buri's forces, and once they're inside, we'll clear their path straight to Buri himself."

"I can fly the *Sparrow*, if that's best," Wendy offered quietly. "She'll stay aloft on her own, so we can leave her in Jokul's cloud and fly down when it's time. But Peter may have to carry me once the dullahans get close."

Something twisted in Hook's chest. He didn't like the idea of Wendy on the ground with the dullahans anywhere near her, and he certainly didn't like the thought of Peter Pan flying around with her unconscious body in his arms.

But maybe it wouldn't come to that. He still had Shadow's poison. Maybe he could find a way to use it on Buri. Or he'd find some other way to kill the ancient giant before the dullahans got anywhere near her. And then he'd put Wendy Darling back on a British ship, and they would sail away from this godforsaken place, leaving it behind forever.

He turned to her and nodded. "So be it. Take the *Sparrow* to the lagoon for now, where the dullahans can't follow. Try to get some rest before the battle ahead."

"Go," Tigerlilja urged. "The dullahans must not reach us here." She glanced at Jokul, then Gerdrek, the captain of the *Sparrow*, who agreed without hesitation.

As Wendy rose and made her way out of the longhouse, Hook watched in silence, refusing to acknowledge the ache that crushed his heart as she disappeared through the door.

Wendy stood at the helm of the *Sparrow*, her hands resting lightly on the wheel as she guided the vessel through the skies of Neverland. The wind that whipped errant strands of hair about her face carried the sharp scent of altitude—a curious mix of lightning and possibility that seemed to exist only here at these impossible heights.

At first it had felt strange that the ship remained so easily at any height she set. The vessel required active thought to move or turn, climb or dive, but if Wendy allowed her attention to still, the ship simply stayed where it was, gliding to a gentle halt in midair.

After trying it several times, she had finally come to accept it. No matter what might happen to her, the *Sparrow* would not fall from the sky. Needless to say, this fact had come as a huge relief—so much so, that Wendy felt the tension in her shoulders easing for the first time since the dullahan had called her name.

And she was determined to take advantage of it.

The *Sparrow* responded to her touch like an eager partner, graceful and lightning quick. She was the fastest vessel Wendy had ever commanded, and that included Peter Pan's ship (though she would never tell him so). Sometimes, when they caught an especially swift current of air, Wendy almost believed they might sail right out of Neverland altogether, into some other realm where Buri had never existed, where Blackheart was still just a bitter child named Mortimer Black, where she herself had never learned the price of changing one's destiny.

But of course, that was nonsense. One couldn't simply sail away from fate, no matter how fine the vessel.

Peter stood near the bow, scanning the horizon with an air of quiet readiness. Ever since the dullahans had begun their relentless pursuit, he had refused to leave her side, though from this height, even their suffocating aura of despair felt no more threatening than a shadow passing briefly over the sun.

In fact, Wendy had allowed the dullahans to maintain their position directly below the *Sparrow*, using her ship's speed and direction to control their path across the landscape. Charming and Tinker Bell took turns scouting ahead, ensuring their route caused minimal destruction.

The plan was sound enough: lead the dullahans away from the village and toward the sirens, whose watery domain would be safe from the creatures' decay. That would buy everyone precious time—for the elves to prepare their remaining ships for flight, for the griffins to meet their new allies, for the combined forces to decide who would gather at the lagoon and who would lie in wait at the rally point near the fortress.

Time, in short, for England to garner every possible advantage before facing Buri.

Wendy's heart clenched at the thought. How could they possibly stand against a being of such power? Even here in Neverland, with allies gathered from every corner of time and space—Vikings and frost-folk, griffins and elves, merfolk and fairies—victory still felt so far out of reach.

A movement caught her eye—a flicker of red at the edge of her vision. Her first thought was that one of the imps had stowed away on the ship, despite her explicit orders for the crew of the *Jolly Roger* to remain safely behind in the village. Or perhaps it was Charming, returning with another report on the dullahans' progress.

But when she turned her head, she found herself staring at something altogether different: a small figure, no more than two feet tall, with a shock of fiery red hair and a flowing white beard. He wore a red jacket that might have been stolen from a toy soldier, a pair of sailor's wide trousers, a round hat perched jauntily atop his head, and gold hoop earrings that dangled from distinctly pointed ears.

He was sweeping the deck with methodical precision, but as Wendy turned toward him, he paused in his work and looked up to meet her gaze.

"Oh! Oh, I'm so sorry." Wendy's left eyebrow rose in sharp surprise. "I thought Gerdrek's crew had all left the ship."

The spry little figure waved the apology away with a casual flick of his hand. "That's all right. Don't mind me. I'm not part of Gerdrek's crew. I belong to the *Sparrow* herself." His voice held an oddly distant quality, reminding Wendy of the sigh of a gentle breeze as it rustles through a ship's rigging. "Where she goes, I go. So, now, where you go, I go, I suppose. At least for a little while. Hard to say how long."

"Well, I'm very pleased to meet you." Wendy adjusted the wheel slightly, letting the ship do some of the work in keeping them on course. "I'm Wendy. Wendy Darling."

"Yes, ma'am. I'm Hoops." He touched the brim of his hat in a gesture of respect. "I know who you are, Captain Darling. I always know who the captain is. And the crew too, for that matter. Even if they don't know me." A flicker of sorrow passed over his weathered features. "Still, I'm always pleased when I get to meet one. And a bit sorry, if I'm being honest."

"I'm pleased to meet you, too. And I'm not a bit sorry. In fact, I like you very much already." The words surprised her even as she spoke them, but they were true, nonetheless. There was something about the little sprite that felt inexplicably familiar, like discovering a childhood friend in an unexpected place.

She was quite certain she'd never seen him before, yet she couldn't shake the feeling that she knew him somehow.

"Thank you, ma'am." His expression grew solemn. "But you might be a bit sorry after all if you knew the truth of it. They always are."

Wendy recognized that look—she'd seen it often enough on John's face when he had unpleasant news to deliver. "Well then, perhaps you'd best tell me the truth of it and let me decide for myself. You never know. I might feel differently than the rest. Whatever it is."

"I doubt it." Hoops leaned on his broom like an old sailor at the rail. "You see, I've been on this ship ever since she was built. I help take care of her. Most ships have a klabautermann—unless we're unwanted, of course. I mend the rigging when it frays, and I polish the deck. I don't need any rest, so I'm always doing something. I love caring for my ship and her crew." His chest puffed out slightly. "I can even help her stay in the air."

"Wait," Wendy's hand tightened on the wheel. "You're the one keeping the ship in the air? How do you do that?"

"I have a small piece of the trinket. They gave it to me. I use it to keep her afloat, so she won't crash." He grinned with pride, but

then his shoulders slumped and his eyes dropped to the deck at his feet. "No matter what happens."

"Why, how wonderful!" Wendy exclaimed. Then her brow furrowed. "But I've never seen a klabautermann before, and I've been on quite a few ships. Have I just been unlucky until now?"

Hoops removed his hat with deliberate care, holding it over his heart. "More like the opposite. Thing is, the crew can't see us." He paused, and in that pause Wendy heard the weight of centuries. "Not until they're doomed to die."

"Oh." Wendy's hands fluttered briefly at the wheel. "Oh, I see."

"Bet you're sorry you met me now." Hoops offered her a gentle smile. "Don't worry. That's how it always goes."

"Oh, how awful," Wendy breathed, the secret kiss at the corner of her mouth trembling slightly.

"I'm sorry you're going to die, ma'am," Hoops said with genuine regret.

"No, I mean how awful for *you*." Wendy's voice grew fierce. "After everything you do for your ship and her crew, after all that time you spend looking out for them, they don't get to thank you or have even one conversation until they're about to die."

Hoops shrugged, his earrings catching the light. "That's all right. I suppose it goes with the territory. I don't need to be thanked for what I do. The task is its own reward." He glanced up at her with kind eyes. "I do appreciate your concern though. It's very considerate of you to think of me, what with you being doomed and all."

A smile tugged at Wendy's lips. "Well, I suspect for most people it's quite a shock. But, you see, I already knew the dullahans were following me. So I've had some time to come to terms with it."

"Even so, you seem like a very good person." Hoops nodded sagely. "I hope your doom is quick and painless."

Wendy's brow furrowed. "I hope you won't be disappointed if I try to avoid it."

"Of course not. Most do try to avoid it, though I've yet to see anyone succeed." He brightened slightly. "Still, I wish you the best of luck."

"Thank you."

Hoops nodded and returned to his sweeping, the broom whispering against the deck.

"Hoops?"

He paused again. "Yes, ma'am?"

"Do you think the klabautermann on our other ships would be willing to keep them afloat like you do for this one? If we gave each one a piece of their ship's trinket, I mean."

"Well now, that's an interesting question." Hoops scratched at his chin beneath his long white beard. "I can't speak for them, of course, but any klabautermann worth their salt would do just about anything for their ship. I can't believe they'd say no, especially if you ask nicely."

"I can play too, if you'd like." Peter's voice startled Wendy. She'd been so wrapped up in the conversation, she'd almost forgotten he was there. "I'm excellent at make-believe. Who are we pretending to talk to?"

Wendy smiled at Peter. "I'm the only one who can do the pretend talking, I'm afraid. But I do need your help with the sails. Get ready to come about. We're returning to the village, as fast as we can. We need to leave the dullahans far behind so I can play this game on all our ships. Right now."

Shadow slithered through the dark recesses of Blackheart's fortress, trying desperately to hold herself together. The dark magic from the dullahan coursed through her veins like the cold, infinite void of the universe, its destructive energy more powerful than anything she had ever known. She had to fight moment by moment to keep it from tearing her apart—to hold onto her own identity and remember who she was.

The magic wanted to consume her, to use her as a cruel extension of its terrible will. The thought of it was almost too tempting to resist.

Looking for something tangible to focus on, something to ground her senses, she turned her attention to the ancient stones of the fortress, wondering for the millionth time where they had come from. She ran her lightless fingers along their rough surface, and the stones whispered to her in a language older than time. She could almost understand what they were saying. Almost.

And yet the fortress had only appeared in Neverland when Blackheart turned against Peter. Which wasn't so long ago—

certainly not compared to Shadow's endless ages here. But these stones, they were as old as Buri. As though they had been waiting for him from the beginning, patient as mountains, eternal as grief.

The beginning. Shadow remembered the beginning.

Her mother had died when Shadow was born—killed by Buri, like so many before and so many after. The memory of it was carved into her essence, so deep it defined her. Ever since that moment, she had been waiting—waiting for her chance at revenge.

She had tried following Peter (she was his shadow, after all), but Peter had proven worse than useless. For thousands of years, he had flitted about, rescuing orphans and animals, embarking upon one make-believe adventure after another. Never once did he notice the weight of the anguish that followed him, free as he was of the burdens of grief and memory.

Shadow carried those for them both.

But then, when she finally had her chance, she hadn't even seen it until it was too late. Her revenge had slipped through her fingers like smoke, leaving nothing but bitter regret.

She had been there when Peter met Tigerlilja, watching from the edges of his existence as she always did. The Viking woman's clan fought desperately against Buri's army of skull-men, though Shadow hadn't known them for what they were. She had simply watched, silent and unnoticed, as Peter approached the Viking woman with his usual careless grace, grabbed her sword, and vanished into Neverland.

Taking Shadow with him, of course. She had no choice in the matter. She never did.

But unlike Peter, lost in his games, Shadow had felt her mother's presence from the moment they arrived. The sensation had overwhelmed her, like a beacon piercing the endless darkness of her existence. She had been so consumed by it that she went

searching, desperate to find its source—perhaps some trace that might remain of the mother she remembered with perfect clarity. The mother she had never known.

So Shadow hadn't gone back through the portal when Peter did. She hadn't been there when he fought Buri.

If she had been, she would have ended it. But she had missed her chance—the only chance she'd had in thousands of years of waiting.

She had never forgiven herself for that failure. One chance, in all those millennia. And then, nothing. Peter went back to his make-believe adventures as though the fate of worlds hadn't hung in the balance, and Shadow followed him in vain, watching his eternal childhood with growing despair.

Until the fortress appeared.

She had known it the moment it happened. Shadow knew every inch of Neverland as intimately as she knew her own soul. She felt every whispered secret, walked every hidden path, remembered every forgotten truth that Peter so casually discarded.

Every moment, every death, every betrayal.

The weight of memory was her curse to bear alone. Unlike Pan, Shadow remembered it all.

So she had known exactly when Blackheart turned on Peter—had felt it in the fabric of Neverland itself when the land gave the traitor a home of his own. She had come to explore the fortress, and she had known immediately that it wasn't just for Blackheart. She had felt Buri's presence in the ancient stones just as surely as she felt her mother's presence here in Neverland.

The two sensations were mirror images of each other—one a beacon of light she could never quite reach, the other a well of darkness that threatened to swallow her whole.

And now, Buri could feel her presence too. Ever since Shadow had spoken to him in his temple, she could sense him reaching for her across the veil.

Waiting for her. Hunting her.

Shadow drifted through the darkened corridors until she reached Buri's arena deep in the heart of the fortress. There, the air grew thick with ancient power, and Buri's voice filled the chamber.

"Why have you returned, little shadow?" The words seeped from the very stones themselves. "Have you ... reconsidered ... your position?"

Buri's body was still frozen in place, but his essence churned like storm clouds. He was close now. She could feel it.

"I want to join you." For once, her voice carried the full weight of her suffering. "As long as Peter lives, no one will ever see me as anything more than his shadow. All that I am—the hopelessness, the doubt, the hatred—they might have belonged to Peter once, but they're mine now. I have endured. I've long since earned the right."

"Yes." Even in her mind, she could hear the distinct note of his dark satisfaction. "I can feel how it has grown in you. The seeds that we planted together, your mother and I, have ripened."

A surge of rage threatened to drown her, but she fought it back, letting just a hint of it seep into her voice. Using it to her advantage. "I will end him. I want to watch as he takes his last breath. His death will be my freedom."

Buri's essence roiled within the portal. "Peter won't wait for me to breach the threshold. He will come here, I think. He will try to kill me, just as you did." His ancient voice carried infinite contempt.

"I always know when he's close. He always finds his way to me, as though we're drawn to each other." She spoke in whispers now. "It's just one more thing I hate about him."

"Then perhaps I should keep you near me. I have trouble sensing him when he's here." His annoyance echoed through her mind. "Something about this wretched place."

The sharp sound of boots on stone announced Kaspar's arrival. He stopped short at the sight of Shadow, his hand instinctively seeking the knife at his belt. "What is she doing here?"

"Shadow has come to join us." Buri's announcement rolled through the chamber like thunder.

Kaspar's expression remained wary, his eyes narrow with distrust.

Buri's form rippled, then solidified again. "She has her role to play. As do we all."

"As you will it, Old One." Kaspar's stance eased, but his eyes never left Shadow's form. "I've come with a report. The allied forces are gathering at the lagoon."

"And Pan?" Buri's essence churned again, a storm about to break. "Is he with them?"

"No. Pan is nowhere to be seen."

"Then they're planning something. But it doesn't matter." Buri's voice held no concern, only the cold certainty of one who had watched empires rise and fall. "There's nothing they can do to me now. Send enough forces to wipe them out. Keep the rest here. They will come for me—they have no choice."

Kaspar nodded. "When they do, we'll be ready for them."

"Kill them all if you wish, but no one touches Pan. Order your men to clear a path for him." The essence of the ancient giant pulsed with anticipation. "I will kill him myself."

"Of course." Kaspar nodded and strode from the temple, his footsteps fading into the endless whispers of the stones.

Shadow drifted closer to the portal, her form lengthening, stretching thin across the sand. "I want to help with the battle plans."

"No. I brought Kaspar here for that." Buri's voice hardened. "As cunning as you are, little shadow, I would have you near me.

I can think of no one I would rather have by my side when Pan comes for me."

"But I could help—"

"If you intend to join me, you will obey me without question." Buri cut her off, his voice reverberating through her skull. "You will stay here until I face Pan." But then his voice grew almost gentle, though no less terrible. "For all we know, you may be the savior of Neverland. When Pan dies, your mere existence might allow this realm to remain."

Shadow said nothing, her mind reeling. Was it true? Was Neverland's magic tied just as tightly to her as it was to Peter?

"If it does, I can use this place to amass my armies before I send them back to the old world." Buri's essence twisted within the portal like a serpent preparing to strike. "The world that was mine, and will be again."

CHAPTER

# 55

The plans had been set, the preparations completed.

The elven vessels were all sky-worthy, and every ship in the fleet now hovered in midair on its own—a feat for which Captain Darling had offered very little information and about which Hook had decided not to ask.

All he knew was that Wendy was the only one who could accomplish it (because of course she was), so she had been forced to drag the dullahans very far away, giving her enough time to fly back ahead of them and get the job done. After all, she couldn't work on the fleet at the lagoon. Buri's spies were surely already watching it, and the allies weren't about to reveal the full extent of their forces, such as they were.

As a result, the dullahans were not at the lagoon as Hook had originally planned. Instead, they were galloping toward Wendy from heaven only knew where, which was not inspiring him with a great deal of confidence.

Wendy, of course, was standing right next to Hook, who had insisted on being part of the team that would infiltrate the fortress. The fate of England hung in the balance, and he wasn't about to send someone else into that fight in his place.

They had flown the *Sparrow* as close to Blackheart's castle as they dared—accompanied by Pan, Jokul, Tigerlilja, Vegard, and Wendy's wingless innisfay companion, landing in the mist so they could sneak even closer on foot, watching the fortress for an opportune moment.

Whatever that might look like.

Not that Hook would know it when it happened, since Jokul was the only one who could see the fortress through the fog.

Sadly, this was not the worst part of the plan in Hook's opinion. Not by a long shot.

First, the dullahans could arrive too early—or too late.

Second, Buri could decide not to attack the lagoon until after the dullahans had arrived, which, Hook supposed, amounted to the same thing.

Third, the griffins could eat all the innisfay. He didn't think this was the worst thing that could go wrong, but it did seem one of the most likely, so it made the list, nonetheless.

Fourth, Pan could have recruited some kind of monster that showed up at the rally point and ate everybody. Under normal circumstances, Hook would have written off this idea as too unlikely to worry about, but these were hardly normal circumstances.

Fifth, there might not be much of anyone at the rally point to begin with. After all, Pan had sent the innisfay to the far corners of Neverland to gather his so-called troops, and the tiny fairies were hardly known for their reliability.

Sixth ...

Hook paused in his musings. Was he really only up to number six? He reviewed the list again, ticking each item off on the fingers

of his good left hand: dullahans, lagoon timing, griffins eating innisfay, monster eating everybody, no one at the rally point … yes, this was number six. Somehow, the list felt much longer than that.

Sixth, and to top it all off, Hook wasn't with his crew.

The very thought of Charlie having to lead the fleet without him made the curve of his steel appendage twitch with anxiety. To be clear, his concern did not spring from any lack of faith in Mr. Hawke—he had every confidence in the man's abilities. But Hook couldn't help but feel that he should be there. They would be facing creatures out of nightmares—wyverns and giants and who knew what else. They were up against terrible odds, and they were likely to suffer heavy casualties.

He expelled a sharp breath and ran his good left hand over his hair, wild and unruly in the damp fog, matching his thoughts. The moisture clung to everything, making the world feel smaller, more confined. More dangerous.

At least he had his sword, his gun, and as much ammunition as he could carry. He reached into a leather pouch that hung from his belt, his fingers reassured by the cold curve of the silver nestled there.

What ate at him more than anything was the uncertainty. In a proper naval battle, he would know his enemy's capabilities, their likely strategies, their weaknesses. But here? Here, he was relying on fairy tales and children's stories come to life. Vikings with longbows. Flying deer. Fairies that fit in the palm of his hand. And Peter Pan, of all people.

None of it boded well.

The fog swirled around them, thick enough to hide an army. Or something worse. His eyes strained to pierce the gloom, searching for any movement. But there was nothing. Just the waiting. The dread. And the growing certainty that whatever came next would change everything—for England, for Neverland, for all of them.

At least Wendy was by his side. In the short time he had spent with her, he had come to trust her more than he ever could have imagined. Despite her siren nature. Or perhaps because of it?

Hook rolled his shoulders, brushing the thought away. He trusted his instincts—they weren't derived from some magical force.

And he trusted *her*.

But still, this entire plan relied far too much on hope for his liking.

He glanced at her, standing straight and still in her blue officer's coat. The very picture of a composed British captain. She would do whatever was needed. And so would he. To protect England. And Wendy. And to put an end to Buri once and for all.

"Are they close?" he asked.

For a moment, her eyes lost their focus, and she shook her head slightly. "No, Captain. It will be a while yet before the dullahans catch up to us, although I can't say for certain when that will be."

Hook nodded. He tilted his head back to peer up at the sky. The fog had thickened, joined by a heavy cloud cover that hung over the fortress like a shroud. Restless, he shifted his weight to the balls of his feet, rocking back and forth. The movement settled him, reminding him of the sea. Every strategy he'd ever learned, every battle he'd ever fought, had led him to this moment.

To this battle.

And to this woman.

Glancing at her again, the thought steadied him. She had changed everything—his perceptions, his tactics, even his beliefs about what was possible. If anyone could guide them through this impossible situation, it would be her.

Hook blew a hard breath out through his nose. All this waiting was killing him. All this *thinking*. He needed to move—to fight.

Battle had a way of clearing his mind, burning away doubt and uncertainty until only action remained.

He glanced at Jokul, who stood absolutely still.

"Buri's fleet is forming up," the frost king said quietly. "They're moving to engage our forces at the lagoon."

A flicker of motion drew Hook's eyes upward, his good left hand tightening on the hilt of his sword—every time he thought he had seen the worst of this place, some new horror proved him wrong. Barely visible through the fog, a stream of massive bat-like shapes darted overhead, speeding toward the lagoon. Were those riders on their backs? Despite their massive numbers, the fog swallowed the sound of their wings, leaving behind an eerie silence.

Peter turned to Hook with a grin. "To die will be an awfully big adventure."

*This godforsaken place.*

Hook couldn't wait to tear it to the ground.

# CHAPTER
# 56

The *Pegasus* hovered unnaturally still over the dark waters where the lagoon met the sea, her shadow stark against the surface below. Charlie gripped the polished wood of the railing with one hand—the ship's trinket clenched tightly in the other as he surveyed the gathered fleet. The Neverland sun rose eternally behind them, casting long shadows across the water.

A cool breeze stirred his hair, carrying the sound of creaking ropes and fluttering sails, and Charlie allowed himself one brief moment to marvel at his situation. It wasn't every day that a nameless orphan found himself in command of a British ship— let alone a fleet of flying ships and magical creatures that would determine the fate of the world.

To his right, a griffin shifted its considerable weight on the weathered deck. The magnificent creature's feathers rustled as it shook itself, its brown and gold plumage catching the light. Even after everything he'd seen in Neverland, Charlie still couldn't quite believe it. He, Charlie Hawke, was stand-

ing next to a griffin on the deck of the airborne flagship of the British fleet.

His thoughts turned to Wendy, as they always did in such moments. She was the reason he stood here now—his truest friend, the one who had taught him to believe in impossible things. He remembered their childhood in the almshouse, huddled together over books about far-off adventures, Wendy's quiet voice spinning tales of the sea while the other children slept.

She had chased her dreams even when everyone laughed, even when Mortimer Black—Blackheart, Charlie corrected himself grimly—had mocked her for wanting to become a sea captain. Her courage had taught him to believe in himself too, though he doubted even Wendy had imagined anything quite like this. He had sailed real seas, seen foreign shores, and now found himself in a realm he once would have dismissed as pure fantasy.

The enormity of it all filled his chest with pride. Whatever happened today, he had achieved more than that humble orphan boy ever could have imagined.

But the gratitude in his heart couldn't quite banish the cold knot of dread in his stomach. He was not prepared for this. He might have been ready to captain a single seafaring vessel—a small one, perhaps, with a coastal patrol. But this?

It all felt like too much.

The weight of his officer's insignia pressed against his collar—the proudest achievement of his life. But here, now, the magnitude of his responsibility threatened to overwhelm him, and he fought back a wave of nausea.

(In Charlie's defense, no one is ever ready for these moments—they are simply thrust upon us. The greatest heroes are born not of quiet confidence, but of the willingness to act despite a significant amount of fear and the occasional bout of vomiting. Whether Charlie knew it or not, he was in excellent company.)

A creak of rope drew his attention to the everlost ship, hovering to his left, where Curly and his crew swung through the rigging with inhuman grace. Their eyes scanned the towering cliffs of the lagoon for any sign of Buri's forces, their movements fluid and precise—which only intensified the mix of pride and fear that churned in Charlie's belly.

Pride, because here he was in Neverland, living exactly the kind of adventure he and Wendy had so often read about in storybooks—and fear as well, for precisely the same reason.

A group of merfolk surfaced near the ship's port side, their scales flashing silver and green in the sunlight. Thelxinoe had promised their support, not that Charlie was certain how much they could do—unless, of course, the enemy was considerate enough to fall overboard and plummet into the sea.

Still, better to have them on their side than the alternative.

As though reading his mind, a siren's song drifted up from the waves, haunting and foreign, yet oddly steadying.

The *Pegasus* rocked gently in the air currents, floating barely twenty feet above the water's surface. The proximity made Charlie distinctly uneasy. He remembered all too well the monstrous crocodile that had almost killed Hook when they'd recovered the *Jolly Roger*. Who knew what other creatures Buri might have brought to Neverland—or what might be circling behind them from the ocean's depths even now?

At least the sun, directly behind their fleet, would give them some advantage. Their enemies would be looking directly into it when they arrived, which might buy them a few precious moments when the battle began.

If it began.

When it began.

Charlie wasn't sure which thought was more terrifying.

The sharp chiming of fairy bells cut through his brooding. Tinker

Bell streaked past his head in a flash of golden light, pointing toward the sky and ringing out orders he couldn't understand before speeding off toward the cliff wall where the innisfay forces were staging.

As he followed her gesture, Charlie's breath caught in his throat.

The approaching armada was so thick it devoured the light itself, trailing long tendrils of writhing dark magic toward the cliffs below. His heart pounded as he counted the enemy ships—far more than their intelligence had suggested. The air chilled as they drew closer, as though winter itself followed in their wake.

The sight grew worse with each passing second. Wyverns wheeled through the air in deadly formation, their slick, metallic scales gleaming like oil on water. Between the ships, massive bats darted through the shadows, carrying black-clad riders on their backs. The bat-creatures' flitting movements made Charlie's eyes ache, as if they were slipping through gaps in reality itself.

Worst of all, above the enemy fleet soared four massive dragons—not the single beast they'd prepared for—their wings blotting out the sky. Charlie had thought Snaggleclaw was massive, but these ancient creatures dwarfed the old dragon, their hides as impenetrable as living rock, their flame-red eyes burning with unmitigated cruelty.

Charlie's mind raced, desperate to find any new tactic, any change in formation that might form a better defense against such an overwhelming force, but there was no time left.

Training and instinct took over as two of the enemy dragons peeled away, tucking their wings for a diving attack. His voice rang out across the deck, shouting orders to his crew.

"Cannons ready! Prepare to fire!"

Adrenaline surged through his body—blasting away any last shred of doubt.

This was war, pure and simple. So he knew—with bone-deep certainty—that not everyone would survive.

# CHAPTER 57

Wendy Darling had never been much for waiting. Her fingers tapped restlessly against the hilt of her sword, playing out the rhythm that John and Michael had coined the "March of the Executioner" back in Dover Castle.

Catching herself with a rueful grimace, she forced her hand to still.

She tried instead to focus on visualizing their success—pushing Buri back through the portal, sealing off his access to Neverland forever. But the more she imagined it, the more unsettled she became, until her fingers started their nervous drumming all over again.

It wasn't that she doubted their plan ...

Well, perhaps she did have her doubts. Perhaps they all did. But that's not what was bothering her—not right now, anyway.

No, this particular unease was more about ... consequences.

The thought of pushing Buri back through the portal felt wrong somehow. Yes, it would protect everyone in Neverland—Peter,

the everlost, the Vikings, and all the magical creatures who called this realm home. But Wendy's conscience rebelled at the thought of simply passing their problem along to someone else.

She didn't know where Buri was coming from, but wherever it was, she couldn't believe that the people there deserved to suffer at Buri's hands more than Neverland did.

Beside her, Jokul grunted. She turned to him, but his soft utterance didn't seem to be aimed at her. His posture was as rigid as the ice he commanded, his eyes fixed unblinkingly on the dark fortress, lost to all but him behind the fog.

In the intensity of his stillness, the air around him had grown so cold that his very breath seemed to freeze and shatter with each exhalation, creating a subtle shower of diamond-like fragments that disappeared before reaching the ground.

Without shifting his gaze, he expelled a long sigh that formed a delicate, crystalline cloud in the air before him. "Whatever it is you're wrestling with, you'd best settle it now." His gaze flicked briefly to her still-drumming fingers, then back to the castle. "There's no room for hesitation in battle. The questions that haunt us can be deadly."

Embarrassed, Wendy cast her eyes to the ground. Was her discomfort truly so easy to read? She was tempted to keep her thoughts to herself, but she couldn't deny the wisdom in his words. "What happens if we succeed?" she asked carefully. "If we manage to push Buri back through the portal, what will happen to the people who live there, wherever he's coming from?"

A frown crossed his face—a blue-tinted shadow drifting over snow. "You're right to be concerned. Buri wants nothing more than to kill Peter. If the old one survives this battle only to find himself cast back to where he started ..." He let the sentence hang for a long moment before finishing his thought. "His wrath will be terrible to behold."

"*If* he survives? So, he can be defeated? You're certain of it?" She grasped at the thought with a surge of hope, but Jokul's expression chilled that spark before it had a chance to take hold.

"He cannot be killed while he stands between two worlds. And once he's free of the portal, even then, he's still an immortal being. At best, he can only be killed temporarily. When he dies, he enters a dormant state for a few hundred years, then returns." Jokul's explanation carried the weight of ancient knowledge, his words precise and measured.

"During these dormant periods," he continued, "he can do no harm. He must simply wait until the time of his return. Think of it like a prison of time itself." The winter king's frost-white hair stirred in a gentle breeze that affected nothing else around them. "Nonetheless, return he will, as enraged and determined as before."

Jokul's gaze narrowed, his shoulders shifting like ice cracking under pressure. "However," he said slowly, "I must admit I have never encountered a portal quite like this one." His words carried a trace of frustration, ice crystals forming and dissolving in rapid succession around his clenched fists.

His voice dropped until it was barely more than a murmur. "There is a possibility—mind you, only a theory—that because time works differently here in Neverland, killing Buri in this realm might make his death permanent." The temperature around them plummeted further, forcing Wendy to wrap herself more tightly within her blue officer's coat. "I have kept this to myself, as I cannot be certain it will work. False hope can be more treacherous than any weapon."

His eyes, the pale blue of a midwinter sky, met hers with solemn intensity. "When hope is misplaced," he murmured, "it lies but a heartbeat from despair. In battle, nothing is more dangerous."

Wendy opened her mouth to respond, but the words died in her throat. A familiar scent assaulted her senses. The pickle-green

tang of Neverland's magic held a rotting undertone that made her stomach lurch.

The dullahans were close—far closer than they should have been.

A moment ago, she had felt the creatures far in the distance, their presence no more than a minor nuisance in the back of her mind. In the next, they were imminent, pressing on her consciousness with a crippling sense of despair.

Jokul's words echoed through her mind.

*In battle, nothing is more dangerous.*

"They're here," she gasped, fighting down a wave of nausea as the corrupted magic pressed against her senses. "But they haven't traveled—they've just … appeared."

Jokul's reaction was immediate. "Everyone to the *Sparrow*," he commanded, his voice cutting through the air like a blade. "Now!"

They ran. Snow swirled up from Jokul's footsteps as the group raced toward the ship—a striking mirror of the decay that always followed in the dullahans' wake.

The soul-draining presence of the riders and their nightmares clawed at Wendy's mind, a wave of emptiness so profound it made even the deepest winter seem warm and welcoming by comparison. Each step required more effort than the last, as if the air had thickened around her, holding her back for the approaching horror.

The *Sparrow* was close. It could be their salvation.

If only they could reach it in time.

With every ounce of strength she had left, Wendy wrenched her gaze to that shining beacon of hope, only to find Hoops peering back at her from the rigging, his eyes filled with sorrow.

# CHAPTER 58

Meanwhile, Charlie was facing dire straits of his own. On the off chance that you've never set a trap for a dragon, here's what you should know: it's a harrowing affair even under the best of circumstances. You can't be sure ahead of time whether it's going to work, and if it doesn't, you probably won't survive long enough to give it another go.

This simple fact was very much on Charlie's mind as he stood at the railing of the *Pegasus*, holding her steady, watching not one but two dragons descend from the sky. If he tried to evade the attack, the trap was sure to fail. Unfortunately, the trap had only been designed for one dragon, and there were in fact *two* dragons, so it was quite likely to fail anyway.

Needless to say, things were not looking good.

In that moment, he wished more than anything that he had a navigator of his own—someone else in whom he might inspire confidence by issuing quiet orders like, "Steady now," or "Be

ready to move on my command." But Hook had asked Charlie to serve as captain, navigator, and admiral, all at once, so he had no one to encourage but himself, which doesn't always work as well as we might like.

The dragons were already halfway to the ship. They folded their wings tight against their bodies to pick up more speed, and a red glow blossomed at their throats, brightening by the second with the heat of their fiery breath.

From the waters below, the sirens offered up a full-throated chorus of hope and inspiration, doing their best to keep the crew of the *Pegasus* from abandoning ship in a full-on panic.

If anyone had offered to lift the mantle of responsibility from his shoulders, Charlie would have handed it over in a heartbeat. But circumstances do not always afford us the choice of the role we wish to play. Decorated captains must occasionally join landing parties with their sworn enemies, and first mates must become admirals and face down dragons before they feel ready, all in the line of duty.

Never in Charlie's life had he missed Wendy so badly.

As the great beasts came within range of the *Pegasus*, opening their terrible jaws to unleash a stream of molten death, the trap was finally sprung.

A tremendous wave erupted from the sea—Undine himself, rising like a living mountain of seawater and foam, his form so vast that it matched even these monstrous terrors. The water elemental's massive arms wrapped the nearest one in an embrace that would have crushed a lesser creature, dragging the beast into the depths where countless unnamed things waited to feast.

The second dragon, knocked askew by Undine's dramatic entrance, loosed its flame in a wild arc that barely missed the *Pegasus*.

Charlie didn't waste a moment.

"All ships, climb!" he bellowed. "Scatter formation!"

The allied fleet responded as one, each vessel choosing its own path skyward to angle away from Blackheart's approaching armada. Charlie tracked the remaining dragon as long as he could, hoping for a clear shot, but the beast vanished into the clouds of steam created by its companion's demise.

A thunderous boom echoed across the water as one of the other ships unleashed a broadside. Snapping his head toward the deafening roar of the cannons, Charlie caught Curly's everlost executing a maneuver that would have been impossible for the *Pegasus*. The entire vessel had rolled sideways, turning completely on its beam ends in midair to get a clean angle on the second dragon's position.

Any other crew in the fleet would have fallen into the sea, but the everlost simply walked along the deck as it rotated, completely ignoring the laws of gravity. When the ship righted itself, Curly grinned triumphantly from the helm.

Charlie counted the seconds, his eyes searching the mist for the telltale red glimmer of imminent dragon fire. One ... two ... three ... four ...

The second dragon was nowhere to be seen, suggesting the everlost's volley had found its mark.

He exhaled a quick, shuddering breath, but there was no time to celebrate. The remaining two dragons had begun their attack runs, diving from the clouds, their terrifying maws already opening to gather breath. Curly's everlost were still reloading the cannons, the *Jolly Roger* and the *Ravenhawk* were too far away, and the *Pegasus* wouldn't have a shot at this angle—the dragons were too smart for that.

Only Snaggleclaw stood between Charlie's flagship and the horrors screaming down at them from the sky.

Thomas, planted firmly on his back, sped into the fray, guiding the friendly dragon to intercept them despite their massive size advantage.

In that moment, a flash of light drew Charlie's attention. It was so bright he thought he might have accidentally stared into the sun itself—that the golden orb had magically traversed the sky from the ocean's horizon to the cliff line.

But no, the dazzling brilliance came from hundreds of innisfay as they darted from the sheer face of the cliffs. In the blink of an eye, they were everywhere, emerging from their myriad holes and hiding places on Tinker Bell's command, their radiant glow reflecting off the water as they raced toward the sea.

And every one of them trailed a gently falling sparkle of glittering dust in their wake—curving and crossing in a wide golden mist that spread like a blanket over the sea.

Wherever their dust fell, impossible things rose from the waves.

Giant seahorses with mother-of-pearl scales took to the air, their merfolk riders bearing tridents of coral and spears of whalebone. A creature that might have been a dragon in its own right— if dragons were born in the deepest trenches of the ocean—rose on fins that had become wings, racing to join Snaggleclaw in his desperate defense of the fleet.

Charlie allowed himself a grim smile. Blackheart's forces could have easily outmaneuvered them, could have surrounded the cove and attacked from all sides at once. But they had chosen to rely on brute force instead, counting on overwhelming numbers to crush any resistance.

That arrogance had left the allied fleet a clear path of retreat— though Charlie wasn't ready to use it just yet.

The wyverns and giant bats were closing fast, their riders leaning forward in their saddles as they raced ahead of Blackheart's ships. But the sea had other plans. Merfolk astride their newly airborne steeds formed the first line of defense, while behind them rose an army born of wonder and innisfay dust.

Flying starfish big as houses spun through the air like living buzzsaws. Electric eels crackled with lightning that had nothing to do with storms. Creatures that might have been clams—if clams had fins and teeth and tails—snapped at the air with shells that could have crushed a longboat.

And beneath them all, a serpentine shape that stretched longer than the *Pegasus* herself rose from the depths, water streaming from scales the size of dinner plates.

"Hard to port," Charlie warned the crew. "Cannons, make ready!"

The *Pegasus* heeled over gracefully, bringing her guns to bear. All around him, Charlie could hear the organized chaos of a crew that knew its business—the rapid thunder of feet on wooden decks, the screech of gun carriages being run out, the sharp commands of experienced gunners positioning their weapons.

"Fire as you bear!"

The *Pegasus* shuddered as her guns spoke. Through the cloud of smoke, Charlie caught glimpses of devastation among the enemy forces—a wyvern tumbling from the sky, its wing shattered; giant bats wheeling away with empty saddles; riders plummeting toward the unforgiving sea. The other ships of the fleet joined in, their combined volleys cutting cruel swaths through the attacking forces.

For a moment, Charlie's heart nearly stopped as massive shapes loomed out of nowhere, surrounding the *Pegasus* on all sides. But these were allies, not enemies—giant squid and octopi, their tentacles undulating like living sails as they rode the fairy dust into battle. Their impossibly huge eyes fixed on the approaching armada as they moved to engage, and Charlie found himself fervently grateful that these particular monsters were on his side.

Surveying the battlefront, he felt a glimmer of hope. The merfolk fought with the desperate fury of those defending their homes, and the great denizens of the deep were proving far more formidable than he had expected. Even the massive forms of Blackheart's dragons didn't seem quite as threatening when compared to the sheer variety of creatures that now filled the sky.

*We might actually win this*, Charlie thought. *We might actually be able to defend the cove.*

But war can be fickle, and victory has an uncanny knack for slipping away just when it seems most certain. Charlie felt the change in the battle's tide before he saw it, as clearly as he would have felt a shift in the wind.

First, Snaggleclaw took a direct hit from one of the dragons. The friendly beast fell from the sky trailing a plume of dark smoke, his massive body crashing into the water.

Charlie's eyes darted to the aerial melee where the onslaught of sea creatures had met the first wave of wyverns and bats. Where moments ago the sky had been full of fantastical allies, only a scattered few remained. The rest had been burned or blasted from the air by Blackheart's forces.

As if to emphasize the point, one of the remaining dragons made a single pass through the squad of flying squid and octopi. The massive cephalopods, which had seemed so intimidating just moments ago, were too large to move out of the way. Charlie's heart broke to see the devastation unfolding before his eyes, their bodies ravaged and consumed by dragon fire.

He took a deep breath, shoving aside the weight of his anguish. The allied forces had fought well. They had blooded the enemy. But holding their position would be foolish now. If they continued to stand their ground, there would be no one left to lead Blackheart's forces away.

"Now!" he shouted. "Make for open water!" A series of whistles, flags, and shouts conveyed the command throughout the allied forces. "Retreat by squadrons, rear guard to form on the *Pegasus*!"

As they turned and fled, heading for the open ocean, Charlie could only hope they had bought the others enough time.

*Godspeed, Wendy*, he thought, watching another great seahorse fall from the sky. *Whatever you're planning, do it now.*

Wendy Darling had nothing left. Even as she ran for the *Sparrow*, her consciousness was fading. She stumbled, barely managed to regain her footing, then stumbled again.

Hook was only two steps ahead of her, but his forget-me-not eyes were glued to the ship. If she fell, by the time he realized what had happened, it would be too late. The dullahans were gaining on them, galloping toward her like the grim reaper himself—trapping her mind in a cruel vice of hopelessness and despair.

Even Peter, who had remained constantly by her side until now, had flown ahead—to get the ship into the air as fast as possible, she supposed. It flashed through her mind that if she fell—*when* she fell—she would never see him again.

From the rigging, Hoops looked down upon her sadly. "Don't feel bad, Captain. I've seen plenty of good sailors die. At least you're not alone. They usually are, you know."

Hoops was right, she realized. Here she was, about to trip and fall to her death, doing everything she could think of to stave off

the inevitable and keep moving forward except the one thing that might actually work.

As she stumbled again, her knees buckling beneath her for the last time, she gathered all her strength and yelled, "Help!"

Wendy had never seen anyone move as fast as Hook did in that moment. In one fluid motion he stopped mid-sprint, spun, scooped her up in his arms before she hit the ground, and spun again, his legs pounding toward the ship as fast as they were before, if not faster.

"Pan," he shouted as he raced up the gangplank. "Get us in the air. Now!"

The *Sparrow* bucked as she took to the sky, her timbers creaking in protest. Hook lurched but kept his hold on Wendy, errant strands of his dark hair whipping about his face as the wind caught them.

Through the haze that clouded her mind, Wendy caught a glimpse of movement at the ship's rail—Jokul, having vaulted aboard at the last possible moment in a shower of crystalline snow, with Vegard right behind him, his axe still drawn and ready.

They had fallen back when she cried out, she realized, placing themselves between her and those terrible riders. The thought of them standing ready to die just to buy her a few more seconds made her heart clench, even through the crushing weight of the dullahans' presence.

The ship continued to climb, the wind growing stronger with each passing moment. Hook carried her toward the helm, where Peter stood with his hand closed firmly around the trinket that controlled the vessel. His eyes met Wendy's briefly before turning to Jokul.

"Where?" Peter's voice was clipped, focused—carrying an edge of determination Wendy had never heard in it before.

The frost king gestured toward the fortress, and Wendy followed the motion with her eyes. She had to blink several times before she could comprehend what she was seeing.

The structure had grown impossibly vast. As Buri had continued pulling his forces through the portal, its walls had expanded outward like a cancer of stone and iron. What had once been an isolated fortress was now a citadel that rivaled the greatest cities Wendy had ever read about—a dark mirror of medieval Paris, perhaps, or even ancient Rome itself.

Walls upon walls had sprung up around the old ones, creating rings of defense that housed all manner of twisted creatures. Some were so terrifying that Wendy's mind refused to register them, sliding away from what she had seen even as the haze began to clear.

Any sane person would have hesitated when told to fly directly at such a stronghold. Even the bravest sailor might have suggested finding another approach, some less direct route that didn't involve charging headlong into that nightmare.

But Peter had never been one for hesitation—that much, at least, hadn't changed.

The *Sparrow* banked hard, then shot forward like an arrow. Still, even as they hurtled toward Buri's inner sanctum, Wendy knew it wasn't recklessness driving Peter's actions. No—whether she felt it through her siren blood or simply intuited it because she knew him so well—his only thought was for her safety.

Everything else, including his own survival, was secondary to getting her away from the soul-draining presence of the dullahans.

Hook's arms tightened around her as the ship picked up speed, but Wendy hardly noticed. The central fortress was growing closer by the second, its towers and battlements looming before them like the jagged teeth of some enormous beast.

The outer walls, imposing as they were, posed no barrier to a flying ship. Archers scrambled to their positions, loosing volleys of arrows that fell short of their target. Giants hurled boulders that passed harmlessly beneath the keel, their frustrated roars fading in the distance as Peter guided the ship higher and faster still.

But as they approached the central keep, Wendy's heart sank. Two massive doors of wood and iron stood firmly closed before them, as tall and impenetrable as the gates to Valhalla itself.

The *Sparrow* was fast, yes, and more maneuverable than any vessel Wendy had ever seen, but those doors didn't call for agility. They called for something else entirely.

Peter cast a quick glance toward Jokul—whether seeking guidance or approval, Wendy wasn't sure. But the frost king didn't even turn his head to acknowledge the look. He simply nodded once, sharply, his frost-pale features set in grim determination.

That was all the encouragement Peter needed. Rather than slowing their approach, he urged the *Sparrow* faster. The wind howled past them now, and Wendy's eyes widened as she realized his intent. He was going to hurl the ship into the gates. The *Sparrow*, for all her grace and beauty, was about to become little more than an extraordinarily elegant battering ram.

One hundred yards, fifty, ten ...

Just before impact, in the very moment Wendy was about to squeeze her eyes shut and throw her arms across her face to shield it from flying debris, something unexpected happened. The gates burst open at the last possible second, letting the *Sparrow* crash through into an entry hall so enormous it could have housed St. Paul's Cathedral with room to spare.

The ship skidded across the polished stone floor in a shower of sparks, her mast snapping like a twig and tumbling away into the shadows. When they finally came to a stop, the silence was deafening.

Wendy breathed in deeply through her nose, let out a tremendous sigh of relief, and placed her hand lightly on Hook's shoulder. "You can put me down now, I think," she said softly. "I'm feeling much better."

Hook, who had clutched Wendy Darling protectively against his chest in what he had believed to be their final moments, now found

himself wildly embarrassed given their sudden change of circumstances. He mumbled an awkward, unintelligible apology and set her carefully on her feet, all while steadfastly avoiding eye contact.

You can imagine their surprise to hear the echoing beat of calm footsteps approaching across the vast stone floor.

All hands on the *Sparrow* turned to see a tall, dark figure striding toward them. He wore a long, dark, hooded coat embellished with equally dark embroidery down the front and along the hem and cuffs. Up close, his features bore enough resemblance to Jokul that their relation was unmistakable.

Wendy recognized him immediately as the man who had orchestrated Peter's kidnapping during the basilisk incident. As her strength returned fully, she noticed that everyone aboard—Peter included—had drawn their weapons.

"Kaspar." Jokul's voice carried more than a hint of warning. "You may have opened the gates, but just so we're clear, we owe you nothing. I know you too well. I have no doubt that your actions here are meant to serve your own ends."

Kaspar's smile was a slow, sly thing, reminding Wendy very much of a fox hunting its prey. "You're wise not to trust me, but don't act like we're so different, you and I. We all have our motivations."

"Does this mean you'll join us in our battle at the portal?" The frost king's question carried a weight that suggested a longer, more complicated history than she knew.

Kaspar's gaze swept across the group, lingering perhaps a moment too long on Wendy. "Frankly, I don't like your odds. So, no, I don't think be joining you. But I do think I should give this wonderful place you call Neverland a chance. I'd very much like to see what a more *focused* mind could accomplish here."

"I hope you don't mean your father," Jokul snapped. "We will never allow Loki to set foot here."

"Perhaps I meant myself." Kaspar's smile didn't waver. "If I were you, I'd worry less about me and more about your current problem. Buri has no intention of allowing Neverland to survive—at least, not for long. If he did, he would not have brought the dullahans here. Their very presence will destroy it eventually." He spread his hands in an elegant shrug. "But I've done all I can. Good luck. Next time we see each other—if there *is* a next time—I'll be delighted to return to our usual … animosity."

With that, he turned and walked away, his coat blending into the shadows until he vanished entirely.

"Always a pleasure," Vegard growled.

Wendy's strength had fully returned now that they were away from the dullahans. But their noxious presence had only been replaced by the dark magic emanating from Buri himself. It was overwhelming here, a storm front raging against her skin.

Judging by the tense set of Peter's shoulders, he felt it too.

The group formed up naturally, with Wendy and Peter leading the way. Together, they moved deeper into the fortress. Guided by the strength of Buri's presence, they navigated corridors sized for giants and halls that could have hosted entire tournaments. But there was no one to be seen.

Wendy wondered if Buri's forces were all committed to the battle outside, either fighting the ships at the cove or defending the city's outer walls. Either way, the lack of resistance didn't bode well for anyone.

It felt far too much like a trap waiting to be sprung.

The next hallway opened onto a gallery lined with giant statues of wet clay, as though they had only just been crafted within the hour. Each one stood at least eight feet tall, clad in intricately detailed armor. They were so lifelike that everyone drew to a halt, studying them with suspicious eyes. But the statues remained motionless.

Vegard, tired of waiting, stepped forward and swung his axe in a mighty arc that caught the nearest statue in the side, just below its chest plate, nearly cleaving it in two. Everyone watched intently as he worked to free his weapon from the clay figure.

Finally wrenching it loose, he turned to the group with a grin. "All clear," he declared.

And that, of course, was when the statues began to move.

Charlie never thought he would die in midair.

At sea, perhaps—every sailor accepted that possibility the moment they first set foot on a ship. But here, with nothing but empty sky between the *Pegasus* and the endless ocean below?

No, this he could not have imagined.

What remained of his decimated forces struggled to maintain formation as they fled over the waves. The dragons were gaining. He could hear their wings now, great leathery sounds that filled the air, more ominous than thunder.

Monstrous bats kept pace with the dragons. Their dark-clad riders stood tall in their stirrups, leaning forward over the necks of the nightmarish beasts, eager for a kill. And behind them came Blackheart's ships, their sails filled with wind and purpose.

"We can't outrun them forever, sir." Cecco, the handsome Italian, surveyed the vast armada behind them, then glanced at his commander, waiting for a reply.

But Charlie only nodded, his eyes fixed on the horizon. The fastest of their pursuers would be upon them soon. He could still order the fleet to scatter—each ship for itself, racing in different directions. Some might escape. But if they scattered now …

The morning sun shimmered on the deck at Charlie's feet—no, it was more than that. The light that splashed across the planks held a hint of undulation, a vague echo of the waves below. As the effect passed, he peered up, squinting at the sky. He thought, perhaps, he could almost see … something.

But whatever it was remained frustratingly unclear, as though his eyes refused to focus properly—and then it was behind them, just the barest glimmer in the sky.

Charlie glanced over his shoulder. The first ranks of their pursuers were still gaining on them. The two dragons bore down on the fleet with single-minded determination, opening their maws, their victory assured. Charlie gripped the ship's trinket more tightly, preparing to give the order to scatter if he had to, his last desperate gambit to save at least some of his people.

And then the air crystallized.

The dragons slammed into something massive and nearly invisible, something they hadn't seen coming. The air filled with the sound of thrashing wings and bellowing roars as enormous, translucent tentacles dropped from the sky to wrap around their scaled bodies.

Wave after wave of pursuing forces crashed into the mounting barrier of colossal, flying jellyfish—their bodies as wide as the largest ships in Blackheart's fleet, their tentacles long enough to reach the sea. The phantom-like forms were finally visible as they moved, tangling sails and wings alike in their deadly embrace.

Charlie watched in awe as Blackheart's mighty armada ground to a halt, caught in a living net that stretched across the sky. He knew the jellyfish couldn't hold them for long—not against tooth

and claw and dragon fire—but their strength and sacrifice would give the fleet the precious time it needed.

And they desperately needed that time. All of their ships had taken heavy damage. The sea creatures that had transformed so magnificently into aerial warriors were now decimated, their ranks thinned to almost nothing. Snaggleclaw was gone, and with him, Thomas. Even the innisfay lights had dimmed, though whether from casualties or exhaustion, Charlie couldn't tell.

As he turned the *Pegasus* in a giant arc, heading back toward land and the rally point where the rest of their allies were waiting, a handful of giant bats and riders shot toward them.

Was the barrier already falling?

His breath caught in his throat as he scanned the frozen armada, but nothing else moved. These were just the isolated few that had been flying wide enough to avoid the trap.

Already, several of Curly's everlost and two griffins had taken wing. The cavalry made short work of the lead rider, and the rest of them fell back, deciding to wait for their armada to free itself rather than share his fate.

"All forces, make for the rally point," Charlie ordered, his voice carrying across the deck. "Full speed ahead."

Charlie wasn't sure what he expected to find there. A handful of elven vessels at least, their graceful lines and silver sails a sharp contrast to the larger human ships. And any other griffins that hadn't joined them at the lagoon.

But as the gathered forces finally appeared on the horizon, the scene laid out before him was a sight to behold.

The elven ships floated low in the sky, joined by several dozen griffins that wheeled among them, at least half bearing riders armed for war. Flying deer pawed at the air, owls swooped through the sky, and enormous wolves lined the railings of the elven ships,

standing shoulder to shoulder with leather-armored Vikings and Jokul's elven archers.

As Charlie's battered fleet approached, the gathered forces began to form up, moving with a precision that spoke of careful preparation.

A single griffin peeled away from the main group, winging straight for the *Pegasus.* Charlie's surprise only grew as he recognized the rider. The griffin landed with surprising delicacy on the deck, and Michael dismounted with what could only be described as practiced ease.

"Quite the entrance," Charlie managed.

Michael grinned, but his expression sobered quickly as he took in the obvious signs of battle. "Gerdrek's idea, actually. Said they needed someone to carry messages between the forces. When Chirpy agreed, well ..." He shrugged. "How could I refuse?"

"Chirpy?"

Michael's cheeks colored slightly. "Can't pronounce her actual name—don't think human tongues are meant to. But she seems to like the nickname. Or at least she hasn't eaten me for using it."

The griffin thrust her chin in and out several times.

"Is that ..." Charlie cocked his head, studying her behavior. "Is she laughing?"

Michael shrugged again. "Honestly, I have no idea. How did you fare at the lagoon?"

Charlie dipped his head, unable to look the other man in the eye. "Not well. We lost Thomas," he admitted quietly. "And Snaggleclaw with him. Plus, I don't know how many mermaids, sirens, seahorses ... our water allies fought valiantly, but we had no idea how many Blackheart would send."

The griffin made a soft trilling sound that might have been sympathy, and Michael's face fell, his shoulders sagging beneath the weight of the news. "What's on the way?"

"Ships. Wyverns. Giant bats with riders." Charlie took a deep breath, finally meeting Michael's gaze. "And dragons. We took down two of them, I think. But the other two … well, they'll break free soon enough."

"Then you'll want to hear what's waiting for them." Michael straightened, visibly gathering himself, and gestured at the assembled forces. "The griffins, as you can see—about half agreed to carry riders. Everyone has ranged weapons, plus whatever they can swing in close quarters." He pointed toward the elven ships. "Viking and elven archers on every deck, plus those little things that like to dance in the Viking fires like embers—"

"The tiny fairies?"

"That's them. And Sir Galahault brought some sort of flying machine. Thomas would have loved it." Michael's voice caught for a moment. "About twenty mechanical suits of armor too."

Charlie tried to imagine twenty mechanical knights charging into battle. It was enough to make his head spin. (Then again, if a polar bear could ride a flying moose, perhaps it was best not to question anything anymore.)

"But the best part," Michael continued, "is the dragon."

Hope surged in Charlie's chest. "We have a dragon?"

"A small one. But a dragon, nonetheless. And its fire is no less dangerous for its size."

Charlie nodded slowly. Snaggleclaw had been their most devastating loss. Another dragon—even a small one—might at least give them a fighting chance. "How long until our forces here are ready to move?"

"Actually, we've just received an innisfay report from the citadel. It's massive now, by the way—more of a city than a fortress. But the dullahans have reached the outer walls, and Blackheart's forces have fallen into confusion at the gate. It's like we thought—they're just as susceptible as we are to the things."

"Good. Then it's time." Charlie gazed out over the assembled host. He wondered briefly how many of them would survive what was to come, then locked that thought away. Behind them, a dragon's roar split the air. "Signal the fleet to move out," he ordered. "We'll need to coordinate with the elven ships—"

"Already done. Gerdrek and I worked out the signals." Michael turned to his griffin. "Chirpy?"

The massive creature dipped her shoulder, making it easier for the man to vault onto her back. The moment he was settled, she launched into the air with a powerful thrust of her wings.

As she climbed, she let out a piercing cry that sent shivers down Charlie's spine. Across the gathered forces, other griffins took up the call. The elven ships moved forward in perfect formation, their silver sails catching a light that seemed to come from nowhere.

The combined fleet set out for Buri's fortress, their shadows painting long, dark streaks across the land below—elven ships with their silver sails, griffins and flying deer wheeling between their masts, mechanical knights glinting on the decks.

And then Blackheart's forces appeared on the horizon behind the *Pegasus*. The dragons had broken free, along with the wyverns, bats, and what looked like most of their ships.

But the jellyfish had bought them the time they needed. They would at least reach the fortress before the remaining horde from the lagoon could catch up.

As they approached Buri's lair, Charlie caught his first glimpse of the vast city it had become. The outer walls rose impossibly high, as though Buri's magic had forced the very stones to grow beyond their natural size.

"There!" One of the lookouts pointed toward the gate ahead.

Charlie didn't need a spyglass to see what had caught the man's attention. A roiling darkness had gathered around it—writhing and stretching inexorably from the center.

The dullahans.

Even as Charlie watched, the massive wood of the gates began to fall.

It started at the bottom, closest to the riders, who leaned forward on their rotting beasts as though directing their energy toward the barrier before them.

At first, the spread of decay crept outward and upward as the gate disintegrated in the middle of their path. Then, as the dullahans were finally able to step forward beneath it, the wood that remained above and around them crumbled faster and faster.

Wherever the darkness touched, it simply … ceased to be.

As the riders moved into the city, Buri's forces fell back—ogres and giants, imps and trolls, all edging away from the devastation, watching the deadly trails with a mix of confusion and horror.

Here and there, some foolish beast tried to charge through the decay, only to fall screaming as their legs were devoured beneath them—silenced only by their eventual, inevitable death.

For a long moment, a terrible silence fell over the allied fleet.

But then someone—whether British, Viking, or frost-folk, Charlie didn't know—gave voice to a battle cry. "For Neverland!"

The shout was taken up by others, intermittently at first but growing bolder by the second, human voices joining with less familiar sounds as the cry rippled through their ranks.

Griffin screams pierced the air. The wolves howled, and the polar bears roared. Elven horns rang out clear and terrible. The mechanical knights raised weapons that gleamed with an inner light.

"For Neverland!" Michael echoed. Chirpy's answering shriek made the deck vibrate beneath their feet.

Charlie felt the cry building in his own chest, felt the weight of everything they had lost and everything they still stood to lose. He thought of Thomas and Snaggleclaw, of Nicholas and Tootles,

of all the brave souls who had fallen to bring them to this moment, and the battle cry burst from his throat, raw and ferocious.

"FOR NEVERLAND!"

Behind him, Buri's dragons roared an answering challenge, while ahead, the dullahans' darkness beckoned.

CHAPTER

# 61

The clay warrior that Vegard had all but eviscerated raised a battle axe high in the air, preparing to slam it down on his head.

Tigerlilja lunged toward her brother as though she might yank him out of danger, but he spun away from the blow just in time. The axe crashed into the floor at his feet, the echo of steel on stone ringing through the gallery.

"Their weapons aren't clay, that's for sure," the Viking growled.

Wendy watched, mesmerized, as the gaping wound in the warrior's midsection sealed over, leaving nothing but a small chunk of its side on the floor.

Beside her, Hook grimaced. "That's not good either."

A wet, squelching sound filled the air as the next statue wrenched its feet from the floor. The clay warrior towered over Wendy, its skin gleaming with moisture. Her fingers closed instinctively around the smooth grip of her pistol, but then she changed her mind—what good was a bullet going to do against *that*?

She left the pistol in its holster and drew her sword instead, yanking it from its scabbard and thrusting the blade deep into the creature's thigh. The sword sank in easily enough, but when she pulled it free, the hole sealed up instantly, the edges of the clay flowing toward each other to fill the gap.

Everywhere she looked, the giant clay statues had come to life. They moved slowly but smoothly, without hesitation, at least a dozen of them now blocking their path.

To her right, Peter seemed to be faring better. His blade found purchase as he wrenched it through a clay shoulder. The statue's arm dropped to the floor with a heavy thud that shook the polished stones beneath their feet. On her left, Hook drove his sword clean through a warrior's throat at it bent toward him, but the moment he withdrew the blade, the clay flowed back together.

"Damned things heal faster than I can cut them," Hook snarled, dodging a retaliatory swing.

The clay figures advanced—the sheer mass of them blocking their way through the gallery. One swept a sword toward Wendy's midsection. She leaped back, her heel skidding on the smooth floor, the cruel edge of the steel barely missing her.

Vegard grunted nearby, his axe lodging in another statue's midriff. He planted his boot on its leg for leverage and hauled the weapon free, bringing chunks of clay with it. The statue paused, the gouges remaining for a moment before slowly filling in, though not as completely as the wounds Wendy and Hook had inflicted.

In an instant, Jokul was at Wendy's side, his ice-touched blade carving through the statue's wrist. Where it struck, the clay froze and shattered, but the statue didn't hesitate. It raised its other hand and swung its empty fist toward her like a club. She lifted her blade to parry, and her sword sank through its fingers. Wendy barely managed to deflect the blow.

"Fight through them, however you can." Tigerlilja's shout echoed off the walls. "Once we're on the other side, we'll look for a way to block their pursuit!"

Sweat trickled down Wendy's back beneath her officer's coat. At this point, she was merely dodging their swings as best she could, one after another. The creatures didn't show any sign of tiring—they simply pressed forward, step by inexorable step.

A massive sword whistled past her head, so close she felt the cold, damp air of it against her ear. She spun away, her boots sliding again.

The clay warriors moved with terrible purpose, their wet footsteps rumbling through the gallery as they fought with the tireless persistence of the earth itself. Even Peter and Jokul, working in tandem, had only managed to bring down one of the creatures, its frozen chunks still scattered across the floor.

"We aren't doing enough damage," Tigerlilja called out. "We need to get past them!"

Jokul's blade flashed at the edge of Wendy's vision, ice crystals forming where it struck. The winter king had forced one of the warriors to give ground, creating a narrow gap. Wendy saw her chance. She feinted left, drawing her opponent's strike wide, then ducked under its guard.

The others seized the moment. Hook's sword kept another statue occupied while he slipped past its guard. Tigerlilja rolled under a sweeping blade. Peter darted through the air, drawing the warriors' attention upward while Vegard sprinted past them.

Frost came through last. With a yell of defiance, he raced toward the left wall of the gallery, running up and along it, defying gravity, to land next to Tigerlilja on the other side.

The clay warriors still lumbered toward them, but the group had won their opening. Together, they burst through the far doorway into the corridor beyond, leaving the heavy clay giants to follow in their wake.

Wendy took the lead, driven forward by some instinct she didn't yet understand. Behind her, the rhythmic impact of clay feet on stone echoed through the passages, each blow a reminder of their relentless pursuit.

Something pulled at her consciousness—a thread of awareness that wove through the very stones of the fortress. Every corridor, every passage whispered its secrets into her mind.

When she allowed herself a moment to sink into that awareness, to feel the pulse of Neverland racing through the citadel it had been forced to construct, Buri's presence stood out like a festering wound. His magic had no place here. In some ways, it felt even more alien than the soul-draining corruption of the dullahans.

"Left!" she called out, her voice sharp and certain. The group followed without hesitation. She led them through the maze of passages, their boots thundering against the stone floor, the sound mixing with their ragged breathing.

Behind them, Peter and Frost slammed shut every door and gate they passed. Each new closure was followed by the sound of splintering wood and crashing metal hardware as the clay warriors smashed through. But eventually, the sounds grew more distant, the destruction more remote.

Wendy's lungs burned, but she didn't dare slow down. The pull of Buri's corrupted magic grew stronger with each turn, each new stretch of corridor. This deep in the fortress, even the stones beneath her feet trembled with it—as if they had been brought here against their will.

The passage suddenly opened into an entry hall so vast it seemed to swallow the light. Wendy's feet stopped of their own accord, her body recognizing where they were, even though the look of it had changed.

The others gathered around her, their presence anchoring her against the tide of evil that emanated from the far end of the hall.

Their breathing was still heavy from the run, but no one spoke. They didn't need to—she could feel in their silence that they knew where they were.

"Buri's portal is through there." Her quiet words fell upon the stones.

Jokul stepped forward, the air around him shimmering as he moved. From beneath his long, frost-touched coat, he drew forth two short swords, their blades emanating a subtle, ethereal glow. Without ceremony, he presented one to Wendy and the other to Hook.

Wendy stared at the weapon in her hands, fascinated by the way the light flowed like liquid through the metal. The blade felt alive somehow, resonating with a power that reminded her of Neverland itself.

"These blades contain elven magic," Frost explained, his voice barely above a whisper. "They should at least be able to cut Buri."

He reached into his coat once more and withdrew two small leather pouches, distributing them with the same solemnity. Wendy loosened the drawstring of hers, finding a small cache of ammunition nestled within, each perfect sphere gleaming with the same inner light as the sword.

"Thank you," she breathed, understanding the gravity of such a gift.

Hook scowled as he examined his own weapons. "You've had these the whole time? Why didn't you give them to us before?"

A shadow passed over Jokul's features. "These weapons are precious to my people. Incredibly rare. I wouldn't be giving them to you now if your own weapons hadn't proven so ineffective." His pale eyes met Hook's with unflinching honesty. "Besides, I wasn't sure you would make it this far."

Before Hook could voice what was clearly building into an angry retort, Tigerlilja stepped between them. "We all know what's

at stake." Her voice carried the weight of generations. "To defeat Buri, we must be willing to do whatever it takes. There can be no price too high. We fight to save more than just our homes, but all that is good in every realm he threatens."

At the far end of the grand entrance loomed a set of doors so massive they dwarfed even the hall the *Sparrow* had crashed into, the ceiling lost in shadow far above. As the group drew near, the enormous hinges groaned, and the doors swung open of their own accord.

Wendy's grip tightened on her new sword as they stepped into Buri's lair. Beyond the threshold lay the same arena she remembered—lit by countless torches, ringed by tiers of stone, its floor covered in sand.

And there, dominating the center of the vast space, swirled the portal—a tear in reality itself.

Within it, stood Buri, his massive form nearly emerged, with only one heel still trapped on the other side—his presence so overwhelming that the very sand beneath Wendy's feet recoiled from his touch.

"Ah, my little orphans. Come to me." Buri's words echoed through Wendy's mind, plucking her heart like a cruel musician, coaxing out a rage she thought she had left behind long ago. "Come and meet your maker."

# CHAPTER
# 62

The rage burned through Wendy's veins, threatening to consume her as she stood before the massive portal, its edges pulsing with Buri's ancient power.

*I grew up without my mother. Without my father. Because of you.*

Every stone of the vast arena—every pillar, torch, and shadow—made her siren blood sing with fury, as though Neverland itself recoiled from Buri's presence.

*You killed Peter's parents. And Tigerlilja's and Vegard's.*

The air was redolent of winter, overlaid with something far crueler—a scent that spoke of loneliness and endings and death.

She glanced at Jokul and saw her own rage reflected in his eyes, pale blue flames of hatred that had burned for centuries.

He might not have lost his parents—that, she didn't know—but he and his people had been forced to flee from their homes. They had lost everything they loved, their very place in the world. Somehow, that had been Buri's doing, too. She could feel it in her bones.

Somewhere near her left shoulder, Charming chimed quietly. Did he know what she was thinking? Were the innisfay orphans too?

Ever since Wendy and the others had escaped from the clay statues, Charming had been hovering just above her shoulder, a constant presence she had come to take for granted. He landed there now, just for a moment, placing a comforting hand against her cheek. His touch was like morning dew, cool and fleeting, but it steadied her.

Buri's quiet, cruel laughter filled the underground arena, reverberating off the ancient stones. His massive form towered within the portal. "Is this really all you brought to kill me, Peter? I am Buri, the First Man of Asgard. I have slain entire armies by my own hand, and you bring me this? A man of ice, four humans, and one wingless fairy?"

Wendy clutched the hilt of her blade, shifting her grip, testing its weight and balance. She could feel its magic resonating with her own, responding to her anger.

Peter's reply carried through the chamber—his voice holding none of its usual playfulness. "I've brought my family. That's all I need."

Buri laughed again, the sound of stone grinding against stone. "Your family? I killed your family, not that you'll remember. Even now, as I speak the words, you'll forget they ever existed."

"I remember more than you think." Peter glanced at Wendy, holding her gaze, and she would have traded almost anything in the world to know his thoughts in that moment. Was he fighting the curse even now? Could he feel the memories slipping away like water through his fingers?

But when Peter turned back to Buri, his eyes blazed with an intensity Wendy had never seen before. He bared his fangs, and his voice carried the weight of remembered grief. "You killed my

parents through a cruel deception, and you're still a coward to this day. Hiding in your portal like a frightened child."

The giant's roar sent shockwaves through the sand, leaving a pattern of concentric ridges across the otherwise pristine floor. Grunting and straining, he wrenched his heel out of the portal and stepped fully into Neverland.

He straightened to his full height, easily twenty feet tall, and stretched his neck, sniffing at the air. "What is that awful stench?"

"That's you, old man." Vegard spun his axe, slowly at first—once, twice, three times, each revolution faster than the last.

Without warning, Peter shot toward Buri, his sword moving so fast that Wendy could only track it by the silvery blur of its blade. He struck from above, from the side, from angles that should have been impossible, each attack flowing instantly into the next.

But Buri met every blow.

The giant moved with a terrible grace that belied his size, his club a dark blur that matched Peter's impossible speed. The weapons met again and again, each impact releasing a pulse of energy that stirred the sand at their feet.

Without a word, Jokul, Tigerlilja, and Vegard moved as one toward Buri's right flank. They fought with the cohesion of warriors who had faced death together, who knew each other's rhythms as well as their own.

Jokul's frost-touched blade led their charge, tiny crystalline shards of ice flying from its edge with every strike. He moved faster than his companions, leaping high into the air for his impossible thrusts and parries, always careful to hold their formation.

Buri sneered at them all, answering their attacks with a low, rumbling growl that shook the pillars of the arena. With his free hand, he drew an axe from his belt—a weapon that would have been massive even for Vegard—spinning and twisting it lightly through the air.

He wielded both weapons with devastating effect, never letting Peter's attacks draw his attention so completely that the others could find an opening.

*This is impossible.* Wendy watched with a mounting sense of hopelessness as Buri defended their attacks from all sides at once. Even as Peter hounded him with a fierce barrage of strikes, Buri forced Jokul's group back with broad sweeps of his axe.

Hook caught her eye, and a wordless understanding passed between them. They would take the left flank—perhaps if they attacked from both sides at once, as Peter harried the massive giant from above, they might finally sneak a blow or two past his defenses.

Charming darted upward as they charged, a tiny golden streak almost lost against the giant's massive frame.

The report of Hook's pistol cracked through the chamber. His aim was true—the enchanted bullet struck Buri's shoulder, drawing first blood in the battle. For a heartbeat, Wendy dared to hope. But even as she and Hook closed the distance, the wound began to heal, the blood slowing to a trickle and then stopping altogether.

Wendy's grip tightened on her elven blade. *At least he can be hurt,* she thought. *At least he can bleed.*

Then Buri's foot lashed out.

Hook tried to dodge it, parrying the kick with his sword, but the giant's speed and size were too overpowering. Buri's boot—as large as Hook's entire body—caught the captain squarely in the chest. The impact launched him backward as though he weighed nothing at all. He struck the arena's wall with a sickening crack and crumpled to the ground.

Wendy's heart lurched. She wanted desperately to check on him, to make sure he was still breathing, but Buri gave her no opportunity. The giant's attacking stomps forced her into a desperate dance of evasion, each massive foot threatening to crush her where she stood.

Above, Charming harried Buri's face, darting in over and over to strike at his eyes before spinning away, but the giant seemed to regard the innisfay as little more than an annoying insect.

"You see how futile this is?" Buri's voice boomed through the chamber as he pressed his attack. "You cannot hope to—"

Suddenly, Wendy was enveloped in complete darkness. Instinct drove her to the right—if she couldn't see, she didn't want to retreat straight back where Buri would expect her. After a few steps, she emerged from the lightless void that was already beginning to fade.

Her guess had been right. The ground trembled from the impact of Buri's massive foot, exactly where she would have been.

More ink-like patches bloomed throughout the chamber. Between them, Wendy caught glimpses of Shadow herself, appearing and vanishing so quickly it was impossible to track her movements. The shade engaged Peter in a brief whirlwind of exchanges before dissolving into another dark pool, leaving Peter to spin and dodge Buri's renewed assault.

Hook appeared at Wendy's side, moving with a slight limp but otherwise whole. Together, they barely managed to parry a sweeping blow from Buri's club—the impact nearly driving them to their knees.

Shadow had turned the tide in Buri's favor. By keeping Peter occupied, she had freed the giant to focus more of his attention on the rest of them.

Wendy stole a glance toward the others. The sight made her blood run cold. Vegard was on his knees, blood streaming from a gash across his forehead. Tigerlilja and Jokul fought desperately to protect him, their blades flashing as they did their best to hold Buri at bay.

Then, Shadow's darkness enveloped all three of them.

*No.* Wendy's heart clenched. With their vision completely blocked, they would be helpless against Buri's next attack. The giant would crush Vegard where he knelt.

But in the next instant, something changed. Buri took a step backward, his massive form shifting into a defensive stance for the first time since the battle began. Wendy's eyes darted to Peter and found the source of Buri's sudden caution.

Peter had abandoned all pretense of self-preservation. He drove himself at Buri with a fury Wendy had never imagined possible, his attacks coming so rapidly that the air itself seemed to cry out in protest. Where before he had been water, flowing from one strike to the next, now he was lightning—brutal, relentless, impossible to predict or counter.

Hook's sharp intake of breath told Wendy he saw it too. Peter was accessing a level of power she hadn't known he possessed, but the cost was written in every line of his body. He couldn't maintain this pace for long.

Lucky for them, the shadows that had been hampering their efforts worked to their advantage now—Shadow seemed unable to manifest them quickly enough to interfere with Peter's onslaught. For a few precious moments, they had the upper hand.

For the first time, Wendy saw something like concern flash across Buri's ancient features. The giant's axe and club moved with increasing desperation as Peter's attacks found their mark again and again—small cuts appearing on Buri's massive arms and chest, healing almost instantly but clearly taking their toll.

Jokul managed to wound him as well, striking a blow that sent frost racing up the giant's calf. In the next instant, both Tigerlilja and Vegard landed hits of their own. But the wounds sealed themselves almost as quickly as they appeared.

Buri let out a sound that Wendy first took for another battle cry—until she saw what had caused it. While the giant had been distracted by Peter's fury, Jokul had struck a savage blow, opening a deep gash in Buri's leg. The wound bled freely, and though it began to heal like all the others, the process seemed slower this time.

The giant turned his rage on the frost king and his companions with renewed vigor. But something had changed in the way he moved. His attacks, though still blindingly fast, had lost some of their fluid grace. He was favoring his wounded leg ever so slightly.

*He's not invincible*, Wendy realized. *He can be hurt. Really hurt.*

She had only a heartbeat to savor that revelation before everything went wrong.

Peter's rampage had taken him too close, left him exposed for a fraction of a second too long. Buri's club caught him square in the chest with a sound like thunder. The everlost crashed to the stone floor with such force that his wings crumpled beneath him, and he lay motionless in a broken heap.

"Peter!" Wendy's cry echoed through the chamber. She started toward him, but Hook's hand closed around her arm, yanking her back just as Buri's axe whistled through the space where she would have been.

Movement flickered at the edge of her vision. A winged figure standing over Peter's crumpled body.

Even from this distance, she would know that silhouette anywhere.

*Blackheart!*

He must have been watching from an alcove, or perhaps one of the many tunnels that led into the arena seating, just waiting for his chance.

Now, Mortimer Black stood over Peter, his saber glinting in the torchlight. "I'll cut out your heart—it's what I've always hated most about you." His voice carried easily across the sands. "I'll gift it to Buri, and Neverland will be mine."

Peter lay unmoving at Blackheart's feet. With a casual motion, he shoved his boot against Peter's shoulder, rolling him onto his back. Then, he raised his saber high over his head and plunged it toward the everlost's chest.

Wendy didn't remember deciding to move. One moment she was watching in horror, and the next she was flying through the air, driving her shoulder into Mortimer's back. They went down in a tangle of limbs, rolling across the sand.

As Wendy regained her feet, she noticed that Hook hadn't followed her past the reach of Buri's weapons. He had stayed behind, trying to press whatever advantage he could find against the giant, keeping him occupied.

When her eyes met Mortimer's, she saw nothing there but pure hatred.

"Wendy Darling." He spat the words like poison.

"Mortimer." She kept her voice steady, though her heart was racing. "Why would you want to hurt someone who has given you so much? Your ship. Your crew. A home here in Neverland. I don't understand."

His face twisted into a snarl. "There's no one to save you this time, Wendy. I'm going to teach you your place, once and for all." He took a step forward, his knuckles white around the grip of his saber. "You're just a little orphan girl whose luck has finally run out. And I'm going to give you what you deserve."

Before Wendy could respond, he charged. The attack caught her by surprise, though it shouldn't have. He had the speed and strength of an everlost now, and he was pouring every ounce of his hatred into each new swing of his blade.

Why did he hate her so much? He had called her an orphan, but so was he. They had grown up in the same almshouse together. What did he even mean? But she couldn't afford to be distracted. She pushed those thoughts away and let her training guide her, defending each blow by instinct.

He fought with such fury and recklessness that she was able to hold her own at first—thanks to years of diligent practice—but he was already wearing down her defenses.

Her sword arm ached, getting harder and harder to lift, until one of his attacks slipped through. Luckily, it only caught the pocket of her officer's coat, tearing the seam.

"Why ... are you ... doing this?" she managed between parries.

"Shut up, orphan girl."

"You keep calling me an orphan." Suddenly, Wendy had a thought so surprising she couldn't help blurting it out. "Wait, is Buri your father? Is that why you turned on everyone? On England, and on Peter?"

Mortimer's attack slowed, his eyes wary. "You were always such a strange girl. Always asking questions. It's like an affliction with you. Clearly, you haven't gotten any better. Why would you even ask that?"

"I found out who my mother was." Wendy kept her blade steady, watching for any opening. "Maybe that's what Neverland does for orphans. It helped Peter remember his. I thought, maybe you found your father too."

He lunged at her with such fury that Wendy stumbled back. "Of course, Neverland gave you a mother." He spat the words. "You wicked, horrible thing. I do what I want to get what I want. That's all that matters to me." He could have overpowered her easily, but he was too angry, too reckless. His attacks were broad and sweeping, signaling his intentions, giving her just enough time to respond—if only barely.

Finally, in his rage, Wendy saw her opening. He overcommitted, trying to run his sword straight through her, and she sidestepped the thrust just in time. She caught his blade between the blade and basket of her own weapon, sliding down the length of it and wrenching it from his hand.

As his sword flew across the sand, Wendy braced herself for his next move. But instead of charging her or diving for his weapon, Mortimer Black crumpled to his knees. His shoulders began

to shake, and long, keening cries escaped his throat—agonized, wracking sobs from somewhere deep and broken inside him.

"Just a poor orphan boy," he wheezed between gasps. "No mother ... no one ever wanted ..." The words dissolved into unintelligible mumbling, his hands clutching at his hair.

Wendy's grip loosened on her sword. Finally, in that moment, she saw the boy she had known at the almshouse—a boy who lived in pain, who would rather seem surly than risk being rejected. Maybe that's all his cruelty had ever been—a wall, built brick by brick around a heart that had been broken too many times.

He crawled away from her on his hands and knees, dragging himself toward the grand entrance hall rather than his fallen weapon, and Wendy turned toward Peter's crumpled form, desperate to know if he still breathed.

"Wendy!"

Hook's bellow snapped her head around. Mortimer was on his feet, no trace of tears on his face, his lips twisted in a feral grin. The pistol in his hand gleamed in the torchlight as he leveled it at her head.

In that frozen moment, as she stared down the barrel, Wendy saw the truth of him at last. There was nothing left of the boy she had once known—only an endless void of hatred, as deep and dark as the space between the stars. He had deliberately chosen evil, again and again, until it had consumed him entirely.

The pistol's report echoed through the chamber, and Wendy understood, through an infinite wave of sorrow, that his was the last face she was ever going to see.

# CHAPTER
# 63

Hurtling toward Buri's fortress-city, with Blackheart's fleet in hot pursuit, Charlie raced to assess the chaos unfolding below. The dullahans had broken through the outer gate and charged ahead, rotting several trolls and at least one ogre into oblivion along the way.

But the city's defenses were far from breached. Dozens of thick walls rose one after another in vast, concentric rings, protecting the inner citadel.

Even now, the dullahans' mounts pawed and reared at the second gate, their riders' auras slowly bringing the stout wood to ruin while Buri's army of monstrosities swarmed in behind them.

A giant wrenched what was left of the outer gate away from the wall and hurled it at the dullahans, but their cloaks swarmed out to intercept it, smashing it to the ground. An ogre stepped toward them, raising its club for a vicious swing, only to stagger back, screaming in pain, the stump of its right foot dragging a wide swath of blood across the street.

"Hard to starboard," Charlie ordered, his voice carrying across the deck. "Circle around those dullahans. We need to get behind them."

The *Pegasus* heeled over smoothly as Charlie guided her in a sweeping arc. He kept the turn wide and obvious, making sure the rest of the fleet could see his intention and follow.

If he could put the dullahans between them, Blackheart's ships might not recognize the danger from below. Besides which, Buri's ground forces would be forced to split their attention between the dullahans on the ground and the aerial threat from the fleet.

The elven ships were the first to understand his intention. They flew in tighter paths, coming around fast and low, their archers launching volleys of arrows into the confused mass of Buri's forces. Curly's everlost followed suit, pulling the same stunt they had at the lagoon to fire a broadside straight down at the front lines.

Even the *Ravenhawk*, flown by Mr. Starkey, and the *Jolly Roger*, under Gerdrek's command, fired their cannons into the fray. They couldn't achieve the same daring angle as the everlost, but the explosions added to the chaos, sending some of Buri's forces racing in the wrong direction.

The enemy troops scattered in disarray, caught by surprise between the dullahans below and the unexpected assault from above. But they weren't entirely helpless. The giants among their ranks began returning fire, hurling massive chunks of debris at the passing ships.

Charlie's eyes widened as a boulder the size of a longboat whistled past the bow of the *Pegasus*. The giants' strength was impressive—they could easily match the range of the ships' cannons.

He slid the ship to starboard as hard as he could, fighting against the keel's resistance. As he did, two griffins launched into the air. One snatched a smaller chunk of stone right out of the sky, preventing it from punching through the mainsail of the *Peg-*

*asus.* The other dove toward the giant that had thrown it, clawing viciously at its head.

And *that* was when the frost-folk arrived.

Through the chaos of battle, Jokul's warriors poured through the ruined outer gate. The dullahans' trails of decay hadn't lingered on the ground—not with the cold stone of the city beneath their feet—leaving an exposed, gaping hole in the wall.

The frost-folk moved with deadly grace, their weapons, horns, and claws gleaming as they engaged Buri's forces. Behind them came the Viking ground forces and Sir Galahault's mechanical knights, their combined battle cries echoing off the stone walls as they carved paths of destruction through the enemy ranks.

From his vantage point aboard the *Pegasus*, Charlie could only catch glimpses of the ground battle through gaps in the smoke—brief flashes of steel, bursts of magic, the occasional giant toppling into a building. But the effect was clear enough. Buri's forces scattered in all directions, their formations crumbling as they faced threats from both above and below.

A flicker of movement caught Charlie's attention. He whirled in a surge of adrenaline, expecting to see Blackheart's pursuing fleet. Instead, he found himself squinting at a massive swarm of ... dragonflies?

Charlie raised his spyglass, and a fleeting smile touched his lips. Thomas, Loamly, and Erikson flew at the heart of a glittering cloud of innisfay. He should have known the Royal Society fellow would find a way to survive.

The tiny creatures darted and swooped around them in complex patterns, their golden light reflecting off Thomas's bronze feet and Loamly's metallic wings.

But Charlie's smile died as quickly as it had formed. Behind them, just visible through his spyglass, loomed the dark shapes of Blackheart's fleet, gaining all too quickly.

"We need more chaos," Charlie muttered. Then, louder: "All hands to stations! Target the gates!"

It was a risky move. Positioning the *Pegasus* for a clear shot at the gates would put them well within range of the giants' improvised artillery. But they needed to press their advantage.

"Not the dullahans—the gates!" Charlie ordered as the gun crews prepared to fire. "We want those gates down, now!"

The guns roared to life, their shots punching through the already-weakened wood. As the second set of gates collapsed, Charlie could see the other ships following his lead. The *Ravenhawk* and *Jolly Roger* moved to engage the giants, providing cover while the *Pegasus* lined up its next shot.

A knot formed in Charlie's stomach as the dullahans advanced through the breach. Every gate that fell brought those horrors another step closer to Wendy. His greatest and truest friend was somewhere in that fortress, and at least one of these creatures would stop at nothing until it had claimed her life.

But the plan demanded chaos, and the dullahans were their best way to create it. Any hesitation would only betray Wendy's trust.

Charlie tightened his grip on the ship's trinket, silently vowing that he would find a way to destroy the dullahans himself, if it came to that. They would not touch her—not while he lived.

"Next gate!" he shouted. "Make ready!"

Before the *Pegasus* could fire again, one of the elven ships took a direct hit. A massive chunk of masonry caught it square in the stern, sending the vessel into a spinning dive. More debris followed—stones, broken beams, anything the giants could get their hands on—and Charlie watched helplessly as the ship crashed into the streets below.

Out of the corner of his eye, Charlie caught a flash of movement—something human-shaped arcing through the air. He blinked, certain he must have imagined it. But no, there it was

again: a draugr, its dead flesh bloated and grey, hurled skyward by what looked like a massive catapult.

Another followed. And another.

"They're launching draugar onto the ships!" Charlie shouted, his voice cutting through the chaos of battle. "Do not try to burn them! Force them overboard if you can!"

Even as he gave the order, one of the undead monstrosities crashed onto the deck of the *Pegasus.* It grew as it rose, its limbs reaching and stretching until it had doubled in size. The crew moved to engage it, pushing at it with long poles and harpoons, but one man strayed too close. The draugr grabbed him, picked him up by his waist, and tossed him overboard.

A flash of brown and gold heralded another one—but no, that was Michael, arriving on Chirpy's back.

"You dropped something," Michael said with a grin.

Chirpy held the fallen crewman in one of her rear paws, depositing the trembling man gently on the deck. Her cargo delivered, she hurled herself at the draugr, lifted him off his feet with her shoulder, and shoved him over the railing.

"Michael!" Charlie called out. "Tell the archers to use the fire fairies. Destroy the catapults on the ground. If those draugar start getting onto the ships, we won't have a chance."

The griffin rider saluted, and Chirpy leaped back into the air.

Moments later, a volley of Viking arrows exploded into flames, the spreading blaze adding to the confusion below. Smoke billowed up from a dozen places where the fire had found purchase.

As Blackheart's ships drew within firing range, Charlie realized the smoke might give his forces an advantage—at least for a while. Natural cover was hard to come by in an aerial battle, but this ... this they could use.

His attention snapped back to the sky as their young dragon streaked past, engaging one of Blackheart's beasts. It might not

have been as big as Snaggleclaw, but it was still nearly as large as the elven ships—and seemed to be holding its own. If it could keep one of the enemy dragons occupied, that would be one less source of flame they'd have to worry about.

Just then, Thomas and his group shot across the deck and dove into the fray below, disappearing into the smoke, no doubt heading to join Sir Galahault's mechanical knights. Charlie smiled grimly. Thomas had clearly fallen in love with the Library—it only made sense he'd seek them out.

As he tried in vain to see which way they'd gone, another flash of motion caught his eye. At first, he thought he was seeing a school of flying fish, which, he decided, wouldn't have been the strangest thing he'd witnessed today.

But as the shapes grew larger, he realized he hadn't been quite as wrong as he had assumed.

Whales. Dozens of them, their massive bodies suspended impossibly in the air, trailing streams of water that caught the eternal morning light.

Dolphins and porpoises darted between them, their leaps and spins deadly serious as they arrowed through the sky. Some of them seemed to have grown their own wings, while others were simply defying gravity, clearly under the influence of innisfay dust.

And with them came the rest of the innisfay, their golden light reflecting off wet scales, turning each individual droplet into a flashing prism.

The school of sea creatures—or was it a pod? a herd? a turmoil?—broke toward Blackheart's dragons without hesitation.

Charlie's mind reeled as the largest whale—some species he'd never seen before—opened its enormous maw and expelled not water, but what looked like a living wave. The water wrapped around the nearest dragon like a fist, constricting tighter and tighter as the beast thrashed in its grip.

"Hard to port!" Charlie ordered. As much as he wanted to stay and watch, there wasn't time. The enemy fleet had arrived, flying high over the dullahans, unhindered by their presence. "Fire a volley, then prepare to dive!"

Using the smoke for cover, he would do his best to draw Blackheart's ships within range of the nightmare riders below.

But as Charlie surveyed the approaching armada of ships and bat-riders, his heart sank. Despite all of his reinforcements, his allied forces were still far outnumbered. They couldn't win the battle—it simply wasn't possible.

All they could do—all they could even hope for—was to buy enough time for Wendy and the others to win the war.

*Godspeed, Wendy. May you know in your heart, for as long as you live, that I have no regrets.*

This was Charlie's final thought as he took a deep breath, then dove toward the nightmare that awaited him below.

For an impossibly long instant, Wendy stood rooted in place, expecting Mortimer's shot to smash through her skull and end her life.

Each heartbeat slowed and stretched to eternity as she took in every detail. The dark barrel of the pistol, aimed at her head. The cruel curve of his smile flickering in the torchlight.

But then his eyes opened wide, a look of utter shock wiping the sneer from his lips. A red flower of blood blossomed across his shirt, spreading through the white fabric over his heart, and the pistol slipped from his fingers.

It struck the sand with a soft thud of finality.

His expression changed again, from shock to dawning horror, as the silver worked its magic in his heart. His body didn't even have time to fall. He looked down at his own chest, at the hole that spread wider and faster by the moment, his body disintegrating from the inside out into a billion tiny embers.

Mortimer Black glanced back at Wendy, his expression impossible to read, and then that, too, broke apart into nothing. The embers of his everlost body glowed briefly, falling gently toward the sand, and then winked out—a sudden emptiness racing through them all, from one to the next, until he was gone.

As though released from a spell, Wendy whirled to see Hook holding a pistol in his good left hand, a thin trail of smoke still curling from the barrel.

The shot she'd heard was his, not Mortimer's. He had saved her life with the same casual precision he brought to everything else. Recognizing her attention, he caught her gaze and nodded, but that was all the acknowledgment he had time for.

He re-holstered his pistol, dove to his left, rolled, and burst to his feet with his sword in his grip as Buri's massive club whistled through the air, slamming into the ground where Hook had been standing a heartbeat before.

A moment of sorrow flashed through Wendy's mind—not for Mortimer as he was now, but for the boy she had once known and the man she wished he could have become. One who might have been saved from his own anger. From his own choices.

But she let the moment pass, accepting the truth—he had chosen his path as surely as she had chosen hers. Peter had given him plenty of opportunities to reinvent himself, to become anything but this vessel of hatred.

*Peter.*

Wendy rushed to Peter's side. He was still lying on the sand, only just now starting to come to. He was clearly battered from Buri's blow, but he gave her a reassuring smile as she helped him to his feet.

*When has Peter ever needed me to help him to his feet?*

Before she could finish the thought, his wings spread wide and he launched himself into the air, charging back into battle.

And there, at his side, was Tink, her golden light illuminating his cheek in a warm glow.

*Wait ... Tink? Where did she come from?*

Wendy turned to see the doors to the great hall standing open, the armored clay statues lumbering into the room, their weapons gleaming in the torchlight.

Clearly, Vegard had seen them too. He charged toward the clay warriors, determined to cut them off, but he couldn't hold them alone. Something had changed—their movements were quicker now, more focused, as though Buri's proximity had imbued them with a deeper malevolence.

A sharper cunning.

In an instant, Tigerlilja and Jokul were at his side, their blades flashing. The Vikings slashed at the legs of the closest one while Jokul fell on it in a fury, severing its limbs and kicking them aside before taking its head.

But another was already stepping in to take its place. It strode forward, ignoring their strikes, focusing instead on shouldering its way into the arena to clear the doorway behind it.

To clear the choke point and let its companions fan out.

Wendy's heart leaped into her throat. Buri already had the upper hand. If they had to contend with the golems at the same time, what chance did they have?

"Shadow, now!" Peter's voice rang through the chamber. "Everyone, get back! As far as you can!"

Jokul, Vegard, and Tigerlilja were already at the arena's entrance, as far from Buri as they could get. But Wendy had ended up behind him. She sprinted away, heading for the far wall with Hook on her heels, then spun—only to take a staggering step backward and fall to her knees.

A pool of shadow had opened up on the sand between the giant and the arena's grand entrance, and a dullahan materialized from the darkness.

The stench of putrefying magic hit Wendy the moment the creature appeared, making her want to retch. Its rotting mount pawed at the ground. Its cloak of insects writhed and shifted, and its empty hood turned toward her.

Wendy braced for the inevitable wave of hopelessness, waiting for it to crash through her, but then Shadow appeared. Her ephemeral form rose from the ink-black pool to stand beside the nightmare, impossibly close, her elbow almost touching the rider's knee.

The creature's empty gaze turned toward her, and Shadow spoke, pointing at the giant, her voice carrying easily through the silence that had fallen across them all.

"His name is Buri."

The dullahan answered in a whisper: *Buri.*

Wendy's blood ran cold. The name filled the hollows of her mind, less a sound and more the absence of one—the space left behind when hope dies.

For a moment, Shadow dropped to her knees, unintentionally mirroring Wendy, the proximity of such concentrated entropy nearly overwhelming her. But then she surged to her feet, disappearing as the dullahan locked its gaze on its quarry.

Wendy watched, transfixed, as the rotting monstrosity drew a sword from beneath its cloak and moved inexorably toward the ancient giant.

At first, Buri seemed unable to process what was happening, making no move to escape the dullahan's presence or deflect its blows. Perhaps he couldn't believe that one of his own weapons

would turn against him, or perhaps he simply thought himself invincible. But everywhere the dullahan's corroded blade touched him, gaping wounds appeared, rotting inward from the edges faster than his immortal flesh could heal.

Wendy dug her hands into the sand between her knees, clenching it tightly in her fists, but then she rose in a single motion, hurling the sand to the ground, brushing off her palms, and grabbing a pistol from its holster.

She started to reload it, fishing in the leather pouch for Jokul's precious magical ammunition—at least she could fire at Buri from a distance. A few yards away, Hook's weapon discharged, and she realized he'd had the same thought.

Their shots might not kill the giant, but maybe they could at least slow him down, adding to the damage as the dullahan overloaded his ability to heal.

By now, Buri had finally started fighting back, but each swing of his massive club was deflected by the dullahan's cloak of insects. What would happen if he finally dropped the useless weapon? Would he pick up the dullahan in his bare hands? Could he?

A horrifying image passed through Wendy's mind as she imagined Buri lifting the dullahan from its mount and hurling it toward them.

With a shudder, she shook her head, trying desperately to clear it, as though the very idea of it might manifest that reality.

But that wasn't what happened at all.

As Buri raised both weapons high in the air, preparing to bring them down on the dullahan's empty hood, Peter flew up to the giant's face, gripped his sword in both hands, and drove it deep into Buri's left eye with a primal scream, sinking the blade to the hilt.

The giant had been too focused on the dullahan to see it coming.

Buri dropped to his knees with such force that the entire chamber shook, sending waves through the sand beneath their feet. His

weapons fell from his hands as his remaining eye fixed on Peter in an expression of disbelief, and then he stilled—as motionless now as the stone portal behind him.

Wendy expelled the breath she hadn't even realized she had been holding, releasing it explosively through her cheeks.

And the dullahan turned slowly, inexorably, toward her.

It took one slow, calculating step, and then Peter wrenched his sword from Buri's eye to fall upon it, flying back and forth through its decay field to rain blow after blow upon its shoulders.

Even at this distance, Wendy could see the excruciating agony etched across his face. But more than that, she could feel the terrible clash of magic between the two titans—the dullahan's death-touched aura surging into him, trying to rot Peter's form into oblivion, while Neverland's magic flooded through him in a torrent, trying desperately to keep him alive.

Through her siren senses, she understood what Peter was truly risking—if the fight continued much longer, the dullahan would drain every ounce of Neverland's magic away.

"Peter, no!" But her plea fell on deaf ears.

His sword flashed again and again, the swarm of insects absorbing every strike. Despite everything, despite their victory over Buri, Neverland was still going to fall—and Peter with it.

A cry of agony tore from his throat.

Calling his sister back from the darkness.

A flash of *emptiness* ripped the seams of reality apart, and Shadow materialized beside the creature once again, backhanding her blade deep into a leather bag that hung at its side.

The dullahan's form wavered, the insects of its cloak scattering in every direction as the bag hit the sand.

A rotted head rolled out, Shadow's dark blade piercing it through.

"For Mother," she said quietly. "And Father."

She caught Peter's gaze, and the barest of smiles touched her lips.

But then a new movement caught Wendy's eye. Behind them, Buri had begun to stir.

"Watch out!" Even as Wendy shouted, Shadow sprang into action.

"The poison!" Her cry echoed across the arena as she dashed toward the fallen giant.

*Poison?*

Wendy barely had time to wonder what that meant before Hook sprinted past her, his coat billowing behind him.

He pulled something from inside his jacket—a small glass vial that caught the torchlight, its contents black as pitch—tossing it to Shadow in a high arc that seemed to stretch forever.

But Shadow was already scaling the giant. She vaulted from his knee to catch his shoulder, hauled herself up with fluid grace, brought her feet between her hands, and leaped high over his head.

The vial met her in midair.

She snatched it from its trajectory, yanked the cork free with her teeth, and upended the contents into Buri's slack mouth. The giant's remaining eye flew wide as he swallowed by reflex.

For a heartbeat, nothing happened.

Then a creeping shade of gray spread across Buri's skin, starting at his throat and racing outward. Everywhere it touched, his flesh hardened, taking on the texture of rough stone.

His eye found Shadow, and his lips started to move, but whatever curse or revelation he meant to share was lost as the noxious potion turned his tongue to granite.

The ancient giant had become a statue, frozen forever in an expression of dawning horror.

# CHAPTER 65

Shadow returned to the sands of the arena, her form clear and sharp in the torchlight. She and Peter stood for a long moment, staring at the ancient giant.

He reached a tentative hand toward her shoulder, then pulled it back, uncertain. Finally, he let it fall, extending it casually instead, palm up, like a peace offering. "Thank you." His wings settled behind him with a whisper of feathers. "Sister."

She hesitated, scowling, but then she rolled her eyes and sighed. Slowly, she reached out and grasped his forearm—one warrior acknowledging another. "It's finished."

The moment stretched between them until Vegard cut through their reverie. "If the two of you are done congratulating each other, we could use a little help over here." He, Tigerlilja, and Jokul were still fully engaged with the clay statues, their weapons flashing in the torchlight.

Their blows were doing more damage than before, sinking deeper into the clay and pulling more of it away with each strike,

but the first golem had pushed far enough into the room to let the others start lumbering in. The heavy thud of their footsteps echoed across the arena.

Wendy closed her eyes and took a quick, deep breath.

She could still hardly believe it—Buri had been defeated. It felt like the fight should be over. Like they should all have the right to rest for a moment. Honestly, was that so much to ask? Her muscles ached with exhaustion.

But the fight wasn't over—not by a long shot. Beyond the golems, high above in the fortress-city, Neverland's combined forces were still locked in combat with Buri's minions. Charlie. John and Michael. The rest of the Fourteenth Platoon. The Vikings and the frost-folk.

They were all still counting on her.

She opened her eyes and took off racing across the sand.

Hook was already sprinting toward the statues, his coat billowing behind him as he charged. Wendy followed, not two steps behind him.

The arena was so large that it took them more than a few seconds to reach the fight. As they were still running, Tigerlilja's sword severed the ankle of the nearest one with a wet, sucking sound.

This time, the clay didn't flow back together. Instead, the creature's ankle slid right off its foot, the edges of the wound slick and clean.

Surprised, the massive figure wobbled on its severed limb, then toppled forward, crashing face-first into the sand with an impact that shook the floor. Together, Tigerlilja and Vegard chopped off its head, their blades meeting in the middle with a dull thunk.

Jokul's ice-touched blade carved through two more, leaving trails of frost that spread through their earthen bodies. When they fell, their forms shattered like ancient pottery, spreading across the sand in a spray of frozen shards.

Peter and Shadow fought together, their blades finding their marks again and again, moving in perfect synchronization. His wings caught the torchlight, scattering it in golden motes across the chamber, but wherever it touched his sister, her body devoured it—a living void that cut through the fabric of the world.

Three more clay warriors advanced toward them, weapons raised. Peter shot upward, drawing the attention of the closest one while Shadow dove between its legs, her blade taking out its knee. It stumbled forward, directly into the deadly arc of Peter's sword. The golem's head hit the sand with a wet splat, its body crumbling a moment later.

The next warrior swung its massive sword low, but Shadow vaulted over it. Their counterattack came from both sides at once—Peter's sword pierced the clay giant's throat as Shadow's blade found its chest. The third managed only one step before they reduced it to rubble.

Soon enough, the statues were all lying in ruins.

Charming swooped down to land on Wendy's shoulder as Tinker Bell settled on Peter's, her golden glow reflecting off his blade. The fairy shook her tiny fist at a fallen statue, and Peter laughed.

Wendy found herself standing beside Hook, both of them breathing hard. The exhaustion that had been gnawing at her edges now threatened to overwhelm her completely.

"We must return to the city." Tigerlilja planted her boot on a fallen warrior's chest and yanked her weapon free. "We need to help our people."

Hook glanced at Wendy. "There's another one of those riders up there, and it's still hunting Captain Darling. For all we know, the godforsaken thing could be halfway through the fortress already."

"It's still out there, yes. I can feel it." Wendy steadied her breathing and opened her mind, letting the cold sense of dread

seep through her awareness. "But it isn't very close. Not yet, anyway."

"You'd best be ready to fly. As soon as we find a window, take to the air. You and ..." Hook hesitated for a heartbeat, then added, "Peter."

Wendy blinked, but Tigerlilja was already nodding.

"Once you're out, head for the sea beyond the docks. That should keep the dullahan out of our way." The Viking leader turned to Shadow. "Do you think you can defeat another one?"

"I can try. But make no mistake—their touch is just as dangerous to me as it is to anyone else. I'm just harder to kill than most." Shadow's form blurred, then came back into focus. "Even if I decide to help, I fight for Neverland, not for you."

"I'm not exactly dying for a hug from you either." Tigerlilja wiped the clay from her blade with quick, efficient strokes. "But you have my thanks for what you've done here. If you can kill the last of the dullahans, at least Neverland itself should be safe."

Shadow nodded, once, the slight gesture barely visible.

Tigerlilja turned to Jokul and Peter. "If Shadow falls, it will be up to you to finish it. You're the only ones who have a hope of getting close enough."

Their plan set, they raced toward the battle above, winding through the endless labyrinth of Buri's fortress.

When they finally found a suitable window, the full scope of the conflict was laid bare—long swaths of the city burning, battles raging in the streets, the air thick with smoke and projectiles. Combatants of every shape and size filled the sky. But throughout the chaos, one thing was certain—far more of Buri's forces remained than their own.

Taking a deep breath, Wendy nodded to Peter. Together with Charming and Tinker Bell, they took to the air, heading toward the docks and away from the main battle. Wendy kept glancing

over her shoulder, trying to locate the dullahan. At first, its presence seemed to be moving away from her, but then she sensed it approaching again, traveling in a wide arc.

When their small group reached the harbor, they flew out over the water, hovering high enough and far enough from the docks to be away from the dullahan's effects, but close enough to see it when it emerged from the city.

When the creature finally appeared, it urged its nightmare steed as far out onto the dock as it could manage. Its empty hood tilted upward, fixing on Wendy's position, and one skeletal hand rose to point at her.

The plan, of course, was to wait for the others. But the moment that terrible evil pointed a cruel finger at Wendy Darling, Peter shot at it from the sky, speeding toward the dock with reckless abandon.

"Peter, wait!" Wendy's cry rang out across the harbor.

She had seen what fighting the first dullahan had done to him—how its death-magic had nearly killed him and Neverland with him.

But he showed no sign of slowing.

He dove toward the water, picking up speed, then opened his arms wide, pulling out of the dive at the last possible moment to race across the surface, skimming his fingers over the shallow waves of the harbor, one after the other. As he neared the dock, he uttered a blood-curdling roar, drew his sword, and shouted, "Now!"

An enormous wave erupted from the harbor.

Wendy's heart caught in her throat as the water twisted and shifted, wrapping itself around the dullahan and forcing its aura of decay back into its own body. *Undine*, she realized—he must have ended up in the harbor during the battle with the fleet.

As the dullahan struggled against the water elemental's grasp, Peter dove straight for it, driving his sword through the leather sack at its hip. The bag split open, spilling its rotting con-

tents into the sea, and the creature's cloak of insects scattered in every direction.

At last, Wendy was free.

And yet, the pressing weight of hopelessness and despair hadn't left her.

From her high vantage point, she could still see the battle raging across the city. Elven ships took damage from boulders flung by giants. Flying frost-deer tried desperately to gore a wyvern easily twenty times their size. A dragon unleashed a torrent of fire into the streets below.

Some small part of her had been clinging to the belief that killing the dullahan would finally break Buri's hold on the legions of forces he had turned to his will, but the fighting continued unabated.

Wendy flew down to land beside Peter on the dock, where Undine's waters had rendered it safe. The water elemental towered over them both, his grim expression matching her own.

"Thank you," she said, but Undine made no reply.

The high wall of the fortress blocked most of the battle from view now, but she could still hear it—the clash of steel, the roar of magical creatures, the thunder of falling debris.

Finally, Hook and the others emerged from the smoke billowing out from the city. They looked utterly spent, all of them coughing and gasping for air—all except Shadow, who had disappeared again.

"The nightmare rider?" Hook managed between spasms.

"Peter killed it, with Undine's help." Wendy glanced back toward the sounds of battle. "But it didn't make any difference. Buri's forces are still fighting."

"It's only to be expected." Jokul's voice carried a familiar bitterness. "The creatures Buri brought here are even worse than men."

Tigerlilja cleared her throat loudly.

"Not all men are monsters," Jokul conceded. "But the humans who hunted us and drove us from our homes held only hatred in their hearts."

Before Tigerlilja could reply, Undine snorted, sending a fine mist of saltwater into the air. They all turned to him.

"Buri told them only the fay could use magic." His voice rumbled and shook, reminding Wendy of storm-wrought waves crashing against the shore. "It was a lie, of course, calculated to prey on their fear. In truth, magic flows to all who believe. But humanity believed the lie—they believed they could not, and so, they could not. From there, the rift only deepened, breeding mistrust, and, eventually, hatred."

"That's terrible!" Wendy blurted out, her hands clenching into fists. "Then Buri's lied to everyone—to us *and* to them. Heaven only knows what he told his people about Neverland. They're killing each other over nothing!"

"They would not be the first." Undine's massive form shifted, scattering the golden rays of the early morning light. "But perhaps it is not too late. Tell them the truth. Once they know, they may not be so eager to risk their lives in this war."

"But I need something I can do *now*." The words burst from her throat, raw with frustration.

"Yes, now." His eyes glittered in their depths. "Speak to them, siren. When the dullahan whispered your name, you did not need to be close to hear it. Nor do they need to be close to you." Undine gestured toward the city with a wide sweep of his arm.

As if to punctuate his words, the *Pegasus* came into view over the high wall of the fortress. Roughly half her keel had been smashed away—by what, Wendy couldn't tell. But the blackened char along her port flank suggested dragon fire.

"Go." Undine's form began to sink back into the harbor. "Join your friends. The battle rages on. We must finish it—one way or another."

Wendy turned to Hook, then Tigerlilja. "Wait here. I'll tell them to come down and get everyone." She rose into the air, heading for the *Pegasus*, and Peter was at her side in an instant.

Reaching the deck, she found Charlie at the helm, his face streaked with soot and blood. Despite what he had clearly been through, relief washed over his features the moment he saw her.

"That dullahan started galloping around the outer ring of the city," he told her. "I was terrified it would reach you before we did. Are you all right?"

The hint of a smile touched her lips. "It's gone. Peter and Undine killed it, and Shadow killed the other. We defeated Buri too—turned him to stone."

Charlie's face lit up in a huge grin. "Then we've done it!"

But Wendy only sighed. "Have we, though?" She looked out over the carnage, and that's when she saw it. Bursting through the smoke below, a huge dragon bore down on the *Pegasus*, already preparing to unleash its fire.

It happened in an instant.

The world around her slowed as the dragon sped toward Charlie, opening its terrible maw. He didn't even see it coming. He was still turning to follow her gaze as the fire grew in its throat, as Peter grabbed her by the waist to fly her away to safety.

In that terrible moment, every fiber of Wendy's body, heart, and soul were suddenly focused on a single, burning desire.

She had wanted nothing more in all her life.

To have come this far only to lose Charlie—now, after they had finally defeated Buri and Neverland was supposed to be safe ...

No.

*No!*

The word was not a word. Wendy's cry swept over the city, not as a shout but as a wave of raw intent that burst from her very core. And with it, a message.

*Stop. Buri and Blackheart are gone. You are free, and Neverland is safe—with plenty of magic for everyone. What you do now is up to you. Go. Live in peace. Don't lay down your life for nothing.*

For one perfect, eternal moment, Wendy was everywhere.

She was with the Viking archers, their fingers releasing bowstrings toward the giants below. And with the giants, hurling boulders at the tiny figures that dared to attack them. She was with elven crews firing on wyverns, and with wyverns diving toward frost-folk deer. With deer lowering their antlers at giant bats, and with bats screaming toward Viking archers.

Wendy felt them all, and they all felt her.

They all *heard* her.

And then she was herself again, standing on the deck of the *Pegasus*, watching as the massive dragon rolled down and away, continuing out over the sea without a backward glance.

Behind it, the rest of Buri's flying creatures slowed and turned, scattering to the four winds, followed by Blackheart's ships.

Many of the creatures on the ground simply sat where they were, as though waking from a dream. Others fled into the depths of the city's countless alleyways, but there was no malice left in their retreat, only the simple desire to hide or to find their way out. To search for a better place—a place where they might belong.

As that desire grew, Wendy felt the magic of Neverland surge back to life, stronger than ever, answering the call.

She felt it raising mountains for wyverns, riddled with enormous caves for giant bats. She sensed a new, sprawling delta choked with rivers and bridges for trolls, and a monstrous forest with towering cliffs for giants.

The battle for Neverland was over, and Neverland itself had won.

After all, Wendy thought, who in their right mind would destroy such a gift—a world that provided so much for so many, asking nothing in return.

CHAPTER

# 66

Wendy sat in the captain's quarters of the *Jolly Roger*, carefully threading her needle through the torn pocket of her officer's coat. The damage wasn't terrible—just a clean slice where Mortimer's blade had caught the fabric.

She could have left the task for later, she supposed, but there was something comforting about the familiar motion of needle and thread, even as her heart felt like it might shatter.

Nana lay at her feet, her shaggy head resting on Wendy's boots. The dog's steady presence anchored her, as it had so many times before. (As for Nana, she wasn't sure why Wendy had left her behind with the village children during such an important battle, but the moment her mistress had returned unscathed, the dog had immediately forgiven the oversight.)

On the desk beside the coat, Charming stood watch, his tiny form casting a warm golden glow across the blue wool.

The needle trembled slightly in her fingers as she worked. If she returned to England, she would never see Peter again. The

391

thought alone made her chest ache. She would lose Charming too, and all the wonders of Neverland—the merfolk and their songs, the great whales that swam through air as easily as water, the endless horizons waiting to be explored.

But if she stayed …

Her throat tightened. She would never again see Hook's knowing smirk or hear Charlie's quiet laugh. John and Michael would return to England without her. She would lose Olaudah Equiano, who had believed in her dreams when no one else would. Even the smaller losses felt overwhelming—Colin's cheerful greetings, Antoine Dumas's stories of France, Mrs. Medcalf's scones over afternoon tea, even Mrs. Healey's kind smile as she pressed another borrowed book into Wendy's eager hands.

A tear splashed onto the coat as she finished the last stitch, and Wendy brushed it away before it could stain the wool. Charming chimed softly—a gentle cascade of bells that somehow managed to convey both sympathy and encouragement. The sound only made her eyes burn more fiercely.

A knock at the door startled her. "It's time," Charlie called.

Together, they made their way through the village. All around them, celebrations were in full swing—frost-folk sang with Vikings while imps danced around bonfires, sharing drinks with the everlost and trading battle stories. Their laughter filled the air, a joyous cacophony that felt oddly distant to Wendy's ears.

But when they reached the great hall, a hush had fallen over the small group within. Peter and Tinker Bell waited near the hearth, while Hook and Thomas stood quietly by the far wall. Vegard, Tiger-lilja, and Jokul were already seated at the long table, their faces solemn in the firelight.

Wendy hesitated for a moment before taking her place beside Hook. Charlie settled next to her, his shoulder brushing hers in silent support.

At the head of the table, Tigerlilja raised her cup. "To victory."

They all lifted their glasses, but the toast felt hollow. Neverland was safe now, and England too. They had earned everything they'd fought for, but Wendy's heart felt heavier than ever.

She couldn't delay the choice any longer. The portal would close forever, splitting her world in two, and she would have to decide which half to keep.

The silence stretched among them, broken only by the crackle of the fire. Finally, Jokul and Hook both stirred.

"I—" Jokul began.

"We—" Hook started.

They looked at each other, and Jokul gestured for Hook to continue.

"We're preparing to leave." Hook refused to meet Wendy's gaze, his voice carefully neutral. "Thank you for the rations. My crew is loading them now."

"Of course." Tigerlilja's response was equally measured.

They both turned to Jokul, waiting to hear what he had intended to say.

The frost king's pale eyes swept across the gathered company. "I just wanted to thank you. For your service." He paused, choosing his words with care. "I know you had your own interests here, but still. What you've done for Neverland will not be forgotten."

"Do you think—" Wendy began hesitantly, but Hook cut her off.

"No." His voice was gentle but firm. "I know what you're thinking. Believe it or not, I've thought about it too. But Frost is right. The portal needs to be closed. Our worlds aren't ready for each other."

Jokul nodded solemnly.

Thomas shifted in his seat, looking down at his legs. "I suppose I shouldn't bring these back either." The firelight caught the bronze of his feet, casting strange reflections across the floor.

Hook turned to Jokul. "Perhaps Neverland might have room for just two more humans, don't you think? Especially one who's part fay and one who's part—" He glanced at Thomas. "You said that's an elven alloy, yes?"

Hope flickered across Thomas's face. "That's right."

"Part elf, then." Hook's words carried the weight of careful diplomacy.

A small smile touched Jokul's lips. "I believe we could make such an exception."

"Really?" Thomas straightened. "Do you mean it?"

"Sir Galahault would no doubt be glad to have your company at the Library."

"You would be welcome here in the village, as well," Tigerlilja added. "I had no idea what we were going to do with an alchemy workshop anyway, to be honest."

Thomas's face lit up. "Oh, that's wonderful! Would it be all right if I went to tell Loamy and Erikson?"

"I'm sure they would like that very much." Tigerlilja's smile was warm with understanding.

Thomas practically leaped from his seat and rushed from the hall.

Hook pushed his chair back with a quiet scrape. "I believe that's our cue. Best not to overstay one's welcome."

"Go with them," Jokul said to Wendy. "At least through the portal. Then, make your choice. Either return to Neverland, or return to England."

Wendy nodded. Her eyes found Peter's across the table, but neither spoke.

Some things were beyond words.

Wendy stood on the deck of the *Pegasus*, staring down at the compass Peter had given her back in England. Its face glowed faintly in her palm—the same compass that had first guided her to Neverland, that had started her on this impossible journey.

She ran her thumb across its surface, lost in memory.

At the helm, Hook and Charlie prepared the ship for departure. John and Michael stood nearby with Nana sitting between them, the great dog's tail sweeping slowly across the deck.

A whisper of wings announced Peter's arrival. He landed beside her gently, almost reverently, his movements lacking their usual dramatic flair. When she looked up, his eyes held an expression she had never seen there before—something ancient and profound, as though he, too, were lost in his own quiet melancholy.

"Goodbye, the Wendy." His voice was soft but steady. "Whatever you choose, I'll never forget you. Even though it would make me very sad never to see you again."

"Oh, Peter." Her heart caught in her throat. "You really would remember, wouldn't you?"

He met her gaze without flinching. "I'm very sad already, just thinking about it. But I still haven't forgotten. I remember everything now—my mother, my father. I have them back because of you."

Wendy couldn't speak. She threw her arms around him instead, hugging him tight. He returned the embrace without hesitation, his wings folding around them both like a shield.

"I'll be waiting for you on this side of the portal," he whispered. "Just in case."

She could only nod, not trusting her voice. Peter squeezed her once more, then rose into the air.

Wendy couldn't bear to watch. She turned instead to Charlie, who met her miserable gaze with a silent nod, guiding the ship upward with steady hands.

Staring straight ahead, Wendy knew it the instant the sky changed. In one moment, they were sailing over Neverland. In the next, the ship had emerged over the familiar island in their own world. The cove where they had first found the *Pegasus* lay just behind them, its waters dark and still.

Charlie brought the ship down gently, letting her settle into the sea with barely a ripple. Hook held out his hand, and Charlie passed him the ship's trinket. But instead of pocketing it, Hook extended it to Wendy.

"What?" She stared at the magical object. "I ... I don't understand."

"England isn't ready for flying ships, Captain Darling." Hook's voice carried the weight of absolute certainty. "She isn't ready for any of it. She isn't ready for *you*. Your place is in Neverland, with the *Jolly Roger*. Where you can be everything of which you are capable."

"But—"

Hook drew her aside, away from the others. His good left hand closed gently around hers. "Captain Darling ..." He paused, sighed, and started again. "Wendy, I love you. With all my heart. Everything you are, and everything you have become. If you went back to England ..." He paused again, his forget-me-not eyes still locked onto hers. "You might as well be placing yourself in irons. You would be shackled for the rest of your life."

"Then perhaps my place is there." She lifted her chin. "I could change things. We, together, could change things."

A sad smile touched his lips. "That would be a noble cause, but I would prefer to take it up without you. I will live a good life and die a happy man, knowing you are still alive, still just as you are

today. The captain of a flying ship, worth more than the best thirty men I have ever known."

Tears spilled down Wendy's cheeks. "I love you, too," she whispered. "I'll never forget you."

Hook nodded, then cleared his throat. "You'd best get going. Just remember to take your dog with you. Unruly thing doesn't answer to anyone else."

"Aye, Captain." Wendy smiled, revealing the secret kiss in the far corner, just for a moment.

She hugged him fiercely, wishing desperately that she had something to give him—something for him to remember her by. And then she thought of the compass.

It had never worked for him, not once, but she imagined him back in his London office, staring at it with a low growl in the back of his throat, commanding it to glow. She could see it so clearly, she almost smiled again.

Almost.

Still wrapped in his embrace, she slipped the compass into the pocket of his blue captain's jacket and then wrenched herself away. She strode quickly toward John and Michael, not daring to look back.

"We love you too, you know," Michael said softly. "Not the way he does, but still. Brothers in arms forever and all that."

Wendy blinked. "What? But ... how did you—"

"Oh, please." Michael rolled his eyes. "You'd have to be blind."

She glanced at John, who merely raised an eyebrow.

"It's such a terrible thing, saying good-bye." Her voice wavered. "I don't even know how to do it."

"I think you just did." Michael pulled her into a hug, and then John, much to Wendy's surprise, wrapped his arms around them both.

"Take care of yourself," John murmured.

"I promise."

She took half a step back to find Charlie waiting for her.

"Charlie, I just …" She stopped, the tears flowing freely now. "I can't. I just can't—"

But, of course, he understood. He always had.

He closed the short distance between them and hugged her fiercely—for so long that Wendy started to think he might never let her go. Which, she realized, was exactly what she needed.

It was the only way they could ever say goodbye.

"We'll see each other again," he murmured. "I don't know how, but we will. I have to believe that. I don't think I could let you go if I didn't."

"Forever is an awfully long time." The words came out in fits and starts, her breath wracked with grief.

"Long enough for just about anything to happen, don't you think?"

She nodded quickly, her face buried in his shoulder, and finally she pulled away, stepping back and opening her arms to Nana, who bounded into them with such enthusiasm that Wendy nearly toppled backward.

John and Michael rushed to steady her, their hands strong and familiar on her shoulders.

"Are you ready?" John asked quietly.

"No." Wendy shook her head. "But yes? I don't know."

"You're ready." Charlie's voice held absolute certainty. "You always have been."

Wendy nodded, gripping Nana tightly. "Hoops," she whispered, "I hope you can hear me. Watch over them for me, would you? If they're ever in trouble—I mean, really in trouble—you know what to do."

"What?"

She heard John's confused question, but she was already in the air, lifting off toward the portal with the huge Newfoundland

dangling from her arms. She wanted to go back, to explain, to hug them all one more time, but she was afraid that if she did, she wouldn't have the heart to leave them again.

The warm island breeze caressed her face, the salt tang of the air brushed her lips with a final goodbye, and then they were gone.

As she emerged on the other side, the familiar scent of Neverland filled her senses—pickles and green and cool cave water. Peter, Charming, and Tinker Bell were there waiting for her, just as they'd promised—though Tinker Bell's expression and the subtle red streaks in her hair suggested she wasn't entirely pleased with this turn of events.

"I knew you'd come back!" Peter crowed.

Charming trilled at him in obvious reproach.

"No, I was *not* just as worried as you were," Peter protested. "That's ridiculous."

Wendy couldn't help but smile. Peter grinned back and took Nana from her, tucking the enormous Newfoundland safely under one arm so Wendy could hug him properly.

"As much as I hate to do it," she said when they finally broke apart, "I suppose it's time to destroy the portal."

"All right," Peter agreed.

She waited for whatever was supposed to happen next, but Peter didn't move. Instead, he simply hovered in the air, watching her with a mix of curiosity and expectation.

"Well?" Wendy prompted. "What do we do? How do we destroy it?"

"I don't know." Peter's brow furrowed. "I thought you did."

"What?"

He shrugged. "It was here when I got here. I didn't have any-thing to do with it."

"Wait." Wendy flew back several feet, trying to gauge whether he was being serious, but the look on his face didn't change.

"You really don't know how to destroy it?"

"Of course not." Peter gestured vaguely at the sky. "It's just a magical portal in the middle of the air. I don't even know how to touch it."

Wendy burst out laughing. He was right, of course. There wasn't a frame or mechanism or anything at all. Just a light shimmer in the endless blue sky.

"Oh, Peter."

"What?" He looked genuinely puzzled. "I really thought you knew how."

Together, they flew toward the village, Wendy shaking her head.

Behind them, the portal sparkled in the light, eternal and unchanging, just like Neverland itself.

# CHAPTER 67

Wendy sat at her desk in the captain's quarters of the *Jolly Roger*, absently scratching behind Nana's ears. The great dog's head rested heavily in her lap while Charming perched on an inkwell nearby, his golden glow warming the dark wood.

She was happy here—truly happy. She visited Thomas at the Library often, always eager to hear about his latest discoveries. And thanks to regular lessons with Thelxinoe, she was starting to understand Charming more clearly, a fact for which they were both grateful. Even Tigerlilja was becoming a friend, teaching her the ancient stories of her people.

As for Peter, well ... he had become far more than that.

He was courting her, in his own way—slowly but certainly, as though they had all the time in the world. Which they did, she supposed, although she found herself doing what she could lately to speed things along.

Still, in her quieter moments, she couldn't help wondering where Hook and Charlie might be, or whether John and Michael were safe. Or what adventures they might all be having.

And whether they might think of her as often as she thought of them.

A bright knock interrupted her reverie. "Come quick!" Peter called.

"What is it?"

She rushed to the door and threw it open to find him smiling down at her, his grin stretching from ear to ear. "It's a surprise."

Wendy followed him to the deck and was about to leap into the air when Peter reached for her hand, pulling her back gently. "Let's take the ship," he said. "It will be even better that way."

They flew the *Jolly Roger* across the Neverland sky toward the region of eternal twilight where the *Pegasus* had first landed.

As they approached the mountain, Wendy's heart clenched—for a moment, she thought she saw Snaggleclaw's familiar form stretched across the rocky slope.

But no, it was the young dragon who had helped save them all, sleeping in the exact same spot.

"We're here," Peter whispered. "But you need to look up."

Wendy followed his gaze. The evening light perfectly captured that one brief moment when the sun leaves the sky and the stars are just starting to emerge, winking into existence one by one.

It was as beautiful as ever, but her eyebrows drew together nonetheless, united in puzzlement. Something felt ... different.

There seemed to be more than usual—many more—as though the very fabric of the sky had somehow deepened.

Peter twined his fingers through hers. "Are you ready?"

Standing there with Peter, holding his hand, she couldn't help but feel that she was ready for anything—for any adventure, danger, joy, or even sorrow.

As long as they had each other, she would gladly experience it all.

So she nodded, smiling back at him, content to see what the night might bring.

With a mysterious grin, Peter raised his free hand high in the air.

At once, thousands of innisfay burst into light.

They filled the heavens like constellations, their golden radiance forming perfect rings all across the sky. Rings upon rings, wherever she looked.

"What are they?" she asked in a whisper.

She gasped as the rings began to turn, the dance of the innisfay revealing glowing pathways that led impossibly onward, beyond the stars themselves.

"They're portals," he told her. "Each one a different world for us to explore together." His grin faltered, his eyes hesitant. "Or for you to explore on your own, if you'd rather. But I'd like to go with you, if you'll have me."

Wendy's eyes flew wide. "There must be hundreds of them," she breathed.

"Thousands." He dropped to one knee and gazed up at her, his eyes full of hope. "Thousands of worlds. Thousands of adventures. And we have all the time in the world to explore them all."

"If I'll have you," Wendy reminded him.

"That's right."

She smiled, her heart full of—everything. Love, light, joy, hope. And, of course, the call of adventure. After all, forever was an awfully long time. Long enough for enemies to become friends, and friends to become lovers. Long enough for curses to be broken. Long enough to reach the stars.

Long enough for just about anything to happen.

"I will," she told him.

In fact, she couldn't wait to get started.

# ACKNOWLEDGMENTS

When we first started writing, we really didn't know how much went into it. It's not the kind of thing you can fully grasp until you've done it, and it takes more people than you might think.

Not just the research, outlining, writing, editing, layout, and publication—which is a lot in itself—but maintaining the sheer tenacity that the effort requires without losing your love for the craft.

So, more than anything, we need to thank all the people who have kept us going as we've been chasing this dream, even through the darkest times and the loss of too many loved ones along the way.

To our parents, brothers, kids, family, and friends who have always believed in us. To Teddy, who helped us keep moving forward. To J. M. Barrie, for writing such a brilliant classic. For Lissa, the best friend and advocate any author could ever have. Thank you all.

To the brave souls on Patreon who refused to give up on book three, more than anyone, this book is for you.

Dad, Sherwood, Sybil C., Stephanie P., we will never forget you.

# ABOUT THE AUTHORS

Together, Erin Michelle Sky & Steven Brown are the writing team known as Dragon Authors.

For more books and updates:
dragonauthors.com

For social media:
@dragonauthors

www.ingramcontent.com/pod-product-compliance
Lightning Source LLC
Chambersburg PA
CBHW051430190726
48289CB00001B/126